SINFUL

A Truth or Lies World Collection III

ELLA MILES

TRUTH OR LIES WORLD COLLECTION SERIES ORDER

ENZO & KAI'S STORY

Taken (Collection I)
Stolen (Collection II)

ZEKE & SIREN'S STORY

Sinful (Collection III)
Broken (Collection IV)

LANGSTON & LIESEL'S STORY

Vicious (Collection V)
Endless (Collection VI)

SINFUL TRUTH

PROLOGUE
ZEKE

I always knew I would die young.

I've known it since birth. From a young age, I would take the blame for Enzo, my closest friend later turned boss. He was always pushing the limits, stealing things he could've bought with a snap of his fingers. He was horrible at thievery, so he always got caught. But I took the blame. Most of my childhood was spent in detention—for every wallet, purse, and laptop Enzo stole just because he could. The man has more wealth than a small country, but it doesn't stop him from showing his power, even from a young age. And I protected him at all costs.

Langston, my best friend and brother in every way that matters, got in trouble in different ways. He preferred to let his fists talk for him—something I understood quite well. We got in more fights than should have been allowed. We both should've been expelled from school, but because of our association with Enzo, no man, not even our principal, would do more than give us detention.

Both men I've protected my entire life. Enzo and Langston are both taller and stronger than any other man I've ever met. But neither man compares to me.

I'm not bragging; I'm humble to my core. But at six foot five, I tower over both of them. My muscles ripple from my body, and men cower at my feet with one glare—a look I've perfected over the years. Yet deep inside, my heart aches to be warm, gentle, anything but the beast I appear to be on the outside. But to anyone except Langston and Enzo, that's what I am—a beast.

My straggly hair and scruffy face only add to that notion. My tattoo ridden body adds fire to my bad boy image. I almost never have to actually use my fists and body to protect my boss, Enzo Black, or rescue my dipshit friend, Langston, when he's in trouble. My appearance more than does enough to scare the shit out of any foe.

But this time was different.

This time wasn't about fighting to keep them safe; this time, I had to sacrifice everything to protect someone more worthy of my protection.

Enzo is my boss; I vowed to protect him with my life the day I took the job at eighteen. After growing up as practically brothers, I would have sacrificed my life for his for free. But this time he didn't ask me to. He asked me to protect another—one more valuable to him than his own. A woman who rests so deeply in his heart that he will never be able to get her out. A woman whose love consumes him.

Kai Miller—a woman I myself love. *No, I'm not in love with my best friend's girl.* Just in love with her strength, courage, and warrior attitude. I'm in love with the way she loves him.

I once thought I was in love like that. But after seeing it, seeing their love grow right in front of my eyes, I know I never have, nor ever will, experience a love like theirs.

Because this is where my story ends—saving the girl. I stepped in front of a bullet for her. The evidence is blood leaking from my chest as my heart pounds over and over and over—each time spilling more precious drops of blood until I'm bled dry.

You would think I would regret my decision to save a woman I didn't love. That I should've reserved this moment for the woman that had captured my own heart instead of the woman destined to be Enzo's equal in every way.

But I don't regret it even now.

My only regret is not knowing if it was enough. *Did I save Kai? Or did I fail? With my death, will she be safe or left vulnerable?*

I will never know the answer. Unless perhaps in heaven, I can look down upon her and see that she survives stronger than ever.

Who am I kidding? If an afterlife exists, I won't be going to heaven; my sins will take me straight to hell.

But then, I'm already in my own personal hell.

The bullet knocked me out, but I became conscious again when the storm pushed me over the railing of the yacht and into the water. The last thing I remember before going underwater was the splash of the salty ocean on my face—then nothing.

How I survived this long, I don't know. But I survived long enough that the yacht my friends were on is no longer here. There is no wreckage for me to cling to. No lifesaver floating in the water. I am stuck in the middle of the fucking ocean in the middle of the fucking night—blackness surrounds me.

I should feel alone. But I'm not. I would prefer to be alone. I would prefer to die quietly and calmly by myself. Even though I did my best to protect those I cared about, I never wanted a martyr's death. However, that is exactly what I'm going to get.

Every nudge of the waves reminds me that I'm not alone here in the ocean. That below me are hundreds of sea creatures all doing their best to survive. That sharks and other deadly creatures could be hiding, inching closer every second, being lured to me as my drops of blood seep into the ocean. Every second that passes is another second closer to death. *But will I die alone, going quietly into the ocean from loss of blood, or will I die violently fighting a shark until the bitter end? Or will the waves finally overpower me, until I drown?*

I tread water with my aching legs, my arms too painful and sore to move. My right arm clutches to my chest, trying to keep as much blood inside my body as possible.

The stars twinkle overhead, taunting me with their beauty and ability to stay alive for so long. My life was short, fleeting. I barely made a blimp on this world. But the stars, they shine forever in a thick layer of darkness draping over us all. They do not fear death; they welcome it. Because even in death, the stars continue to shine for sometimes thousands of years later.

I know my death will be the same. What was taken granted before —the friendships, the brotherhood, will be turned into more. But I only hope it gives Enzo and Langston the strength to face our enemies. And I hope once they're safe, they can move on.

I continue to tread water as each second passes by in what seems like an hour, so slowly I'm not sure I'm moving at all. I should be grateful; these are my last moments on this earth. Despite the pain I'm feeling in my body, the beauty of the night being stranded in the middle of the ocean doesn't go unnoticed. The moon creeps up higher in the sky—a full moon that turns the dark skylight.

The moon will be the last thing I see before I close my eyes— before I die.

I can already feel myself fading—my will to live leaving my body as my legs tire beneath me. My breathing is slow and heavy; my lungs are filling with a little saltwater each time I try to breathe. I'm not able to fully keep my head above water any longer.

This is the end. The end of my story. And what a sad story it was.

No!

My story wasn't sad; I did what I always thought I would do—give up my life to save another. One more worthy, one meant to change the world. And Kai Miller will change the motherfucking world.

My long hair falls over my eyes, but I don't have the energy to brush it off my face so that I can stare up at the beautiful sky. And one of my last acts before sacrificing my life was giving a scrunchie to Kai to keep her hair back so she could fight without worrying about her hair in her face.

I smile, thinking of that moment. And how it felt to do something so simple and kind for a woman so amazing as Kai. I lived for moments like that. I just never got to have those moments with a woman I was in love with.

I close my eyes, deciding it's better this way, that blackness sends me to my death instead of looking at the hair in my eyes. My throat makes a strangled sound as more water enters my chest. I've always loved the ocean, dying in it doesn't seem like such a bad idea. I'd rather die here than be buried on some hillside with a tombstone that my friends feel compelled to visit and bring flowers and all that bullshit. This way, I'll just be gone.

Maybe they'll think of me the next time they are on the ocean, feel me in the wind that blows through their hair, but that's it. They won't feel obligated to me in any way other than just living their lives.

The pain starts, and the panic sets in as my lungs continue to fill more and more with saltwater instead of the oxygen they desperately desire.

I may let the ocean take me, but I don't want to drown. I want my death to be easy and quick, as do all humans. So I remove my hand from my chest, letting the blood spill quicker from my wound. But I think the saltwater—the very thing that's trying to kill me by drowning me—is also saving me. Because my blood should be flowing much faster from my chest. Instead, the water pressure is keeping the blood within my veins.

Dammit.

I kick harder, determined to die at least on my own terms. I try to get my chest above the water, I try floating on my back, but the waves fight harder, pushing me back under.

No, I will not let you win.

I force my legs to kick, my arms to paddle; I urge my body to float. *Dammit, float!*

But my heavy body doesn't have the buoyancy to float. My arms are exhausted, barely doing more than a toddler would who has just learned to splash in a pool of water. My legs carry all my strength—but my strength floated away with Kai, and Enzo, and Langston. My strength is still on that yacht. My strength is gone.

The pain is the only thing keeping me alive. The agony triggers adrenaline—the need to survive deep in my body. But I don't want to survive, not like this. I don't want to spend hours more floating in this water waiting for death to come.

So much for quick and painless.

My death may not be painless, but it will at least be quick. I'm done suffering. And I know I have enough willpower left in my body to die on my own terms.

Drowning it is.

I take a couple more deep breaths, trying to get one or two moments of comfort, security, and warmth inside my body before I take the plunge, but when you're dying, even that simple breath of oxygen isn't comforting. It's pain and pain and pain. It is all I feel. It is all I think about—the pain.

I've never been one to fear death, and I won't let myself be scared right now. Even if I could feel fear, the pain wouldn't let me—my body trembles as my muscles fatigue. My chest makes an awful wheezing sound with each anguished breath. My eyes burn as more saltwater enters them. And my heart—my heart pumps harder and more distressed with each thump, trying to decide between holding on and giving out as the pain possesses my body.

It's time.

My body switches from trying to survive to just trying to get rid of the pain. I need to end; the suffering is too much. So I take one more big breath, and then I dive under the heavy waves and into the darkness.

Death should come quickly but not painlessly. I have to endure more torment in order for the pain to stop. But right now, with every nerve-ending in my body begging me to make it stop, it's a trade-off I will gladly endure.

Deeper into the darkness, I descend.

Deeper.

Deeper.

Deeper.

I force myself to kick as hard as I can to get as deep as I can because I know that once my lungs start filling with water, my fight or flight response will kick in again, and I'll try to save myself. And I can't handle any more moments of pain.

With each kick deeper, I feel my lungs tightening, the pressure constricting around my body, intensifying the discomfort.

Just a little further, I think.

If I can get just a little deeper, I won't be able to get to the surface fast enough when I start to panic. This is the end, being surrounded by nothing but water, darkness—alone.

But then I feel it, a jolt in my body, a reverse in direction. Instead of traveling deeper into the depths of the ocean, I'm making a break for the surface.

What the hell?

I have no idea what's happening. *Did my body spontaneously change directions? Or am I already dead, and an angel is grabbing me and taking me to heaven?*

I don't know, but I don't have the strength to fight it. So I let whatever force is pulling me back toward the surface do its job.

Time moves fast again as I hit the surface. My mouth opens, gasping for air, getting just enough oxygen to keep me firmly on the side of living instead of dying.

I feel a hand over my face sweeping the wet mop of my hair clear from my eyes and mouth, making it easier to breathe. I don't know how I'm staying afloat because I'm not kicking or treading water, I'm completely dead weight.

But once the hair is gone from my face, I hear a sigh relief.

I open my eyes and come face-to-face with my savior. *And what a face it is.* Striking brown eyes loom into mine, examining my face quickly and thoroughly to ensure that I am alive and not dead. Long dark hair frames her face parted perfectly down the middle, like a model coming out of the water instead of the sea monster I must look like. Her red lips pout, disappointed in something she sees in me. But all I can think is her lips are magical.

This can't be real. I must be imagining some perfect woman in my last moments here on Earth. I'm not really here; I'm still deep within the heart of the ocean. But if my fantasies are going to try to give me one last moment of pleasure before I leave this earth, I'm not gonna fight them.

The woman grabs my arm harshly and jerks me toward her.

"Come on," she says.

Come on? I'm not sure what she expects me to do, I have no energy to swim, there is no way I can save myself; I'm drowning in the middle of the ocean with no boat, island, or person to save me. But I let her pull me, assuming she's a current dragging me deeper into the ocean, waiting until my lungs give out.

She pulls hard, and I feel my body moving, dragging behind her. I don't know where we're going or what she wants me to see before I die, but it seems urgent. Probably because she knows I only have seconds left to live. Maybe it's something beautiful like a seahorse or whale or dolphin—something beautiful she wants me to see before I die. But all I can think is that there's nothing more beautiful than her.

She swims harder now, more determined than before. But I'm not desperate or hurried, not in the final moments. I study everything about her. The way her arm darts into the water with beautifully tanned skin that shows just how much time she spends in the sun. I watch her toned legs kicking with the efficiency of a dolphin. I watch her ass bob up and down over the waves in bright red bikini bottoms.

If only she were real. If only I found a woman like her while I was still living.

But then Kai would be dead. There would've been no one there to save her if I had fallen in love with a woman like this. Because there's no way I would've sacrificed myself to save a friend when I had a woman I loved who desperately needed me to live. Maybe that's why I never found love. Because it would've made me a worse version of myself.

"Can you help me at all, you big oaf?" The woman says, throwing her head over her shoulder, shooting daggers with her eyes in my direction.

I smile. I don't know why the woman is so angry at me, but I devour the look on her face.

When I don't move to help her, she huffs and then starts kicking wildly again, lugging me along behind her.

I see the sky changing from dark to light. It must be the light that everyone talks about seeming just before they die. And I know my time is almost up.

The woman sees it as a sign to swim faster in the water.

Until she suddenly stops.

I don't care why she stops. With us no longer moving, I can study her features more clearly, I can see the light freckles dusting over her nose, I can see the gold flecks in her otherwise dark brown eyes, I can see the streaks of red in her hair as the sun catches it just right, as it begins to rise over the horizon behind her.

And I know in this moment she is my angel. She is here to take all of my pain away. And I'll forever be thankful for her.

She shakes her head at me again, disappointed, but I don't understand why.

She reaches for something behind her, and my gaze runs along her tanned arm to the tip of her red painted fingernails as she grips the first rung of the ladder.

A ladder?

She hosts herself out of the water, dragging me to the ladder behind her. I grip on automatically, and then I'm pulled into a boat.

We both fall to the wooden deck, exhausted and panting heavily.

"I don't know why I risked my life to save you when it's clear you wanted to die," she says.

"Die?" I ask.

She nods. "You dove under the water just as I shouted that I was going to throw you a lifesaver."

My eyes widen. I have no idea what she's talking about. I never heard her speak before I went under.

Her eyes soften as she realizes I didn't hear her. I was just an anguished man, who was tired of the pain and needed to end his life on his own terms.

She quickly looks over my body until she sees the blood oozing from my chest where the bullet hit me. She grabs for a towel behind her and holds it to my wound, applying pressure with her hands.

"Is this real?" I ask. *Or is this the end? The pressure of the ocean squeezing out the last drops of oxygen from my lungs?*

"This is real. You are on my sailboat off the shores of Saint Kitts. We can make it back to the island in about two hours if the weather is in our favor. Do you think you can hold on that long, sailor?"

I nod.

She gives me the faintest hint of a smile or at least what I assume for her is a smile. Her lips thin, her eyes turn bright, and her cheeks shade pink.

"You're my angel," I say.

She shakes her head. "I'm no angel."

"What's your name?"

"You can call me Siren."

Siren—such a beautiful, unique name. A name that for thousands of years meant death to any sailor who met a siren. But this woman isn't like the mythical stories. This woman saved my life.

I close my eyes, needing rest.

She strokes my face, running her hands through my long hair.

She starts humming, and it's the most beautiful sound I have ever heard. Calming, entrancing, enduring. If I could stay awake, I would, just to listen to her voice.

"I shouldn't have saved you," she says. But then she's right back to humming and singing with her heavenly voice.

She's wrong. I will make her see that risking her life was worth it. She saved me. Now I owe her. And I never relent on a debt.

CHAPTER 1
SIREN

THREE MONTHS LATER

I was raised to tell the truth, no matter what. It should be my greatest virtue. Instead, I consider it my greatest weakness. Maybe it's because of how I learned the skill that makes me feel this way. But the truth of the matter is that I can't lie.

Can't—as in can't physically make my mouth form the words to tell a lie. I know that's hard to believe, but it's my truth.

It started when I was three. My best friend in the world at the time, Gavin, ripped my favorite doll out of my hands, so I pushed him. He ended up crying for the next twenty minutes, loudly enough that my father came to check on us. When he asked me what happened, I lied. I said he had fallen and hurt himself, not because I pushed him. That was my first lesson, my first mistake.

What my three-year-old self didn't realize was that my father had been listening to Gavin and me fighting in my bedroom behind the door. He heard me shove him. He knew I wasn't telling the truth. And I paid for my sin, dealt by my father's belt.

At three, I didn't quite realize what sinning was, but over the years, my pastor father and religious mother drilled the message into me.

Lying was a sin equal to murder in their eyes. Whether it was the smallest of white lies or biggest of lies, it made no difference in their eyes.

It was a sin.

I was a sinner.

And so I had to be punished.

But I also learned another important lesson in those first few years of life; I'm not a fast learner. The daily beatings did nothing to stop my lies. I didn't lie about anything big—just normal childhood fibs.

Did I eat a cookie before dinner? No, I lied. *Slap.*

Did I finish all my homework? Yes, I lied. *Slap.*

Did I drink alcohol at the party? No, I lied. *Slap.*

And over and over again. *I lied. I sinned. I was punished.*

It took me almost eighteen years to finally learn my lesson. Eighteen years of groundings, spankings, beatings. Eighteen years of being wrecked and broken—until the lies finally stopped.

I can't lie now, even as a thirty-two-year-old woman. I got pulled over for speeding last year. When the cop asked me if I knew I was speeding, I said yes. I couldn't lie, I couldn't fib and say that I didn't know the exact speed I was going. I said I knew I was going exactly twelve miles over the speed limit. I got the ticket.

But it's not all bad. Telling the truth has saved me as many times as it's gotten me into trouble. For example, when I was twenty-one, my boyfriend at the time and I went through an adventurous sex phase. We tried all the toys, positions that we could find. One drunken night my boyfriend thought he was shoving a dildo into my ass turned out it was a spiked paddle. I bled, we got scared and ended up in the emergency room. Normal, rational people might fib, embarrassed by the truth. But I told them exactly what happened and got medical care much faster.

But sometimes a lie could save me, even from the smallest of things. When my friend, Rue, asked me how her butt looks in her new dress, I told her the truth—it makes her butt look too big. Times like those, I wish I could lie. I wish I could spare her feelings, my cheek when she slaps me, and the turmoil our friendship goes through every time I tell her the truth when she's looking for me to lie.

It's my burden, my curse, and my greatest strength.

My sailboat floats into the harbor of Saint Kitts with just me aboard. It's a beautiful day, but *why do I have a sinking feeling in my stomach every time I come back here?*

I try not to focus on the feeling in my gut; after all, I've learned not to trust it. It's led me in the wrong direction many times before.

I tie off my sailboat, and then I hop down to the shaky pier. The wood beneath my sandaled feet is worn, the paint stripped from the harsh weather here. Each step I take, the wood creaks, the pier sways. All it would take is one mediocre storm to wash this all away. Yet, somehow day after day, year after year, the pier and the small town relying on it, remains.

I strut down the pier with my bag thrown over my shoulder. Even though I've been a resident of this island for years, it doesn't stop the men's eyes from stalking me as I walk.

Each gaze says something different.

I want you.

I'm imagining you naked.

You don't belong here.

This is a man's world.

I've learned not to let the inappropriate stares and whispers bother me. There was a time I would have pummeled each and every guy who dared to look at me or comment about my appearance. But I've learned it's not worth my time. Sometimes, my body is even an asset.

I've considered dressing more conservatively, at least when I'm here. But that's not who I am. And honestly, I like the stares. The stares expose each man's true self. They tell me the men I should stay away from. They tell me the honest men from the pigs.

My clothes are a test. My jean shorts barely contain my ass; the front pockets hang lower than the hem. My cut-off shirt reveals my tanned stomach and dips down, showing my more than adequate cleavage. And my hair is loose in a long mane of thick waves. The island is windy, and my brunette locks are constantly in my face. But when I flip my hair, it's the ultimate test. The men can't resist a good hair flip. It's like I'm calling out to them, alerting them to a hot female in their presence. And every man on the pier failed.

I smirk as I walk off the pier with my duffel bag over my shoulder. I find my white 1980 Toyota Land Cruiser parked right where I left it three months ago when I was last here. Three months—such a long time, but it also feels like no time has passed at all.

I prefer the sailboat to the island. The ocean is unpredictable; you never know if you will live or die. You have to constantly be on your guard. You have to be prepared for anything.

I unlock my car and toss the duffel bag in the back seat.

I guess life on the island is the same. Each day is a struggle to live. On the ocean, it's just me and the water. Here—there is more than one danger I have to deal with. The men on the island are my biggest threat.

I climb into the driver's seat and turn the key in the ignition, which, I'm happy to say, starts. I've come back from many trips when the car wouldn't start. Or it was stolen. The fact that it starts is a win. I back out of the beachside parking lot. It's one of only three free spots you can park in long term.

A shadow crosses in my rearview mirror. I slam on the breaks to avoid hitting the tall man standing behind my car.

"Shit."

I grip the wheel like my life depends on me hanging onto the wheel. I pant heavily as beads of sweat form on my forehead. I run my hand through my hair, changing the direction of my part from left to right. And then I let my eyes flicker up to look into the rearview mirror and pray I didn't hurt the man. Hopefully, he's still standing.

But when I look into the rearview mirror, I don't expect what I see.

The man is still there, but his face is only barely visible in the mirror. He towers over my SUV. He's standing in ripped jeans and a snug white T-shirt that barely fits his bulging biceps. His body is tall, fit, and rugged. But that isn't what draws me to him. His face does. It's a face I've seen before. Dark scruff clings to his chin, not in the messy I-don't-care-what-I-look-like kind of way that most men on the island wear. His looks like it is a part of him. It's tidy and neat. His hair is pulled back into a messy man bun. Not something I would usually be attracted to, but on him, his hair brings out the beast below the surface. But his eyes are what have me captive. I recognize the brown ambers of his eyes.

The same eyes I pulled from the ocean a little over three months ago.

He's alive.

I wasn't sure if he would make it. When I pulled him from the water and saw the damage his body had been through, I was afraid I would arrive in town with a dead man in tow. Somehow he hung on, even though he was clearly hallucinating. He called me his angel. But I don't think he meant that I was an angel because I saved his life. At one point, I think he actually thought he was dead, that he was in heaven, and that I was a real angel.

But this man lived long enough for me to get him to the island. I shoved him in the back of this very beater. I glance at the backseat that is still stained red with his blood. No matter how much scrubbing I did, I couldn't get it out. I knew for sure he was going to die as I drove him to get medical help. But again, he proved me wrong. For a man so intent on dying when I first jumped into the water to save him, he sure as hell fought to live once I pulled him out.

Even though he survived the hours it took to get to the island, the car ride to get medical help didn't mean he was out of the woods. Our small hospital doesn't have the same level of equipment and care most hospitals have. It wouldn't have been enough to save him. Which is why I didn't drive him to the hospital. I drove him into danger, but it was the only way I could think of to save his life.

And it paid off. The man is alive. Despite me almost running him over with my car. *How ironic would that be?* It took every ounce of energy and determination I had to save him three months ago, only to run him over with my car and kill him in a split second now.

I never thought I'd see him again. I thought one of two things would have happened by now. He'd either be dead or gone. No one stays on this island long term if they know what's good for them. They flee the first chance they get. Sure, tourists always say they'd love to live here. But they don't really mean it. The island is paradise and hell. Its beauty draws men in, only to torture them with regret as soon as they make the island their home.

So what is the man still doing here?

What was his name again?

I pushed his name from my mind. I knew I couldn't keep his name in my thoughts. His name would haunt me. When I saved him, I knew there would be unforeseen consequences of my actions. It hasn't happened yet, but it will.

Enzo?

Kai?

No, neither was his name. Just names he muttered in his sleep.

The man's eyes cut to mine, and I think he remembers me as his head tilts to the side to try and study me better. But he can't see me, at least not enough of me to make a positive ID. My windows are tinted to help keep the burning sun out of my car and so I can't be seen.

He can't see me.

But maybe he senses the change in the air—the familiar unease growing in my belly with him near. I don't know why everything changes with this man near. And not in a good way. I've never felt my pulse race so quickly, my stomach flips in unsettling ways, and I'm nibbling nervously on my bottom lip, like that is somehow going to help.

"Zeke," one of the men from the pier shouts in our direction.

Zeke—that was his name. It fits him. It's a powerful sounding name. And he must be a powerful man to have survived this long. The island wears people down, but he looks better, stronger. I study him closer, trying to decide if he has money. His clothes don't give me any designer, rich person vibes. The man shouting for him is just a fisherman who doesn't make a lot of money. All the signs say he is nothing. Probably doesn't even have enough money to buy a plane ticket off the island. Or maybe he has amnesia and doesn't know where to buy a plane ticket to? Or even how to access his bank account?

No.

This man doesn't carry himself like he doesn't know who he is. He stands tall and proud. The twinkle in his eye tells me he's a man that likes to laugh and live well, yet he prefers to use his size to intimidate any person he perceives as a threat. The look now is meant to tell me to back off, that he could kill me with his fists alone. I don't doubt that he could, but I also see the softness in his eyes. It's a deadly combination. He can make any man fall to his knees in fear, while every woman would fall to their knees in front of him for a very different reason.

Zeke knows exactly who he is. He's a burly man who knows how to use his body to get what he wants. I can't imagine a man like him doesn't have money.

So what is he still doing in a place like this?

"Zeke, you coming?" the man on the pier asks.

Zeke nods but doesn't stop looking through the rear of my car straight to my soul.

He can't see me. He can't see anything.

Finally, Zeke looks away and starts walking toward the pier.

I exhale a breath, pushing the air too quickly through my lungs, so it almost hurts to breath. And then I zip out of my parking spot, trying to put the events behind me. I can't think about Zeke. I can't think about anything other than my job.

But I can't help but glance in my rearview mirror as I drive away from one of the most attractive men I've ever seen. A man I can't read.

Is he a good or bad man?

Who am I kidding? All men are bad. I've learned that lesson enough times by now. Even the good ones have an evil streak. Even the good ones will damage my heart until it is no longer recognizable. Until my heart is no longer mine.

Thump-thump.

Thump-thump.

Thump-thump.

Damn, stupid heart speeding up just thinking about Zeke.

My heart still hasn't learned its lesson. Not that I have a heart left to give. My heart is no longer mine. I haven't had anything truly mine in a very long time, including my own body.

But it doesn't stop my heart from yearning. From yearning to know more about Zeke. To wondering if he could be the one—the one who is different. The one who could stop my pain. The one who could save me.

Ha—I don't need saving. I chose this life. I want this life. Any other life would make me weak and vulnerable. My life makes me strong.

I've already chosen my fate. I know how my story ends.

Saving Zeke was a mistake, I know that as I watch his shadow disappear from view. He wasn't just any sailor who wasn't experienced enough and fell victim to the sea—he's different. He's going to wreck my perfect little world, blow it up in a way I'm not prepared for.

Saving a man should absolve me of my sins. But instead, saving him will cost me everything.

CHAPTER 2
ZEKE

I can't shake the strangest feeling as I walk down to the pier. I'm not even sure what my body is reacting to. *The beat-up Land Cruiser almost hitting me?*

No, that was hardly life or death. The car stopped long before it got close to me.

But I can't shake the déjà vu feeling. Maybe because I've passed that beat-up SUV parked along the beach every day I've been coming to work. And to see it actually move put me into shock. *Yea, that has to be it.*

I stare down at my arms, where goosebumps have formed, and hair is sticking straight up as if warning me that danger is nearby.

I glance back as the car speeds off down the highway.

There can't be anything dangerous about a person who can barely afford a car. Most people think that poor people are more dangerous than rich. That poor people are desperate and addicted to drugs. That they will do anything to survive. Anything to get the drugs—not true.

Sure, poor people can be dangerous. And yes, some are addicted to drugs. Stealing petty amounts of money or robbing someone at gunpoint, if they happen to get ahold of a gun, is the most damage they can do. Yes, that might end in a death or two, but it's nothing compared to the damage a rich person can do.

A rich person has more to lose, and that makes them more dangerous. A rich person can hire an army to take out the threat. They have endless weapons at their disposal. They can pay off the police to ensure there are no consequences for their actions. Rich people can make anything they want happen. I know—I've worked for a rich person my entire life. I've seen what wealth can get you.

Whoever was in that car was not a threat. Whatever fucked up spidey sense my body was trying to use to warn me is broken.

"Zeke, get your fucking ass over here if you want to get paid!" Wayne says.

I shake off the strange feeling and continue walking to the pier. I don't speed up my steps. That's not who I am. I may follow orders, but I don't change who I am. I'm the gentle giant—calm in the face of fear. And I don't like being disrespected. I don't like working for bosses I don't admire. And Wayne has not earned my respect.

"What do you want, Wayne?"

"It's Mr. Hill."

I stand, towering almost a foot taller than him. My muscles ripple and contract in ways his never will. He may write my paycheck, but I'm not going to pretend I won't kill him if he fucks me over.

"What task have you arranged for me today, Wayne?" I ask, continuing to use his first name.

He frowns but doesn't fight me on it. An audience has formed around us as his men stop their work to watch our inevitable fight.

I still don't understand why Julian Reed has Wayne as his number two. I haven't learned everything there is to learn about Julian, but I do know he's smart, powerful, and ruthless. He's a lot like my old boss, Enzo Black. He just doesn't have quite the empire or money that Enzo has. His money is newer. His empire is just starting out and focused mainly on selling drugs as far as I can see. While Enzo has his hand in everything.

"I need you to load the speed boat with the cargo from the truck. Think you can handle that before lunch?" Wayne says, his eyes threatening to fire me. He hates me. If it were up to him, he'd have already fired me—*do us both a favor.* But it's not up to him. It's not even up to me. I was saved. I owe a man my life—something I can never repay. But I'm doing my best before returning to my real life.

"It will be done within the hour," I answer.

"No way. You're underestimating the amount of cargo that needs to be transferred. There is no way one man can get the job done within the hour."

"Are you saying I'm not a man of my word?"

He folds his arms across his chest in a grumpy way. "I'm saying there is no way you can load the boat with all the cargo in an hour."

My eyes deepen, and my jaw twitches. I hate being underestimated. "Care to make a wager on it?"

He shrugs. *Pussy.*

"If I get it loaded in under an hour, you pay me double," I say. I don't care about the money. I care about putting this motherfucker in his place.

"And if I win?"

"I work for you for a month for free," I say, even though I don't plan on staying that long. I won't lose this bet. I know my capabilities.

The crowd of men around us *oohs* as the wager is placed.

Wayne grins, extending his hand to me. "I love having workers I don't have to pay." His eyes dart over to two of his men that are currently working a year for free. I wouldn't call them workers so much as slaves. They do all the work everyone else doesn't want to do. And not only do they not get paid, they get treated like dirt.

Wayne looks at his watch. "Time starts now."

I shake my head at the dirty bastard as I walk at my normal, casual pace over to the truck. He thinks he's being tricky by starting the time without warning and without me anywhere near the truck, but he's just digging his own grave deeper. The more he messes with me, the more I want to end his life.

I look into the back of the loading truck. There are a dozen crates that usually take two men to lift, and at least fifty bags that need to be carried over. I look in the corner where the dolly is, but one of the wheels has popped off, and the other has a flat.

Bastard.

Guess I'm getting my workout in this morning.

I'll start with the crates first. They are the hardest to move because no matter how strong I am, I can only lift one at a time. Then I can work on the bags which I can transport more quickly.

When I walk out of the truck, carrying one of the crates easily between my arms, I hear the gasps from the men around me.

I snicker. I just wish I could watch Wayne pissing his pants. Julian Reed isn't going to be happy he has to pay me double wages.

Forty-five minutes later, I lift the last five bags, toss them over my shoulder and then start carrying them to the boat.

"Zeke," Julian shouts from his car.

Thank God. I'm tired of dealing with Wayne.

I toss the last of the bags into the boat and then find Wayne's gaze. "You owe me double."

His face goes white in front of his boss.

And then I head over to Julian's car.

Julian glares at Wayne. "He's having you move cargo?"

I nod.

He shakes his head. "Sorry about him, he can't recognize good talent when he sees it."

I shrug. "I think he's just threatened."

He laughs. "Probably."

"You have something better for me to do?"

"Get in," he nods.

I climb into the backseat next to him. And then his driver starts driving as Julian presses the button for the partition to go up.

Julian is dressed in a sharp suit. He looks more like a banker than a drug dealer. I don't understand the appeal of suits. I guess men wear them when they want to look powerful without having to put in the work to gain muscles. Muscles that automatically earn you respect from other men when you walk into the room.

"I think it's time we put your skills to the test," he says.

I nod. I like where this is going. If I can do something big enough to repay the debt I owe him, then I can get off this island. It's beautiful, sure. But it's not home.

Julian saved my life three months ago. He pulled me from the ocean before I nearly drowned. He brought me back to his mansion and flew in the best doctors to take care of me. He said the doctors at the local hospital couldn't have saved me. And after driving by it a few times, I realized he was right. They couldn't have saved my life. I was lucky he did. Julian knew if he saved me, I would owe him. I know he didn't do it out of the goodness of his heart. He saw how large I was and took a chance that I would be able to pay him back in a way worth his time.

"What do you have in mind?" I ask. *Please let it be something that earns me my freedom.* I'm not really his captive. I'm not his slave. But I can't leave in good conscience until I pay him back. It's just the way I am. I've worked for him for two and a half months now. As soon as I healed, I got to work. He insisted on paying me for the work even though I said I would do the work for free. All the time, waiting for a moment when I knew I could finally leave, my conscience clear.

It's taken all of my strength to stay. All I wanted to do was get on the first plane back to Miami. I had friends who depended on me. People I needed to protect. But I knew if I returned in the shape I was in, I would only get them all killed. Just like what happened before. I wasn't as strong as I should have been. And it almost cost me my friends' lives. It almost cost my life. I won't put them in danger again. And I'm afraid if I don't leave here with Julian's good graces that I will be putting them in danger. I will be creating a new enemy.

So that's why I've stayed mute about who I worked for before coming here. At first, I pretended I couldn't even remember my life before. And I sure as hell won't be telling Julian about my boss now. Even though this guy is small fries compared to the great Black empire.

"I have a deal that needs arranging. Wayne hasn't been able to close it for me. And the timing isn't good for me; my biggest client needs my attention. I can't be seen courting another client at the same time. You understand, optics in this business are everything."

"Of course," I say.

"I need someone I can trust. Someone smart to go in my place.

Someone who can close the deal. Ensure he chooses me to be his partner. That I'm the one he trusts to manage his shipment. Are you the guy to make that happen?"

He pulls a cigar out of his jacket and lights it. He doesn't offer me one. He knows by now I won't take it. I've been too focused on healing to take pleasure in any sort of vices. My lungs still burn when I breathe from taking in too much saltwater. I can't add smoke inhalation to my list of injuries.

"I can be for the right price."

He laughs. "I assumed you were a good negotiator. Name your price. Want ten percent of the deal?"

I shake my head, my eyes darkening, showing how serious I am. My lips thin, and my shoulders straighten, making me look more powerful. More dangerous. "If I do this, then my debt is clean. I owe you nothing. We are done. You are no longer my boss, and I'm no longer your employee. I've repaid you for saving my life."

Julian's lips twitch. He takes another drag of the cigar and then slowly exhales until the back of the car is filled with smoke.

My lungs ache as I inhale the smoke. My throat itches with the need to cough and remove the fumes. My eyes water, and will be red the rest of the day. But I don't cough, scratch, or cower. I don't show weakness.

Julian wants me to handle a drug deal with a man he is desperate to work with. He's trusting me with this task. I can't show him any weakness. He needs to know that no matter what, I will get the job done.

"Sure. You do the job; you owe me nothing. Although, I hope after you get a taste of working for me, and the money and bonuses that come with it, you will reconsider working for me on a long term basis."

I don't respond. I don't want to lead him on and think that I will work for him. But I don't want to insult him by saying there is no amount of money that could ever make me work for him. My boss is Enzo Black. He's earned that right. He's one of my best friends. I don't want to work for anyone else.

"He's a lucky man," he says.

"Who?"

"Whoever you worked for before I found you. It's obvious you risked your life for him. That you will do anything to return to work for him, even though you've been here for months, and he hasn't even tried to find you."

Because Enzo thinks I'm dead, and he has a woman he loves that he has to protect at all costs.

"I would love to have a man work for me with that kind of loyalty."

You have to earn it. Show that even though you do some bad things, you are fair and honest and do the right thing when it really matters. You will sacrifice your life for mine just as I would mine for yours.

Julian will never be that kind of boss. He likes money and power too much. From what I've seen, he's fair with how he treats his men. He pays them well for the jobs they do, but that's as far as it goes. He's not friends with his men. He doesn't treat them like equals. And he thinks his life is more important than theirs.

"Who is your boss, anyway?" Julian asks, causally taking another puff of his cigar.

But there is nothing casual about his question. He's very curious to know who my boss is. And I don't plan on telling him a damn thing. I'm loyal; I'll protect the Black empire with my life.

"Right now, you."

He chuckles, almost choking on the smoke cloud that surrounds us.

"Good answer." He reaches into his briefcase and pulls out a small stack of papers. "Memorize everything on these, then burn them. We don't leave a paper trail." His eyes focus on mine as I take the papers. He's not sure if I'm anything more than just muscle. He's still not sure I have any brains behind the armor I wear. It's a mistake many men before him have made.

But my brain works just fine. Even after almost drowning and bleeding out in the middle of the fucking ocean.

I'll memorize everything on these papers with no problem. Then I'm going to get Julian this fucking drug deal and get off this fucking island.

But as my eyes skim the papers quickly, I realize Julian isn't the man I thought he is. His soul is darker than I realized. His greed for money has no bounds. And I just walked into his trap.

Because what I'm reading isn't something I would ever do. I've done some bad things in my life. Stolen. Threatened. Beaten. Tortured. Killed. But this is a line I don't cross. I don't traffic humans, and yet that is exactly what Julian is asking me to do.

CHAPTER 3
SIREN

*W**hy did I end up parked in front of the biggest mansion on the island?*

Because I'm stupid.

Because I'm begging to get caught.

Because I like living in danger.

Because I'd rather be trapped in a beautiful cage than continue to live in my own personal hell.

Because I'm desperate.

I consider using the doorbell, but that's really not my style. I don't ask for permission. I never have. I take what is owed to me, even if others disagree. And then I deal with the consequences.

So I walk around to the back of the large all-white building that is just as fake as the man who lives alone inside. The house is three stories tall and the size of a football field. Water weaves through the compound, separating the various buildings from the main house. It looks like an expensive resort, instead of where the devil lives.

I hate this house.

I hate this island.

And I'm finally going to do something about it. A plan forms in my head as I walk to the back door. I'm going to steal something. Something valuable. Something I can easily sell and use to get off this island. Something I can use to start a new life. Something I can use to hide away. Something this man won't even miss.

Who am I kidding?

Julian will realize something is missing from his precious mansion. He lives for his things. He loves the status they give him. He's a little OCD about it. I wouldn't doubt he spends his nights counting all the expensive things in his mansion. They're the only things that can tolerate living in his presence.

I pick the lock on the back door and crack it open, waiting for an alarm to sound. None does.

I've never stolen anything before. That's not the kind of person I am. But I'm desperate. And if anyone deserves to have something stolen, it's Julian Reed.

I step one foot inside, waiting for his army to descend on me. Again, nothing happens.

I grin.

This might actually work.

That, or he'll find me and kill me. Either way, I won't keep living with this pain.

I walk through his house, my hands tempted by all the objects in his house—the paintings, the gold-plated sculptures, the finely threaded fabrics of his furniture. All are too big for me to take. I need something small. Something that can easily be sold.

Jewelry, I decide.

I head up the staircase in search of his bedroom. I'm sure he keeps some jewelry up there.

I haven't seen any sign that he is home. But Julian doesn't scare me. He's a fucking drug dealer who thinks he's a bigger deal than he is. He's a nothing—a boy playing with his daddy's money.

And if he catches me, I'll offer to suck his dick or something to get out. He's a good looking man, even if he is evil.

I find his bedroom. It's dark, and the door is closed. I lean my ear against his door—nothing.

I open the door. It creaks, but no one comes for me. No one knows I'm here.

I step inside. I consider turning the lights on but decide I've tested fate enough. However, I'm not good at seeing in the dark, no matter how much my eyes try to adjust. I don't make a good criminal. I'm just hungry and desperate enough to try anything.

My hand finds the wall, and I walk with my hand against it until I reach an opening—the bathroom.

My hand trails over the counter as I search for a jewelry box, anything that contains something expensive that can be easily sold, but not easily missed.

Jackpot.

I find a box sitting out in plain sight on the middle of the counter. I flip it open and dig to the bottom, hoping to find something that will change my life.

I pull out a bracelet, dripping in diamonds.

I grin—this would give me a new life.

I go to put the bracelet into my pocket, when a hand grabs me out of the darkness.

I close my eyes, hoping this is all a dream, a figment of my imagination, my worst nightmare. That when I open my eyes, I'll be in my bed, not here, stealing from the most dangerous man on the island.

But when I open them, I'm still in the darkness. And Julian is still gripping my hand.

"What are you doing?" he asks, his voice curious more than angry.

Think, quickly! I can find a way out of this.

I stare at the bracelet.

"I'm—" Fuck, I can't answer.

"Are you the new maid?" he whispers into my neck. He releases my wrist, but his heavy breath has me captured. His body is pressed against my ass and back, and he sweeps my air off my neck so he can own that part of me too.

I breathe out with a shaky breath, but can't force my lips to say *yes.*

"Is there a reason you are cleaning in the dark?"

The power is out.

I couldn't find the light switch.

I prefer the dark.

So many lies fill my head. But none of them can flow through my lips.

"I'm not the maid. I came here to steal something of value I could use to get off this fucking island. Something you wouldn't miss. Something I could use to start a new life." *Something to heal my pain and fix my problems.*

The lights flick on in that moment, and I'm exposed. The lights shouldn't make a difference, but they do. In the dark, I could have spilled all of my secrets but in the light...I want to close up every thought I have and hide them away from this man.

Julian Reed is well-known on the island. I've served him in bars where I worked as a bartender numerous times. But seeing him now, pressed against me, the first two buttons of his shirt undone, his hair slicked back, and his eyes focused on me and not some business deal he's working on, I realize how intimidating a man he is.

"What's your name?" he asks.

Lie.

Don't tell him the truth. Keep all of your secrets.

I can't lie, but I refuse to answer.

His eyes light up when he realizes this.

"You can't lie, can you?"

"No...I can't."

He shakes his head as he brushes more of my hair off my neck, fascinated by me.

I'm silent. *I can't lie.* Every time I try, my body or words betray me. *Even if it could have saved me now.* If I had just pretended to be the maid like he guessed, I would be safe.

"What's your deal, pet?"

"Pet?"

He grins as he puts his hands in his pockets as if trying to make me more comfortable by preventing himself from touching me. I'm not falling for it. I know this man will hurt me before the night is over. He'll rape me. Torture me. Kill me. Him putting his hands in his pockets doesn't make him any less of a threat to me. I turn to face him.

"Yes, you are now my pet. Unless you tell me your name, and I like it better than 'pet.' Then I might call you by your name instead."

My lips beg me to lie. To tell him any name. I don't want him to know who I am, but I don't want him to call me pet.

He cracks his neck back and forth casually, waiting for me to answer.

"You're an intriguing creature, pet."

My eyes burn red.

He laughs, and then one of his hands reaches out automatically.

"I'm going to enjoy you so much, pet."

"No," I whisper, trying to step back as his hand strokes my face, but there is nowhere for me to go. I'm trapped between him and the counter at my back.

I turn my head, trying to be as defiant as I can.

"I'm sorry. I shouldn't have broken into your house and tried to steal from you. Let me go. I'll owe you. I'll work for you for free."

He tilts his head, studying me. "Will you now?"

I nod, hoping to god he needs free labor more than he wants to do bad things to me.

"I don't think you really have a say in the matter, pet. You broke into my house. You stole from me. Now you have to pay the consequences."

"Are you going to call the police?"

He laughs. "No, pet. I'm not going to call the police."

"What do you want from me then?"

"I want your fiery spirit."

His eyes heat over my body.

"I want your perfect lips that can't spill a lie."

I gasp as his thumb traces over my bottom lip.

"I want to own your desperation."

He spins me around, and then I'm facing the mirror again. His hand is on my throat and hip. And I'm pulled tight to his rough body.

I can't breathe, but not because of how he is holding me. Because I'm waiting for the rest of his words to fall. I'm waiting to hear what my fate is.

"I want to harness you. I want to teach you how to use your assets to my advantage. I want to own your body. I want to control your mind."

I'm never breathing again. Maybe if I stop breathing, I won't live long enough for any of his words to come true.

"And what if I don't do what you want?" I ask, with words bolder than I'm feeling.

"Oh, pet. I always get what I want."

CHAPTER 4
ZEKE

There has to be a different way I can repay Julian.

That sentence has played in my head over and over and over. Every day of the last week, I've tried to come up with a different plan—a different way to pay him back.

He saved my life. *I could save his.*

But he never puts himself in any danger. I've never seen a leader of a criminal organization keep his hands as clean as he does. Instead of doing the dirty work himself, he always has his employees do anything remotely risky. And the few times he has to take meetings in person, he does it in his mansion, where I know he has plenty of security features.

My old boss was in the security business. I know security when I see it, even though his is well hidden. I can spot the cameras, the infrared, the panic buttons. I can spot the bulletproof walls.

Julian knows he has enemies. He knows he is exposed if he puts himself out there. So he hides. People know who he is, but he rarely shows himself in public. Somehow, that makes him even more powerful.

But it makes it very difficult for me to be able to save his life to pay him back.

I'm stuck in the horrible position of getting him a partnership with a man who traffics humans. And I don't see a way out.

I could run away. Not repay my debt.

But Julian's not the kind of man who lets a debt go. He would come for me. And in turn, he'd come for my boss. He'd come for the Black empire I'm desperate to protect.

No way will I let that happen.

But I really don't want a permanent mark on my soul.

I step out of my beat-up truck and look up at the enormous warehouse sitting on the edge of the island. It doesn't look like anything special. Just four walls with a tin roof. It looks like any other storage facility. But this one has one main difference. Instead of storing merchandise or supplies, this building stores people like animals.

"Ah, you must be Mr. Zeke," a man says as soon as I step out of the car.

He's dressed in a sharp-looking suit just like Julian. But unlike Julian, this man has a gut that sticks out, defeating the purpose of the suit. He looks weak, not powerful.

"It's just Zeke. You must be Oscar," I say as I walk to him and force myself to extend my hand.

He takes my hand and shakes it. And I can't resist squeezing his hand a little too harshly.

He just grins at my forceful handshake.

"Mr. Reed has said many good things about you. He said you were his best up and coming man. That you could easily be his number two."

I nod. "I'm the best at my job." My stomach churns bile into my throat. I'm good enough to actually do this job; to convince this man that he should work with Julian and me. I have the skills to ensure shipments happen swiftly and accurately.

"Come, come. Let me show you around, and then we can talk business," Oscar says, extending his hand to lead me toward the building I want to empty and burn to the ground.

I don't smile, as opposed to the petite man as he leads me into the building, showing me around the building like he's giving me a tour of the Louvre instead of where humanity comes to die. Good thing I almost never smile. Frowning feeds into my scary appearance. It makes me look more menacing.

Fuck, how did my life lead me here?

I've seen a lot of sinful shit in my life. I've seen more men killed in front of me, by me, than I ever thought I would. I've tortured people. Watched the life leave their eyes. I've known women who were raped. But nothing in my life could prepare me for what I saw when I entered this building.

I could feel the fear, pain, and anger the second I entered the building. I have an uncanny ability to feel emotions emanating from nearby people. I don't understand it. I can sense things others are feeling. I haven't even seen another person so far on our tour, but I've never felt so much pain in one place before.

"This way," Oscar says excitedly.

I glare as I follow the pudgy little man.

He opens the door, and I step through to a room I wasn't expecting to see.

"What's this?" I ask.

He grins like he's about to show off the Sistine Chapel instead of his demonic headquarters. "This is where we hold our main event. We only hold an event here twice a year for our biggest clients who spend the most money. It's an auction of sorts. We parade our best women in front of them, and the highest bidder wins the prize."

A low growl escapes me as he speaks about selling women, but the asshole is too busy to notice as he gloats about how he turned this part of the warehouse into a fancy showroom filled with tables, bars, and a stage that shows off the women's best assets.

"Why don't you hold more frequent events here? That way, you wouldn't need us to transport and sell your remaining women for you. You would get all the money yourself," I say, hoping this man is just an idiot, and once I point out the obvious, he will have no need for us. Sure, I'll fail the task Julian gave me. But maybe he'll let me try again with a shipment of drugs or weapons, anything but people.

He sighs. "It would make business a lot easier. But it's just not feasible. The richest people in the world come here for the event. It's our biggest money earning night of the year. But we hide it under the guise of the weekend-long yachting event. That's how we keep suspicions low. The men all stay at the Four Seasons, the luxury hotel where the event is held. They all attend, and then we sneak them here under the darkness of the night. Our little island would get too much press and attention if the richest in the world were all flying here on a monthly basis on the same weekend."

I frown. "But this island is beautiful with plenty of luxury hotels. Why couldn't you just house the women here, and when one of the buyers comes, bring them here individually to have their pick?"

"It's too expensive to feed the whores while we wait for the men to come to us. And even though this is one of our most profitable nights, not all of the men can travel to us. Sometimes we need to go to them. Which is why we hire out. You take on all the risk, while we get all the reward."

Tell me about it.

"So then why would we want to do business with you if we take on all the risk?" I ask.

He raises his eyebrow. "Because we aren't the only ones who get a reward. If we strike a deal, then we split profits fifty-fifty. And the amount of money we pay is bigger than the petty little drugs and weapons Mr. Reed currently moves. This would put him on a whole new level. Supposedly, Mr. Reed is the best at transporting things while flying under the radar."

"He is," I agree.

"Well, that's why you are here. To prove to me you can handle the job, not question why I run my business the way I do."

"No, I'm not here to convince you of anything. You know of Julian's reputation. You can see I mean business."

He laughs. "I don't believe anyone who shows up in ripped jeans and a man bun is serious about doing business with me. And I don't think anyone who calls his boss by his first name respects him."

I snarl, this time, he hears it. He freezes.

"I'm here to see if we can strike a deal. But I won't let my boss enter a relationship with a man who is an inadequate business partner. I'm doing my due diligence.

"And if you don't already think we are a good partnership for you, then you are an idiot. You didn't choose our island for the scenery. You chose our island because of Julian. You knew he was the best at transportation. You need him; he doesn't need you. He will be just fine without your business. And I respect Julian greatly. And he respects me, which is why we are on a first-name basis."

Oscar's eyes dart side-to-side as he takes me in—how fucking serious I am.

"Then he sent the right man. Because I don't do business with desperate men, and that's exactly what I thought Mr. Reed was when he called trying to get my business. You just changed my mind." He turns to continue the tour.

"We want sixty."

He pauses, his head swiveling to look at me.

"You heard me. We want sixty percent. And we want half of it upfront."

He narrows his eyes. "The deal was for fifty-fifty. That's my final offer. It's the arrangement I have with all of my partners. I capture the women and hold them for no more than a week. Then you arrange deals with buyers and transport them. It's a fifty-fifty arrangement."

"No, it's not. Finding sellers, vetting them, and then transporting the women takes a lot longer than grabbing them and holding them here for a week. We could have to hold onto the women for weeks, months even. We take on the risk of selling and transporting them to a client who could be working for the cops, while you sit back here protected from everyone.

"If we get caught, we go to jail. We lose everything. While you just lose your partner. We want a bigger cut—sixty," I say, hoping this will ensure we don't have a deal. If I push him hard enough, he will back down and say that he won't do business with us. And if Julian asks, I can tell him I didn't think it was a good deal because we deserved a bigger cut. And I'll personally find him a deal that will make up for the lost income—one selling drugs, not people.

"You better be worth it, Zeke," he says with a frown.

Dammit.

"Come on, let me show you where we store the women. Then I can see if we have a suit that fits you. You aren't showing up for the biggest night of the year dressed like a bum."

I frown. I'm not wearing a fucking suit. That is not my style. And I'm tall and bulky enough to know there is no way he will find a suit big enough to fit me.

I follow Oscar behind the stage, trying to prepare myself. But nothing could prepare me to see women in chains. And not the kinky, consenting kind. The kind no woman has the strength to break free from.

I prepare myself to hear begging, to see tears, but these women don't look at me as their savior. They think I'm just like Oscar. They think I'm a villain that one of them will eventually be sold to. They don't know I would never buy any of them. If I could, I would set them all free.

Instead, I look at hollow eyes, tight lips, and women trying to hide their bodies from my view.

"They are bewitching, aren't they?" Oscar says, grabbing one of the women by the chin and lifting her face up to examine her like an animal.

I tense, but don't react. *How can this be real? How can people be this cruel?*

"We already have a transporter for this group. But we will have over a hundred women for you in a few weeks."

A hundred women—fuck.

"And then we will have a new shipment for you in three weeks after that if the first deal works out. So I suggest you move quickly."

We will get another hundred women in less than a month—fuck, fuck, fuck.

We walk further down the hallway to where there is a large cage filled with twenty women. Each of them is shackled at their arms and legs as if they would have the strength to get through the metal bars holding them in.

"These are the women for tonight. The most beautiful, attractive high priced women we could find. Some are virgins; some are women from high-class families. All will go for more than a million a piece."

Jesus Christ.

"But if Mr. Reed wants first pick, of course, that can be arranged for the right price. Take a look," Oscar says.

I'm sick. I'm seconds away from puking up everything I've ever eaten. My face turns green, but I'm not going to let Oscar know that. I don't have a plan. Not yet, but I will.

I look over the women with a deep scowl, knowing I can't save them. I can't protect them.

I glance at the last woman, and my heart stops. I squat down in front of her, getting a better look at this exquisite creature.

The most alluring eyes look back at me. This woman isn't scared. She's full of fight. I see the wheels in her brain turning, determined to find a way out of this situation. She's not going to go down without fighting.

But she's going to lose. I know the amount of security Oscar has. I can't save her. If I find her leaving, I will be forced to capture her and turn her back in. She needs to accept this is her new life. It will be easier for her.

But the fight in her eyes, long gone in the others, isn't the only thing that makes me pause looking at her. There is something else about her. Something that has my brain spinning, trying its best to remember why I know her. A wash of déjà vu crashes through me when I look at her.

"Aww, this one is going to go for the highest price tonight, guaranteed. She's beautiful and a fighter. The others are already broken. She's going to make me a lot of money. I'd guess three million. The men prefer a fighter. They want to be the one to break a woman. And she is begging to be broken."

"Where did you find her?"

"This one washed ashore during the last storm. The ocean finally gave us a gift for once."

The ocean.

Julian didn't pull me from the ocean.

This angel did.

Siren—that was her name.

I still owe Julian for getting me medical attention, but I don't owe him as much as I first thought. Because Siren was the one who pulled me from the ocean. She stopped me from drowning. She put her hands over my wounds to keep me from bleeding out. She sang to me to keep me calm. She dragged my lifeless body to her car. She brought me to the only person on the island with the money and power to save me.

And what did the world give her for saving me? Imprisonment and the verge of being sold into sexual slavery.

She glares at me. She remembers me. And she hates me. She blames me for her predicament. And she thinks she saved a monster. She thinks I'm just like the men who took her.

I stand up. "How long until the event?"

"Three hours."

I nod. "We better get ready then."

"Excellent." Oscar starts gabbing about everything still to be done. I barely listen, though. All I can think about is Siren. About how she saved my life. And now, I have to save hers.

CHAPTER 5
SIREN

I hate silence. But I hate the sound of sniffling even more. It's like someone is stabbing my ears with knives. That's the reaction I feel every time I hear a sniffle, a cough, a muffled cry. Not because I care or have a heart for the other women who are captured with me. I do, of course, have a heart. I want them all to find their way out of this mess the same as me. But right now, I can't think about escaping because my brain is consumed with sniffle, drip, sniffle, cough.

Fuck, I grab my ears with my hands trying to get the sounds to stop, trying to get the anxiety building in my chest to dissipate. But it only grows. There is a name for my condition—misophonia. It means normal, ordinary sounds cause a visceral reaction in my body. Usually, I can avoid the sounds. If someone is slurping too loudly at a coffee shop, I can leave. If my friend is chewing too loudly at dinner, I can talk over the noise. If someone is sneezing on the bus, I can play music louder in my earbuds.

But I can't do any of those things right now. I'm stuck in a cage with a dozen terrified women. A hundred more are tied up nearby. All of them releasing a cacophony of various noises in the otherwise silent room. No one dares to talk, too afraid they will become the first victim to be beaten, raped, or sold.

None of them understand it doesn't matter if we are the first or the last; we all face the same fate. We are all about to be sold like cattle. We have all lost our dignity, our human right to freedom. We are now property.

Deep breath in and then out, I practice my calming technique, and I feel the anxiety lower an inch from my throat to my chest. Most people think anxiety is all in your head; it isn't. It takes over everything in your body. Your stomach aches, your chest pounds unable to catch a breath, your throat closes up, your mouth runs dry, and even your bones throb from the anxiety. Relieving a single one of those pains is a success in my book.

"What do you think is going to happen?" the woman to my right whispers into my ear. She's dressed in a gray suit, with a white blouse underneath. Her blouse is now covered in dirt, her mascara is running down her face, and her hair looks like it hasn't been washed in a week. I would guess a week ago she was a high-powered lawyer or business-woman—now she's nothing but tears. But she is strong enough to ask me a question in the silence even though there are guards watching us. I admire her bravery.

"They are going to sell us," I say flatly, not sugarcoating our outcome.

The woman grips her neck, as if she can't believe her fate.

"For what purpose?" her voice is weaker now.

I blink rapidly, looking at her. *She can't be serious?* Does she not realize there is only one reason to sell another human being? *Money*. These men want money. And the men who are buying us want power. They want to control us, live out their sick fantasies, rape us, torture us, and, the kind ones, kill us.

But I see her trembling hand; I see the tears welling up in her eyes, the way she bites her bottom lip. She's about to break out into an uncontrollable sob. That's a sound that will rip right through my body and bring back every drop of anxiety I was feeling.

"What's your name?" I ask.

"Alice."

She doesn't ask for mine. She's too focused on her own fate to see that she isn't the only woman who is about to face the same outcome.

"Okay, Alice. Are you married?"

She shakes her head.

"Have a boyfriend?"

Again she shakes her head no.

"Kids?"

No—she was probably too focused on her work to date. She seems like a smart, ambitious, gorgeous woman in her late twenties. She probably never bothered to date. Now, I'm sure she wishes she did. Then maybe she'd have that love to focus on. That strength to pull her through this. That hope that her man would come and save her. That fairytale that love conquers all, that it ultimately wins.

I laugh.

"What's so funny?" She asks.

"Sorry," I say, thinking about how love only makes you weaker, not stronger. By not falling in love, this woman proved her ultimate super-power. She is strong enough to handle anything on her own.

I grip her shoulders and look her straight in the eyes. "Alice, you are strong. You have not only survived these last twenty plus years without a man, but you have thrived. You have become a fierce, badass woman. No matter what happens, you lived a great life. And you are strong enough to handle whatever is coming your way. Remember that."

My words are meant to be a pep talk, but it seems to have the opposite effect on Alice, who bursts into tears. A domino effect of emotional distress rips through the group until the entire room is crying, sniffling, sucking in tears—all the things I hate.

Dammit.

Sighing, I bring my knees up to my chest and my long brown hair around my ears, trying my best to tune them all out.

"Stop that racket, you stupid whores!" a guard yells, pounding his gun against the bars.

The room instantly falls silent, and I find myself liking the guard a bit more for making the room go silent again. *How fucked up is that?*

Our cell door is opened, and three guards enter the small cage holding me and eleven other women. We are all handcuffed at the hands and feet, but I don't think the cuffs are needed for most of the women. They are all too terrified to run or fight. They've already accepted their fate.

The guards start grabbing women up off the floor until they are on their shaky feet. I refuse to be pulled up by my hair or arms, so I stand before a guard can get to me. I will not be afraid—I refuse. As long as I don't say that I'm scared, I won't be. I can't lie to myself and say that I'm happy or unafraid. Deep down there is some fear, but as long as I can't focus on it, then I'm not lying or telling the truth. I'm just focusing on other things.

A guard reaches me, seeing me standing eye to eye to him. I'm tall, even without heels.

"Are you going to be a problem?" he asks, eyeing me before uncuffing my ankles.

I raise an eyebrow. "Only if you try to hurt me."

He huffs and then grabs my arm roughly. I fight, trying to pull my arm free as I kick at his legs.

He shakes me; I fight harder.

He stops, I stop.

He sighs. "Fine, we will do this your way. I've dealt with your type before, and I'd like to have children someday."

I grin when he releases my arm. I'm the only woman left in the room. He correctly guessed that I would kick him in the balls if he manhandled me too much.

"This way," he points to the exit of the cage.

I start walking untouched.

He verbally commands me to walk down the hallway to a small room where three women wait for me.

I spot a chair in the center that's meant to glamorize me—make me look like a woman again instead of a gaunt invalid that hasn't been fed in a week.

"Sit," the man says.

I sit, knowing he is the least of my worries.

"I'll be right outside the door. Don't give them any trouble, or I'll break your wrist."

"You can't do that. I doubt the men who are waiting for us want to buy broken women."

He frowns. "That's why I said wrist instead of foot or nose. The men won't be able to tell your wrist is broken. The swelling won't happen until after you've already been sold, and by then, we can just say they were the ones who broke it."

With that, he walks out, slamming the door.

The three women all put their heads down, none of them looking me in the eyes as they begin to work on my hair, face, and nails.

"Why do you work for these men?" I ask.

None of them answer me.

Two of the women murmur something low and quiet to each other. It's then that I realize they don't speak English. Two of the women look Hispanic. One of the women is black and doesn't chat with the other two. I look like a mix of the three women.

My skin is tan in an exotic way. I don't know the nationality of my birth parents, but I would guess I'm a mix of several ethnicities. My adoptive parents always treated me as if I were a bad person for having an unknown origin. My culture is a strength—I am a mix of everything and hence know more of the world because of it.

The women chat again.

"Why do you work for these men?" I ask in Spanish.

All of the women freeze but don't answer me. They heard and understood what I said, though.

So I try again. "Help me. Or at least help them," I say in Spanish.

Nothing.

One woman files my fingers harder until I'm not sure I'll have a fingernail left.

I sigh.

"They won't answer you," the third woman says.

"Why not?" I ask, looking into her eyes. She meets my gaze, and I realize she's old enough to be my grandmother. The other two women are closer to my age.

"Because they are afraid. Everyone is afraid. They risk facing the same fate as you if they help you."

I look at the two beautiful women working on my hair and nails.

They aren't wearing any makeup, they wear their hair back in buns, trying to hide their beauty.

"The only reason they aren't sold is that they can do hair and makeup."

I nod. "And you? Will you help?"

The older woman grabs my hand and places it between her two hands, trying to comfort me. It works, my insides warm a little at the touch.

"Do I look like I'm strong enough to be able to help you escape?"

I sigh.

"I can't help you or any of the other women escape. But I can offer you words."

I nod for her to speak, even though I don't think words are going to be able to help me right now.

"Give them hell."

Three little words—*give them hell*.

I scrunch my nose, and she laughs.

"I see how much fighting spirit you have inside you—use it. The ones who last—the ones who make the men fall in love with them are the ones who eventually gain control. They become the masters.

"You have what it takes. You will not only survive, but you will become powerful. You will rule. You will have the ability to one day put an end to this. So give them hell."

Give them hell.

I nod. *That, I can do.*

She smiles at my reaction and then gets back to work at plucking my eyebrows.

The rest of my time with the women is silent as they work. They paint my nails, curl my mud-brown hair, decorate my face in makeup, and wax off every piece of body hair. Then they leave me alone with a rack of lingerie and a robe.

They didn't have to tell me what to do, I already know. Pick out the piece of lingerie to wear on stage.

I don't want to wear any lingerie.

But the guard's words haunt me. If I go for more money, I will be better taken care of. I'll be more valuable. So I need to choose what I wear carefully.

I look over the garments. Most are white—innocent.

I laugh, I'm not innocent. I'm not an angel. Those were the words I said to Zeke. *I'm not an angel.* But neither is he—the bastard. I saved his life, and he repaid that debt by being an even bigger schmuck than I thought possible.

Fuck him.

Fuck them all.

Give them hell.

I grin when I find the last garment on the end of the rack. I put it on and stare at myself in the mirror before I put the robe on, covering my body.

Just as I finish veiling myself with the robe, the guard opens the door without knocking.

"Time to go back to your cage," he says.

I stand taller than him now in my heels, and the lustful look on his face as he takes in my appearance tells me that even with the robe on, I would go for a lot of money. But once I take the robe off, my price will skyrocket.

He clears his throat and holds the door open for me. I brush past him as I strut.

And I hear him curse under his breath. I smirk, feeling powerful.

He may not be able or willing to save me. But someday, I'm going to find a man who can—a man who is willing to risk everything for me. Then I will have all the power.

I walk back to the cage where the other eleven women sit. This time, none of us are handcuffed. We are all wearing robes covering the intimate pieces of our bodies that will eventually be exposed. Every woman's hair is styled, her face painted. Each looks a little different. Some look like innocent angels; the youngest woman even has pigtails to make her look younger. A couple of the women have dark red lips to make them look older and more mature. But all of the women look more terrified instead of determined.

The apparent man in charge enters the cage with two of the guards. One of the guards has a notebook and pen in his hand. The boss takes his time walking around the cage, studying each of us like he's trying to determine how much we should go for.

I want to stick my foot out and try to trip him, but I resist the urge as he starts pointing to women and assigning each a random number. I realize he's deciding the order in which we will be trotted out on stage. He's starting with the women he thinks will go for the least and ending on the most expensive.

He hasn't pointed to me yet. Maybe because he's forgotten I exist as he walks around the circle.

I swear my foot sticks out on its own accord. Next thing I know, he stumbles over the heel of my foot.

I pull it back to my body quickly. I'm afraid, but knowing if I'm punished, it will be minimal. They don't want to damage me right before the show.

The man squats down in front of me, looking me in the eye. I think he's going to yell at me. Punch me. Make me feel some pain for tripping him.

Instead, he grins crookedly, a toothpick sliding out between his yellow teeth.

"Twenty," he says, looking at me. "She will easily go for five mill. Maybe more, she has a fight to her the men can't resist. They will all want to be the one to break her."

Five million dollars, holy hell.

Maybe the advice the woman gave me was bad? If I give them too much hell, then they will want to break me.

The man walks out and through a door to what I realize is a stage.

I can hear the sound of music playing in the next room. The show is about to start. And I can practically feel every heart in the room speed up at the sound.

A few minutes later, one of the guards is dragging out the woman labeled number one. She's one of the youngest. I would guess seventeen or eighteen. She's still a baby in many ways. And she's about to be thrust on stage and sold.

The guard pushes her out and leaves the door to the stage open so we can all see to the stage. I don't know if it's meant to intimidate or encourage us to be able to see how the previous women are treated.

But the first woman stands in the middle of the stage, gripping her robe nervously as men yell out numbers in the crowd.

After a few minutes of her being on stage, the man in charge asks her to disrobe. But she only grips it tighter.

He snaps his fingers, and two of the guards rip the robe from her body. She crumbles to the floor in tears, trying her best to cover her almost naked body.

All of the women in the cage turn away, looking away from her humiliation.

One by one, each woman is dragged to the stage and faces the same fate. Most sell for between one and three million. Each is forced to disrobe. Each is humiliated and frightened beyond possibility.

But I won't be. *Give. Them. Hell.*

I plan to.

The guards outside the cage start drinking, enjoying the fun and amount of money their boss is making, which will obviously trickle down to them.

And then I'm the only woman left in the cage.

My heart speeds uncontrollably as I prepare for my turn. I'm not sure what I'm going to do, but I won't cower. I won't let them have my power.

Finally, the man who has been my guard walks to the entrance of the cage. He motions for me as I stand.

"Your turn." His eyes light as he says it, as if he wishes he had enough money to bid on me.

"Give me a shot of tequila."

"What? No."

"I'll go for more than double any other woman here if you give me a shot. You can tell your boss it was because of the shot of liquid courage that helped me to perform. You will have gotten your boss more money and maybe a new strategy to help future women."

He frowns but hands me a shot glass. He grabs a bottle as all eyes of the other guards focus in on us. He pours the tequila into the shot glass and fills it to the rim.

"You owe me, and don't worry. I plan to collect on my debt," he says, threatening me.

But I won't be threatened. He can't hurt me. No man can. I know what it's like to be betrayed by a man. And the only way a man can hurt me anymore is if I give them my heart—something I will never do again.

I throw the shot back into my mouth.

I feel the warm liquid trickle down my throat and warm my stomach.

It's my last moment of happiness, the last moment that is truly mine before I walk on the stage.

I hand the shot glass back to my guard, and then I strut up the stairs to the stage. I'll give them hell alright. The men will wish they never captured me.

Because I'm about to tap into my power tonight. I may not win the fight, but by the time I'm through with them, I will drain them all of their power.

Even if it's the last thing I do.

CHAPTER 6
ZEKE

This is my nightmare.

Men are sitting at small circular tables scattered throughout a dark floor. Each table can sit three men max, but only a couple are filled. Most men are sitting by themselves with a phone in one hand, a drink in the other, and cigar puffing out of their mouths.

Each man is assigned a scantily dressed waitress to do more than just serve drinks. They are here to tease the men before the show, so maybe they will open their bank accounts wider.

"What can I get you, sugar?" The waitress assigned to me asks.

"I'm good," I say, lifting my barely drank scotch.

She gives me a knowing look as she eyes the scotch.

"Got a weak stomach, sugar?"

I growl—she's just trying to goad me into drinking more so I'll be more hasty with my money. But I need my wits about me tonight.

A man at the table over must hear our conversation because he starts murmuring to the man on his right.

Great, I'm going to be known as a pussy.

Fuck—I can't let that happen.

Not because I care what people think of me, but I can't draw any suspicions. I need Julian to think I'm an equal to him. And if Oscar thinks of me as a pussy, then he'll tell Julian.

I down the expensive scotch.

"Another," I say.

She picks up the glass, her eyes brightening, and her hips swaying as she walks away from me to retrieve another drink.

The lights dim even more, until the only lights left in the room are the single candles on each table.

Oscar walks out onto the stage as a spotlight follows him.

"Welcome, friends. I have quite a show for you."

Some of the men applaud and hoop excitedly, while others stare at their phones like they couldn't be more bored.

I do neither. I reach for where my drink once sat and find the table empty. I need my damn waitress to get back with my glass, so I have something to squeeze to death while I try to think of a plan.

"The first beautiful woman I have for you is more girl than woman. Let's hear it for Chaste."

The light flickers to stage right as a young blonde woman is pushed onto the stage by two guards. She stumbles, falling to the ground as she grips the thin white robe around her body. She doesn't realize the robe is practically see-through in the bright stage light. We can already see her body. A body that looks barely older than fifteen.

Jesus Christ. I glance around at the men. They are sick. Not only are they selling women, but they are selling underage women.

The waitress finally returns with my drink, and I down it. I'm going to need a lot of alcohol to get through tonight.

"Keep them coming," I growl at her as I crush the glass in my hand, not caring who sees.

"Of course, sugar." She brushes her hand over my shoulder in a seductive way before she walks away. But the most attractive woman in the world could strip naked in front of me and offer to suck my dick, and I wouldn't get turned on right now. I'm beyond pissed that men are this disgusting.

Oscar starts the bidding at half a million.

That number quickly shoots up to over two million for the young virgin.

But Oscar isn't satisfied. He snaps his fingers, and the guards return to the stage. Her rope is ripped from her body until she is standing in white lingerie, revealing small breasts, a flat stomach, and bony hips. She's so young. Untouched. And scared to death.

I skim the crowd trying to memorize every face of the men who are bidding on her—reserving a special place in my memory filled with the torturous thoughts of what I'm going to do to them when I'm finally a free man who can come after them.

The woman sells for $2.5 million.

And seconds later, another woman is dragged onto the stage to do the whole show all over again. This one is slightly older than the first, but just barely. She wears the same face of terror as the girl before her.

My stomach contracts tightly at the sight. I could easily vomit I'm so angry and disgusted. Instead, I sip on the drink my waitress brought me.

"Young women aren't your thing? Don't worry, they always save the more mature women for the end. You would think the young ones would be the most popular, but they aren't. The young ones the men can get all the time.

"Just flash some money in a twenty-something's face, and she will do anything for you. It's the older women—the ones who have a career, a husband, kids, a life. The smart ones are hard to get. They aren't as easily broken as the young ones." She sighs. "Around number fifteen is when I expect you to start bidding, stud."

And then she's gone. I'm not going to bid. If I do, it will be just so it's not obvious that I'm a traitor. But I won't win a woman.

I'm here to protect.

That's what I do—protect people. But I can't protect any of these women. Not without getting a lot of them killed, myself included. I just came back from the dead; I don't want to return so quickly. I would risk it if I had a real shot at getting them to safety, but I don't. I don't have a big enough truck to transport all of them in. I don't have a boat to help them escape. I would just be leading them all to their deaths.

They might prefer it to where they are going, but I can't be responsible for getting them killed.

Another woman appears on stage, gripping the robe like it's her only lifeline. The only thing keeping her safe.

Is it..?

The woman finally looks up into the crowd of dark faces.

No, it's not Siren.

But the next woman could be.

What the hell am I going to do?

I can't let her be sold. I can't let her become a sex slave. She saved my life; I owe this to her. It's as if fate stepped in and is requiring me to save her life. I'm in the right place at the right time to protect her. Just like she was in the right place at the right time to save me.

But how do I save a woman currently being held by my boss' client?

I could kidnap her.

Take her at gunpoint.

Or sneak her out before she was transferred to her new owner.

I could get a boat or a plane out of here. Take her anywhere in the world.

But Julian would know. He has enough resources to come after us both. We would always be running. She would never really be safe.

And I could never return to my life before. I would never bring them into more danger.

Besides, I'm not sure if I could rescue her without us being caught. There are cameras, guards, and locked doors between us and a chance at freedom. I might not even get her out the door.

More women are brought on stage, each more terrified than the one before. The girls being shown now are women, not girls—most in their late twenties to early thirties. Some even have a tan line where a wedding ring used to rest.

Only two women left—one is Siren.

I hold my breath as the second to last woman is pushed out onto the stage.

Blonde.

Not Siren.

Fuck.

Only one woman left. And then the show will be over. My time is up. I need a plan—now.

I don't listen to the bids. I can't focus on anything except the anxiety in my chest as I wait for Siren.

The room falls silent again, as the woman is dragged off the stage.

"We saved the best for last. This woman is exotic, beauty itself. She has a mane of hair. Red fuck me lips. Eyes like fire. Flawless skin. And tits for days."

The room cheers in anticipation of the last woman. There are only twenty women to be sold and thirty men to buy them. It ensures that the last woman goes for the most. Not all men will leave with a woman, at least not a woman from the select group. I'm sure they can go backstage and have their pick of the rest before they are shipped out.

But they don't get the honor of having one of the "best."

I wait for the familiar push and stumble of Siren onto the stage. But it doesn't come.

Instead, *click, click, click.*

The room is silent except for the click of her heels against the hard wood of the stairs.

The entire room takes a deep breath as she appears on stage. And the oxygen in my lungs vanishes entirely.

Siren doesn't get pushed into the center like any of the other women. She struts, owning the stage like it was her idea in the first place.

There is no fear in her eyes, just anger.

She flips her long tresses of brown hair from one shoulder to the other so her eyes can shoot daggers in each man's direction. Her lips purse tightly, prepared to bite us all for putting her in this situation.

And the robe barely covers her body with a simple tie; she doesn't bother to grip it tightly like the other women.

The room is still silent, glued to the goddess in front of us as she takes center stage.

What is she doing? Does she think if she seems willing she won't be sold to such a monster?

But then her face turns wicked. Her eyes shine with the fiercest fire. And her middle finger flips us all the bird.

I laugh at the fierceness exuding from her.

"Fuck you all," she says.

I bite my bottom lip, more entranced with this woman than I've ever been before.

Hoops and hollers and whistles from the men around me tell me I'm not the only one infatuated with her—she has the entire room under her spell. I don't doubt if she started ordering men around, they would do as she asked. Several of the men are clearly submissives, looking for a strong woman to tell them what to do.

But those aren't the men that scare me. It's the other men. The men who haven't bid on a single woman yet. Who have lifted their gaze from their phones to look at her now. And they are looking at her like they want to devour her. Like they can't wait to break her. They see her as a game they plan on winning.

"I told you I saved the best for last. Who wants to start the bidding on our wild stallion here?" Oscar says.

"I'm not a fucking stallion. I'm a woman!" Siren shouts at him.

He just grins—loving her performance, knowing it's going to get him more money.

I smell sex and money in the air—a battle is about to happen.

I tear my gaze from Siren to look at the men who are pining to win her. So many fucking erections fill the darkened room.

Fucking disgusting.

I close my eyes, trying to break the image from my head. I take a sip of the scotch, washing the repugnant feeling down.

And then I open my eyes, looking up at Siren, who is now stripping out of her robe and throwing it angrily into the crowd.

She's not dressed as an angel, like most of the women. Or black like the last third. She's in a red, fiery number. One that matches her red lips, but shows more of her skin than I want any man to see. Because it doesn't cover any of the important parts of her. It's just a sea of red straps twisting across her body. Her beautiful tits are on full display—the perfect size for her frame, curvy but not fake.

Her nipples are pointed in the chill air, and I pretend they are that way just for me. I'd love to lick and taste them and listen to the purrs and moans leave her lips as I tease them. My eyes travel down her firm stomach, complete with the light outline of her strong abs. And her bare pussy is highlighted with two red straps on either side hiding nothing. If she's going to be sold, she's going to do it on her terms.

I feel my body responding to her, giving her all the control. My cock pushes against the zipper of my slacks.

My cock is a fucking asshole.

I'm turned on by a woman about to be sold. A woman defying us all by giving away the goods before she is even sold. I wouldn't doubt that she would drag a random man on stage and fuck him just to prove that she is in control—not us.

It's true. She wins this round. *But what about the next?*

What about when she isn't on stage?

What about when she's one-on-one with a man stronger than her?

A man who has a gun?

And a team of men working for him?

Will she always win?

Men start throwing their numbers up, pushing the bidding higher and higher, faster than they did for any of the other women as she continues to curse and spit into the audience.

Her outrage only drives the energy and bidding higher. The men all think they will be the one to break her. To control her.

And I'm just as sick as they are because I want to control her too. I want to mark that beautiful skin of hers. I want to claim that mouth and stop her from cursing anything except my name. I want to spread her legs wide and lick every drop of sweetness spreading between them.

I want her.

I want her to be mine.

I want to fight for control.

Suddenly, my hand goes up, indicating I want to bid.

"Five million, to number fifteen," Oscar says, grinning at me like we just agreed to do business together.

What am I doing?

I'm disgusting.

No, I'm saving her.

This is the only way. I have to buy her. Take her as my slave. Then I can find a way to set her free.

"Five point five million, to number twelve," Oscar says.

I grind my teeth together and then drink the rest of my scotch. The bidding has only started, and already it's higher than any of the other women's final total.

Siren is worth it. It's clear she is stronger than the other women. Her spirit is unbroken. Her desire is insatiable. Her body is flawless. She deserves to be worshipped by a king, not sold to a monster.

Her eyes track from the man who just bid on her back to me. And I swear she can see me. Not just see me, but see through me. She knows even though I claim to be bidding to save her, I'm just like every other man in this room. I'm disgusting. I'm sick. I'm a fucking bastard who doesn't deserve her.

If I win her, she will be my ultimate test. I always knew I was going to hell. I knew I was a sinner. But she would be my ultimate sin. She would confirm the darkness in my heart. Because I'm not sure I could resist her. And she knows it.

It doesn't stop my hand from raising again.

"Six million, to number fifteen."

I stare at my opponent across the room, but I can't make out his face in the darkness. I don't know how high he's willing to go. I don't know how much money he has or is willing to spend on Siren.

But I'm determined to win. She's mine, not his. I'm willing to bid everything I have on her; I just hope it's enough to win her.

CHAPTER 7
SIREN

"Seven million. Really? You bastards think that's all I'm worth?" I shout out at their disgusting faces.

I hear chuckles and whistles as I reveal more of my body to them. But I don't care. I want whoever buys me to know he doesn't own my body. I've already shown myself to every man in the room. If I could have every man touch me, fuck me, ruin me for my new owner, I would. But Oscar would never allow that to happen, so I don't try.

I just strut around the stage, acting like I own it, cursing, and flipping them off every chance I get. Which only makes the crowd cheer more.

What am I doing? Why am I making more money for these assholes?

Because it hides my fear, it makes me feel powerful—in control. And it's the only thing I have left right now that's mine.

My dignity is gone.

Soon my strength, my choices, and my body will be too.

This moment is the last of any control. So I'm going to make it my most powerful.

There are only two men left bidding on me.

My fate will soon be decided.

And I don't know which man to cheer for. I don't even know who the two men are. The darkness covers their faces from me. The candlelight on the table is barely enough to make out the light of the men's eyes.

But even if I could see their faces, they are both monsters. One might be less evil than the other, but that is the best I can hope for. Otherwise, they wouldn't be here.

"Eight million."

Holy fuck.

My mouth drops open. The last woman went for five million. They are bidding eight on me and don't show any signs of slowing down.

What will be expected of me for eight million dollars?

What sexual acts will be required of me?

Will I have to fuck other men? Or will I be the buyer's prized possession?

Will he keep me alive longer because he paid more, or will he enjoy ruining me faster because he thinks I can't be broken?

The room stills as the two men continue to go back and forth, bidding against each other in half a million increments. Eight point five million. Nine million. Nine point five. Ten.

At the rate they are going, it doesn't seem like either of them will stop.

I don't move onstage. I don't flip them off or curse. I'm frozen. It's only now do I wish I was still wearing my robe to cover up.

None of the men's focus is on me; it's on the two remaining bidders. It's a game. And I can hear the bets from the other men in the room about who is going to win me.

Win me—ha. I'd like to see a man try to 'win me.' It can't be done. I'm not a possession.

"Twelve million," Oscar shouts.

The room falls silent; we all turn our heads in the direction of the other man. He leans back, out of the candlelight of the table. He's alone. He didn't bring a guard or companion to help him discuss. And I haven't seen him reach for his phone to secure more funds. He's doing this completely on his own.

Finally, I see the man lead forward until the green of his eyes flickers in the candlelight.

Gorgeous.

Consuming.

Evil.

Just the kind of man I would be attracted to if we met in a club. The wrong kind of man. The dangerous kind. The kind who will destroy me the second he gets the chance.

That's what is so fucked up about this. If he had just asked me out at a bar—bought me a drink, I would have ended up in his bed for less than the twenty bucks he'd spend on drinks. He could have gotten me with a pleasant exchange of words.

I enjoy sex. I would have spread my legs and tried any weird fantasy he had. Instead, he's dropping a small fortune, ensuring his place in hell, and fucking with my life.

I should thank him, though. Because if the other scenario had happened and he was a good lay, I might have gone out with him again. I might have fallen in love with him before I realized what a monster he is. This way, there is no chance of me falling in love. No chance of a broken heart. Just a broken leg if I don't behave.

"Twenty million," the bidder says in a deep, gravelly voice. The kind of voice that says this ends now. I'm already his, and he won't let any other man win.

Oscar drops his mic, and silence turns to murmuring. Every man in this room has money. Every man in this room could drop that kind of money to buy me if they wanted to, but these men also like a bargain. They like a good deal, and they won't spend a fortune on one woman when they could buy five for the same price.

I let my eyes drop, making sure my pussy hasn't turned to gold or something, and that's why this man is bidding so high. But it hasn't. I don't have a clue why he thinks I'm so special to him.

Everyone turns their head to the other bidder, waiting to see what he'll do.

"Twenty-five million," he says casually, but I can hear the fear in his voice. This is as high as he can go. He won't bid again.

"Thirty," the other man says almost immediately.

Heads snap back and forth, giving me whiplash.

"Thirty million going once."

Silence.

"Twice."

Nothing.

"Sold."

Sold—that word is going to change my life. Most likely for the worse. But maybe I can find a way to use the situation to my advantage. I was just sold for $30 million. *I'm valuable. Use it.*

Before I realize what's happening, two of the guards have me by my arms and are forcing me off stage.

I try to speak, but one look from the guard who has been relatively nice so far shuts me up. I guess when you are worth thirty million dollars, no one lets you talk or walk or do anything on your own—at least not until the transaction has been made.

My robe is shoved at me.

"Put it on," the guard says.

I do, happy to have clothes on again. I look around and realize I wasn't brought back to the cage where I was held with the other girls. I'm back in the dressing room, except this time there are no beauticians waiting to style me. This time it's just me and the two guards.

"What happens now?" I ask as I tie the sash tightly around my waist and fold my arms across my chest.

"We wait for the money to be deposited. Then you will go to your new owner," the guard says.

"I'm not property. You can't just sell me."

He grins. "We already did."

Fight—that is who I am. I fight.

I don't care that these men have more muscle in a single-arm than I do in my entire body. I don't care that they have guns while I only have nails for a weapon. None of that will stop me from fighting.

I run full force in the guard's direction—angry, pissed, and uncon-fined. At the last second, I kick my foot up, using the pointed heel of my shoe to dig into his groin.

I hit my target.

I grin as he doubles over in pain.

I hear the other guard coming at me from behind, and I elbow him, hearing the whoosh of the blood spilling from his nose when I break it. I feel invincible in this moment. I can take on two grown men, no problem. Where I come from, you learned to be scrappy or you didn't survive. I'm a survivor.

I'll sneak out the back and never return.

I'll hot-wire a car and then steal a boat. I'll be gone from this god-forsaken island. *I'll be free.*

I reach for one of the men's guns, when a deadly voice stops me.

"I wouldn't do that if I were you."

My hand falls at his words. *What the fuck?*

I don't let men control me. I don't let a voice like that penetrate my armor. But his does. His pushes through my outer shell and cracks through like lightning splitting a tree in half. He splits my soul.

I swallow and then reach again, pushing his stupid voice down.

"Stop, Siren."

My hand freezes midair.

Stop listening to him. But there is something so commanding in his tone. Something that makes me want to listen to him. His voice convinces my heart he knows what's better for me than I do. *It's a lie.* My brain knows it, but my heart is easily tricked.

I turn slowly and come face to face with the man who will haunt me the rest of my life, even though I already know from his voice who he is.

"You can leave," Zeke says to the two guards.

"Yes, sir," they both answer before leaving Zeke and me alone in the room.

For a moment, I think Zeke might be my savior. He may have bought me to set me free. But no man spends thirty million on a woman just to set her free.

Maybe he does?

Maybe this man is good?

Maybe he realized he owed me after I saved his life?

A life for a life.

"You owe me," I say, raising my hope. I shouldn't do it. I've been burned by too many men before. I've learned better than to trust a man. I'd be better off trusting a weasel.

"I owe you nothing."

Damn, his voice vibrates through me. A wisp of his hair falls out of the man bun in front of his face. His eyes darken. His jaw tenses. And his lips hide whatever truth he dares to never speak.

I burn down his walls with the glare in my eyes. But he doesn't move. Or flinch or show any weakness.

"I saved your life."

He shakes his head. "Julian Reed saved me. You merely transported me from the middle of the ocean to this island. I owe you a voyage to a destination not of your choosing."

I frown. "What? That makes no sense."

He steps forward. His presence fills the tiny closet of a room. I want to back away, but I don't dare show weakness. His body towers over my much smaller frame. He's a giant compared to most men. He has at least a good foot on me, even in the heels. And he fills out a suit like no man I've ever seen.

But I know he's not comfortable in it. He's not a suit kind of man. I've seen the callouses on his hands. He prefers work to commanding, although he's good at leadership. *He's probably good with his hands too.*

He cocks his strong head sitting on his thick, veiny neck. *Jesus, this man is huge.*

"Doesn't it, though? You are the reason I'm on this fucking island. You're the reason I now owe a debt to Julian. You are the reason I was in the right place to buy you."

"You can't just buy me! I'm not for sale!"

He snaps his jaw shut. "I just did, sweetheart. I just fucking did."

I stand on my tiptoes, trying to look taller. "I will never obey you. I will never be yours. I never lie. I always tell the truth. I will destroy you before you ever lay a hand on me."

He studies me a moment. "I'm sure you believe every word you are saying, but only time will tell who will end up destroying who."

Zeke turns around and starts walking for the door. "Come," he says, without looking back at me, barking orders like a dog.

If he thinks he can just order me around, he's wrong.

He walks out the door.

I stay.

But then I hear the cries of the women in the building. Zeke may be a monster, but so far, he hasn't touched me. He hasn't beaten me. He hasn't threatened me.

I'll follow him, but only because if I stay, the men who will claim me are worse.

I exit and find Zeke holding the door open to the parking lot.

"I'm not a patient man, Siren. I paid thirty million dollars for the pleasure of ordering you around. I suggest you follow my orders in a more timely fashion."

I grit my teeth together. "Or what? You'll punish me?"

"Yes, Siren. You may always tell the truth, but I always keep a promise. I owe you a debt. You took me hundreds of miles to the nearest island. Someday, I'll repay the favor. Until then, you're mine to do as I please."

"And what do you please?"

"Right now, I want you to shut your smart mouth and get into the car."

He holds open the door of his beat-up truck.

I frown. So much about this man I don't understand. He has thirty million dollars to just blow. And yet he drives around a crappy truck. His suit is obviously a rental, he fills it out, but it's not properly tailored. This man is hiding something, and I'm going to figure it out.

I climb into the passenger side of the truck, choosing to pick my battles when it comes to Zeke. The man I saved. The man who will ruin my life. I should have known he was a jackass like every other man.

CHAPTER 8
ZEKE

What am I doing? My mind races as I drive down the gravel road in the dark through the middle of the island. The truck jostles back and forth roughly with each spin of the wheel. I've cracked the windows to let in the cool, salty air. The air conditioning barely works on this truck, and I didn't think I'd live here long enough to bother fixing it.

I'm treating Siren like I own her. *But do I really have a choice?*

If I started treating her like the princess she is, then Julian would start to get suspicious.

But could I treat her like a human? Tell her I only bought her to save her?

I chance a glance over at her. She sitting as far back as she can get in the seat, her legs are crossed, causing the robe to hike up danger-ously high on her thigh until I can almost see the red, strappy number underneath. She's still wearing the pointed heels, but I think it's because she knows she can use them as a weapon, not because they're comfortable.

I was shocked when I entered the room and found her beating up on the two guards. She has skills—training someone taught her. She knows how to use her body as a weapon. She's dangerous. I will have to be careful with her.

But the most surprising thing is her fearlessness, even now that she's sold. She's mine, and yet she's only sitting as far away from me as possible because she's disgusted, not because she's scared.

I envy her. I want to live my life completely unafraid. Another quality that makes her dangerous.

"Fasten your seatbelt," I bark at her.

She gives me a dirty look. "Why? We are going twenty miles an hour. There are no other cars on the road at this time of night. I think I'll be fine. And don't pretend to care about my safety."

"I want to protect my investment. Buckle. Your. Seatbelt," I growl, hating how she defies me. *Can't she see I'm only trying to help her? Keep her safe?*

She flips me off. *Apparently not.*

I consider my next move. I could force her. I could do it myself. Or I could convince her to see things my way.

I choose option number three. I need her to obey me because she has no other choice. I need her to stop fighting every little order if I'm ever going to figure out how to save her.

I can't tell her the truth. *At least, not yet.*

Julian could have this truck bugged. The home I rent from him is surely bugged. He's a paranoid man who doesn't trust anyone, and he thinks I'm hiding something. I am, just not what he thinks. And until I'm free of him, I can't risk telling her the truth.

I press on the gas, going faster than safe on the bumpy, unpaved road. Siren is thrown up from her seat, until she's gripping the ceiling to keep her head from bumping into it.

"What are you doing?" her voice breathy.

Damn, I like the sound of her voice.

"Driving."

"No, you're trying to get us killed."

I shake my head as I put one hand out the window, feeling the wind as I pick up more speed. "I like to feel the wind."

"Slow down."

"I don't follow your orders. I give the orders. And you will find I only give orders once." I drive faster, watching Siren be thrown around in the truck. She's barely hanging on now. Her hands are gripping the seat, the ceiling, the frame of the window—anything she can hold onto to keep her in the car instead of bouncing out of it.

"You've made your point. Slow down," she hollers, still not giving in to my orders.

I drive faster, purposefully losing control more as I drive, running over several bushes and getting dangerously close to several trees as we bounce down the hill.

"Fuck," Siren curses when I turn head-on toward a large palm tree.

She reaches for her seatbelt almost automatically. I don't think she even realizes that she is giving into my command. As soon as she has the belt buckled, I swerve away.

"Are we dead? Did you hit it?" She asks, her eyes closed tightly, and her red lips turned ghost white.

I smile, liking her afraid, relying on me.

"Nope, we are still very much alive."

"Dammit."

She slowly opens her eyes.

"Are you going to slow down, now?"

I step on the gas. She doesn't get a reward for doing what I asked her to do five minutes after I asked it.

She sighs and grips the seatbelt now firmly across her chest.

Siren is feisty. She's not like any other woman I've met. She was the only woman out of a dozen to completely own the stage, to not let us take control of her.

She's the only woman I've ever met who doesn't want me for my money, protection, or access to my hotter, richer best friends.

Because you bought her, you idiot. That's the only reason she's in this car. A woman like her wouldn't look twice at a man like me. I have money sure, but not enough to please her. I don't have any power. I work for a powerful man. I protect. I risk my life for others. I could never fully be hers.

"What's your last name, Siren?" I ask.

She gives me the finger, her signature move.

"Where are you from? Do you live on the island?"

She raises her eyebrows at me. "You really think I'm going to answer your questions?"

"Yes."

"Why?"

"Because if you don't, there will be consequences."

She rolls her eyes. "I'm not afraid of your consequences. We aren't always going to be in a car where you can just pick up speed to get me to do what you want."

"No, but I can think of other ways to get you to do what I want." My eyes threaten her with danger, but I would never physically hurt her. I've never hit a woman, and I don't plan on doing it now. But Siren doesn't know that. And right now, I need her terrified. I need her to stop resisting and let me save her.

She goes quiet.

Good, maybe my threat worked.

"Are you married?" I ask, hoping to god she isn't.

Wait...what? Why do I care if she's married? If she is, it would be easier for me, not harder. I could just drop her off with her husband. She would become his problem to take care of, no longer my concern.

"You've never done this before, have you?" Her eyes focus on me.

I swallow hard but don't answer.

She smiles. "What is *your* full name, Zeke?"

I clench my jaw.

"Where are you from?" she asks.

"Are you married?" she asks.

She leans back, smiling smugly, thinking she's won.

She has.

But she won't again.

I turn the wheel hard, driving hard into a small ditch on the side of the road.

She squeals crazily with the fear of death in her eyes.

Then suddenly, we stop as I slam on the breaks.

"You're insane," she pants, holding her hand over her heart as she tries to catch her breath.

I grab her wrist, needing her to look at me, needing her to take me seriously.

Of course, there's a fucking spark at our touch.

We both stare down at the surge going back and forth between our skin. *How is it that the first woman I've felt butterflies for is also a woman I can't have?* I fucking bought her, even if I save her, even if I get her to freedom eventually, she won't forgive me for this. She'll always view me as an asshole.

And I will have to treat her like one until I can find a way to set her free. I don't have a choice. Julian will be watching my every move. And he'll kill us both if he thinks we aren't on his side.

But it doesn't stop my heart from doing fucking somersaults in my chest at her touch. *Maybe when I set her free, I could seduce her? I could court her? Make her fall for me by bringing her flowers, chocolates, do all the romantic things I used to be good at? Maybe that would be enough for us to have a chance?*

I lean in close, until I'm all but kissing her. She licks her lips in anticipation of a kiss that will never come. I'm in control here, not her. She doesn't get to decide my actions. I give a command; she follows it. Or there will be consequences.

"What is your last name?" I ask, my voice booming so loudly it even scares even me.

"Martinez."

"Where are you from?"

"Costa Rica."

"Are you married?"

She holds up her left hand. There is no ring or tan line where one used to sit. She's not married.

I release my grip, and we both take a deep breath, like it's a race to get all the oxygen we can before the other takes all of it.

I stare at her. Consuming all of the information she gave me. *Siren Martinez. From Costa Rica, not here. She's not married.*

That last fact warms my cold heart more than it should. She's not married, *but that doesn't really make her yours.* I don't have a real claim on her. What I have is temporary. All we have is chemistry. And fucked up debts to each other. And half-truths and lies.

We could never have a real relationship even after all of this is over.

Even though she isn't married, I'm sure she has a life waiting for her in Costa Rica.

And I have a life waiting for me in Miami.

We would never work.

I grip the steering wheel again; my point made—if she doesn't follow my command, there will be consequences. This one was simple. I scared the shit out of her with just my voice. I may not hit her, but I can find other consequences for her not bending to my will.

She doesn't know that I won't physically hurt her, but she's a smart woman. She will quickly figure it out if I'm not careful, and then she will try to run. And if she runs, Julian could find her before I do. And he's a real monster. The kind that will hit a woman. The kind who will rape her. Torture her. Kill her.

My eyes water thinking about any man hurting her. I don't know how I've already grown attached to her. *Was it because she saved me? Did I fall in love with the sound of her voice when she sang to me? Her skin when she touched me? Did I grow soft watching her on stage? Or was it this moment watching her do everything to defy me that made me fall for her?*

I don't know. But my heart definitely has a soft spot for her. That's my problem. I let people in too easily. And then I get fucking hurt. But Siren is innocent. She has a big heart. She wouldn't have saved me in the ocean if she was a cold criminal. I owe her my life.

When I get to my house, I'll get to work on debugging it, so I can eventually tell Siren the truth and form a plan to get her off this island —to get us both off this island. But until then, I will have to make Siren fear me. Fear will keep her weak, malleable. Fear will break her spirit. Every time she fears me, it will hurt. But it's the only way to protect her.

CHAPTER 9
SIREN

Zeke turns the car down a familiar road. The last road on the island I want to be on. A road I've traversed before. A road that became my most painful mistake. A road that led me to be sold as a sex slave.

I shift uncomfortably in my seat as the seat belt constricts across my body. I can't breathe. I can't go back. *Not here...*

I squeeze my eyes shut, hoping to block out the impending panic attack. But it's too late to stop it. The panic lives in me now.

"Siren?"

Zeke's voice breaks through the fog. It's so calming and assuring. His voice can stop the panic; his alone has that kind of power.

My eyes open cautiously, looking into his profound, intimidating eyes.

He narrows his gaze, trying to figure out what I'm hiding behind my panicked eyes. But I'll never tell. I'll keep my secrets.

But I hope Zeke spills his.

His truth is the key to escaping. *Who is Zeke? What makes him tick? Where did he come from? What motivates him? Is his heart as evil as every other man's on this island?*

I need the answers. Because with the answers comes power. I can take back control. I can earn back my freedom.

Zeke turns his attention back to the road as my breathing calms at his command. But he didn't order me to breathe. He didn't instruct me to be calm. My body responded to his on its own.

Fuck me—why does my body have to be attracted to such a cruel man? Now that his gaze is off of me, I almost want it back. I forget about any panic and only feel him. His stare makes my toes curl, my heart flutter, and my lips wet.

I'm a sex slave that wants to be fucked by her master. *How sick is that?*

I won't let it happen, though. I won't let him rape me. I will fight every second. If he asked, I might give in. I like sex as much as any other warm-blooded woman. But Zeke won't ask for sex; he's the kind of man who will demand it—the kind of man I hate.

I hear the gravel change to pavement as the road changes under the tires of Zeke's truck.

I swallow the lump in my throat and turn my gaze to the most beautiful property on the island. All white—like an angel descended to make everything pure. But there is nothing pure about this place.

I want to ask if Zeke lives here, but I don't want to give away my own truths. I don't want him to know I've been here before, so I stay silent. It seems is Zeke prefers it—silence. He doesn't speak unless he has something important to say.

We drive past the main house, Julian Reed's home.

I hold my breath the entire time, hoping we aren't going to make a stop here, praying Zeke didn't buy me just to give me to Julian. I know it's not going to happen. Julian was the one who sold me to Oscar, who, in turn, sold me to Zeke. There would be no reason for Julian to buy me back. But it still worries me until we drive past the main building.

There are dozens of buildings on the property. Most belong to Julian's servants. I don't take Zeke as a servant, but he could have become one of Julian's employees.

Lights guide our way down the paved streets until we stop at a house on the edge of the property. This one isn't lit up like the rest. It seems to be hiding in the shadows, instead of shining brightly in glory like the rest of the buildings do on the property, proudly displaying their wealth. This house is still massive, but it's hidden beneath overgrown vines. Paint is chipping on its exterior. And based on how dark it is, I wouldn't have guessed anyone lives here.

Zeke shuts off the car and steps out without a word to me.

I sit in the car as he walks around the front of the truck, still not looking at me. I expect him to open my door and escort me inside, but he doesn't. He just walks tall and confidently toward the front door of the house. His ass is swaying nicely in his suit pants. He opens it, not needing a key. Apparently, he doesn't lock the door. He walks inside, still not giving me any attention.

Maybe he forgot about me?

Maybe he wants me to run so he can chase me? Punish me?

I don't know what game Zeke is playing at.

He hasn't given me an order.

And yet, every bone in my body is begging me to get out of the car and follow him inside.

I could run, try to escape. But I wouldn't dare, not with Julian Reed lurking nearby. Zeke can't be worse than him. *Right?*

I saved Zeke's life, even if Zeke doesn't see it that way—I did. That has to count for some kindness on his part.

I fold my arms. *Maybe I'll just stay right here in this truck?* Zeke can't hurt me if I don't follow him inside.

Car lights from the road flash in my direction. And suddenly, I don't want to be alone anymore. I want inside.

I jump out of the car and half walk, half run inside the open door. Convincing myself that for the amount of money that Zeke paid, he will protect me. At least until he gets what he wants from me.

I pant heavily as I look around the foyer of Zeke's house for him. But I don't find him immediately.

I hear car tires squeal behind me. I sense an approaching man. I feel the danger nearing.

I need Zeke.

My eyes widen as I try to search, but I can't see in the dark. And I have no idea where the light switches are or if they will even work.

Maybe this isn't even his house? Maybe this is just the dungeon he plans on keeping me in?

I grip the edges of my robe between my breasts, holding it tighter to my body.

"Zeke?" I ask into the shadows.

A light flickers on as Zeke appears in front of me. He's leaning against a pillar, his arms folded across his chest. He's lost his suit jacket already, his tie is gone, and his collar has been loosened, exposing the dark hair of his chest. His sleeves are rolled up until I see the start of his familiar tattoos. I remember them covering his body from when I saved him.

"Yes, Siren. Did you need something?" he asks smugly. *He's won.* He's showing me he has the power—the control. I followed him inside, and he didn't even have to say a single word.

I look like a desperate woman who wants to be controlled. I look weak—vulnerable. *And I fucking hate it.*

There is a knock at the door, and Zeke looks from me to the door. Like I might run to the man behind the door for help. He doesn't know the only man in the world who can truly terrify me is behind that door. I would trust Zeke time and time again over Julian.

Zeke doesn't give me an order, but he senses my fear. And he feels me move behind him, using him like a human shield as he goes to the door. I consider running and hiding, but I don't have the chance before Zeke opens the door.

I take a deep breath and then puff out my chest, determined to not let Julian see my fear.

"Julian, what do you need? I wasn't expecting you at such a late hour. I thought you had a client you needed to attend to," Zeke says, not showing Julian any respect.

Interesting—everyone shows Julian respect. In fact, I've never heard anyone call Julian anything other than Mr. Reed.

"I saw your truck drive in just as I got back, and I wanted to have a chat about how your meeting with Oscar went," Julian answers as he steps inside, pushing Zeke back even though Zeke never invited him in.

Zeke doesn't relent. And the two men's shoulders collide in a show of testosterone and power.

Zeke gives Julian an angry look as Julian smirks.

I'm not sure which man won, but clearly, neither of them plans on backing down.

Zeke doesn't bother to shut the door. I hope that means he isn't planning on letting Julian stay long.

Julian spots me, and my world stops.

The evil glint in his eyes brings me back to that night. The night I met him and became acquainted with the man, the monster, the devil. That was the night I learned just how vile he truly is.

Julian runs his tongue over his bottom lip as if remembering that night as well.

"And who is this beauty? Oscar said you had bought yourself a little treat at the event; I just didn't expect you to buy this exotic creature," Julian says.

Zeke studies Julian carefully and then my reaction to his words.

My fist tightens around the robe until my knuckles are white. Anger heats my cheeks and straightens my back until I'm at eye level with Julian in my heels. But fear—fear licks at my heart.

Julian notices the anger.

But Zeke, he notices the fear.

"Yes, I couldn't resist her," Zeke says. The way he says it seems like I'm the one with the power, but he's just teasing. It's clear he doesn't plan on letting me have any.

Julian's attention flickers back to Zeke as Zeke walks in front of me.

I exhale a small breath when Julian can no longer get a direct view of my body. I don't know why Zeke is standing in front of me. *Did he see the way Julian was looking at me? Is Zeke possessive? Does he not want to share me? Or is he protecting me?*

"Oscar seems to think I'm the man for the job. I'll have the deal closed and the shipment handled by the end of the month," Zeke says.

"Yes, Oscar told me. It seems that by buying the slut, you ensured your loyalty to him. Especially since you were the highest bidder of the night," Julian says.

"As I've said before, I'm the best. I do good work. You have nothing to worry about. These house calls aren't necessary," Zeke says.

Julian steps closer to Zeke, but I realize it's so he can look at me, not him. "I didn't stop by because I didn't believe you could do your job. I consider you a friend, Zeke. I thought we could discuss how our nights went over a drink and enjoy your new pet."

That word—*pet*. It's like being pummeled with bullets when he says that word. I hate it. I never thought I could hate a word, but I hate that word.

Zeke laughs, completely unaffected and unaware of how Julian is gazing at me like I'm his, not Zeke's. I see the promise in Julian's eyes; he will come for me. He will remind me of our night together. He isn't finished with me.

"Goodnight, Julian."

Julian looks from me to Zeke. He's been dismissed—without an explanation of why he can't stay.

My mouth gapes. It's clear Zeke is currently working for Julian, but he doesn't let Julian boss him around. He's his own man, with his own desires and own control on life.

Julian frowns, but he doesn't argue with Zeke. He'll save his fight for another night. At least, that's what his eyes promise me.

Fuck.

Zeke doesn't walk Julian to the door. He stands solid, an unmoving statue. He won't let any man come into his house and order him around, that much is clear.

"The door," Zeke says, his voice booming as Julian exits.

For a moment, I don't think Julian is going to shut the door. I think he's going to leave it open. But at the last second, he changes his mind and closes the door behind him.

Huh? Maybe I'm not the only one under Zeke's spell.

Zeke turns and looks at me. He looks menacing, like a beast. He's muscle, tattoos, and hair. The suit he wears is practically bulging off of his body. It's clear he doesn't belong in it. He's too manly for a suit. Too big. Too much beast.

"Come," he says as he starts walking.

I consider defying him. But Julian is too close. I won't defy him when the alternative is Julian.

Zeke walks down the hallway, but he doesn't turn on any lights. He just walks. And I follow, desperate to feel more in control.

I want out of these clothes. I want to wear something more respectable. I want out of this caked-on makeup. I want a bubble bath. I want food in my belly. And a bed to sleep in.

But I doubt I will get any of that. I'm sure he's leading me to some shackles for my wrists and ankles. Then to my cage. And if he isn't a patient man...he'll try to rape me.

I start looking for a weapon. Something I can use to prevent that from happening. But it's so freaking dark I can't see anything. I assume that's part of his plan to keep me captive.

Suddenly, he stops.

"Sit," he commands.

I look around but can't see a foot in front of my face. I doubt he wants me to sit in a chair anyway. So I start to sit on the floor.

"Stop."

I stop mid crouch.

I hear the scraping of a chair being pulled out. "Sit here."

I feel for the chair he's placed in front of me and take a seat, I realize at a table.

My heart thumps, trying to guess what is going to happen next, but I can't figure Zeke out. He's the most mysterious man I've ever met. When I saved him, I thought he could be different. I thought he could be one of the good ones, but it turns out he's working for Julian, and I'm now his slave. I can't gleam any more since he hardly speaks, though.

I hear him banging around, opening drawers and cabinets. *What is he searching for? Rope? A knife? Something to hurt me with?*

I hold my breath as I feel around on the table, but I don't find anything for a weapon.

Finally, Zeke returns, plopping something on the table in front of me.

"Eat."

"What?"

He sighs, taking the seat next to me. "Is your hearing bad? Or do you just like asking questions you already know the answer to?"

I frown, even though I doubt he can see it. "I don't like being ordered around."

"And I don't like having to work out, but it doesn't stop me from doing it every day. Now eat."

I cross my arms. "You working out and me taking orders from you aren't exactly comparable."

"Eat," he huffs, like he doesn't have the energy for this.

I grin. I'm learning something about him already. Talking must wear him down. If I can exhaust him, he'll be too tired to rape me. He might even let his guard down and tell me more about himself.

"How do I know you haven't poisoned it?"

"Why would I spend millions of dollars on you only to poison you?"

"Fine. How do I know you won't drug me?"

"You don't. But you're hungry, so you don't really have a choice."

"How do you know I'm hungry?" My stomach growls, giving me away.

"Because you are. Oscar wanted you to look your best so he could earn top dollar. That means skinny, not bloated with food. You're hungry. Eat."

"I can't eat in the dark."

He growls loudly.

It shakes every nerve in my body, causing me to tremble. But not in fear—in excitement. I like the way his voice sounds. I like his commanding echo. If we were in a consensual relationship, I would want him to boss me around in the bedroom. But we aren't, which means I have to fight.

"Then, I guess you won't eat."

I hear the sound of him chewing his food.

And I stare into the darkness at the table in front of me. *Why does he like living in the darkness?* Just another question without an answer.

I want to defy him. I want to go without eating, but I'll need my strength to face him. To have a chance against him.

So carefully, I feel around on the table until I find a fork. Then I move it around on my plate, and I stab a piece of food and lift it to my mouth. I smell it hesitantly—broccoli.

I curl my lips down in disappointment. I could go for some French fries or a burger or pizza—something heavy on the carbs. But of course, mister zero percent body fat and all muscle only eats vegetables.

But once I put the broccoli in my mouth, I don't care. It practically melts in my mouth. I don't know how it's cooked so well. I put my fork down on the plate again, but realize I'm stabbing meat instead of broccoli this time.

I frown. I'm going to have to nibble on the meat with my teeth. I'm sure he didn't give me a knife.

Hesitantly, I feel around on the other side of my plate, and there I find the sharp edge of a steak knife.

I have a weapon!

As quickly as I lift it, I feel Zeke's hand grip my wrist.

I freeze. At his touch, my hair rises on my arms, wanting to feel more of him. My breath catches, and my heart slows. I bite my lip, waiting to hear what he says.

"You show your thoughts easily, Miss Martinez. If you are planning on killing me with this knife, I suggest you have a plan to kill Julian as well. Because the only thing standing between him and you is me." He releases my wrist and goes back to eating. I decide it's best to only use the knife to cut my steak instead of Zeke's throat—at least for the time being.

How did Zeke so clearly read my thoughts? No one can ever read me. I'll have to be more careful, so he doesn't learn my secrets before I learn his.

We continue to eat in silence. Zeke finishes eating long before I do, and I can feel his heavy gaze on me as I keep eating, even though we are eating in the dark. I'm glad it's dark, so I can't see the look in his eyes. *What would I find there if I could see his eyes? Want? Lust? Desire?* I don't want my body to react to any of those feelings. I'm not in a place to handle them. So I just focus on eating.

A moment after I finish, Zeke grabs my plate and silverware and whisks them away. Again he doesn't speak, but I hear his heavy footsteps. He's walking away, and before I can make a cognitive decision, I'm following him.

Zeke didn't give me an order, but I'm already eager to follow his unspoken commands. *What will happen when he actually gives me an order? What then? How much of my soul will I lose while Zeke holds me hostage?* Not much, since I barely have any soul left to lose. I'm barely hanging on to who I am as it is.

I'm usually defiant. I'm a fighter. I will fight if Zeke tries to harm me, but somehow I've turned into an obedient dog, trying to figure out how to please my new master without him even speaking a word. It's because I'm exhausted and just want to sleep in peace. I don't want to get hurt. I don't want to face Julian.

Zeke walks through a hallway, again in the dark. I hear him open a door at the end of the hallway and step inside. I follow, assuming it's the cage he plans on keeping me in.

But when I walk inside and see the moonlight shining through a large window, I'm shocked to see the most beautiful cage he could have created for me.

A large king-sized bed is the focus of the room, with shiny white sheets sparkling in the moonlight. The floor is dark wood, in deep contrast with the bed, making it look like it's floating on water. The windows are large and look out over the cliffside to the ocean beyond —the only place where I feel at home.

I look to Zeke, who is opening a dresser drawer.

"Is this my room?" I ask, my throat dry as I speak. It doesn't make sense if it is. *Is he buttering me up with a soft, beautiful bed before he rapes me? Or does he prefer to do his damage in the clean white sheets?*

"No."

No? Then what am I doing here if it isn't my room?

I start slowing backing away, not liking being in the same room with Zeke when there is a bed he could easily destroy me on.

He closes the drawer and faces me just as I get to the door. He doesn't seem surprised that I'm trying to escape. He doesn't draw a gun or try to prevent me from running in any way. He seems in complete control standing there facing me.

"Leaving?" he asks with an amused expression.

"Yes. If this isn't my room, then I shouldn't be in here." I take another step back toward the door, but face Zeke as I do it. I won't ever turn my back on my enemy.

"Who says I'm giving you any of my rooms?" Zeke answers.

I narrow my eyes. "Then where will you keep me?" *Please tell me there isn't a dungeon or cage somewhere on this property.* I'm starting to think Zeke didn't go to that auction planning on buying me, but something changed, and he did. He's not prepared for me.

Zeke's eyes cut to the bed.

I swallow. He wants me in his bed. He's not going to wait to rape me. He's going to take what he wants right here, right now.

He tosses something at me, and I catch it automatically.

"Put it on," he says before he turns around.

I glance at my hands and realize it's a T-shirt—one of Zeke's T-shirts. I'd rather sleep in this than what I'm wearing, but I doubt I'll be sleeping at all tonight.

When I look up, I see Zeke undressing. He's slowly unbuttoning his shirt and pulling it out from his pants. But he isn't facing me. He's giving me the privacy to change without him looking. So I take advantage. I disrobe and remove my uncomfortable, strappy number and then slip the T-shirt over my head. I feel more comfortable in the shirt that hangs down to just above my knees, but I do wish I had underwear to sleep in.

Zeke is still undressing away from me. His shirt is gone now, and he's working on his pants.

My teeth scrape over my bottom lip as I take his backside in—strong and masculine. His hair is still up in a man bun on top of his head, and it gives me an unobstructed view of every muscle and tattoo on his back.

Most of the bidding men in that auction room were disgusting, gross, unfit monsters. But Zeke has the body of a god; he didn't need to buy one in order to have his choice of women. Tattoos are inked into his back, and when he drops his pants, I groan at the sight of his tight ass in his Calvin Kleins, fitting to his muscular ass like a second layer of skin.

Turn around. Show me your package.

He does, and my eyes bulge. *Holy hell!* I've never seen a package so perfectly formed beneath a man's boxer briefs. But his has me mesmerized. I want to unwrap him and see what's underneath. I want to turn him on and see how big his erection can grow. I want—

"My eyes are up here, Siren."

Fuck, I've been caught.

I glare at him. "Just getting a good look so I know where to aim when I cut off your dick. Because I will knife you before I ever let you stick your cock anywhere near me."

He cocks his head. "Really? Because the heat in your eyes, the flush in your cheeks, and drool pooling in the corner of your mouth tells me you'd rather ride my cock than cut it off."

I grit my teeth as steam boils inside me. *How can he be so infuriatingly good at reading me?* I always hide my emotions. It's my signature trait. But not with him. With him, he sees the real me, and that terrifies me. He could discover my secret, and that would be worse than him raping me.

Zeke walks over to me, and I freeze. I try to hold my expression so he can't tell if I'm terrified, turned on, or am about to attack him. He stops just in front of me and both of our breaths heat. He exhales into my hair, while I inhale his bare chest.

My breath rises harder in my chest, and I lick my lips in anticipation of a kiss before I remember that he owns me. He isn't going to kiss me; he's going to fuck me—destroy me, ruin me.

I glance up, and his dark eyes read mine. For a second, I think he's trying to tell me something with just his eyes, but I'm probably reading too much into it.

He reaches around me and closes the door behind me before locking it.

"You can sleep on the left side of the bed," he says before he turns and walks to the right side of the bed.

What?

I watch Zeke climb into the right side of the bed, and I swear he's snoring as soon as his head hits the pillow.

He's not going to rape me, at least not tonight.

But can I really sleep in the bed next to him?

I tiptoe over to the bed, hoping like hell I don't wake him. If I do, he might change his mind and realize he's hornier than he is exhausted.

But he doesn't stir. I glance at the floor. I could sleep there instead of in his bed. But I wouldn't get a minute of sleep; the floor is too hard. I glance at the door Zeke locked. He locked it from the inside. I could leave no problem.

But where would I go? What security measures does Zeke have in place? And how far would I get before Julian would find me? Could I sleep in a different room?

No.

I need to earn Zeke's trust. Make him fall for me. Learn his secrets. That's the best way to get free.

Stop being a fucking pussy.

I pull the slick covers back and climb into the heavenly bed. I close my eyes as my head hits the pillow, expecting to feel more petrified than I have in months. But instead, I feel the heavy pull of sleep as my heart calms next to Zeke's light snoring. He could hurt me as bad as any man ever has. He could kill me, end me. But somehow, I feel more protected than ever.

CHAPTER 10
ZEKE

I don't sleep. How could I, with the most gorgeous, intelligent, quick-witted woman in my bed?

I pretend to snore initially, so Siren would trust me enough to sleep next to me. But it was all an act. I'm learning I can be a good actor when I want to be.

I should have locked Siren up in one of the other bedrooms. I should have tied her up with ropes. I should have ensured there is no way she could escape while simultaneously fueling my new fantasies about having Siren tied up.

But I'm not that breed of monster. The only promise I've silently made to her is not to hurt her. So I won't. I might manipulate her. I might do cruel things, but I'm only doing them to protect her. If I can avoid physically hurting her, I will.

And given her reaction to Julian Reed, there is no way she will voluntarily leave my property. She's too afraid he will hurt her. So in her mind, the safest place she can be right now is my bed, even if that confuses her. Hell, it confuses me.

It's been ages since I've been this attracted to a woman. Siren is hot, sure, but she's so much more. I want to know everything about her. I could listen to her smart mouth put me in my place all damn day.

I want to know every snarky comment in her beautiful brain. And I want...hell, I'm desperate to kiss her red-stained lips. Just once, I want to fight back with my lips pressed against hers instead of riling her up with my own careful words.

There is so much I want to say to her. But I can't, not until I know Julian isn't listening to our every conversation.

And what was with Siren's reaction to Julian anyway? Yes, he's a very intimidating man. Anyone could look at him and tell that he's evil. But Siren didn't show a moment of fear on that stage when she was in a room of dozens of wealthy, horrid men. A man like Julian shouldn't scare her, unless they have history together.

It was clear they have met before. And that meeting wasn't a pleasant one. Siren doesn't even fear me—the man who bought her for millions and she thinks is going to rape her. And yet she fears Julian.

I have to find a way to get answers. But I don't want Julian to know that I realize he knows Siren. Or at least, Siren knows him. He's such a bastard he probably hurt her and then forgot about her. And when he saw her with me, he wanted to destroy her all over again.

I need answers from Siren, which is going to be hard. I also need to stay as far away from her as possible.

I glance over at the angel of a woman, perplexed that she doesn't call herself that. Sure, she has a potty mouth. And I believe her when she says she'd cut off my dick before she lets me touch her, but she's still my angel and probably my downfall into darkness.

I'm generally a good man, at least when it comes to women. I don't lead them on. I don't date. I give them a good night or two, and then I move on. But with Siren, I know one night wouldn't be enough. I want to do dirty, offensive things to her. I want to own her, just like I paid for. I want to break her and then put her pieces back together, so she owes me a thousand unrelenting debts.

My hand reaches out, wanting to brush her strands from her face, but I stop at the last second. I can't even let myself have a taste. I have the ultimate level of self-control, but with Siren, I'm going to fall into the depths of hell after one drop. I want her too much. If I get one taste, I'll be hooked. I won't be able to keep my promises not to hurt her. And I'll become like the men I'm trying to protect her from.

So I keep my hands to myself. The less I touch her, the better.

But the longer I stay in bed with her, the less control I have on my body. Especially when she starts making adorable snoring noises in her sleep.

I have to get out of here.

I jump out of bed, not caring if I wake her. I have work to do. I have a house to debug, a debt to Julian to repay, and figuring out how to sell women while saving them at the same time. Not to mention what the hell I'm going to do with Siren to keep her safe once I've repaid my debt to Julian and ensured he won't follow me when I leave.

I grab my jeans and T-shirt from the closet and then walk down the hallway to the bathroom. Why the hell this house doesn't have a bathroom that connects to the bedroom is beyond me. Siren doesn't stir as I leave, and even if she does, she won't leave the safety of the house. I don't have to worry about her escaping.

I walk into the bathroom, flick the shower water to cold, remove my boxer briefs, and stand under the cold spray. I'm desperate for it to knock some sense into me and ease the pain of my night-long erection.

But when I look down, my cock is still hard, aching to be inside Siren.

Fucking hell.

I fall forward and put my hands on the wall of the shower. I let the cold water fall over my head and down my back and chest. I close my eyes as I pant heavily, trying to get the images of Siren out of my head.

I try to think of anything else—Julian, the old lady who gets me coffee at the cafe down the street, a peanut butter sandwich, the work I need to do to the beat-up truck. *Fucking anything*—but my cock is still hard.

I want to jack off, but I know if I do, Siren's body will be what I get off to. Her body on stage with a few tiny straps hiding only part of her skin, but not the most intimate parts.

I'm sick.

I won't pleasure myself to her being forced onto a stage for others' enjoyment.

I start thinking about all the men who saw Siren basically naked.

All the men who have probably rubbed their dicks to the image of her they have branded into their heads already.

My stomach flips at that thought. I hate that any man has ever seen Siren that exposed, basically naked. And with that thought, my erection immediately disappears.

My job is to protect those I love, those I owe a debt to, those that are innocent. I owe Siren a debt. I won't let her fall into any other category.

I turn off the water, get dressed, and then walk back to my bedroom.

Siren is awake, with the covers lifted up to her chin like that will protect her from me.

"Are you hungry?" I ask.

She shakes her head.

I walk over to her side of the bed and pull a bottle of water out of the nightstand and set it next to her. I've kept a few bottles of water in the nightstand so I could take my medications the first thing in the morning.

"I'm going to work," I say.

Her eyes widen, and a smile forms behind her lips. She thinks she can plan. She can search my house to find dirt on me. But even if she did, there is nothing here. She will find no personal detail about me if she ripped this house apart room by room.

I walk to the door, though, as a plan forms to keep her safe. She's safe in my house, sure, but she's safest in this bedroom. She won't be tempted to run away if she can't see how easy it would be for her to run down the beach and away from Julian's property. Here she won't be tempted to leave.

"Enjoy your cage until I get back," I say as I close the door and pretend to lock it from the outside. But there is no lock on the outside, although she doesn't know that.

I hear her run to the door and pound on it hard.

"Zeke! Don't! Don't lock me in here!" she shouts from behind the door.

"It's for your own good. I wouldn't want you to wander and fall into the hands of a man who isn't as kind and patient as I am."

"I'm claustrophobic!"

"Good thing that room is huge then."

"What about food?"

"I asked, you said you weren't hungry. I'll be back by dinner time."

I start backing up as she keeps pounding on the door but doesn't once test the door handle. She believes me. She truly thinks I locked her inside the room.

"Zeke...please." Her voice is soft and begging.

It should make me want to help her. I'd help any other woman who spoke to me that way. I'd tell them the truth. I'd find another way to contain them. But not with Siren. Siren's sultry plea makes my cock hard. It twists me into a one-track man who wants to devour her.

She's safer locked in my bedroom.

So I walk away and hope Siren doesn't realize the door isn't locked. She's as free as she was before she was kidnapped, but I'm not the devil she thinks I am. I'm much worse. I'm the kind who pretends to protect her but ultimately destroys her—just as soon as my beast within breaks through.

If Siren is smart, she'll run. She'll save herself before my beast escapes. Because when he does, she'll never be safe.

CHAPTER 11
SIREN

ucking bastard.
    Asshole.
    Buttmunch.
Jackass.
Coward.

Zeke fucking locked me in his bedroom. And it pisses me off. *I'm not an animal he can just lock up!*

But apparently, I am. That is exactly what he did. He locked me up and is holding me hostage.

And now what do I do?

He expects me to wait until he returns so he can order me around and have his way with me—I don't think so.

That sure as hell isn't happening.

My thighs clench, my nipples pebble, and my mouth runs dry just thinking about Zeke. I slept next to him all night. Somehow, my dreams were all about him. *Dreams*—not nightmares.

In them, he wasn't much different than the man I've come to know since he bought me—the strong, silent type. He would just look at me and I could tell everything he was thinking—exactly what he wanted me to do.

95

And I did it. I undressed slowly. I touched myself, spread the moisture between my legs over my lips so he could see how wet I was for him. He was commanding without saying a word. And I wanted to follow his every desire.

But then I woke up. I remembered no matter how attracted I am to Zeke, I will never fuck him. For a split second, when I saved him in the water, I thought he might be the rare good guy who would never hurt a woman. But now I know the truth.

He locked me up simply because it was the easiest course of action. He knows he doesn't need to tie me up, although he might try to just for his own twisted enjoyment.

Currently, a simple lock on the door is the only thing between me and freedom.

I fold my arms over my chest as the air conditioning kicks on and chills my arms and legs. I'm still naked except for Zeke's oversized T-shirt.

I should find more clothes.

I should break down the door or one of the windows.

I should run.

But I can't.

The island is too small. Zeke could find me easily. Or Julian...I won't risk Julian finding me. So I'll stay.

I walk over to the dresser and pull out drawer after drawer until I find a pair of sweatpants. I put them on, feeling less naked, even though I have to roll the waistband several times and tie the string around my body to keep the pants up.

I may not be able to escape, but at least I can find out more about Zeke. I can gather as much ammunition possible on the man. I need him to get me off this island. I need answers.

So I dig through all of the drawers in his dresser. All I find are clean boxer briefs that somehow already smell like him. I inhale the sweet mix of ocean, fresh-cut grass, and intangible man. I find socks, T-shirts, and jeans. All I learn is that he likes his clothes casual, yet designer.

I dig through the nightstands on either side of his bed. I find water bottles, pain pills, and a tattered copy of Moby Dick. He reads apparently. Or at least he likes this particular book.

I find nothing else I might expect from a monster like him. Nothing kinky. No BDSM stuff. No handcuffs, ties, whips. I don't even find a condom. *Maybe he isn't into safe sex? Maybe he's one of those sick bastards who likes to impregnate women and then beat them until the baby no longer exists?*

Fuck.

I slam the last drawer shut, trying not to think that way anymore. *Zeke isn't an angel, but he can't be that big of a monster, can he?*

I sit back on my heels and look around the room. There is no door other than the one leading to the hallway. No closet to search through. No bathroom to rummage through. I've officially run out of things to search in the first fifteen minutes he's gone. And I've learned practically nothing about Zeke.

Wait...there is no other door! No bathroom!

I stand up and look again. That can't be right. This room is too beautiful and grand for a bathroom to not be connected to it. But there is no door. There is no place for another door to be; it would ruin the enormous ocean vista out the windows.

My belly rumbles. I place my hand on my stomach and frown. Not only do I not have any food for however many hours Zeke is gone, but I don't have a bathroom.

I sigh.

I won't let him win. He's just doing this to agitate me and rile me up, so when he returns, I'll fight harder. That's probably what his sick mind is thinking. That's why he didn't touch me last night. He knew I was too exhausted to fight hard.

I eye the big bed and climb back under the sheets. I'm not tired since I'm used to only getting a few hours at a time. And despite it not being the smartest thing I've ever done, I slept just fine with Zeke next to me all night.

My pussy pulses and my tongue runs over my lips just thinking about Zeke.

Dammit!

I can't want him. He's a horrible person. But then again, I'm always falling for the wrong men. Time and time again, I find myself lusting over a man who deserves to be thrown in prison, not in my bed.

You make bad decisions, that's why I don't let you make any decisions for us anymore, I think to my crotch.

But it's been so fucking long since a man touched me, brought me to the brink of ecstasy, pounded into me until only pleasure cascaded through me. I may not be able to find a good man, but I can find a to-be-confirmed-bad boy. A complete stranger I can fuck and abandon before I get to know him. Those are the only good guys anyway, the kind whose shit I don't know about.

For now, my fingers will have to do. I don't have anything else to do for the hours that I have to wait for Zeke to return anyway.

I lay in the middle of Zeke's bed, under the cloud-like covers. My eyes scan the room, looking for the camera I'm sure the bastard has hidden in here. The windows are hard to plant a camera on without it being noticeable. I look up at the light fixture—a strong possibility, but I don't see anything out of the ordinary to indicate a camera. Then I look to the door.

I narrow my eyes on the door handle as I try to spot anything there that shouldn't be—bingo. The screw on top of the door handle is bigger than the one below it. It appears to be more flat, more like a nail than the screw underneath. And I guarantee if I got out of bed and walked over to it, I'd be able to see a tiny lense instead of a screw.

For a moment, I consider ducking under the covers to touch myself. Keeping silent, so even if he guesses what I'm doing, he will never be able to see me. Just like he will never be able to touch me.

But what's the fun in that?

I've never been the kind of woman who shies away from owning who I am. I'm a strong, confident, sexual woman. And I own myself; no man owns me.

Pain fills my heart when I speak the words to myself, in my own head. Because I can't tell a lie, and those words are all lies.

I throw the covers off my body and push the sweatpants down off my hips before spreading my legs wide, giving the camera the perfect view of my body.

He's supposed to be working, but he might be watching me right now on his phone, and I plan on giving him one hell of a show.

I lift the shirt up off my head and then shake my locks, letting my hair fall down in my face. I bite my lip, wishing I had some red lipstick and fuck-me heels on to really bring the message home, but I don't.

I own me.

I own my body.

I own my mind.

My soul.

My heart.

No man will ever claim a single part of me as his. And even if a man does, I will fight to get every part of me back.

I arch my back and puff out my chest as my hand twists my nipple between my fingers.

I let the images come of men I've fucked before—men that were excellent in bed and hotter than gods. I don't think about what the men did to me after. How they all betrayed me. I just let their expansive chests and rippling abs fill my head. I let my mind drift over each and every one of them, like they are nothing but objects for me to get off to.

But then my mind stops and flutters to a man it shouldn't.

No!

I open my eyes, pushing him out of my brain.

I take a deep breath—and Zeke fills my nostrils. I smell him everywhere. On the pillow, the sheets. His smell turns me on.

And I know who I'll be thinking about as I pleasure myself—my fucking master.

It's wrong...so fucking wrong. But I can't stop myself from thinking about Zeke. Not when I'm dripping and I haven't even touched myself yet.

I let my hand slide down my stomach and between my thighs, I find my lips and let my long fingers rub over the whole area taking my time as moisture covers my fingers.

I look straight into the camera as one hand pleasures myself. *This is what you are missing, bastard! This is what you'll never get! You will never touch me. Never hurt me. I have all the power here, not you.*

I rub my fingers up over my clit, as it grows more sensitive. I imagine Zeke's big hands touching the sensitive bud. His tongue lapping, as more my slave than master. But as soon as he makes me come, the roles change. I'm his.

How I would beg, plead, kiss—do anything for his cock to stretch me in that uncomfortable, delicious way his large cock is surely capable of, where most men come up short. Zeke would fill me to my limits. He's a big guy, and I've seen the outline of his partial erection. The real thing would be the stuff of dreams.

Just thinking about what Zeke could do to me if he chose to fuck me like a man instead of a monster brings me close, until I'm at the place where if I don't stop, I won't be able to stop the impending orgasm. But I don't want to stop. I want to come over and over. Until I drive him crazy. Until he knows if he fucked me tonight, I wouldn't feel anything but my own fingers on my pussy—I'd be numb to him.

As I come, I use my other hand to flip off the camera. The release as I come is huge. I feel it in every nerve in my body. It cascades down my body like a waterfall overwhelming all of my nerves in my body.

It's a big fuck you to every other man in the world. I don't need a man to make myself come. I don't need a man to make it the best orgasm of my life. I don't need a man...

Dammit, there I go lying to myself again. Because I got off to a man —Zeke.

I let the orgasm roll through me before I get up. I walk naked over to the door, and then I give the camera both of my middle fingers.

"Fuck you! I will never be yours! You will never touch me. You will never fuck me. You don't fucking own me!" I slam my hand on the door and jump back when it creaks open the tiniest bit.

What the...?

I expect Zeke to walk through the door. *Did he choose this moment to come home?*

I swallow, realizing my little show might have been a bad idea. As much as I wanted Zeke to come home and let me out of my cage, I was safe as long as he wasn't here. With him here, I'm in danger full-time again.

I'm suddenly very self-conscious of my nakedness and fingers that smell like sex.

He won't fuck me. I won't let him.

Lies. If he wants to fuck you, what is your scrawny ass going to be able to do about it?

I stare at the door, waiting for Zeke to pull it open. He doesn't.

I push my hand on the door, and it opens.

I walk out and look at the other side of the door. There is no lock. The door only locks from the inside.

The fucking bastard—Zeke lied to me.

I hate human traffickers, and thieves, and rapists, and murderers. But liars—I hate them most of all. Other monsters show you exactly who they are. They don't hide their horns; you can tell they are the devil right from the start. But liars—they pretend to be better than all the rest. They like to play games, deceive, and trick you into a false sense of security before they rip out your heart and stab it to death.

Zeke is a human trafficker. One look at him tells me he's also a thief, a rapist, and a murderer. But I thought at least he could be honest about who he is. Instead, he'd rather play games and test me.

Fine, if he wants to play games, we will play games. But unlike him, I won't lie and cheat. I'll win while telling every damn truth I have. Even if he's too stupid to believe me—I'll win.

CHAPTER 12
ZEKE

The day dragged, but it's finally time for me to go home. It's eight o'clock in the evening, and I know Julian has a few guests coming over to occupy the rest of his night, which means I can get the hell out of here. I'm tired of talking to Julian about contracts, men who I can trust to transport the women, and the plan for selling them. I'm tired of pretending I find Julian's way of making money admirable. Although, I never verbally agreed with him. I never said anything to the contrary—lie by omission.

Why I thought I owed Julian a debt though is ridiculous. This man is a coward and a greedy criminal. He knew I could help him, so he let his doctors treat me. He didn't save me—not like Siren did.

I should have left the island as soon as I was strong enough to go. I could be back with Enzo, Kai, and Langston by now. Or at the very least in a cabin hiding out until I healed enough to not be a burden on my friends. I shouldn't have stayed.

But I wouldn't have seen Siren again. She would have been sold to a different man, one who would have already raped and beaten her. She'd probably already be dead.

My heart rages just thinking about what would have happened to Siren if I hadn't had been there that night, if I hadn't saved her.

I shake my head. *I haven't saved her yet*. She's not safe until she's off the island. There is something I'm missing between her and Julian. Some dark past I'm not aware of. But I'm going to find out, and Siren is going to be the one to tell me.

"Good work today, Zeke," Julian says as he takes a puff of his cigar.

I nod.

"Want to stay for a drink? I heard you drank at Oscar's, so it seems like your self-imposed sobriety has ended."

I nod. "I figured my body had done enough healing; it's time to get back to the real world. But I'll take a rain check on the drink."

Julian smiles, evilly. "Of course. You have more important things to get back to. I was surprised to see you up so early this morning at work; I assumed you had a long night breaking that one in."

My insides curl as he speaks about Siren like she's a horse needing domesticating instead of a woman. I don't give him confirmation of what I'm feeling inside.

"Need anything else before I go?" I ask instead, trying to change the subject.

Julian takes a long puff on his cigar as he rests his other hand across the back of his expensive red couch.

"No, but I plan on cashing in that rain check on Friday night."

I raise an eyebrow.

"I'm having my closest friends over then. They will be our best bets at securing buyers for the women."

I cringe on the inside. I'm going to actually do this—sell women to monsters. I don't have a choice if I want to protect my friends—if I want to protect Siren. I need to do the job, earn Julian's trust, and then get the fuck out of here.

"I'll be here then."

"Good, and bring your pet."

"Pet?" I ask automatically, not understanding what Julian is talking about, until I remember the previous night. He called Siren a pet.

"Yes, that beautiful whore you spent so much money on. Someday you'll have to tell me how you earned so much money to waste on a creature like her. But I can understand the intrigue. I understand wanting to harness that kind of power."

"I don't think she'll be up for meeting anyone so soon. Not after what I have planned for her."

Julian grins. "Just make sure she's still breathing. It doesn't matter if you've tamed her yet. Or if she's broken and bleeding. The men will be drawn to her no matter what. They will see the high-quality women we have. They will spend more money and want more of our inventory."

I try to think quickly to keep Siren at home instead of in Julian's clutches, but it's not my strong suit. I'm a methodical, careful thinker. Give me a month to make a plan, and it will run perfectly. I can protect others quickly with my body, but not my wit.

So I just nod and leave. I won't let Siren anywhere near Julian or his men. But I have a couple of days to figure out a plan.

I drive the truck home and park it in front of the house. It's time to see if Siren has escaped or not.

She's attracted to me. Her eyes speak volumes. She wants me. And she's terrified of Julian. She thinks I will protect her against him. She's right. But she doesn't get to know that.

She didn't run.

I open the front door and immediately realize I'm wrong. She fucking ran, but only after trashing my house.

Furniture is kicked over, papers are scattered everywhere, and dishes are shattered all over the floor. My eyes fume as I take in all the damage she did.

I understand she doesn't want to be a hostage, but this is unacceptable. I haven't been anything but hospitable toward her. I fed her last night. I gave her a comfy bed to sleep in. I've protected her all day from Julian. And this is how she repays me—by breaking everything in my house and then leaving.

I walk over to the liquor cabinet, hoping she didn't shatter my whiskey because I'm in desperate need of a drink. *That fucking pain in my side of a woman*—she spilled every drop and then shattered the bottle for good measure.

Other than last night, I haven't had a drink in months. And now, when I desperately need it, she took my relief from me.

I decide to go shower and wash the anger away before I decide to search for her or not. But a creak stops me.

I look down the hallway to my right, the opposite direction of the bedrooms. And I can sense her presence without seeing or hearing her.

She's here.

She didn't run.

I take my time walking down the hallway. No one can make me rush unless I want to. And I don't fucking want to rush into that room. Because I'll break my promise not to hurt her if I do.

I take a deep breath before turning the corner to the sitting room. It's my favorite room in the house, so it doesn't surprise me Siren was drawn to it. But if she destroyed this room too, I'm going to throw her ass out, and she can figure out how to deal with Julian on her own.

The room is perfect, untouched. However, instead of being empty and mine, as usual, Siren has taken over the room as her's.

I stand in the doorway and growl, making my feelings known without having to speak.

Her eyes drift up from the book in her lap and the glass of red wine in her left hand.

"You going to speak, or are you just going to stand there?" she asks, with a knowing smirk on her lips. I'm starting to believe her now when she told me she wasn't an angel.

"I'm not the one who needs to speak. You do," I say, still standing in the doorway. If I enter the room, I'll lose my temper, and I have no idea what I'm capable of doing to her. I've never been this pissed off with a woman before. She ignites feelings I didn't even know I could have.

She raises an eyebrow and then casually takes a sip of her wine. "I don't think so. I think you have things you need to say first."

I lose it.

I'm to her in one giant step. I shove the book out of her hand and down the glass of wine, needing alcohol in my system to settle my nerves as I press her deeper into the chair.

Her eyes bulge as she grips the armrests of the chair.

"You destroyed my house! Do you know how much damage you

caused? Do you know how much money I've already spent on you? How much troub—" I stop myself before I reveal my real thoughts.

She glares at me. "You lied to me! You said you locked me in the bedroom and didn't actually lock the door. You made me feel like an idiot. You locked me in a room with no bathroom or food. You made this all into one big game. This is my life! And I won't be lied to."

I laugh in her face. Breaking down was a mistake, because it causes me to move closer to her and straddle her in the chair. And now I can smell her. And she smells like sex.

What did my little vixen do while I was away at work? She's been very busy if she had time to destroy my house, read a book, and pleasure herself.

"You're mad at me because I lied to you?" I laugh again, not able to contain how ridiculous she's being.

"Yes," she hisses, completely serious as her face inches closer to mine. So close I could lean forward an inch and our lips would touch. I wouldn't even have to pretend it was a kiss. Just our angry words colliding.

"I hate to tell you, Siren, but lying is by far the least offensive of the crimes I plan on committing when it comes to you."

She stops breathing as she looks at my lips. She wants to kiss me too. I can tell in the way her breath hitches and her parted lips moisten.

But I'm too angry to let her have anything she wants. "I own you, Siren. You are mine. I can do whatever I want with you—including lie. But my lies should be the least of your worries."

Slap.

My head whips so hard to the side so fast I don't even realize what just happened. For a second, I think that Julian or one of his men have attacked and punched me square in the jaw. But when I turn my head back to look at Siren, I realize the swing came from her. She's tiny; I have no idea how she was able to give her slap so much power.

It may be hard to believe, but I've been slapped by women before. None of which I completely deserved—until now. I earned every sting zipping through my jaw right now.

Siren is panting heavily underneath me. Her body is on alert, and if

I say anything else stupid, she will slap me again with the full force of her petite body. She's definitely been taught how to defend herself. *From who?* I don't know. But that wasn't your average slap.

"Is that all you got? Because that pathetic tap won't stop me from getting what I want." I lower myself on top of her, until my body is pressing down on hers. Until my cock is resting against her stomach. Until she can barely breathe beneath me.

"Then rape me already! Get it over with! Stop playing games and get it over with!" she cries before her hand comes up again to slap me. I stop her automatically this time, more prepared than I was before.

I push her hands down into the armrests on either side of her. Now all she can move are her lips, as my head blocks any other movement. But her lips alone are dangerous enough.

"Do it. Rape me. I'd like to see you try. I'll cut off your dick before you have a chance."

I lean down until our lips are aligned but stop short of kissing. Her pink lips are taunting me in a way I can't resist, and her damn fucking smell is pulling me to her like a magnet. My raging hard-on is getting uncomfortable in my jeans. I didn't think this position through when I pinned her to the chair, because it's more torturous for me than her.

"Who says I want to rape you?" I say, my eyes searing. It's my biggest lie yet. Okay, I don't want to rape her, but I do want to fuck her—badly. I'm not sure I've ever wanted anything more.

Her eyes flicker down to where my erection gives me away. "He does."

I smirk. "Only a weak man lets his cock make the decisions. And I'm not a weak man. I'm a smart businessman who likes money."

She snickers. "You sure as hell don't look like any businessman I've ever met. And you aren't very smart with money if you are willing to drop thirty million on a woman when you could easily pick up some woman at a bar with your body."

"I am focused on my money, which is why I don't want to rape you. It's like driving a brand new car off the car lot. You would instantly lose your value if I was the one to break you in. As you said, I spent too much money on you to let that happen."

Her face drops into concern as she struggles carefully against my body. I'm so close she can barely move without our lips touching. And she won't give me that satisfaction.

"Then, what do you want from me, if not my body?"

"I want to sell you. We are going to Julian Reed's Friday night. He's inviting some of the richest men in the world. Men that would make the boys at the auction seem poor. I'm going to sell you and double my money."

Her mouth drops open, speechless.

All of my words are lies. I don't want to sell her; I want to protect her. And selling her to Julian Reed would be sentencing her to a life of torture. But she doesn't know that. I need her to fear me. I need her obedient. Especially if we go to Julian's. I don't need him suspecting I haven't touched her yet.

"Now, slap me again, and I'll make sure you go to the most ruthless man instead of the one with the biggest pockets. Understand?"

She nods slowly.

"Good." Although, I'm not sure I like her so silent. Her body lies to me, I can feel it. There is no way she's actually attracted to me. No way her nipples are hardening in my direction. No way the scent of sex is growing. No way she is licking her lips because she wants me. When she speaks, she tells the truth. She's told me as much before. She hated it when I lied, probably because she's a horrible liar. I need to get her talking.

"How do you know Julian Reed?"

I expect her to pretend she doesn't. I expect her to at least attempt to lie first—she doesn't.

"No," she flat out says.

"No? I don't think you get how this works. I ask you a question, you answer."

"No."

I growl.

"You just admitted you wouldn't hurt me because you're selling me to another man. You won't damage me before you do that. So no, I'm the one with control now. And I'm not going to answer your questions."

"I have a better idea," I retort.

She blinks, waiting for me to speak, but she still thinks she holds all the power.

"You always tell the truth. That's what you told me before, when I bought you."

She shifts beneath me but doesn't confirm or deny the truth.

"And you hated it when I lied to you, which means for you, telling the truth is your most important value. Something you won't waver on easily."

Again, she doesn't speak.

I smirk. *I have her.*

"Fine, you don't want to answer my questions, you don't have to."

She grins, thinking she won.

"But there will be consequences to your silence."

She narrows her gaze at me but doesn't move. She can't; I'm still holding her down to prevent another inevitable slap.

"You either tell me the truth, or I'll commit a sin." I don't tell her what the sin will be, but the look in my eyes gives her a clue. I won't be the gentleman I'm used to being. I'll unleash the beast. And once I do, there is no going back.

CHAPTER 13
SIREN

Tell me the truth, or I'll commit a sin.

Those words are going to be the death of me someday.

This man is all about playing games, because it's the only way he can beat me. He wants ultimate control over me. He wants me to spill all of my secrets and willingly give him my body. *Not going to happen.*

We both stare back and forth, neither of us backing down.

I refuse to be scared of his silly game.

And he refuses to show me any emotion other than absolute stillness.

Zeke's hands are still on me, but he's not manhandling me the way I might expect him to. His body is pressed against mine as he sits on top of me, and his hands have mine pinned to the armrests, but he isn't exerting all of his physical strength over me. His presence alone would have me bolted in place. He's so intense, unmoving, like a rock that can't be swayed by anything, even the wind.

He's a man of steel, only speaking words when necessary—only applying force when he needs to. Because he knows the costs of exerting his physical prowess on others. And he only reserves that for the most serious situations.

I'm the first to move, squirming beneath his hard body. I feel his erection against my stomach. He doesn't try to hide his attraction to me. He displays it proudly. And as much as I want to make a snarky comment about him being turned on by me—I can't. Because it would be a lie to tease him for his attraction when I'm equally turned on.

My self-pleasure session earlier did nothing to squash this deep craving in my core that has now spread to the tips of my fingers and toes. Every nerve, muscle, and bone in my body is screaming—I want Zeke.

I want to tug on his man bun sitting on top of his head, until his hair falls gruffly to his shoulders, turning him into more beast than man. I want to feel his stubble against my thigh. I want to feel the power of his hands as he pushes inside of me with his impressive cock. I want to fight back, determined to ride him instead of letting him fuck me. I want him to tame me, convince me that having a man in my life is a good thing.

I want to lose all control and forget how horrible men are. How selfish, egotistical, assholes all men are. I want to forget about him buying me. I want to pretend our only interaction before today was when I saved him.

I want...

I swallow. *It doesn't matter what I want.*

My eyes drop back to Zeke, who hasn't moved and gives me no clue of his thoughts. But I know that he's thinking. Every move he makes is calculated, including when he is as still as a statue.

His silence is driving me mad. I want answers. *I need answers!* I need to know the man beneath the shield. So I can hurt him, demolish him, and be one step closer to freedom.

I shift again, pretending I want to get away from him, while accidentally thrusting my hips up into his erection.

His lip twitches. *He notices.* His body stills, except for his eyes. It's less than a second, but I see them roll with pleasure.

Why isn't he going to try and have me, then? He wants me this badly. Does he really want to sell me to Julian or one of Julian's friends?

"Truth or sin. What does that mean?" I finally ask.

Zeke looks down at my hands gripping the armrest. With an

unspoken promise, he releases me. I expect him to be hesitant and wait for me to slap him again. But he doesn't. He trusts me. *How foolish of him.*

Zeke stands up and walks over to the far side of the room. He returns with a second wine glass and a bottle of wine. He fills his glass, then mine. This bottle is one of the last of his alcohol supply to survive my tornado. I destroyed or hid all the rest.

I take the glass from him; our fingers tingle when our hands brush. *Stupid body, always choosing the wrong men.*

Zeke takes a drink, and so do I. He has this unyielding power over me. I almost wish he'd speak. I can fight back word for word. I can use my snarky wit to knock him on his ass and put him on the defensive. But I can't fight back without him talking. I can't resist his pull. It's like gravity pulling me to him, commanding me to follow his unspoken words.

I clear my throat, trying to break free from the spell. "What do you mean?" I ask again.

He doesn't let my question or uncomfortableness speed up his answers. He takes his time, drinking more of his wine as he waits me out.

I try to sit up taller in the chair while he stands over me. But it's no use. With his six foot five frame towering over me as I sit in the chair, I can't help but feel small.

Finally, he kneels in front of me. Reducing his power, but making me more uncomfortable now that we are eye to eye.

"Better?" he asks.

My mouth is dry. *How can he read me so easily?* I shake my head, trying to wash all feeling from my body.

He raises one eyebrow. "Hmm, well then make up your mind, Siren. Should I kneel or stand?"

"Sit...in a chair." *Like a normal person.*

He shakes his head slowly. "That wasn't one of the choices. Kneel or stand?"

My eyes flicker back and forth, trying to read his. "Kneel," I whisper.

He nods and continues to kneel.

Holy hell. Why is this big, muscular, powerful man kneeling in front of me? And why is it the sexiest thing I've ever seen?

He finishes his wine and sets it down on the end table next to me. He still hasn't answered my question.

Then he reaches for my wine glass. I let him take it. I don't need more alcohol in my system if I'm going to have a fighting chance against Zeke. He's not like other men. And that terrifies me. I don't know how to play him if he's constantly two steps ahead of me.

But when he reaches for the glass, he grabs my fingers too. He lifts the glass to his own lips and drinks. His eyes looking up at me as he drinks from the glass I'm holding.

I change my mind; *this* is the sexiest thing I've ever seen. It's such a simple move, but I can feel his touch, his breath all the way to my core. My toes tingle and my pussy drenches just from his lips being so close to my fingers. His hand is touching mine in a controlling but kind way.

I bite my lip, trying to keep from gasping and moaning while he drinks. When he finishes the last drop of my wine, he takes a deep inhale.

I think he's breathing in the wine, but the mischievous look on his face tells me otherwise.

"It appears that you have already sinned," he says.

I blink rapidly. *Can he still smell my cum on my fingers?* My cheeks heat at his accusation. I shouldn't be the least bit embarrassed; I'm a grown woman who can touch herself as much as she wants. I practically paraded naked around his house. I flashed his cameras, showed him how I came. I thought it would be a big fuck you, but right now, I think it's a big fuck me.

"How do I know?" he asks, asking my unspoken question out loud.

I nod.

He shakes his as he releases my hand. "This is how the game works. You want answers, you have to be willing to give everything. You have to risk the highest price in order to get the truth."

"Touching myself isn't a sin."

"Yes, it is—*to me.*"

I cock my head, not understanding.

"You belong to me, Siren. You. Are. Mine. You don't get to touch yourself without my permission. Your pussy belongs to me. Your pleasure belongs to me. You touched what is mine. To me, that's a sin."

His words infuriate me, and somehow also turn me on. No man has ever talked about owning my pussy or pleasure like that.

"You don't own me," I whisper—not terrified, but not strong enough to say the words so loudly. Not because I'm scared of Zeke, but because on some level, I want a man to lay claim to my body. I want to be controlled. I'm tired of having to do every-fucking-thing for myself. I want a man who can make me come better than I can.

Zeke leans forward until his mouth is against my ear. "No, Siren, maybe I don't. Because to truly own someone, the other person has to willingly give himself back. But soon, I will. Because you are on the verge of giving me everything."

He sits back. And once again, I'm left speechless.

"So, how does this silly game of yours work?" I ask, clearing my throat.

He sits back on his heels. "I ask you a question. You tell the truth. And if you don't want to answer, you have to let me commit a sin against you."

"And what about me? Do I get to ask a question? Do I get to commit a sin if you don't answer?"

"Yes," he answers, surprising the hell out of me. I assumed this would be one-sided. But this might be exactly what I need to be able to get my own answers.

"And if we choose to answer the question, how do we know we are both telling the truth?"

He lets out a breathy growl as if the question I asked is ridiculous. "We both know the answer to that."

I run my hand through my long hair, wishing Zeke would do the same—come unhinged a little, let his hair down, and stop controlling my every thought. But he doesn't. His hair stays high up on his head, locked away with a black scrunchie.

"You told me you can't lie. And I believe you."

"I can too lie...I um...fuck," I breathe, not even being able to lie about lying.

He smirks. "See? You can't lie."

Now it's my turn to growl.

He smiles in a charming, bright way—*fucking asshole.*

"Fine, but someday, I might figure out how to lie and how will you be able to hold me accountable?"

He leans forward again. "Because if you find a way to lie with your words, your body will betray you. Your cheeks will shade just the slightest darker pink. More blood will flow to your lips until they are as red as a poisoned apple. Your eyes will dilate. You'll fidget just the tiniest bit more. And your body will melt under my scrutiny."

As he speaks, everything he says happens to my body. *How can he control me that much?*

"And how will I know you aren't lying? You've already lied to me."

"And you figured out I was lying within an hour of me being gone."

"So? I don't expect our game to last an entire hour."

"I suspect you are a fast learner."

I laugh. "I'm really not. I'm the worst learner. It takes me forever to master a skill. I have to put in way more than my ten thousand hours to learn something. But once I master it, I never forget. I don't have to practice anymore." *Why the fuck am I telling him this much about myself?* I'm just willingly spilling all of my secrets.

His eyes widen at my admission.

I clamp my mouth shut to keep from admitting any more stupid secrets.

"I grew up in New Orleans. My mother is in prison; my father died when I was five. I worked as a mechanic for a few years in my early teens. I met my first girlfriend in college at the University of Texas. I studied biology, but never finished my degree."

My mouth slowly unclamps at each of his admissions—wow.

"Did I speak the truth?" he asks.

I think back to how he delivered each sentence. I close my eyes, trying to remember every syllable he spoke, the inflection, and any clues his body gave away. Most people would have said there were no clues—nothing to give away if he spoke the truth or not. He delivered his words with the same calm stillness he does everything else with.

No—he didn't tell the truth.

When he is speaking the truth, he is passionate about what he says, and his voice is husky and intoxicating. My body would follow any command he'd give. I could listen to Zeke talk all damn day.

His voice was still deep and sexy, but it was slightly different. If he spoke a command in that voice, I wouldn't have had to listen to his order unless I wanted to.

His body was more tense than still.

His eyes glazed over just a little, trying to hide the truth.

"You lied," I say.

"How did you know?"

I shake my head with a light smile. "I'm not telling you my secrets."

He narrows his eyes in a scowl, which only brightens my smile.

"Fine, don't tell me what my tells are. But you trust that you will be able to tell when I'm lying?"

"Yes."

"And if either of us is caught lying to the other, then he, or she, gets to commit the ultimate sin."

I swallow the lump down. I don't have to ask what he means by 'ultimate sin.' There is one universal sin that all people, animals, and culture believe is the worst—murder. If I lie, and he catches me, then he will kill me. If he lies, I kill him.

These are the ultimate stakes. The highest bet either of us can put on the table. But we both want each other's secrets.

Zeke wants to know about my relationship with Julian, while I need Zeke's secrets to use against him and free myself.

We are both willing to risk everything for the truth.

I nod, silently agreeing to his terms.

Most men would want to hear my words, not Zeke. All forms of communication are equal in his book.

"We can only play max once a day," Zeke says.

I agree. I don't like endless prodding and questions about my life.

"Follow up questions have to be asked the next day."

I nod.

"And you don't have to reveal anything other than the basic answer to the question. Elaboration happens with further questions."

Again I nod, agreeing. I will have to be careful with how I ask my questions to get the most answers from Zeke, while trying to keep my big mouth shut. Zeke is clearly used to keeping his answers simple, so I doubt I'll get more than one sentence. He might even try to answer me with a single word if I'm not careful.

"You first," I say, assuming he will ask me about Julian, and I'm not sure if I'll answer or choose sin. I don't want to talk about Julian, but I don't want to let Zeke commit a sin against me. He could choose anything from kissing to raping me—anything but killing me.

And I have no idea what question I'll ask him.

Zeke licks his lips, and my eyes are glued to his sensual mouth and rough five o'clock shadow darkening his square jaw.

"Do you find me attractive?" Zeke asks.

"What?" I gape.

He reaches up to his head, and pulls the scrunchie from his head and puts it on his wrist. His hair falls down, making him look like the human prince from Beauty and the Beast.

I can't blink, I can't breathe, I can't speak. My body is beyond attracted to him. He already knows that. I may hate how my body reacts to his, but it's not something he has to ask me to know it to be true. If this is the question he's asking me, it's a waste of a question.

He waits, patiently, still kneeling in front of me. "What will it be? Answer the question truthfully, or do I get to commit a sin against you?"

"The sinning part—can be anything you choose?"

He nods, his eyes like fire ready to burn me the second I refuse to answer the question. "Anything except murder."

I nod. I was right in my understanding of what a sin could be. And I can't believe I fell for his twisted game. He likes torturing me before he beats and rapes me. It's more fun to think it's my fault he's hurting me than to just fucking do it himself—*fucking coward.*

This is the easiest question, but also the hardest to admit. We both already know the truth, but I know nodding won't be enough this time. He wants me to verbalize my feelings. Whether I answer or not, he wins. He either gets me to admit my attraction, which he will use against me, or he gets to rape me.

I grit my teeth in anger at his ridiculous question. He doesn't care about Julian or getting honest answers from me. He just enjoys the slow torture. I won't let him win. He doesn't get to hurt me tonight. I won't let him. I'll answer him. Words and teasing won't hurt me.

"Yes," I answer, refusing to give Zeke more than a single syllable answer. Luckily, it's enough to please him.

His face darkens, and I can tell he's thinking about all the dirty things he wants to do to me.

"Your turn," he says.

I think for a moment through my red, angry cheeks and grinding teeth. I'm not going to waste my question like Zeke did. Although, from the amount of rage I'm now experiencing, he didn't waste his question. He got me riled up and unfocused.

"Do you enjoy taking women as your slave?" I spit out in anger. *Yes, my question sucks and doesn't get me any real answers.* But I'm pissed. I want him to admit he's a monster, just like I had to admit I find him attractive.

I tap my fingers hard against the soft fabric of the armrests, wishing my nails could make an annoying tapping sound to unnerve him. I glare at Zeke, demanding an answer. A simple yes will satisfy me, just as I answered him.

"Sin."

I blink rapidly. *Wait...what?*

"I won't answer your question. I choose sin."

I'm speechless. I gave him an easy question, and rather than answer me truthfully, he'd rather let me commit a sin against him. I search his eyes to see if he set a trap, but I don't find any there.

My wheels turn, trying to come up with the perfect sin to inflict upon him. After a few moments, I grin slyly when I find the right one. Now to figure out if Zeke will keep to his word and take my wrath.

CHAPTER 14
ZEKE

Why didn't I ask her about Julian? Why didn't I ask the most important question?

I know why. Once I get an answer, this will end. She will go free. She will no longer be mine. Our time together will be over.

I don't know how I know exactly, but I know. The question is too important. The truth she is hiding is too big. I can see it in her surprised eyes when I didn't ask the obvious question. By not asking, I got more information about how important the answer is than if I had asked. Sure, I might have gotten to commit a sin if she wasn't ready to share the answer with me. But once I start committing sins, I won't be able to stop—not with Siren.

Why did I choose sin instead of answering her question?

Because I had no choice—I either lie or tell her the truth. And even though she thought her question was an easy one, it wasn't. I'm not the man she thinks I am. I didn't want to buy her like I would a car, but I had no choice.

Just like I have no choice but to choose sin instead of truth. I can't tell her the truth, and she would know if I lied—so sin it is.

"What is your sin?" I ask, still kneeling between her legs, staring eye to eye with her. When I first knelt in front of her, it was to get her to trust me; now, it's tempting me in ways I never imagined. Being so close to her and not being able to touch her, not being able to rip her sweatpants off and devour her sweet pussy—*kneeling was definitely a mistake.*

"Hmm," her lips purse as she contemplates her decision. I know she is going to push my limits even further. She knows she is my weakness, and for some reason, I'm not letting myself have her. The lie I told was that I'm going to sell her to make a profit as long as she is untouched. But I'm not sure she bought that lie.

Siren thinks I'm ruthless and cruel, but I'll protect her with my life. I've already moved her into the very limited circle of people who I would defend no matter the cost.

Her eyes darken as they go back in forth in search of finding something in my eyes. But I'm as blank as a sheet of paper. I won't yield any truths outside the game.

"I'm going to need some real clothes," she says.

"No, that's not part of the deal. You get what I decide to give you."

She frowns and folds her arms over her chest, lifting her legs up into the seat, trying to get as far away from me as possible.

"I knew you were a liar and would go back on our deal."

"I'm not going back on our deal. You can commit any sin you want. I just don't have to fund it or supply you with clothes or anything you need to commit the sin."

She shakes her head. "I have nothing. I own nothing. You've given me nothing! How am I supposed to commit a sin when I have nothing to work with?"

I shrug. "That's not my problem."

She pouts for a second, then says, "I can use anything I find? Anything I own or lay claim to in order to commit my sin?"

I narrow my eyes and lean forward, not sure where she is going with this. "Yes."

She hops over the side of the armrest and then starts running through the house.

She's going to be the death of me; I can feel it.

A second later, I chase after her. I'm fast, but due to my height and weight, I'm not as nimble as she is. She can hop over and dart around the various pieces of broken glass and furniture before I even see them.

She's out the front door before I get to the foyer. But I'm out the door in two giant leaps. She's running for my truck—the driver's side. My keys are still in my pocket; she can't start the truck. *Right?* But I don't stop to recall if the keys are still in my pocket or if I accidentally left them in the truck.

I run to the passenger side.

Siren is sitting on the driver's side. Her hands are on the wheel, and her seatbelt is already fastened.

"And where do you think you are going without the keys?" I smirk.

She bites her lip, trying to hide her mischievous grin. "I'm not going anywhere without the keys. Thanks for bringing them."

And with that, she starts the truck and puts her foot on the gas, flooring it.

Damn it, I'm a fucking idiot!

I'm used to older trucks, the kind where you have to put the key into the ignition to start it. But even though this truck has already been beaten to death by the previous owner, it has a key fob. You don't need to put it into the ignition, but I usually do out of habit. I consider jumping out of the truck, so the key is no longer in the vehicle. But I'm not sure removing the key fob from the car at this point will even shut the truck off. She could drive anywhere. She could get free.

It could be a good thing...unless Julian finds her.

I grab for my seatbelt instead and buckle myself in as she drives dangerously fast through Julian's compound.

"Where are we going?" I ask.

She smirks. "This is my choice—my sin. And I'm not telling yet. You'll just have to wait and see."

I silently punish myself for coming up with this game. I thought it would get Siren to trust me enough to spill her secrets. And it might over time, but right now, all I've accomplished is cursing her and myself to hell.

Siren takes a hard left turn off Julian's property onto the main gravel and sand road. My body gets thrown into the window as she turns.

"Slow the fuck down," I curse under my breath.

"Fucking hypocrite," she chuckles back.

"What did you just say?"

She turns toward me, her eyes no longer on the road as she drives faster. "You heard me."

I growl and sit back in my seat, my hand instinctively grabbing the door handle as she takes another sharp turn too fast. *She's right; I'm a hypocrite.* I drove fast just to get her under my control. She's just doing the same thing.

But one way or another, I'm going to be the one driving the truck home. Whether her ass is in it or not.

Siren flicks on the radio to fill the silence. She bobs her head to the music and mouths the words along to the song. But she doesn't sing. I haven't heard her sing since the night she saved me. *Maybe I imagined it?* I don't know how much of what I remember is real or made up. But after spending more time with Siren, I don't think I will ever forget a single second of my time with her.

I wait for her to start singing along, but she doesn't.

Finally, she stops in one of the local towns, parking the car illegally in front of one of the storefronts.

"What are you doing?" I ask, my heart still racing from the death-defying ride over here.

She unbuckles her seatbelt happily, like a teenager about to go shopping with their father's credit card at the mall.

"Getting new clothes," she says, before swinging her door open.

"With what money?" I ask as I jump out of the truck to go after her. It's only then that I realize my wallet is missing.

How the hell did she pull that off?

I don't have a clue. She must have been a thief in a previous life. I really need to ask questions that will give me some actual answers about who Siren is.

She skips up and down all bubbly as she heads into the first department store. I follow and corner her before she can use my money to buy some clothes. My body presence alone corners her between two racks of clothes.

"Give me back my wallet."

She tosses it to me. And then darts under my arm.

Wait...that was too easy.

She struts across the store and starts talking to one of the employees. And then she flashes me one of her *I'm going to kick your ass one day* smiles and hands the woman my credit card.

I'm searing. I'm sure actual fumes are coming out of my ears. She thinks these games are going to protect her. Her strategy is to keep her secrets by torturing me so I'll want to surrender to her. *Think again.* She has no idea who she is messing with. I'm going to wreck her.

♡

AFTER SIREN'S LITTLE SHOPPING SPREE THAT INCLUDED BUYING half a dozen jeans, a couple of heels, and twenty designer shirts, she's finished spending my money. We are back in the truck, this time with me in the driver's seat and her in the passenger seat.

"Time to go home," I say.

She shakes her head. "You think that was my sin?"

I frown. "Yes, you just spent thousands of dollars on clothes. I think that counts as a sin."

She laughs. "Not even close." She kicks her feet up on my dashboard. "We are going to the bar on seventh street. That is where I'll complete my sin."

I sigh. I'm tired, and I don't feel like fighting her. I need her to trust me. And I need this night to be over. Tomorrow I have more important things to deal with—mainly Julian.

So that's how I end up driving Siren to a bar.

She practically sprints out of the car the second I stop, assuming I'm going to try and stop her after I drove her all the way here—she has a lot to learn about me.

I take my time getting out of the truck, after making sure I have my wallet with all my credit cards.

I walk into the crowded bar, taking in its steely decorations, making it look more like a dance club than a bar. It feels like every tourist on the island is packed in this place.

I find Siren at the end of the bar already flirting with a man, clearly ordering her a drink.

I walk up behind her. I know she can feel me behind her because goosebumps have risen on her arms.

She's wearing jeans, heels, and some black strapless shirt that makes her toned shoulders easy for my teeth to sink into. I've never been into biting during sex, but her shoulders taunt me in a way that makes me want to try sinking my teeth into her. Pleasurably watching tiny drops of blood drip off those sexy shoulders would ease the fury she boils inside me.

She doesn't turn around, and I don't need her to in order to get my message across.

I lean down close to her neck. I don't have to lean down much now that she is wearing heels—heels I'm secretly happy she bought because they are sexy as hell.

"If you ask anyone in here for help, if you try to run, if you tell anyone the truth...there will be consequences."

She shivers at my throaty words.

"But I hope you do try to run, because I enjoy chasing. And I'll enjoy inflicting the punishment even more."

She stops breathing as my words sink in.

My threats are real. I don't want her to run. Julian is too infatuated with her. He would find her, rape her, and sell her. Threatening and inflicting consequences is the only way to show how serious I am about protecting her.

I walk away to go order a drink and sit in one of the booths to wait for her sin. I'm already afraid I know what it's going to be...and I'm not sure my restraint is prepared for what she's about to do.

CHAPTER 15
SIREN

I've enjoyed teasing Zeke all night.

I didn't think I'd enjoy driving Zeke's big, worn-down truck, but I was wrong. I understand now the thrill of feeling power over the world when you drive it. The truck drives like it doesn't give a fuck that it's run-down and should be scrapped for metal. It drives like it owns the road, and anyone in its way needs to get the fuck out.

I get it; I'm the same as the truck. A little rough around the edges, but more powerful than anyone suspects at first glance. And I loved using that power to make Zeke regret ever buying me.

When I stole his wallet, the look of shock on his beautifully sculpted face will stay with me forever. I don't know what he thought of the move—if I had practiced stealing before or if I got lucky. And I'll never tell him the truth.

I've had a fun night—until Zeke breathed down my neck. Until his words held promises and threats of what would happen if I ran. He doesn't know I have no intention of running. He may suspect I'm scared of Julian, but he doesn't know why. He doesn't know Julian would hunt me to the ends of the earth without Zeke's protection.

But Zeke's heated threat almost makes me want to run, just so he will chase me. Just so he can *punish me.*

I don't run, though. Instead, I let the handsome man I found the second I walked into the bar order me a shot of tequila. We both take the shot. Then I stroke the stranger's strong forearm, flash him a bright smile, and wink before sauntering off.

I felt Zeke's gaze on me the entire time, but if he thinks flirting with a stranger at the bar is the sin I plan on committing against him tonight, he's in for a surprise.

I strut across the room to the dance floor, making eye contact with a man dancing seductively with a woman.

My turn—my eyes and body say.

The man's gaze finds me immediately. What can I say, I know how to attract men to me like a moth to a flame. I will burn every single man who thinks he has a claim to me.

I scrape my teeth over my bottom lip and bat my eyelashes at him, then I wait. He will ditch his date for me.

And right on cue, he does. The woman yells and scowls at the man, but he isn't listening anymore. I have him thoroughly under my spell.

"Dance with me," he says.

I crook my finger under his chin. "Let's see if you can keep up."

I don't introduce myself or ask for his name. This isn't serious. This is about sex, even if we never get to the physical act. We will dance, and it will be as close to sex as you can get with your clothes still on.

I grab his neck, he grabs my hips, and then we are moving, grinding on each other through the thick crowd of people. We only need a second to learn each other's style. And then we are effortlessly moving across the floor—our bodies dancing on top of each other. I push; he pulls. The sexual tension between us is palpable. If I had control over my life right now, we'd end up in the closest hotel room.

Instead, this is all I get.

I give the man everything I have while dancing with him. I don't search to see if Zeke can see me. If he's smart, he will pull out his phone and get buried in it, instead of watching me.

I know Zeke wants me, but for some reason, he isn't going to touch me until he decides if he wants me more than he wants to sell me to Julian. I'm about to make that decision so much harder for him.

Suddenly, I feel like I have more eyes on me. The room has circled around me, and I know that Zeke is watching.

Good. I'm about to murder his heart.

The dance ends, and I pull the hot man I'm using flush to my body. Our mouths pant over each other, but I don't kiss him. And I don't let him kiss me.

The crowd claps and hollers, cheering us on—wanting another dance.

But I have a better idea to give them a full show.

While my dance partner inches closer to grabbing my ass, I look over his shoulders and find the DJ behind him.

I crook my finger at him, and he runs toward me.

"Can I use the mic, and can you play 'Truth Hurts' by Lizzo?" I ask.

"You can have whatever you want," he says with a wink.

I look back to my dance partner. "Can you sing?"

He chuckles. "They don't care if I sing. But I can show you off."

"Good enough."

The DJ returns with the microphone, and the song I requested starts.

My hot dance partner spins me around, and I start singing with him dancing around me.

As I sing, the room quiets. I've always been a good singer. I've sung numerous times in the shower or car, but never publicly. But I don't doubt the power of my voice.

The man holds me in his arms, swinging our hips together as I belt out the song.

My eyes find Zeke's. He's sitting at a round table directly across from me. The crowd has parted, and Zeke has the perfect view of me. So I sing for him. I let him know he will never have me. I will never be his. And I can have any man in this room.

I up my game, teasing the man holding me and walking over and touching or rubbing against every other man in the room. But it's not enough. I want my sin to hurt Zeke.

So I turn to my dance partner, rip off his shirt to the hoop and hollers of every female in the room. And then I kiss down his chest as I sing before rubbing my ass on his hard-on.

The song ends, and I'm covered in sweat and exhilaration. My dance partner leans down to kiss me, but I move at the last second, and his kiss falls to my shoulder. My eyes lock with Zeke.

I could let him kiss me, *but I didn't.*

I could let him fuck me, *but I won't.*

As long as you behave, this is as far as I will go. I'll never make you imagine me with another man unless you give me reason to.

"Thank you for the dance," I say to my partner before strutting over to Zeke.

Zeke watches me carefully and finishes his drink before waving the hot waitress over.

She smiles at him brightly while bending over so he can see down her blouse as she takes his order. But he doesn't look; his gaze is still on me. And I can see the agitation in his eyes at having to watch me dance all over a shirtless man, and knowing that every man in the room wants me—*I can choose any of them.*

My sin worked; he's pissed.

But then Zeke grabs the waitress and dips her over his lap. She laughs hysterically as he whispers something close to her lips. She nods enthusiastically at his words.

And then he leans down and kisses her, with his eyes still locked on mine. He asked if he could kiss her. So he is capable of asking a woman for permission before he takes what he wants. He just won't do that with me.

I thought my flirting without crossing the line was a good sin. I was wrong—Zeke's sin is better. He damaged me worse than I injured him, and it isn't even his turn to sin. I don't think I can handle what he will do when it is.

CHAPTER 16
ZEKE

The second my lips touch the waitress's lips, I know it's a mistake. I thought the kiss would hurt Siren, pay her back for all the flirting, dancing, and rubbing on that man she did. But the kiss feels wrong in every way.

I asked the waitress if I could kiss her before I did it. I'm not the kind of man who takes something from a woman without asking before. But Siren saw me ask—and she's pissed. Because she thinks I would never ask before I took from her.

As my lips press against the waitress's thin, pink lips, I feel awful. This kiss is good, simple, not too wet. When I shove my tongue between her lips, I taste the sweet wine she must be sipping between customers behind the bar. It's pleasant and awful.

I'm not the kind of man who feels a rush of emotions with a kiss. I've never fallen hard for a woman I've been intimate with before. Never experienced that head over heels feeling for another woman. And I sure as hell don't feel that now kissing Samantha—at least that's what her name tag says. In fact, I feel the opposite. I feel regret, remorse, and stupidity.

I should not have kissed her.

I should not have taunted Siren.

I thought that I would pay her back for hurting me with her sin. But instead, my move backfired, and I ended up damaging myself more.

Siren's face full of disappointment and anger is like a shock to the heart. I didn't realize how much I cared about what Siren thought of me until now.

I thought the kiss would make me stop thinking about Siren. I would realize I just needed to get laid to forget about her. But the kiss made my obsession for Siren worse and did nothing to quell my desire for her. It just showed me how a kiss from any other woman isn't enough.

I want Siren.

I want to kiss her.

I want her in my bed.

I want her writhing underneath me as I thrust into her.

I want her riding my cock on top of me as she digs her nails into my chest.

I want...fuck, I can't even think it. Because I want so much more than just a good fuck when it comes to Siren.

When Siren committed her sin against me, I thought I was going to lose my mind. But not out of jealousy like she wanted me to feel. Sure, I wanted to be the one she was dancing all over. I wanted to be the man whose cock she rubbed with her curvy ass. But watching her move, listening to her sing, seeing her confidence as she took control of the entire room—I could search a lifetime and never find a woman like her.

I always knew I'd need a strong woman if I were to ever settle down. My lifestyle requires a woman who can hold her own—a powerful woman who doesn't put up with any man's shit.

Siren is that woman.

And I'm torn between setting her free and finding a way to make her mine, for real.

I know she wants my body. She's made that clear. But she could never love the man beneath the hard exterior. Because unlike her, I commit sins every day. I steal, beat, and murder. I'll even end up selling women if it comes down to it, because I'm only truly loyal to a small handful.

And she will never get past any of that. I could bring her chocolates and flowers every day of her life. I could court her and take her to fancy dinners, dancing, and movies. None of that would matter. She's already seen the worse part of my heart. She will never see me as anything other than cruel.

But it doesn't stop my cock from hardening or my heart from hoping she was brought into my life for something more than just saving me in the ocean.

"I get off in an hour. We could get a room at the hotel down the street," the waitress says, still sitting in my lap with her hands around my neck.

Shit, I'd completely forgotten about her.

"Sorry, a work thing came up. Thanks for the kiss." I try to smile and give her my best apologetic beam, but from the hurt look on her face, she thinks I'm the kind of man who will kiss a woman and then dump her when he finds a better-looking woman to take home. And she's right.

She stands but turns at the last minute, and I already know where she's headed with her movements. She's going to slap me.

But she's not as fast as Siren. She's not practiced the movement enough. So I grab her wrist before she even winds back to slap me.

She frowns, glaring at me like I'm the devil. If she only knew how true her thoughts were.

I dig into my wallet and pull out a couple of twenties. I hand them to her. "Thank you for the drinks."

At first, I think she's going to reject the money. But she grabs it hastily and shoves the wad into her bra before stomping off.

Siren laughs, like what she witnessed was the funniest shit she's ever seen—me getting told off and almost slapped by a waitress. But I see past her light chuckles. She's hurt—I hurt her with that kiss. It was my intention, but seeing the pain behind her eyes makes me regret my decision even more.

Finally, she stops laughing and walks over to me. "I thought I was the only one who got to sin tonight."

"You telling me that kiss hurt you? Because that would mean you are jealous of a waitress. It would mean you want me to kiss you. I know you find me attractive, but I thought you thought more highly of yourself." *I'm such an asshole.*

This time Siren doesn't take my bait. She just walks away.

We walk toward my truck in silence.

"Any chance you want to let me go?" she asks, her voice heavy. She doesn't look up at me. She just stops next to the passenger door like she's ready to accept her fate, but she'd rather run.

"Never," I answer honestly. *I never want to let her go.*

She sucks in a deep breath, and I swear I see tears in her eyes. Siren doesn't strike me as the type that cries often. So the fact that this moment is when the tears start surprises me.

Finally, she nods and then climbs into the passenger side. Without fighting me about who is driving.

I take my time climbing into the driver's side, hoping she will have stopped sobbing by the time I climb in.

She hasn't—her crying has gotten worse. Tears are pouring out of her eyes, and her voice is wailing in pain.

What's happening?

I don't understand why she's crying so much or in so much pain. But the fact that I can't ask—the fact that I can't touch her, can't console her, hurts me worse than watching her dance with that man. It hurts worse than watching her kiss another man. It hurts worse than knowing she's fucked another man.

It hurts, seeing her in this much anguish. It hurts so much that I almost want to let her go. This is the worst sin she could ever commit, hurting and not letting me do a damn thing to help her. This sin destroys me. This sin will be my undoing.

CHAPTER 17
SIREN

My tears break him.

I didn't expect them to. I've just had so much emotion floating through my body I needed a release. I promised myself I would stop as soon as Zeke got into the truck.

But as soon as I saw his face, felt his nervous energy, and saw him fidgeting with the steering wheel and keys like it was his first time driving, I knew the tears just became my sin, not the flirting and dancing.

For a second, I thought I should have kissed my dance partner, because that jealousy would have hurt Zeke the most. Turns out, jealousy barely registers on his radar.

But seeing me in pain, that hurts him.

Huh.

Is that why he hasn't raped me despite wanting to? He's torn between what he wants and not being able to handle seeing me in pain?

I keep crying, and the pain deepens on his face—so I cry harder, seeing how far I can take it before he completely shatters. I need to know his limits. It's the only way to destroy him.

My sobbing turns to heartbreaking wails, the kind women use only after the worst happens to them—the loss of a spouse or child. But my cries aren't acting. I'm not lying with my howls. Everything I'm letting out is exactly how I feel.

I'm trapped, and I've lost everything and everyone important to me. Even if Zeke lets me go, I still won't get back what I lost. I'll never be whole again.

Suddenly, the truck stops. My eyes are red with tears blanketing my vision, so I can't tell if we are back at Zeke's house or if he stopped somewhere else.

He unbuckles and climbs out. I reach over for my seatbelt and fidget with it until I finally get it to unlatch.

Zeke opens the door before I'm finished. He doesn't say a word. He doesn't tell me to stop. He doesn't comfort me with his body, even though his presence does strange things to mine—excites and soothes.

I move to climb out, but his body blocks me.

"What?" I ask, as the tears continue to fall.

He doesn't answer with words. Instead, I'm lifted up in the air and flipped over his shoulder until my face is staring right at his glorious ass.

My sobs are stifled as it's hard enough to breathe flipped over like this, let alone cry.

Zeke carries me like a caveman away from the truck. I try to lift my head up to see where we are, but all I can see is his ass and then eventually the sand below his feet. Then I hear the crashing of waves.

Why are we on the beach?

The waves get closer, and I realize what Zeke is planning on doing.

I fist my hands and start pummeling his back with my fists.

"Don't. You. Dare," I say firmly between hiccuping sobs.

He doesn't speak or stop walking.

I watch the bottom half of his jeans get swallowed up by the waves. And then I'm being flung onto my back into the cool water.

I stay under the water longer than I need to. I love the water. I used to want to be a mermaid when I grew up. It took until I was a teenager to realize mermaids weren't real. I couldn't spend my life swimming in the water, rescuing dolphins, and saving sea creatures. I had to grow up and get a real job.

But sometimes, when I'm all alone in the water, I pretend my life is different. I pretend I'm just a mermaid, living her best life as a magical creature that won't let anyone hurt her.

I close my eyes as I come up out of the water. My heels somehow get washed from my feet, so my bare toes touch the smooth sand that feels like home. My hair covers my face, so I flip it back as I gasp in a deep breath, and the tears stop.

Despite hating that Zeke just threw me in the water, it did the trick. The water is where I feel alive and safe. There is no way I could cry right now, even if I wanted to.

I find Zeke's gaze on me.

"Enough," he says.

That one word vibrates through my body. And I feel it in all the ways he meant it—as a command and a question. He wants me to stop hurting, yet he's also asking if I've had enough. If I'm over whatever was hurting me because he can't handle my pain anymore.

And he can't be gentle with how he helps me get over my pain. Surprisingly, I don't want him to be. I want someone who knows when I'm hurting and puts an end to it abruptly.

I've never had a man care enough about me to do something about my pain, even in this unconventional way.

Zeke is now standing waist-deep in the water a foot from me. The waves wash up again, striking me in the back and Zeke in the chest, but it doesn't stop the intense connection we share. We aren't touching, yet in the water, I feel him. *All of him.* I feel his pain. It's a pain I don't understand. He's a powerful man with more money than sense. *What could he be possibly be hurting about?*

But it's there—his heart is bleeding as badly as mine is.

We stand there for another minute. Both giving the ocean everything we can never give to each other. Our pain. Our secrets. Our *truths.*

And when everything has been spilled, I nod.

Zeke turns with the nod and starts walking to the truck. He doesn't wait for me to follow. I could run. I could swim into the ocean, and he would never catch me. But I don't because now I'm curious about the man. The only man who has ever shown that he cares about my pain.

That man also happens to be my current owner, who might sell me on Friday. And I'm more confused than ever about who he is. *What kind of man is Zeke?*

We both climb into the truck soaking wet. I've lost both shoes and sand clings to my brand new jeans.

Zeke again doesn't look or speak to me as we drive. But I squirm a little, hating that I'm getting saltwater and sand all over his car.

"Don't worry about it. I'll have you clean it out tomorrow," Zeke says, with—*wait, is that a grin?*

I try to hide back my own smile, but I can't. I don't know how I went from pissed, to crying, to smiling in a matter of minutes, but I did. Zeke did that.

"I'm not your maid. I think you have enough money to hire someone to clean your car."

He raises an eyebrow. "But then I wouldn't get to see you in a slutty maid outfit."

I shake my head. "That is never happening."

"We'll see," he whispers.

Yes, we will see—and it's not happening.

As we drive past Julian's house, the joking moment we had before turns serious. My fear returns at just the sight of his property. Today is Wednesday. That means I only have one more day to convince Zeke not to bring me to that house. One more day to convince him not to sell me. One more day to put an end to all of this.

As I climb into Zeke's bed after showering, I know one day won't be enough.

CHAPTER 18
ZEKE

I still don't understand what happened yesterday. How did I go from being pissed and hurt, to wanting to take away all of her pain?

Siren is a strong woman, but she's still a woman—still human. I forgot that because she always acts like a superhero. She acts tough and resilient, like nothing could ever hurt her.

But last night, I learned she hurts just like all the rest of us; she just hides it better until the dam finally ruptures. And last night it burst.

How stupid was I to bring her to the water? I knew it would help her. I knew it would stop her tears. But it also sharpened our connection to each other. She learned things about me last night she shouldn't have. She learned I have a soft spot for her; I'm not as cruel as she thought. Which means I'm going to have an even harder time controlling her. An even a harder time keeping her safe.

I open my eyes, and instead of staring up at my white ceiling, I see Siren straddling my body—and what a sight she is. Even with her messy hair and sleepy eyes, I want her. I could get used to waking up this way every morning. Yet, I don't think she's straddling me because she wants a quickie before I go to work. She wants something.

I grumble and roll my eyes. "What do you want?"

"A rematch."

I sigh. "A rematch?"

"Yes, I want another game of truth or sin tonight."

"Fine," I rub my eyes and then stretch my arms up over my head. I expect her to jump off me now that she's gotten what she wants, but she doesn't. She continues to straddle my waist, and if she moves a few inches lower, she will be greeted by a particular part of my body that would be very happy to get better acquainted with her pussy. She's wearing a layer of shorts and panties, but that barely separates us.

"Anything else?" I ask, rubbing my head. *I think I'm getting a headache from her.*

She grins brightly. "You aren't a morning person, are you?"

I growl, and she finally jumps off me. "No, I'm not. So I suggest you remember that before you wake me up like that again."

I get out of bed and pull on my jeans. I showered last night, so I don't bother today before I head into work. I have to meet Oscar today.

"Going to work?" she asks, her voice hesitant.

I nod, as I pull on a white T-shirt run my hand through my long hair, before pulling it up into a man bun.

"Are you going to lock me in a room again?" she snickers.

"Nope, you already learned that trick."

"But you are going to leave me here, alone?"

I turn toward her, raising an eyebrow. "Why shouldn't I? You already destroyed everything in my house. There is nothing left for you to damage."

She frowns. "Aren't you worried I will run?"

"Are you going to run?"

She doesn't answer.

I sigh. "No, I'm not worried. For one, I live too close to Julian's property. He has cameras everywhere. He would see you run. He would chase after you and only return you to me after he's had his turn with you. You already seem to know that, though, so I know you won't run."

She pulls the covers up over her body, immediately changing her demeanor when I talk about Julian.

I finish gathering my wallet and keys—not worried at all that she will still be here when I return. But I pause at the door, because I don't want a repeat of yesterday.

"I'm renting this place from Julian. And he sees everything that goes on in his house," I say, eyeing the camera in the door.

Siren's eyes go wide. I hacked the camera last night when I couldn't sleep to see what she did yesterday when I was gone. The sight of her pleasuring herself drove me insane. I deleted the footage, hoping Julian or his guards hadn't seen it yet. It was a risky move; Julian could notice my hack and the deleted footage. But I couldn't stand for him to see Siren like that.

I don't tell her that, though. Maybe it will get her to behave today to know Julian is watching her, not just me.

"And if you get bored, you can always start cleaning up the mess you made yesterday."

She snaps back to life. "You aren't going to hire someone to clean up and get you new furniture?"

I shake my head. "I'm really not. Why would I when you would just destroy it again?"

She pauses. She doesn't have a smart retort for that.

"Have a good day, Siren." And then I'm gone to go meet Oscar and hope I can find a way out of the mess I've found myself in.

OSCAR SMILES AT ME AS I PULL UP AT THE WAREHOUSE WHERE HE holds the women. The same warehouse Siren was held in just a few days ago. It makes my stomach flip to think about it.

Siren deserves so much better. She deserves to live the life she wants. She deserves to be happy with a man who can give her everything. She deserves to have the big house and two-point-five kids with a dog, if that's what she desires. I don't even know her well enough to know what she wants.

Is she a dog or a cat person?
Does she want kids? How many?

What was her job before she was captured? Does she want to return to that career or start something new?

Where does she want to live?

Does she want to get married?

No, none of those questions matter. Because I will never be the man to give her any of those things. There are only a few questions that actually matter. *What is her relationship to Julian? And where does she want me to drop her off?*

"Zeke? Are you listening?" Oscar asks.

"Yes, sir." *Fuck, now I'm calling Oscar 'sir.'*

"Good. Follow me."

I follow Oscar back into the depths of hell. I have to force my legs to follow him instead of running back to my truck and getting the fuck out of here.

But once inside the warehouse, there is a new stillness in the air. I don't hear the heavy breaths of the women afraid to breathe, let alone move. I don't hear the hustle and bustle of his men moving supplies around. It's almost eerily quiet.

Oscar notices my change in expression. "Our other shipper picked up the women last night." He grins. "It's a great feeling to know all my hard work paid off, and the money has hit my bank account."

I squeeze my teeth down to keep from chewing him out before clobbering him into the ground with my fists. I'm grinding my molars so hard I'm sure I've rubbed off a layer of enamel, and Oscar can hear the sound of my teeth destroying each other. But if he notices, he doesn't react. He just continues to talk about the women he sold like they were cattle.

I need to get out of here. "When will you have a shipment for us?"

He smiles. "Two weeks."

Shit.

That's not enough time for me to form a plan on how to save them. That's barely enough time to make a real plan to try and sell them.

I'm screwed.

And so are the women he's about to take.

My soul will forever be tarnished. There is no forgiveness for men who sell people. I'll be banished to eternal damnation. I won't be able to look at myself in the mirror. And I sure as hell won't be worthy of a woman like Siren, even to kiss her. My lips alone would burn her like fire. She's pure; I'm evil.

"How many?" I ask, needing as much information as possible.

"We should be able to do two-hundred easily."

Fuck, it's worse than I thought. Two hundred women. I'm having a hard enough time saving one woman; there is no way I can save two hundred.

♡

I SLAM THE DOOR AS I RETURN TO THE HOUSE. I NEED A DRINK—NO, I need six. This is hopeless. There is nothing I can do. I don't have the money to buy two hundred women while secretly letting them all go free—no one does.

Fuck, I'm spineless. I should be going into Oscar's warehouse guns blazing, trying to kill every man who works for him. That's the only way to save the women.

I'd have to kill Julian too, but he's been very careful. He has more men working for him than he lets on. If I attack him, I need to know every single one of his men, or I'll spend my life running and looking over my shoulder.

It's too late, anyway. Most of Oscar's men are already out somewhere kidnapping women. I don't know who they are or how to stop them. In two weeks, the women will be mine. And I'm still clueless as to what I'm supposed to do.

"You're back," Siren says, leaning against the door of the kitchen as she holds a high-ball glass filled with amber liquid.

"Where did you get that?"

She grins. "I made sure not to break all of your glasses and liquor."

I walk to her.

She doesn't retreat. She stands her ground.

I stop inches from her. So close, yet so far. I take in a deep breath. I can't even smell the liquor. All I smell is her—a fresh, citrus, watery scent.

She wags her finger in front of me. "You aren't getting any of this. This has to last me the entire time I'm here, since you refuse to restock the liquor cabinet. I'm not sharing."

"You destroyed my liquor and glasses! And most of my fucking house! I shouldn't be the one to replace any of it, you should."

She bites her lip to hide her growing smile. She likes riling me up.

I hold out my hand. "Drink."

She scrunches her nose and makes an adorable purse of her lips like she's contemplating it. And then she goes to pour the contents into my hand.

I stop her before she tilts the liquid into my hand.

"Don't play with me—I'm not in the mood for games."

"That's too bad, because you already agreed to play our game tonight."

I huff as I pry the glass out of her fingers. "I need a dozen drinks first."

I down the liquid as I release her hand. When I glance back, she has two more full glasses in her hand. She quietly holds one out to me.

I set down my empty glass and take the new one, noticing the sparkle in her eyes. She likes playing games. And this time, she's out to win. She'll either learn more about me or get to commit another sin. And I have a feeling last night's sin was child's play compared to the plans in her head.

"I shouldn't have bought you."

"Oh? Why not?"

"Because you are going to be the death of me."

She smirks. "I'll drink to that."

We clink our glasses together. Our eyes never leave each other, even when we tilt our head back to drink the smooth whiskey.

The liquor isn't all I drink in—I greedily gobble up her body. She's wearing a pair of ripped jeans that hug her luscious hips. She found new heels, thank god. I almost regretted last night just because she lost her heels. A snug red top completes her look. She's let her hair down in long waves, but she's not wearing any makeup, not that she needs it. Her lashes are long, cheeks blush pink, and lips redder than any lipstick could match. She is beauty—makeup would only hide who she really is.

Her eyes take in my appearance as well. From my muddy boots to my overworked ripped jeans; my white T-shirt clinging to my body and covering enough of my tattoos that she can't tell what any of them are. She frowns when her eyes stop on top of my head.

I smirk—she doesn't like my man bun. I can see her imagination working, wishing my hair would fall down to my shoulders again. Most women hate my hair. They'd prefer me to chop it off. I don't know why I don't. Other than I've always worn my hair like this, and I'm too lazy to get a monthly haircut to keep up a shorter style.

She clears her throat as if to clear her mind. She's ridiculous for thinking about my body at all.

"Ready?" I ask.

She nods.

I follow her through the kitchen to the sitting room, the only room other than my bedroom she didn't completely destroy.

"What do I have to do to get you to spend some of your millions to hire someone to clean up this mess?" she asks before we reach the sitting room.

Her eyes meet mine again, and she blushes when she sees the heat in my eyes. She would have to willingly do some very dirty things for me to clean up her mess—things she will never voluntarily do.

Siren sits in the same armchair from last time we played this game. I notice the bottle of whiskey on the end-table and make a mental note to hide it after our game, if there is any left. I'm tired of her having the upper hand.

This time, instead of sitting on top of her or kneeling, I pull up one of the other chairs in the room and face it right across from her. This way, I won't miss a single expression she makes.

"Ladies first," I say.

She taps her fingers against her glass as she contemplates her single question. *Is she going to try to get answers from me, or is she going to try to get me to let her sin?*

She sighs, and I know I've already won before she even asks the question. Because tonight she is going to choose answers, even though she's burning to commit another sin. She thinks, in the long run, having more answers might mean losing this battle but eventually winning the war.

Unbeknownst to her, Siren has already won no matter what answers I give or sins she commits. She's already gotten me to silently vow to save her. In a few weeks, she will be free while my soul will belong to satan.

"Where are you from?"

I cock my head, trying to understand where she is going with this. *Why does it matter where I'm from?* It doesn't. *So what game is she playing? Does she think if she gets me to answer an easy question today that I'll answer a harder one tomorrow?*

"Are you sure that's the question you want to ask?" *More like a waste.*

She closes her eyes as if it pains her to ask. "Yes, my question is, where are you from?"

This is an easy question to dodge the truth on, while still giving her the truth. Before I came here, I lived in Miami. I spent most of my life there. At least I did when I wasn't out on one of Enzo's yachts.

But telling Siren I'm from Miami would be risking Enzo and my friend's lives. If Julian is listening, he would have probably heard of Enzo Black. He would know he's from Miami. He could piece together Enzo is my real boss. And I don't want Julian to know.

Siren doesn't realize the question she asked matters. She just wants to break through my walls and learn more about me. She wants to see if she can hitch a ride back to my home town. She can't—I would never take her to Miami.

I could tell her I'm from the ocean, but that would piss her off.

So I answer the only way I can. "New York." The place I was born. I lived there for less than nine months, but technically it answers her question. It's where I'm from.

Siren grins. "Zeke, from New York. I can work with that."

I frown, realizing now why she wanted to ask the question. All that is missing is my last name, and she would be able to search me in any database. She won't figure out my last name, but even if she did, New York knows nothing about who I really am.

She tucks her legs under her body, happy with her choice of question.

I shake my head. *How can she go from strong, gorgeous woman to sweet, innocent girl with one giddy smile and tuck of her legs?*

"Your turn," she says.

I could ask her the same question—use her strategy against her. I already know her first and last name. All I need is a location to find out everything. Although, if I wanted to research her right now, I could. I could find out everything with just her name.

But I'd rather find out everything from her. At least, until I'm forced to find out the truth. I'm nervous to face the truth, though, because honesty has a way of ruining everything. And I don't want whatever is flaring between us to disappear quite yet.

So I don't ask her where she is from. I consider my question for a moment, but I know the question I want answered.

"Who hurt you? Who made you hate men?"

Her eyes blink slowly, surprised by my question. She doesn't realize she wears her pain like a suit of armor. She oozes pride and defiance, a will to never let any man hurt her ever again. She is a woman who doesn't need a man.

Maybe it was getting kidnapped and then sold that made her hate men? Although, I think her hatred started long before Oscar found her. *Was Julian the one that hurt her? Or does her pain extend back a lifetime?*

Once she gets over her surprise at my question, her mind goes there—back to the day a man hurt her. Her body trembles slightly as she remembers. Her fear and pain ring through her body. Her eyes cloud over. She is no longer in this room—*she's there.* With *him*—I just don't know who *he* is.

I hate seeing her in pain and regret my decision immediately.

"Siren?"

Her head snaps to me, and her vision is gone.

"Who hurt you?" I ask again, with more caution in my voice. Now I must know. Because after I get Siren to safety, I'll hunt this predator down and kill him for ruining such a strong woman.

"Sin," she whispers. "I won't answer your question. I choose sin."

My shoulders fall; I won't be getting an answer out of her, at least not tonight.

I nod. "I reserve my sin until tomorrow." I stand to exit. With her memories of a vile man fresh in her mind, she isn't safe if I'm still here with her.

She hugs her knees to her chest. "Tomorrow is Friday."

"Yes, tomorrow is Friday."

"Julian?" she asks, her eyes pleading me to say I'm not bringing her, but I can't promise her that. I can't let Julian know I'm saving her until she's already safe.

"We are going. I'll decide tomorrow what my sin will be. Whether I sell you or claim you as my own. I expect you in bed within the hour, or you will have more than one punishment. Don't try to run; I won't be the only one who hunts you."

And then I leave, knowing within minutes, Siren will be in my bed next to me, hating me. Her hatred is for the best. Tomorrow I will commit a sin; it just isn't the sin Siren's expecting.

CHAPTER 19
SIREN

I didn't sleep—not for a single second. I don't think Zeke slept either, although he never opened his eyes. His body tossed and turned in the bed as much as mine did. There was no snoring, no slow steady-rhythm breathing, no lifeless slumber.

We didn't sleep.

But we didn't talk either.

We didn't share our racing thoughts.

But Zeke didn't have to ask to know what I was thinking. He knows I'm terrified of Julian; he just doesn't know why. And he's not going to know why. Even if I end up going to Julian's tonight, Zeke is still going to be clueless as to the truth. But tonight could change everything for me—and it terrifies me.

As soon as dawn starts shining in through the bare windows, Zeke jumps out of bed. The room may be beautiful, but there is no way to sleep in, not when there aren't any curtains to keep the light out.

He doesn't speak to me as he walks down the hallway to the bathroom. I hear the flick of the water on.

And I carefully climb out of bed. When I hear the shower door open, I know now is my chance.

I need to run.

It's the only way I can stay safe.

If I start running, I will always be running.

Julian and Zeke will always be chasing me.

But I'd rather run the rest of my life than be ruined forever.

I tiptoe quickly through the house until I get to the back door. I don't want to run out the front. The front door leads to Julian; the beach and the ocean are to the back.

My plan is to swim out into the ocean and let the current carry me toward the pier where I can steal a boat and get off this island forever.

I open the door carefully, yet it screeches a little. The sliding door is rusty and in need of some WD40. But I can still hear the faint sound of the shower in the distance.

I take a deep breath, and then I run. Stripping my clothes down to my bra and underwear as I go. Down the steps. Across the beach. And into the water.

My safety.

My peaceful place.

My sanctuary.

The waves splash against my face as I sprint further into the water, and the feelings of security consume me. *My plan will work. I'll be safe, at least for tonight.* Tomorrow, I'll deal with the consequences of my decision. I just can't go to Julian's. I'd rather die than go back there.

Finally, I'm far enough out into the ocean that I can barely keep my head above the water as I wade. I dive under, feeling the connection to the water. I kick hard...once, twice, three times before I surface again and start breast-stroking down the beach. Each time I take a breath, I feel more alive than the previous. This is where I belong, chasing waves, not running from monsters.

Why didn't I do this the first night Zeke bought me?

Because as freeing as this feels, I'm also sealing my fate—I'm not really free. This is temporary. I have a lot of work left to do to make this permanent.

I dip back under the water, but this time I don't move with the wave. I'm jerked back by my ankle.

When I surface, I find myself pulled tightly against Zeke's shirtless body. I pant heavily, but I don't know if it's from the physical exertion or being so close to Zeke's body.

When I realize I'm not fighting, I push hard against him. He can't take me back. *He can't take me to Julian.*

But as soon as I break free, he grabs my wrist again, pulling me to him harder than ever. His force and our tension bruise my wrist.

"You're mine, Siren. I get to decide your fate, your future, your present."

"No," I pull hard, but his grip doesn't change. He's stronger than I will ever be. It doesn't stop me from fighting with everything that I have. "Let me go."

"No," he growls, pulling me up out of the water by my wrist until we are eye to eye.

He's pissed. Scared. Angry. I've never seen him so emotional before.

I stop fighting at his expression.

I'm not even sure I can breathe anymore without his permission.

"You. Are. Mine. You will follow my orders."

I nod, silently surrendering to him. My plan failed. I give in. And if Zeke didn't already have my fate planned out, he knows now. He can read on my face what will happen if he sells me to Julian.

"It's for your own good," he says so quietly that I'm not sure I even heard him.

I shake my head. Zeke has no idea what he is sentencing me to. He drags me through the water back to the beach. He doesn't stop. He doesn't breathe hard. He walks like he's walking on a treadmill, not dragging my ass through waves and sand.

When we reach the shore, Zeke throws me down harshly onto the sand. I fall, twisting, landing on my back, and my impact covers me in coarse sand. I'm only wearing my bra and panties, and I don't care what parts of me Zeke can see. This moment is the furthest thing from sexual.

Zeke stands over me, like the god he thinks he is. He may not have physically hurt me yet, but one way or another, I will be injured by the end of the night. Either Zeke will decide he wants me, in which case he will finally use me, or he'll sell me to Julian. And I'll get wounded worse than anything Zeke could ever imagine doing to me.

I close my eyes to keep the tears at bay. Running was a mistake. There is no way I was getting off this island, not when Julian owns every boat here. My only chance is Zeke. Him keeping me. He may only have a sliver of a heart, but at least he still has a piece of one. He may try to rape me, abuse me, torture me. But Zeke doesn't have Julian's experience. With Zeke, I have a chance at escaping. With Julian, I'll be dead by the end of the week.

"Don't sell me," I whisper.

Zeke doesn't answer. He doesn't flinch. He's not moved by my sobs.

Come—he commands with his body as he walks off. He doesn't even bother to speak to me.

My head falls as I push myself up off the sand. Running right now would only exhaust me. Zeke would catch me again, and bruise my other wrist. If Zeke is going to sell me to Julian, then I need all of my strength to fight my new enemy.

So I follow Zeke's command and accept my fate.

The rest of the day sludges by. We don't talk to each other. We eat in silence. And I spend most of the day in the shower, getting all my tears out and letting warmth sear my body. Once I'm inside Julian's house again, I'll be flooded with freezing fear.

I wear the most conservative, unflattering clothes I can find when I do finally get dressed. My baggiest jeans, tennis shoes, and an over-sized sweatshirt. Even though it's warm outside, I need as many layers of protection as I can get. I wear my hair up in a high ponytail, using one of Zeke's scrunchies. At the last minute, I spot Zeke's razor next to the sink. I slip one of the blades out and into my back pocket. It's not much, but at least it's a weapon.

Strange how, in the last few days with Zeke, I haven't searched for a weapon. I haven't been afraid that Zeke was truly going to hurt me. This just proves how wrong I was. He may not be the one to lay a hand on me, but he's going to cause my suffering all the same.

Zeke's reflection pops into the mirror, just after I stash the razor. I stare at him blankly. If he realizes I have the blade in my pocket, he doesn't say anything.

We both stare, defying each other with our glances, but neither giving in. Any lust I felt for Zeke is long gone. I don't know why I was attracted to him for a single second. Physically he might be beautiful, but his heart is black. It doesn't matter how gorgeous he is on the outside, if he's a monster on the inside.

Zeke turns, and I follow automatically. We both walk slowly through the house. The sunset warms Zeke's appearance through the windows as we walk. He's wearing his usual jeans and a T-shirt, but this time he's added a leather jacket. I also see where he's carrying a gun in the back of his jeans.

He doesn't usually carry a gun; at least he doesn't around me. When I was going through his house, I didn't even find a gun locker or stash. Apparently, there are things in this house he's still hiding from me.

If Zeke's carrying a gun, it means he expects trouble tonight.

I'm not sure if that reassures me or terrifies me more. Julian is Zeke's business partner. He shouldn't expect any trouble going over for dinner to sell me to him. But he does. His steps aren't as purposeful as they usually are, almost like he might falter and change his mind.

We reach the front door.

Please, stay. We don't have to go. At least let me stay.

I feel his eyes cut back to me, but he doesn't turn his head full around to look at me. Maybe if he did, he'd choose differently. But he doesn't. He walks out to the truck, leaving me to follow.

Out of defiance, I leave the front door wide open as I exit. If Zeke notices, he doesn't care since he doesn't bother to go back and close it.

He just starts his truck and drives. Julian lives close enough that we could walk, but driving is probably better. I would purposefully walk at such a slow pace, it would take us all night to get there. Unfortunately, Zeke drives like he can't get to Julian's fast enough.

After parking the truck, Zeke gives me a look I can't read, and then we both step out. Now that I'm here, I won't show fear. I'll walk in on my own will. And I'll fight with everything I have.

Zeke knocks once. It's loud enough to vibrate through the entire house.

I stand next to him proudly. I won't cower behind him like I did last time I saw Julian.

Of course, Julian isn't the one to open the door. That would be beneath him, so one of his men does. He nods at Zeke and holds the door for us to enter.

My eyes dart all around. My heart thumps on high alert the second my foot crosses the threshold. I'm ready for whatever Julian is going to do to me.

But I never get to the second step. I feel hands go all over my body as multiple men grab me. My mouth is gagged. My arms are pulled apart in either direction, and my ankles are tied together roughly, reminding me the tiny bruise Zeke caused when he grabbed my wrist was nothing. This is what real pain feels like, what real fear is like. I'd been spoiled living with Zeke these last few days.

The men start dragging my body away. I didn't even get to fight. I didn't have time to grab my weapon before I was ambushed.

Zeke doesn't even realize what happened until the last second, as I'm being dragged away.

His eyes connect with mine to witness my terror. Instantly, I force my pupils to change. *You did this. This is your fault. You knew better than to bring me here. Any pain I experience is on you. I hope you can sleep tonight knowing my pain is your fault.*

And just before I'm yanked out of his view, his eyes change too. Maybe it's my own stupid hope imagining the split-second change in his expression. Or maybe it's real. But I swore he promised me he wouldn't let anyone hurt me.

When I'm pulled into a dark room with half a dozen men, I realize it doesn't matter if the look in his eyes was real or not. Zeke won't be able to keep that promise.

CHAPTER 20

ZEKE

"Where is he?" I say, as I tear through the house looking for Julian.

One of his servants runs next to me, terrified. He tried to lead me to a sitting room, where he said Mr. Reed would join me in a minute.

I don't think so. I want to see the man—now.

I march up the stairs and find a locked door at the end of a hallway. A door I'm sure leads to his bedroom.

He better not be naked or fucking a woman right now, or I'll kill him. Nothing would stop me.

I kick the door down in one swift kick. He's not naked on the bed, thank god. I march through the room to the bathroom and find Julian spraying some aftershave on his face like nothing is happening —*fucking moron.*

"What the hell do you think you are doing?" I'm fuming. I thought I could hold back some of my anger, but I can't. I never agreed to Julian tying up Siren and dragging her to god knows where as soon as I entered his house. I agreed to bring her. I agreed to show her off in front of potential clients—nothing more.

Apparently, my rage isn't afraid of ruining everything by throwing a punch at this man. I do it anyway.

The crack of his jaw is music to my ears.

But one punch isn't enough. I grab his shoulders and shove him into the closet door behind him. His head bounces off the door as his eyes see stars.

I snarl. The man may be the leader of a criminal organization, but he can't fight for shit. He hasn't defended himself. He hasn't tried to throw a punch. He hasn't even reached for a gun.

He starts sliding to the floor, but I grab his shirt collar and hold him eye to eye with me. His feet dangle on the floor.

"What. Did. You. Do?" I growl. I'm not letting him go until I get some answers. And depending on his answers, I still might not free him.

He spits blood out to the right as he cracks his neck and takes his time answering me. I'll give him credit—he's not cowering in front of me like I'd expect an inexperienced man to.

"Put me down, and I'll tell you," Julian says, adjusting his jaw side to side.

I place him on his feet, but don't let go of the collar of his pristine white shirt. Somehow I managed not to get a drop of blood on it. I'll change that quickly if he doesn't start talking.

"I needed to make sure your pet was secure while we had dinner," Julian says.

I shake my head. "She's obedient to me. You didn't need to tie her up in order for her to behave herself."

"But then you might be distracted, and I need you on your game in order to convince these men to place a big shipment. Getting the deal with Oscar means nothing if we can't sell the women for a high price."

"You had no right to touch her. She's mine. I'm the one who has been slowly breaking her in. I'm the one who paid millions of dollars to enjoy her, not you."

"And I'm the one who cuts your paychecks so you could afford to buy her in the first place."

I raise my eyebrows. "You paid me thirty million dollars? Hmm...

because my bank account says you've paid me far less. I guess I earned that money long before I ran into you."

"You wouldn't be alive without me. You owe me."

I don't argue. "Where is she?"

"She's safe—locked up in a room in the basement with a dozen guards watching over her. They are under strict instructions to only tie her up and protect her with their lives. I know how much she's worth to you. I won't let any harm come to her. But my offer still stands, I'll buy her from you. Name your price. From your reaction, I can tell the sex alone must be worth every penny."

I growl again.

He smirks.

I'm still gripping his shirt.

But his eyes hold no fear. He's in control. He's the boss, not me. I've never been the boss, even when I worked for a good man, my life still wasn't my own.

I could probably ask for sixty million, and Julian would pay it. He has the money. And he wants to take something from me, even if he pays for it.

But I'd never sell Siren. Even though she thinks differently—Julian will never touch her.

"Siren isn't for sale. She's mine," my voice is throaty and low, deeper than a crack of thunder.

"We'll see. I'm guessing you'll be begging me to buy her soon."

Julian's eyes glance down at where I'm still gripping him. "Now our guests will be arriving shortly. It's time to go make some money."

I release him, hating this. I want Siren with me, not locked up somewhere. When I get her home, I'm going to pay for her being locked up. I'll have to sleep with one eye open because Siren will certainly try something. This is definitely worthy of her cutting off my dick.

Julian wipes the blood from his mouth. The bruising won't set in until tomorrow, so his guests will never know I hit him. Then he grabs his suit jacket and puts it on before I follow him downstairs to the dining room. His other guests have already arrived.

"Welcome, everyone. Sorry for the delay," Julian says, walking up to the first man.

"So glad you could make it, Mr. Palmer," Julian says.

"I would never miss a dinner of yours, Mr. Reed," he answers.

"This is my right-hand man, Zeke," Julian says.

I shake the man's hand sternly, even though I'd rather rip it off. I can see his dark heart without knowing anything about him.

Julian introduces me to a short, balding man and his wife next—a Mr. and Mrs. Gibson. Bile rises in my throat, realizing a woman is involved in buying other women. Somehow it seems worse that she would betray her own sex.

The last man I'm introduced to is younger, closer to my age. He, like me, doesn't like to be called by his last name. Instead, he goes by Rafael.

Julian motions for us all to take a seat. Julian sits on the end of the table, and I'm seated on his right with everyone else filed around.

Servants stream in, pouring everyone a drink, and bringing out appetizers. I force myself to eat calamari even though I'm not the least bit hungry.

"So tell us, when will the next shipment be in?" Mr. Palmer asks.

Julian shovels food into his mouth. Apparently, he wants me to answer the mundane questions.

"Two weeks," I say.

Mr. Palmer sounds surprised, "So long?"

"Yes, we want to ensure we get the highest quality for you to choose from."

"Hmm," his wife, Mrs. Gibson, murmurs, not believing me.

"We also hand-deliver your selection to ensure your order gets there swiftly and without any complications," I say, like I'm talking about a shipment of drugs instead of women.

Everyone nods.

"Tell me, what type of women and how many each of you might be interested in? We'd like to make the best selections for you," Julian says.

We go around the room listening to each of Julian's guests describe in vivid detail the kind and quantity of women they want to buy. It's clear we won't be able to get rid of any more than twenty to this group of buyers, but they have connections who would be happy to take more if the quality is high, according to Mr. Gibson. And these four would pay fifty million dollars a piece for a high-quality woman.

"Again, you still haven't convinced us of the quality of your women." Mr. Palmer says, shoving half a lobster into his mouth after drowning it in butter.

Julian smiles. He snaps his fingers.

My next sight hits me down to my bones.

Siren is dragged into the room, tied up with ropes and three men guarding her. Her mouth is gagged, and she fights hard against the ropes.

Julian nods to one of the guards, and he rips the sweater from her body. The look in her eyes is one meant to kill.

She fights harder, and I have no doubt if she fought for long enough, she'd find a way to free herself. You can see it in all her body language. And everyone in the room witnesses it too. I quickly look around and see how much every person in the room wants her—*my woman*.

My blood boils red. I can't make a scene here. It would ruin everything. I need Julian to think I'm as bad as him, so when I leave this damn island, he will have no reason to follow. I'll have paid my debt.

But after this, after what he did to Siren, I can't just bounce. Julian will pay for this.

CHAPTER 21
SIREN

I'm not a woman who asks for help often. But today—I'm asking for help. Because I already know how this ends.

I have rope burn all over my body. My agitated skin will have marks and welts for at least a week where the rope digs into my skin. At least the physical marks won't be permanent. But the emotional scars, they will stay with me forever.

This isn't my first time in Julian's house. I know what he has planned next. And being tied up, dragged out in front of a group of people enjoying dinner, while embarrassing, is nothing compared to what comes next.

I try to get free, but I'm not strong enough to take on three grown men, much less the ropes binding my arms and legs. I shake my head, trying to get the gag to loosen from my mouth. I manage enough for my cries to start sounding less like moans and more like real words. But I can't get the gag off, and my cries for help sound like I'm enjoying myself, not afraid for my life. So eventually, I force myself to remain silent. These people don't deserve to hear me.

My eyes defy every person in the room. The single old man. The gross couple. The young man. Julian snickering at the head of the table. And finally—Zeke.

I shouldn't have looked at Zeke. I know it immediately when our eyes lock. He can't help me, and that devastates me. Because he's the only one who can...

Once I look at him, I can't look away. I plead for him to help with my eyes. And his eyes respond with *I can't.*

Everything else in his body screams a different promise. *I'll burn this fucking island down for you.*

His face is red, his nostrils flare like a bucking bull, and his jaw ticks with the full force of his anger. The veins in his neck bulge as blood circulates faster, flooded with adrenaline. He's suffering under the stress of a decision—saving me and ruining his relationship with Julian, or doing nothing to save face.

I don't know which he's going to choose. If logic wins out, I'm toast. But I can tell his heart thinks differently. His heart wants to save me.

I almost wish he wouldn't save me. I'll ruin his soul, and he won't deserve the pain.

Zeke's body has hardened, and I can't tell if his muscles are pumping up ready for a fight, or his brain won and his body is just tense as he forces it to stay in his chair.

Unfortunately, Julian decides not to stay in his chair. He stands and takes his time walking over to me.

"All the women we bring you will be of similar quality as this one. Expensive breeding, exquisite body, and a fight you will enjoy taming."

I scream as I pull against the ropes as Julian approaches.

The woman laughs. "She's wonderful. Is she for sale?"

Julian looks at Zeke, who looks like he's going to murder everyone in the room.

"Sorry, I don't believe she's for sale," Julian finally answers. "But worry not, we will only bring you women of the same caliber."

There are murmurs throughout the room.

"Come, see for yourself what a treat she is," Julian says, waving the group over.

No.

I won't let them touch me.

I have too much self-respect.

I have control over who touches me and who doesn't.

Zeke sits up straighter, seconds away from launching himself across the table. I want him to save me, but not from this. *This, I got.*

So I give Zeke a wink. He blinks rapidly, not sure he saw me do it. It makes me smile slightly. He cocks his head, confusion on his face.

This time, I save myself, but you owe me, Zeke. Soon, I won't be able to.

He nods at me, and then I focus on my target—the woman. She disgusts me more than anyone else here. And if I take her out, this charade will stop. They will focus on helping her, not on parading me around the room for their pleasure. They will hate me.

The old man approaches and grabs my chin—I let him. He inspects my face like a racehorse he's about to buy.

The next man grabs my waist, pulling me toward him until I smell his whiskey breath and plump belly against my stomach. At least his stomach protrudes enough to shield me from feeling any erection he might have under all that blubber.

The young man keeps his distance, observing from afar. He pretends to be uninterested, although I know differently. It doesn't make him any more moral than anyone else here.

Finally, the woman approaches. She takes her time looking me over with a bright smile, and then, she goes for my breast. *Not today, lady.*

The guards are holding my arms tightly out on either of my sides, with the third guard standing behind me. My feet are tied together at my ankles. I can't break free of the ropes, so I use them.

As the men hold me up, I throw my weight back onto my arms, lift my legs, and kick her hard in the chest with both my feet.

The woman falls back, like she's just been shot.

I laugh beneath my gag as the guards stand in shock, not sure what to do. The potential buyers bend down to help the woman. She struggles to breathe, and she'll have a nasty bruise over her heart for a few days. I'm sure I'll get punished for the move by the guards or Julian, but it will be worth it.

Julian walks over, observing my victim calmly, and without any intention of helping. Instead, he turns and looks at me with fury in his eyes.

Serves you right for treating me worse than an animal.

"Get her out of here," Julian says to the guards.

I'm starting to get dragged out, when Zeke stands up.

Yes! Now is the time to save me. Because if I leave this room without you, the scars they'll inflict will never leave me.

Julian steps in front of me, facing Zeke. I can see the side of Julian's expression. He's telling Zeke to fix this. Close the deal, or else.

Or else what? What does Julian have over Zeke?

When my view of Zeke is unblocked, I look at him, but he's no longer looking at me, he's looking at the mess on the floor and how he's going to salvage it.

No...

Zeke...

Julian returns his gaze to me, and I see the devil in his eyes. I know what comes next.

The guards pull me out of the room, away from Zeke.

Zeke doesn't follow.

He stays. He sentences me to my fate.

If he lets me leave with Julian, he won't be able to save me.

The guards drag me up the stairs and into Julian's bedroom. I'm tossed to the floor. My body slams against the wood floor. The guards leave as Julian enters the room.

The familiar sound of the lock on the door closing behind him skyrockets my anxiety.

Julian takes his time walking over; he's like Zeke in that way. *How could two men be so similar and yet treat me so differently?*

Julian yanks me to my feet, and I'm left standing in the middle of the room, still tied around my arms and legs. My mouth is still gagged. I have the ability to fight—to at least delay Julian's fury and give Zeke more time to rescue me.

But I'm frozen. I can't move. I can't react. Julian is the only man in the world I can't fight back against.

It wouldn't make sense to most people. But it's my reality. That's why Julian scares me more than most men. Every other man I can fight against. He may still win, but at least I have a chance. With Julian, I'm helpless.

Julian undoes the button holding his jacket together. He slips it off carefully and hangs it over the back of a chair in the corner. Then he slowly rolls up his sleeves. Each of his movements taunt me. My imagination is worse than what will really happen—or at least that's what I keep telling myself.

Julian grins at me as he takes a step closer, and I don't back up. He's won already. He controls me.

"Such a pretty girl, but you didn't dress very pretty for me tonight, pet."

I close my eyes. I need to disappear, at least in my head. It's the only way to survive.

But Julian won't allow that. *What fun would he have in hurting me if he couldn't see the pain all over my face?*

He grabs my chin and uses his other hand to pry my left eye open. It burns being forced open.

And then he spits.

I close my eye quickly, but some of his saliva still enters my eye —*disgusting.* I try opening, but it stings. I blink, trying to see again, but I can't. *What was in his saliva? Pepper? Alcohol? It's fucking alcohol.* I smell the whiskey.

"Look at me, pet."

I can't, I try to say, but it comes out as a moan.

I look at him with my good eye, and his lips curl up higher, loving my sounds.

I won't make any more. That was the last you will get from me, you bastard.

I swallow down the pain. It's just my eye. I'm sure with some water, it will be better. My eye is the least of my worries.

I have to frequently close and re-open my eyes so I don't seem like I'm crying. It's when I have my eyes closed that he chooses to attack.

His hit is a semi-truck right to my jaw. It takes my breath away and gives me a splitting headache. I'm sure I heard bones break. It will take me weeks to be able to eat properly.

I fall to my knees from the explosion of pain in my head. I try to open my eyes, to prepare for the next attack.

"You can thank your boyfriend for that. He punched me in the jaw; it's only polite to return the favor."

Zeke punched Julian? Somehow that makes me feel a little better. I'm not sure what Zeke and Julian's relationship is exactly. Zeke doesn't call him Mr. Reed like everyone else, and Julian doesn't seem to care. Yet, Zeke still works for him, makes money for him. I don't understand.

"And this, this is because I like breaking pretty things."

No!

It's too late. My breath is gone as he kicks me in the chest. My ribs crack, and I'm afraid my heart stopped at the jolt.

I fall over to my side. *I'm helpless. Powerless. I can't win.* And Zeke will be too late. I already know.

I look to the door through my burning tears. The tears from my left eye spill to the right. I close my eye tightly, but some of the drops get in, burning my right eye as well.

I close them both tightly, refusing to open again. I have no hope that Zeke will come, at least not until it's all over. For all I know, he's already sold me to Julian. That's why he let him take me. And he's downstairs getting the other men to agree to a payment of their own.

Zeke will leave here rich, while I'll leave here broken and in someone else's charge.

I feel more hits, but they barely register. He's already broken me; everything else is just scattering the pieces. The first hit is always the worst; this is nothing.

Until everything changes. Getting hit is one thing, but getting raped...

I feel him rip my clothes with a blade pushed against my skin, leaving my bindings intact, until I'm wearing only my underwear.

I beg through my eyes, giving him one final plea, hoping he has some level of consciousness beneath his rough exterior.

Please.

I hold my gaze on his as a single tear falls down my face. Then another, and another.

"God, I love it when you beg."

With one final rip, I'm naked except for the ropes. I have no clothes left to protect me. Julian is done beating me.

I was wrong when I said the first blow is the worst. If I was only getting beaten, that statement would be true. But what comes next will obliterate me. There will be nothing left of me to put back together.

Siren will be gone. And I don't know who will replace me.

CHAPTER 22
ZEKE

I don't like that I can no longer see Siren. But being locked away somewhere is safer than being in this room, with these horrible people. As soon as I finish closing this deal, I'll get her and leave.

I still have a sin to use against her from our game yesterday, but I've already sinned enough. I'll answer any question she has and let her commit any sin against me.

Because I failed her.

I didn't protect her.

She's spent her night tied up in ropes because of me.

I walk over to the huddle of men and the injured woman Siren kicked in the chest. *Serves her right.* I wish I could do the same to all of them without pissing off Julian.

"Need any help? Should I call for the doctor?" I ask.

"No, no, that won't be necessary," the woman's husband says. He strokes her face. "Feeling better, dear?"

Dear? God, they disgust me. He's calling his wife by an endearment when they came here to buy another woman for him to stick his nasty dick into.

She nods, and the men help her sit up. She grasps her chest, her breathing hard and painful.

Good.

"She just knocked the wind out of me. That was some woman," she says.

At least she got something right; Siren is definitely some woman—she's my woman.

"Maybe we should continue these discussions next week? You should probably get some rest; you took quite a hit," I say, just wanting this night over. I'll wine and dine them again; I just want to get Siren out of here as fast as possible.

"No, no. That won't do. We have a flight scheduled for tomorrow afternoon," the husband says.

"Well, would you like to discuss some numbers then?" I ask. *Please say no. Say you don't want to do business with us after Siren hurt your wife.*

"Yes, let's do."

Ugh.

I spot a stack of documents in the corner of the dining room Julian seems to have had drawn up for this meeting. *Where is Julian anyway?*

I spot one of the servants. "Do you know where Jul—I mean, Mr. Reed disappeared to?"

He nods and whispers. "He had some blood on his shirt. He's just changing but said to have you finish up here."

I sigh.

I pick up the documents and look them over quickly, knowing the faster I get this finished, the faster I get to see Siren. I'm not waiting on Julian to get back.

The contracts discuss the payment and delivery timeline the client would like for "goods." No mention of selling women. Smart not to put something so incriminating down on paper.

I sit down in Julian's seat, not because I want to sit there, but because it gives me the best view of everyone.

"So how many would you like delivered to you? We can offer a slight deal on larger orders. But if you want the absolute best we find, those come at a premium price." *Fuck me.* I deserve everything coming my way for this meeting alone.

The wife and husband exchange glances, and then she looks at me giddily. "We want the woman who was here before."

I cock an eyebrow. "The woman who kicked you?"

I don't understand why they would want Siren when she nearly killed this woman. If she wasn't tied up, I have no doubt she would have succeeded.

"Yes, we want her. I love a woman with that much spirit. A woman like her takes so much longer to break. We will pay a premium price for her," the wife says.

"She isn't for sale," I answer.

The wife looks to her husband, who takes over. "I'm sure we can come to a financial agreement."

"She's not for sale." *No woman should be.*

"Twenty million."

"She's not for sale," my voice is annoyed and deep. *He's pushing me too far.*

"Thirty million."

"She's not for sale."

"Fifty million."

"She's not for sale."

"One hundred million."

The room falls silent—all eyes go to me. Julian would kill me for not taking the deal. He just offered a hundred million for Siren, more than triple what I paid for her.

It's an insane amount of money.

But once again, I have to state the obvious.

I stand, putting my fists down on the table, rattling the tableware. "She. Is. Not. For. Sale. She's mine." My voice shakes the entire room, like an earthquake just hit the house.

Everyone is silent. No one says anything while I stare them down.

This is not a negotiation.

This is not something I will back down on.

If it's the last thing I do, I'll make sure Siren gets off this island and safely away from these people.

Rafael breaks the silence. "I'll take five at ten million a piece. Plus, I have some close friends who will each want at least five as well."

I write down the deal. I don't care about negotiating for more money at this point. I just want this over.

I slide the contract and pen over to him.

He reads it over carefully and signs it before sliding it back to me.

I nod at him.

"It was pleasure doing business with you, Zeke. Tell Mr. Reed I retired to my room for the night and look forward to doing more business with you in the future."

I nod again but don't shake his hand. I can't stand to touch any one of them right now.

He picks up his drink and then whistles casually as he walks out.

"I want three," the older man says.

Again, I fill out the paperwork, then he signs and leaves.

I turn to the remaining couple. "And what can I do for you?"

"We want your best ten. If they are as good of quality as you claim, we will pay up to fifty million a piece."

I nod, agreeing.

I fill in the blanks on the contract and then slide it over to the couple to read.

The couple takes fucking forever to read every word of the contract. It's probably a smart move considering who Julian is, but my anxiety is rising with every passing minute.

I expected Julian to have returned by now, but he hasn't. *Maybe he's letting me finish the contracts by myself? He thinks we will get a better deal if I do the negotiations? Or he wants me to show how skilled I am?*

But it makes me feel uneasy. I don't know where Siren is. Julian knows he can't touch her. I would kill him for a look in her direction, let alone a touch. He promised he would unleash her as soon as the meeting was over. So hopefully she's just locked up in a room somewhere.

But if I know my girl, she's pissed. She should be making a lot of racket, slamming on doors and stomping her feet to show me how disappointed she is in me. But I hear nothing.

Either Julian's house is more soundproof than most, or Siren is still tied up.

I glance over at the couple, imploring them to fucking sign the papers already.

Finally, they sign.

I stand and rip the papers from them, preparing to exit the room. "Excuse me," I say. It's the last words I ever want to say to any of them. Because if I meet them again, I'll kill them all for thinking women are items for sale.

When I exit the dining room, I crane my neck, trying to listen to any sign of Siren. But I hear nothing.

Where are you, baby? I know you hate me right now, but you need to tell me where you are.

There is a door that leads down to the basement, and a grand staircase that leads upstairs. *Which should I choose?*

I see a servant standing, watching me from the hallway.

He doesn't speak, but his eyes tilt up.

She's upstairs.

I run up the stairs, three at a time.

My breathing picks up as I look left then right. There is a long hallway to each side. With closed door after door.

I hear a noise from my right. The tiniest of cries—Siren's.

No.

No. No. No.

Please no.

I can't have failed her this badly. *Please, don't let her be hurt. I won't survive seeing her in pain. That's my greatest weakness. Fuck, no.*

I run down the hallway and twist the door handle. It's locked.

I step back and kick with everything I have. The door splits, but it's thicker than most. A door built to keep sound and people in.

Fuck. Why did I bring Siren tonight? I could have closed that deal without her. I should have stood up to Julian.

I kick again, and the door splits enough for me to push through the splintered wood.

The sight I see destroys me.

Siren is naked on the floor. Ropes still bind her arms and legs. Her mouth is still gagged. But otherwise, everything that made Siren herself has been beaten out. So much blood covers her skin. Bruises are already coloring her broken layers. Her legs are spread, and Julian is settled between them.

I don't know if he's entered her yet.

But I already know I failed. No apology will ever be enough to make this up to her. She will never forgive me for letting this happen—*never*.

And I'll never be able to forgive myself.

But what guts me the most is her tears. *Her beautiful, fucking tears.* She's been completely ruined. She doesn't cry unless she's really hurting. I could snap her arm, break every bone, and she wouldn't cry. She's too proud. She wouldn't want to give Julian the pleasure of seeing her in pain.

Yet, here she is showing him every drop of pain—showing me. And it's all my fault.

I explode—headfirst at Julian.

I pound him into the floor with all my might, getting him as far away from Siren as I can.

And then I start punching, over and over and over. "I'm going to kill you! You hear that? You're a dead man!"

More punches. More kicks.

I forget about everything except killing this man. I'm a trained killer. One snap of his neck. One jab to the throat. One shot of my gun. One slice to the heart. There are so many different ways I could kill him—so many choices.

But I don't want to kill him quickly; I want him to die slowly and tortuously for what he did. For the mess he caused. And how much I'm going to have to clean up after he's dead. How many more men are going to have to die because of him.

I'm going to spend the rest of my life running and fighting, away from my family of friends, until I've killed every man loyal to this bastard. Instead of being free of him in a matter of weeks.

It will be worth it though to avenge Siren.

Moans...*Siren! I completely forgot about her.*

I punch Julian hard one more time in the face, knocking him completely out. I need to tend to Siren; then I can decide his fate.

I run over to Siren and find her stirring, groaning in pain. She shivers from the cold, and if I'm not careful, she'll lose too much blood to recover.

Siren has to be my focus right now as much as I want to kill Julian.

I consider pulling my gun out and shooting him dead. But that wouldn't be enough to satisfy me or Siren. She's going to want him tortured. I'll come back for him later.

Right now, I need to protect Siren.

I pull my shirt off and wrap it around her body as best I can. I loosen the gag, and it falls around her neck.

"You're going to be okay; I've got you," I whisper into her hair, not caring if Julian hears me or not. She's mine, not his. If I choose to be kind to her, that's my prerogative.

"This is going to hurt, just for a minute. But I'm going to make you feel better soon. I promise."

She sighs, her eyes still shut with tears falling quickly. I lean down to kiss her cheek but stop short. I don't get to kiss her when I'm the reason she's in pain.

The stench of alcohol hits my nose—her tears. The bastard poured alcohol into her eyes; no wonder she's crying.

Carefully, I place my arms under her neck and legs. I force my eyes to avoid looking between her legs. I don't want to know if he raped her or not. Because if he did, I wouldn't be able to leave without killing him first.

Once Siren is settled in my arms, I stand and face Julian, who is starting to stir.

"This isn't over," I say.

He coughs up blood. "You're right; it's not."

I kick him one more time for good measure, and then I leave. I race down the stairs, trying my best not to jostle Siren too much, but I know she needs out of this house as fast as possible.

My truck is parked out front, and I'm grateful I drove the truck instead of walking. But I don't want her out of my arms, even for the two-minute drive to my house.

So I push the driver's chair all the way back and hold her in my lap as I drive home.

"Please, be okay. Please, forgive me. Please..."

I can't open my eyes, but I'm still aware of everything happening.

I hear Zeke kick Julian's ass.

I feel him carry me in his arms. I should hate him. He's the reason I'm hurting. But in his strong arms, I feel safe, protected.

Stupid mind thinking I could ever be secure with a man.

I feel him holding me tighter to his chest on his lap, like a wounded bird. *That's what I am? Wounded? Broken? A goddamn disaster.*

I feel every bump in the truck as he drives us back, but I try my best not to whimper. I want to be back at Zeke's house as soon as possible, even if I have to deal with a little extra pain.

And then I feel Zeke carry me into the house. He flicks lights on as he goes. I moan as the brightness stings my eyes even though they are still closed.

"I'm sorry, but I need to be able to see your wounds to help you," Zeke whispers, like each word pains him.

Even though the gag is gone, I still don't speak in anything but moans and groans. Julian took my voice, along with everything else.

I hear Zeke sweep something onto the floor, and then he lays me down on the dining room table.

I shiver as the cool hits my back.

"Hold on," Zeke says.

I chuckle on the inside. *There is nothing for me to hold onto, you idiot.*

Time does weird things when you are in pain. A second later, or maybe an hour, Zeke returns. He places a thick blanket over me.

"I'm going to check over your wounds, okay? I need to stop any bleeding and make sure nothing needs stitches."

He waits. He's asking me for fucking permission to heal me. *It's too fucking late to ask for permission now, you prick!* You should have asked me before you bought me. Before you tried to sell me.

He waits a second longer, then curses under his breath. He must have decided he's out of time to get permission.

He checks over my head first, placing a bandage on my forehead. I hear him hiss when he gets to my jaw. But he doesn't say anything.

He examines my neck next. He must decide it's okay, because he quickly moves to my chest and stomach.

He gasps—*it must be bad.*

I feel something stick into my arm. He's giving me drugs. The warmth spreads quickly, and I instantly feel light as a feather. I'm floating above all the pain. It's still there, the pain, but it doesn't control me anymore.

I try to see what he's doing, but it's still too painful to open my eyes.

I feel his hands work on my stomach. He's probably stitching me up, but he must be very skilled at it because I don't feel the stick of a needle or the pull of thread.

I feel him cut the rope from my arms, remove the gag dangling from my neck, and re-wrap the blanket around my torso. Then he frees my legs as well.

The blanket is covering most of my body, but I feel him hesitate before lifting it up to see between my legs.

Almost instantly, he lowers the blanket again. Either I look normal, or there is too much damage for him to fix.

And then I feel his hand against my face, stroking me gently.

"I need to wash out your eyes," he says.

He's right, but I don't want to open my eyes. I'm not sure how he knows my eyes need washing out.

"I'm going to get some water, and then I'm going to stop the burning."

He doesn't ask me for permission this time, knowing I won't answer him right now. I hear the faucet run, and then he's by my side again.

He takes my hand and places it on his forearm.

"Squeeze hard," he commands. I do as he says. Gently opening my left eye, he begins flushing out the alcohol.

I squeeze his forearm as he pushes more water through my eye. Eventually, I feel the sting soften. He lets go of my eye, and I close it gently to prepare for him to flush the other one.

He doesn't give me time to think about the pending pain. He just moves to the next eye and does what needs to be done. I squeeze hard as pain stings my eye, but it too dissipates.

Zeke stops.

And I keep my eyes closed.

My breathing steadies.

The discomfort eases.

And Zeke—he's still here.

Time passes as my exhausted body falls into a restless sleep from the drugs Zeke pushed through me. At first, I fight it. I don't trust Zeke, or any man, when I'm under the pull of drugs. But I need rest to heal.

"You're safe," he whispers. "I won't let anyone hurt you. Ever again. Including me."

And with those unreal promises ringing in my ears, I drift to sleep.

I WAKE IN A SOFT BED. I'M LYING IN THE MIDDLE WITH PILLOWS ALL around me. I'm in Zeke's bed, so I expect to see him sleeping next to me.

But when I open my eyes, I find him kneeling next to the bed, his head bent, his hands clasped together and folded. I recognize the position—my father was a religious man. He'd pray every night before getting into bed.

Zeke can't be praying, though? Is he?

"Are you praying?" I ask, looking at him suspiciously.

His head pops up suddenly. All kinds of emotions cross his face—joy, fear, pain. His face finally settles on a reserved expression hiding his emotions.

"I'm not religious. And if God exists, I would be one of the last people he would listen to. But I had to try. Your heartbeat was so weak. I couldn't understand why. You didn't lose much blood, from what I could see. I assumed you were bleeding internally. And if you were, I wouldn't be able to get you to a decent hospital in time. All I could do was pray."

My mouth drops.

"What did you pray?"

"I begged for you to stay."

I gulp. He looks so sincere—in so much pain, watching me.

I don't know how long I've been out, but it doesn't look like he's slept. Julian's blood still speckles with mine all over Zeke's clothes. His hair is barely held up by his scrunchie. His eyes are bloodshot. And he looks to be in physical pain.

"Are you injured?" I ask.

"Not physically," he answers. *Just emotionally.*

I blink, not understanding how he's hurting emotionally.

"You didn't sell me?" I meant my words to be a statement, but they come out as a question. *Did he sell me? Was he just pissed at Julian for touching me before the money had been transferred?*

He's silent a moment, still as a statue. But his eyes pour into mine, giving me everything. Then he says, "I lied. I never planned on selling you and I never will."

What? My eyebrows reach epic levels on my forehead. *He lied?*

"I know it means you get to kill me now, but can you at least wait until I apologize first?" he smiles gently, testing the waters with me.

It's a damn gorgeous smile—complete with a shy dimple I didn't notice before, but all I can focus on is what he just said. *He wants to apologize?!* I don't think anyone, especially a man, has apologized to me before.

"Can you reserve your punishment until I finish speaking?" he asks.

"You didn't lie during our game."

He nods.

"Then I don't get to punish you. The rules only apply to the game."

He nods again, with a brighter smile, but then he exhales harshly. "I'm sorry."

Two words.

Words that change my life.

My heart starts hammering faster.

My breath is deeper.

Colors are more vivid in the room.

And Zeke's smell fills my nostrils fully for the first time.

I come alive with those words.

Zeke studies my expression as he speaks.

I close my eyes to keep new tears at bay. "Again," I whisper.

"I'm sorry," he says.

"Again."

"I'm sorry, Siren. I'm so sorry," his voice cracks in pain. It's the most beautiful sound. *So fucking beautiful.* I've never heard anything so beautiful.

He clears his throat and tries again. "I'm sorry I lied to you about selling you. I'm sorry I brought you to Julian's. I'm sorry I let the guards tie you up. I'm sorry I let them take you away. I'm sorry I let Julian hurt you. I'm sorry..." and then he's not speaking anymore.

I open my eyes and watch him break. Tears are falling.

Down.

Down.

Down.

Tiny droplets coat his cheeks and drop to his shoulders.

I've never seen a grown man cry. Up until this point, I didn't think men ever cried, at least not in front of other people.

But here he is crying for me. For my pain. For what he did to me.

I don't understand this man.

I don't understand why he bought me.

I don't understand why he didn't protect me.

But the most surprising thing...I don't know when I started falling for him.

It's the stupidest thing I could have done—*fall*.

Zeke may care for me, but he's also going to get me killed one day. I shouldn't want anything to do with him, yet I do. I want to experience everything with him.

He was the first man to save me.

The first man to say he's sorry.

The first man to promise to protect me.

And that means everything.

I might risk my heart again, even if I already know the outcome. Maybe for a little bit, I can live in this moment of pure happiness. It may not be love, but it could be fucking close.

"What happened?" I ask, needing to know everything.

"Julian played me. He wanted you, and I was stupid enough to think he was on my side. I'm sorry."

I nod. That's who Julian is. He has this ability to hide his monster until he's ready to show it to you, and by then it's too late.

"I'm going to kill him for touching you."

More tears spring to my eyes. I want that so badly, but it can't happen for so many reasons Zeke has yet to realize.

"No, I don't want you to."

He frowns.

"Just keep me safe from him. Promise?"

"I promise."

And I'll hold him to that vow.

"What happened?" Now it's Zeke's turn to ask.

"Julian...hurt me."

Zeke wants to know more. *Did he rape me? Did he push inside me?* That's what he's really asking.

"Was I too late?" Zeke asks.

I pause. That's such a complicated question to answer. I try to think, but most of what happened is a blur. My brain pushed it out. Whether Julian raped me or not doesn't matter. Because what he is really asking is—is it too late for us? Too late to change our future? Too late for us to choose love over hate?

And that answer is going to hurt.

Him.

Me.

"Yes, you were too late," I answer honestly with burning tears.

Zeke's eyes scorch too.

I wipe my eyes, needing to change the subject.

"How about that sin you still have to commit? What will it be?" I ask, needing him to do anything, make me feel anything but this heartache.

Zeke could have been the one. The one to be strong enough.

Man enough.

Loving enough.

But now it's too late—and I may have just missed my one chance at ever knowing love.

Zeke smiles sadly. "I've sinned enough for one night."

I sigh. I agree. But we need something to get rid of the tension—something to push our thoughts away from what happened.

"How about a new game of truth or sin?" I ask.

He nods—of course, he does. Right now, I don't think Zeke would deny me anything. And somehow that terrifies me.

CHAPTER 24
ZEKE

I was too late.

I was too fucking late.

Those two words, *too late*, will end me.

I thought we might be at a beginning after I saved her, not an end. I finally finished debugging the house. I can tell her the truth. I'm ready to face Julian Reed head-on. I could get her out of here.

But now, I don't know.

She hates me, with good reason. If I told her the truth right now, she wouldn't even believe me.

And now she wants to play a game of truth or sin.

Like I have the energy for that.

But I'll deny her nothing right now. I'd bring her Julian's head on a platter if she demanded it. I'd jump into a fire just so she could watch me burn. I'd do anything, fucking anything, for her.

And she knows it.

So if she wants me to play, I'll play. But I don't want to hurt her. I can't sin against her. That is the one request I can't fulfill.

"I'll play under one condition," I say.

She frowns. "What?"

"If you don't answer the question, you get to choose your sin against me, not me." My voice is vulnerable. I'm telling her exactly who I am in this moment—weak, weak for her.

She's wanted control this entire time. Well, now she has it, all of it. I'm giving it all to her—every single drop. I have nothing left. I won't order her with my voice or my unspoken commands. I'll ask nothing of her, ever again.

She nods and gathers herself.

I've long given up stopping the heavy flow of tears. I rarely cry. But I am a sensitive person, so it does happen, just usually not in front of someone else. I can normally wait until I'm by myself to let loose.

"You go first," I say.

Lines form around her eyes and mouth as she thinks. It's adorable as always and distracts me from the physical pain on her face.

"Why did you buy me?" she asks.

She chose her question well tonight. And I don't know whether to answer her with the truth or let her commit a sin. I'll give her whichever she needs.

So I take my time, reading her face. She wants the truth, but not all of the truth. She's not ready to face why I bought her. She's not ready to learn I bought her to save her.

She wants the other half of the truth.

She wants me to tell her I want her. I longed for her. I couldn't resist her.

So that's how I answer, "Because I wanted you. I've never wanted anything more. Not another woman. Not money. Not a fancy car. Not an expensive yacht. Not a luxury trip. I've never felt so much want, so much need in my entire life as I did watching you on that stage.

"Even if I didn't have the money to buy you, you were mine from that night. Nothing would have stopped me from claiming you. Not another rich asshole. Not Oscar. Not Julian. Not a calvary of a hundred men. You were mine. And I was yours from the moment I saw you."

It's the first time I've mentioned ever belonging to her as much as she belongs to me. It was a slip of the tongue, but completely true. I've been hers for a lot longer than she's been mine.

A tear drips, slowly at first, then speeds down her cheek as more moisture pushes it faster, and gravity pulls harder.

I reach out and wipe the tear from her eye. It's such a normal act—something any couple would do for the other. But we aren't a couple. She just admitted we will never be.

I was too late.

I don't know if she meant Julian succeeded in raping her before I got there, or if she just meant too much has happened for us to move forward. Maybe she meant she could never forgive me for letting Julian lay a single finger on her. For buying her in the first place. For letting her think I would sell her.

I've sinned too many times for any truth I speak to heal us. Our wounds are too deep. Permanent scars have already formed.

"Your turn," she says with a deep breath.

I pull my hand away from her cheek. And I feel loss. So much loss.

She grips the bedsheets, pulling them tightly to her chest as she waits for my question. I don't know if I want to pull a truth or a sin from her. I want answers, especially after what happened with Julian, but I don't know if I have the strength to hear her past with him. She also, more than anyone, deserves to commit a sin against me.

So I ask the question. The only question I need answered truthfully.

The question that holds my end.

I don't understand how I know, even now, but her truth will change everything.

"How did Julian hurt you before?"

Her eyes drift up to mine, and she bites her lip. I can tell more than ever that she wants to tell me the truth. She wants to pour her soul to me.

And yet there is something stopping her. Something preventing her from screaming the truth.

"Truth or sin?" I ask. *What's it going to be?*

"Sin," she answers.

I suck in a breath, preparing myself for her sin.

She's weak—she shouldn't get out of bed. She might choose to postpone her sin. Or she is going to have to choose something simple she can do from bed.

She pats the side of the bed next to her. Apparently, she's already decided on her sin. She knew before she answered what it was going to be.

I feel a lump in my throat. My heart is racing. My muscles are aching, trying to figure out what she is going to do.

I'm so close to her. I want to kiss her, taste her. I want to worship her body until she begins to forgive me. Until she no longer thinks it's too late to give us a chance.

"What do you want? What's your sin?" I ask, unable to wait, unable to contain myself any longer.

Siren moves hesitantly toward me. Her body inches closer and closer. I prepare myself for a coming slap, punch, or hit. I won't stop her. I deserve any pain she wants to inflict my way.

I try to keep my eyes open. But my reflexes will stop her if I see it coming, so I sit on my hands and close my eyes and wait.

I breathe slowly in and out, waiting for the pain to hit me. I'm begging it to. *Maybe I'll feel better if I'm hurting even a fraction of the amount she is?*

But what I feel is the opposite of pain.

Her lips brush over mine, ever so slowly, sparking something deep inside, bringing me back to life.

My eyes fly open at her touch. Our eyes lock as her lips hover over mine. I don't move. This is her sin, not mine. But it takes all of my self-control not to devour her.

And then, everything changes. She grabs my neck, pulling my head to her in a forceful kiss I've been dying for since the moment I saw her in the water swimming toward me.

My hands fly up, gripping her head and deepening the kiss. My hungry tongue pushes into her mouth, tasting every drop of her. So sweet, sassy, and delicious.

She moans against my lips, kissing me again and again. With promises of what could be.

These kisses are nothing like I've ever felt before. These kisses are life itself. I hold her firmer, and she tugs hard on my hair, letting it fall down the way she likes.

I could be the man for her. Her beast in the bedroom, her protector during the day. I could give up everything else for her—my job, my friends, my home. I feel it the second our lips touch.

She's everything I've ever wanted, and nothing I knew existed.

When she nibbles on my bottom lip, I'm done. *I'm hers.*

Completely.

Wholly.

Entirely.

Hers.

And she knows it. She smiles back against my lips.

But then she grips my hands, and gently pushes them away from her face, so she can pull back.

I feel empty without her touching me.

"It's too late," she says sharply.

It's then I realize her sin. Siren kissed me, showing me everything I could have. Everything missing from my life. Everything I could have had if I were a better man. Then she took it all away with three little words.

Fuck—this is my life now. I'll forever feel empty without her. There is no going back to a life without her.

I can't have her.

I was too late.

CHAPTER 25
SIREN

Why did I kiss him?

That kiss was painful.

Well, not the kiss part. The kiss part was great. It was magical, passionate, and everything I've been missing.

Cheesy, but it's true.

And now...now, I'm ruined. That kiss ruined me worse than anything Julian could ever do.

We don't speak after my sinful words. We both just collapse into the bed, so close but not touching, as is our life together. Close, but never together.

Not as friends.

Not as lovers.

And soon, not even as enemies.

I don't think I can sleep, but soon the darkness pulls at me. I'm still physically exhausted, so even though I'm anxious, sleep still wins.

I hear a vibrating sound on the dresser.

Zeke jumps out of bed and grabs his phone.

"Yes?" he answers grumpily.

He listens for a minute while looking at me to see if I'm awake. He

191

must spot the white of my eyes staring back at him because he doesn't stop looking at me.

"Tonight?" he asks.

Fuck, no. He can't go anywhere near Julian. It was just last night that he had to save me from him—that they fought.

But then I notice the rest of the room for the first time. The IV pole, the bags, the medications, the gauze. That's a lot of IV bags if I was just out of it for a day. I've been unconscious for days, possibly weeks.

Which means it's time for Zeke to transport the women. To sell them to the highest bidder. To confirm he is just as bad as Julian.

For a long time, I thought Zeke might be different. The way he treated me these last few days. Nursed me back to health. He's never laid a hand on me, and it makes me believe he is a good guy. Or at least not a bad guy.

But if he sells those women, he's just as evil as Julian. Just as wicked as every other man in my life.

Zeke hangs up the phone, and my attention goes back to him as he walks toward the bed, with indecision in his eyes.

"Don't," I say.

He pauses and looks at me with sadness.

"Don't go. Stay."

His eyes get big as he looks at me. He doesn't nod. He doesn't answer me with words.

And for a moment I think he is going to go—that he's going to leave me.

Instead, he pulls the sheets back and climbs into bed. And then he puts his arm over my body. It's not sexual; he doesn't even pull me to his chest. He just rests his arm over my body with a promise to protect me always.

I wait until he falls asleep for me to close my eyes. And I'm asleep within seconds of my eyelids falling.

But when I wake up, I already know the truth. Zeke is a bad guy. He's a monster. He's gone.

If it wasn't too late before, it is now. I will put up with a lot of things, but not this. *Never this.*

CHAPTER 26
ZEKE

This ends tonight.

The three words play over and over in my head as I slip out of bed in the middle of the night. As I walk quieter than a ghost through my house and out to my truck.

I consider walking the quarter of a mile to Julian's house but think better of it. I might need the truck. And I want to save all my energy for Julian.

Tonight, Julian dies for his sins.

He dies for tying Siren up.

He dies for touching her.

For hitting her.

For almost raping her.

He dies.

The second he chose to touch her; he sealed his fate. Death is all his future can hold. I can't let him breathe another second for what he did to Siren.

Julian ruined the best thing in my life. In one night, he took every chance at happiness away.

Maybe Siren and I still wouldn't have ended up together. But I had hope. Hope for her. For me. And for us.

193

I could have asked her out on a real date. Brought her flowers every day for a year to apologize for buying her instead of telling her the truth from the start—that I bought her to keep her safe.

Siren could have forgiven me for keeping her in the dark and pretending to be a monster. But she can't forgive me for failing her. She can't forgive me for hurting her.

I was so close to being able to tell her everything. I got rid of the bugs in the house. And I had a plan for how to pay off my debt to Julian without becoming a human trafficker myself. I could have told her the truth. Every move I've made has been to protect her.

Now, that's all gone—because of Julian.

I don't have a shot in hell. Siren deserves better. A man worthy of her. A man with honor and goodness in his heart.

I will never be that man.

Unless killing the bastard who touched her is honorable.

I don't know anymore. I just know it has to be done.

It won't give me any more points in Siren's book. She won't look at me with want in her eyes. She might even hate me for killing yet another man. She may think no one deserves to be slaughtered, even a demon like Julian.

But it has to be done. Julian has to die.

I didn't realize tonight was going to be when he dies until Oscar called, saying the shipment is ready for me. It's been almost two weeks since Julian laid a hand on Siren. She's been sleeping and recovering while I played doctor, hooking up IVs and medications to keep her alive.

Tonight became *the* night the second Oscar called. My time is up. I either kill Julian and every man who works for or with him, or I traffic women.

My choice is easy.

Even if I'll spend the rest of my life running, hunting down lead after lead, connection after connection of men who work for Julian. Men who, after today, will become my enemy.

I may never return to my previous life. I may never work for Enzo Black again. I may never get to joke with my best friend, Langston. Or see if Kai finally tamed Enzo.

I will live my life alone. My only purpose will be killing and ensuring Siren's safety. I'll have to watch Siren from afar. Watch her get a new job, move into a new place. Date other men. Marry a man. Have kids with another man.

It will be torture, but a worthy life. Because if I have to spend the rest of my life protecting Siren, then my life is worth something. I'll have spent my time on this earth doing something honorable instead of wasting it away, committing the worst crimes.

I pull up in front of Julian's house in my truck. It's the middle of the night, but Julian surely already knows I'm here. He doesn't have the security features my former boss did, but he's paranoid enough to have a solid security system.

He knows I'm here.

I prefer it that way. I don't want to sneak into his bedroom while he's sleeping and shoot him dead. I'm not that kind of guy.

I want a battle.

I want to know the best man won when I kill him.

I want him to look into the whites of my eyes as he bleeds out in front of me.

When I step out of my truck, I slam the door extra hard, ensuring my presence is known, if it wasn't already.

Then I pull out my gun, load it, and cock it. I hold it to my side as I walk calmly to the front door.

I don't ring the doorbell.

Instead, I kick down the double-bolted door with my massive foot and step inside.

My ears are alert, listening for any sign of Julian or his guards. I will have to take out his guards too, but I hope when I finally get to Julian, it will end with just the two of us fighting.

My eyes scan the darkness, and I see a shadow move in the living room.

Cautiously, I hold my gun out as I move through the dark entryway. When I get to the living room, I see Julian seated in a chair towards me, waiting.

Shoot him. Now.

End this.

But something stops me.

And then, it's too late.

The lights flick on, and I see thirty men surrounding Julian.

I don't drop my gun, though. I've been outnumbered before. I have a fifty-fifty chance of winning, killing every bastard here.

If it was just me I had to worry about, I might take those odds. Fifty-fifty is pretty good when it comes to a gunfight. Technically, just fighting a man one on one is fifty-fifty odds, because all it takes is one shot—one bullet to hit me in just the wrong spot for me to lose. But one on one, I've never lost before, so I consider my odds much higher.

But with this many men—fifty-fifty.

There is a fifty-fifty chance I live or die.

A fifty-fifty chance I return to Siren.

A fifty-fifty chance I can protect her.

A fifty-fifty chance Julian finds her and finishes what he started.

I can't take the chance. Because if I fail, Siren is who will pay for my loss, not me. Sure, I'll be dead, I won't even realize I lost. But I won't have to suffer the consequences like she will.

I look around at the thirty men I've never seen before. Julian's operation is bigger than I realized. *Where has he been hiding this army?* They are muscular, confident, and know how to hold a gun from the looks at them. Any one of them could do the job Julian asked of me. *So why does he want me?*

"We've been waiting for you," Julian says, with a grin.

I don't lower my gun, and none of the men draw theirs. It's like they know Julian isn't really in any danger. That's either a mistake on their part or mine.

Fuck—I've already lost.

Julian snaps his fingers and looks at the man on his right. "Load up. Zeke will be right there to lead you."

The men all file out of the room. Now's my chance. It's just me and Julian.

I don't lower the gun, but I don't pull the trigger either. I wouldn't be shocked if Julian already has a man near my house, ready to attack Siren if anything goes wrong tonight.

I put in extra security measures at the house. I even left a gun under Siren's pillow to protect her. But it won't be enough if I don't return.

"I'm done," I say.

I lower my gun. I mean it. Julian still needs to die, but it doesn't have to happen tonight. I have to put Siren first. I have to protect her at all costs, which means returning to her as fast as possible and then getting us off this fucking island.

Julian folds his hands and cocks his head up as he looks at me. "You owe me a debt, Zeke. I saved your life."

I toss my gun in front of him. "And consider this me saving yours. I should have killed you for what you did. You touched what was mine without permission."

I study his face. His has caked-on makeup to cover the bruising on his face. He's still injured two weeks later.

Good.

I'd rather him be in the hospital right now, or better yet, six feet under. But knowing he's bruised and hurting brings me some level of satisfaction.

Julian shakes his head. "I don't accept."

I frown. "You don't have a choice."

"I have thirty men who say otherwise."

I growl.

"But I'm willing to negotiate; I'm a fair man. I think we can come to an agreement if you want out."

I don't like the sound of this.

"I'll give you a choice for paying your debt off. You can either transport the women to their new owners and ensure we get paid more than a fair amount for each, or you can buy your freedom."

My chest rises and falls heavily. Julian doesn't own me. I shouldn't have to pay for my freedom. But right now, I'll do anything if it means I don't have to fall deeper into the depths of hell.

"How much?"

Julian twists his mouth, thinking for a moment. "Let's see, the going rate for a person seems to be what? Thirty million?"

I narrow my eyes. It's the amount I paid for Siren. He wants me to pay him the same amount to earn my own freedom.

"And since I'll most likely lose my account with Oscar over this, since none of my current men have any brains when it comes to business, I'll require a bonus. Your pet will do."

The money was one thing; adding Siren means the choice isn't even an option. I will never betray Siren again.

Julian grins. "Money and one girl, or you sell two hundred women. I would think the choice is easy since two hundred is more than one. One girl can't mean that much to you, can she?"

Fuck him.

He knows.

He knows I've never touched Siren.

Never fucked her.

He knows I only bought her to save her. And he knows I don't want to sell the other women; I'm not that kind of man. This is a test, and no matter what I choose, I lose.

"Which will it be? Pay for your freedom and give up one girl? Or become the monster you hate and sell two hundred humans into slavery?"

I already know my choice, and I hate it. I hate him. But I never had a choice.

"I need to ensure Siren will be safe. That you won't touch her. No man will."

Julian nods. "What do you want me to do?"

"I already have a new security system in place. I will be able to see everything that goes on inside my house. I want you to place three of your best men on guard outside of the house. I want you to hire a cook and nurse who you trust to cook and take care of Siren while I'm gone."

"Done."

"You won't touch her. You won't go near the house. You will never lay a hand on her again."

"Are you finished?"

"No, I'll do the job. But you won't get the money until I return. Until the job is over, and I know Siren is safe."

Julian frowns. "And if you screw me over, what I did to your pet before will seem kind compared to what I will do."

I suck in a breath. *I can't fail.* If I do, Siren's life will be on the line.

I hold out my hand, and he shakes it.

Then, I turn to find the thirty men who will work for me while I do the job.

A job that will destroy my soul.

A job that will consume my heart.

A job that will turn me into the devil.

I can't save them. That's the lie I keep telling myself. Because I can save them. And two hundred is greater than one, but I choose Siren instead. It's a choice I will never regret.

CHAPTER 27
SIREN

It's been twenty-three days.

Twenty-three fucking days.

I haven't heard from Zeke for twenty-three days.

And it's driving me mad.

Sure, he has guards posted outside my window protecting me, but they're probably keeping me inside as much as they are keeping people out.

And sure, I've had a private chef come cook for me the most delicious food every night. He's even been teaching me how to cook.

And yes, a home nurse came over every day to check on me while I was healing. Once I'd healed, she still came to bring me movies, books, and entertainment. She would talk about gossip in town, and the horrible storms we've been having.

But none of that matters. Zeke isn't here.

And I'm trapped in his fucking house.

I don't know what's happening, and yet, I know. He's doing the job Julian asked of him. He's trafficking women. Even after everything Julian did to me, Zeke is still making that man money.

Fuck him.

He's nothing but a spineless coward. He should have told Julian to go fuck himself, find himself a new number two. Instead, he went in the middle of the night, the second Julian called. Zeke put Julian above me—again.

I'm done. I'm so done. As soon as Zeke gets back, I'm ending this.

I'm done being captive.

I'm done waiting for Zeke to decide what to do with me.

I'm done.

I hear the front door slam shut—Zeke.

He's finally back.

And I'm ready to give him hell.

I run through the house full of rage, ready to tell him off. To demand answers. To finish this.

But I stop in my tracks at the sight of him sitting on the stairs and kicking off his shoes.

Zeke looks horrible, like he hasn't slept in a month. His boots are covered—in mud, blood, water, and god knows what. His jeans are splattered with more dark red spots. His leather jacket has rips in it. And his once white T-shirt looks more gray than white. He now wears a full beard, having not shaved for twenty-three days. And his hair is technically in a man bun, but most of his hair has fallen out, and he hasn't bothered to fix it.

Maybe I shouldn't pounce yet?

I should let him have a day.

A day to shower, eat, sleep.

No.

This is war. He deserves everything that is coming.

"Where the fuck have you been?" I shout, folding my arms and sticking my hip out as anger consumes me.

Zeke doesn't look up. He just unties his second boot before slipping it off.

"Did you hear me? Or did you lose your hearing the twenty-three days you've been gone?"

His head snaps up—pain. His sight lasers through my heart. He's hurting so fucking much.

Well, too bad. He's not the only one in pain.

"You don't get to just leave me for a month on my own trapped in this house!" I shout, walking toward him.

He stands up. "Watch your mouth, Siren. You have no idea what I've been through."

"I have no idea what you've been through? Are you fucking serious?"

I push him square on the chest. He doesn't move, but it still feels good. Instead, he steps around me.

"I know exactly what you've been through because it's been the only thing I've been thinking of this entire time," I scream.

I follow him, and when he turns down the hallway, I push again. This time, he's off-balance enough to take a small step back.

"You've been tying women up."

Push.

"Threatening their lives with your gun."

Push.

"Locking them up in cages."

Push.

"Transporting them to far off countries in the back of vans and cargo holds."

Push.

"Making calls with the most disgusting men in the world."

Push.

"Negotiating costs and pushing prices higher and higher so you and Julian can make more money."

Push.

Zeke's body is pressed flush against the wall now. I'm unhinged— my body relentlessly pushing his against the wall over and over.

I can't remember being this pissed with a man before. *But why?* He did his job. He's just like Julian and every other man on this island.

Because I was stupid enough to think that Zeke might be better. That he had a speck of good in a sea of bad, but he's just like all the rest.

"Do it," I say, shoving again.

He frowns, not understanding what I'm saying.

"Rape me! Hurt me! Be a fucking man!" I push again. "You've

already hurt hundreds of women. I'm not any different than any of them. Stop pretending you are the good guy. You're not a good man. You're evil. The devil!"

Zeke doesn't move, even when I push him again.

My body is boiling. I'm red, exhausted, and angry, but I can't stop. I need this to end. One way or the other, I need this over.

"Stop pretending you need the excuse of the stupid game to sin!" I cry.

This time when I launch myself, my body falls into his. I'm too exhausted to hold myself up anymore. Too angry.

Zeke holds me gently in his arms. My head rests on his chest, and his arms hold me up at the elbows.

We are both still for a moment. I pant heavily against his chest as I watch his rise and fall. My ear is pressed against his pec, and I can hear it—the thumping of his heart. It's accelerated. Beating as fast as mine.

I look up and see the pain on Zeke's face, mixed with desire. He's desperate for me, yet he still exercises restraint.

I'm tired of him being a gentleman to me when he's a monster to everyone else. I need to see the real him. It's the only way.

I lift my head from his chest.

He freezes as if he can read my mind and already knows where this is going. If he just stays still, he'll be able to resist.

But he's a man, a monster—he won't be able to stop himself.

I rise on my tiptoes, and then, I kiss him.

I melt as soon as our lips touch. His are so soft, so welcoming, so *mine*.

Fuck, where did that thought come from?

He tilts his head, letting me in more as his deep voice strains against his vocal cords as I slide my tongue into his mouth.

Yes, stop resisting—show me who you really are.

I grab his neck, holding his lips to me as we kiss harder, our mouths begging for more. For more than a kiss can give.

It's an endless kiss—wet, and hot, and delicious. I love everything about it. How he moves his tongue, how his lips part, even the scruffy hair on his face against my cheeks.

It's what I've been searching for forever. But it's not real. This isn't the real Zeke.

At the same time, we push each other away, until we are arms-length apart.

Our hands still hold each other. His hands claw my shoulders, and mine graze the surface of his biceps. We pant hard and fast. Neither of us is getting enough oxygen right now to think clearly.

"Why did you stop? You know you don't want to," I breathe out.

His eyes turn in his head. He's fighting his self-control—hard. And his dick is winning.

Yes, just a little more, and I'll have you. You'll show me your true monster, and then I can use it against you. But what will it cost me?

"Why did *you* stop?" He throws my words back at me.

"This isn't about me. This is about you. About the monster you've become."

He shakes his head with a sexy grin as he wipes his mouth with the back of his hand. *Like that's all it takes for him to get rid of me—ha.*

"Oh, beautiful. You really think I'm the only one with a monster inside?" His eyes meet mine. "If I'm a beast, you're a tiger. Just as vicious, just as willing to devour innocent prey."

I narrow my eyes.

And we both attack again.

He goes for my hair; I go for his jacket.

He pulls my hair back, tilting my head as he lays another kiss on my neck as I push his jacket off.

He grabs my neck, pulling me tightly to him, not willing to let me go. I grab the V of his shirt and rip it all the way down the middle until I see his rippling muscles and tattooed body.

His hand tangles into my hair, fisting it back, giving himself better access to my lips. I want more, and so does he.

I grab his scrunchie and rip it out of his hair as he pushes my shirt up as he feels my smooth stomach.

Progress.

But then, he snaps back.

I reach for him, but I feel nothing but air.

He's glued to the wall, his hands stuck to his side.

I laugh. "You afraid?"

"You have no idea," he pants.

I touch my swollen lip with my finger. *I want more. And now I'm afraid. Because I'm not supposed to want him back.* I'm supposed to be in control. But a few kisses and I want him as badly as he wants me.

"I have an idea." I grab the hem of my shirt and lift it over my head.

He groans at the sight.

He didn't realize I wasn't wearing a bra when his hands were all over my stomach.

His eyes flutter up to the ceiling, as if not looking is going to save him. He already has my body ingrained in his head. There is no escaping.

"Zeke?" I say, my voice dropping to serious levels.

His eyes carefully drop back to me, attempting not to catch a glance of my boobs, of my nipples hardening for his touch.

"Yes?" He answers.

"Kiss me."

We charge at each other. This time he grabs my ass, and my legs wrap around his body. I feel his erection push between my legs; my nipples rub against his chest as our mouths collide.

*This is what has been missing—these kisses. This...*I've never felt whole kissing another man. I've never felt protected and safe. But Zeke forces me to feel all of it.

His lips are evil liars, but incredibly sexy and talented liars.

I'll call him out on the lying later. Right now, I just want to kiss him. Enjoy my last moments of pleasure with this man.

He spins us around, until my back is against the wall, and breaks the kiss far too soon.

I pout.

He chuckles, giving me a wink, before he dips his head down and finds my nipple.

"Ah, fuck," I moan, holding onto his head to keep him from pulling away again.

I thought his tongue was talented in my mouth, but it's reaching new levels on my nipple. The sensation radiates all over my body. I'm throbbing between my legs, needing so much more than he's currently offering. This can't stop. Not until...

Until I let him fuck me?

Because that can't happen. I can't reward him like that for all the shitty things he's done. Even if it's a reward for myself too.

Once again, Zeke stops.

This time I do too.

What the hell are we doing?

We can't keep doing this.

We hate each other.

We want to destroy each other.

And kiss each other, lick each other, fuck each other...

Zeke rests his forehead against mine as we breathe into each other's mouths. I see and feel the pained expression on his face. It's the same one I wear.

I'm so confused.

He is too.

What are we doing?

No, better question—*what is he doing?* If he wants me, then he has the power to take me. To force me. To take what he wants from me. He paid for it. *So what's stopping him from taking it?*

I don't want him to take anything. Being raped by a man I kinda, sorta find attractive is still a horrible experience. It's still rape. It will still top my list of worst nights.

I reach down between our legs, and find his dick, squeezing hard.

He howls and shoves me hard against the wall, forcing me to release my grip.

I've awakened the beast with my touch. I can see it in his eyes. I wanted to know who he really is—*this is it.*

This man standing before me, with long, wild hair. An untamed beard. Tattoos covering as many scars as muscle. A ripped body he used to torture, rape, and kill. Life-taking hands. And a brain filled with dirty thoughts about me since the second he bought me.

That's who he is. And he's one push away from acting on it. From proving me right—that he's a monster.

Zeke sees into my mind. He reads my thoughts. And he takes back control.

"What did Julian do to you to make you so scared of him? What did he do to you before?"

I shake my head. "Playing this game doesn't make you any less of a monster. You've wanted to rape me ever since you bought me; just because you've earned the right to commit a sin doesn't make you any less of a sinner."

"Answer the question, and I won't get to sin."

I grit my teeth together. This is the moment. The moment where the truth mixes with sin. This is the moment where I find out the truth of who Zeke really is.

How do I want to learn the truth about him? By speaking my own truth? Or letting him sin?

I'm not ready to share my secret, not until he's spilled his first.

But if I choose sin, will I forever feel guilty for him raping me? Because I gave him the power to do it?

No, I won't. If I choose sin, it doesn't give him permission to violate me in that way. Even if I choose sin, I will still fight back. I won't let him get that far.

"Sin," I answer.

His eyes gloss over with that single word. He needed, and feared, that answer.

Your move, big guy. Your move. Let's see what you got. Because I'm about to castrate you.

My legs are still wrapped around his waist. I'm still gripping his shoulders, but that doesn't mean I've given him permission to fuck me.

Maybe if he asked first, but he won't.

He makes a decision in an instant; then he's carrying me through the foyer. I assume he's going to take me to the bedroom, but he doesn't. He takes me to the living room.

Huh? Not a bed kind of guy? Or does he not want to bother having to change the sheets after the ensuing bloody battle?

He finds the large ottoman in the center of the room, kneels in front of it, and sets my ass down on the edge.

"Lean back," he says.

I frown. If he thinks I'm just going to lay back and take it, he's crazy.

"I said, lay back," his voice deeper, more powerful than before.

I fall back automatically.

Shit, now what?

I slip my hand slowly in the back pocket of my jeans and grab the knife I hid there. I hold it to my back as he unbuttons my jeans and slowly slides them over my hips, then down my body.

I purse my lips and breathe out slowly. *I've got this—he won't touch me without getting castrated.*

Next, he grabs my lacy panties. He takes his time undressing me.

And then I'm naked.

I close my eyes, trying to calm myself. He's still not undressed, so I have time before he fucks me. He's a slow, gentle giant. He won't speed up just to rape you. He's waited this long. He's a patient man; he'll wait until he's good and ready.

I grip the knife tighter, preparing myself.

I feel his hands on my inner thighs; he gently spreads me apart.

This is it—the moment I need to attack before he does something he can't take back.

"Siren?" he asks.

My eyes open and look at him.

He smirks at me, but his eyes say something else. They ask for permission.

Permission for what?

His eyes dip down, and I realize what he's about to do. His jeans are still on. His hands have my legs spread, and his face is positioned just over my pussy, ready to devour me.

He wants to fuck me with this mouth, not rape me. That's his sin —giving me pleasure.

I blink several times, completely confused.

How could this be? How is he this guy, not the monster? Or is he only this guy when he's around me? And he's a monster around everyone else?

Zeke hovers over me, waiting for some sign of permission. Technically he never asked with words, but we've never needed words to communicate.

Yes—no.

How do I decide? My body is begging me to let him kiss me there. I already know it will be the most explosive orgasm of my life. *But is that giving in? Being weak? I shouldn't—*

But I feel my hips move up on their own accord.

Zeke grins broader before he licks his lips.

Wait, I didn't answ—

His tongue licks over my slit, and I realize my hips made a much better choice than my brain would. One stroke of his tongue and I'm his. I don't care what he's done. I don't care how evil his heart is. I don't care how many people he's killed or how many lives he's stolen.

Feeling his tongue between my legs, over my most sensitive area while he kneels in front of me, expecting nothing from me in return, is everything I've ever wanted in a man.

And god is it sexy to see him giving instead of taking from me.

I lean up on my elbows so I can watch him lick me. At first, he's slow, so achingly slow. But it only intensifies everything. I can feel every lick, flick, and breath coming from his mouth.

And then he narrows in on my clit.

Too much. My legs close in around his head.

He grins as he licks over my clit more, and his hands slowly spread me wide for him again.

"I think your clit likes my tongue," he says.

"Mmm," is my response.

"Keep your legs spread, or I'll stop," he commands.

I frown. That's an impossible task, but I see why he commands it from me. He removes one hand from my leg and puts two of his fingers in his mouth before I feel them pushing at my entrance.

I tighten at first, resisting anything entering. *It's been a long time, too long.*

He removes one finger and tries again, being so slow and patient with me, waiting until my body accepts him before he pushes.

He licks faster, moving out of his usual slow movements for me. I arch, my muscles relax, and his finger glides inside me.

"Fucking, wow," I get out.

"If you think that was good, just wait. I'm about to have you screaming and cursing my name."

I like his promise. And I can't wait for him to deliver on it.

He slides his finger out, and I curse the emptiness I feel. I want him inside me—more than just his finger, but I'm not ready to tell him that yet.

He starts pushing in again, but this time a second finger joins in. I feel an intense tightness as he pushes further.

"Relax, baby," he whispers over my clit, licking faster.

I look at his eyes. They scream, begging—*trust me.*

I do. Fuck, I do.

I let go.

Of my expectations.

My fears.

My observations.

My pain.

My truth.

I'm just here, with a man doing incredible things to my body.

As soon as I let go, Zeke takes complete control. His fingers thrust inside me with expert ability. His tongue licks and nips at my clit. And his eyes promise me the world.

Our eyes lock until I can't look at him any longer. Everything is too intense.

And then I explode all at once, throwing my head back and clamping my eyes closed. My back arches, my toes curl, and my legs tighten around his head. My pussy clenches down in a ripple of throbs, releasing my orgasm on his fingers.

What. Just. Happened?

My brain seems to thaw, and my first thought is blissful bewilderment.

I smile up at the world, because for the first time, it brought me something good. Even if it was only supposed to last for this short time, I wouldn't trade a single bad thing in my life if it meant giving up these few minutes with Zeke.

I hear him moving.

I sit up, and then he's draping a throw blanket over my shoulders.

He scoops me up, and we move to the couch before he sets me down on his lap.

His eyes drop down to my lap.

Mine follow.

"Oh, um..." I start, trying to explain why I'm gripping a knife.

He chuckles. "If you castrate me, I deserve it." He leans forward and kisses my forehead sweetly. I can smell myself on his breath. *Jesus, I smell delicious on his face.*

I expect him to try and take the knife from me; he doesn't.

Slowly, I come back to life. To the real world. And he just gave me the most beautiful sin. It felt dirty, wrong, but oh-so-delightful.

I consider thanking him, but it doesn't feel right, so I don't. But I do have my question. I know what I want to ask him.

"Who are you, Zeke? A beast or a monster?"

He tucks my hair behind my ear as he grips my neck, stroking me with his thumb.

"Is there a difference?" he asks hesitantly, afraid I'll say no.

"Yes."

He nods and then leans back against the couch. I tighten the blanket around me. I hold my breath, waiting for his answer. *Will he choose beast or monster?* If he says monster, there is no saving him. He's cruel down to the bone. And this ends here.

But if he says beast, it will give me hope. Beauty was able to tame the beast in the end. The beast had a heart. The beast could still love, even though he sometimes did cruel things. And that makes all the difference to our future.

"Sometimes, I'm afraid that I'm a monster."

I suck in a breath—*dammit.*

"But after spending time with you, I've realized I'm a beast."

I smile—*yes, my beast. My gentle giant. My anchor, keeping me calm and protected while I wait out the storm.*

I got my answer.

But Zeke doesn't stop there. He tells me his whole truth.

"I lived in Miami. I was born in New York, but I moved to Miami shortly after. I worked for..."

No. Please, no. Don't say it.

"Enzo Black. He was my best friend and boss. We mainly handled security and created super-yachts for our rich clients. But during my time with him, I did horrible things. I stole, threatened, killed. But every time it was to protect my boss, my friends."

No...my heart is breaking.

"I almost died saving them."

No, no, no.

He tucks a finger under my chin.

I can't breathe.

"Until you. You saved me."

I exhale. *I can't do this.*

"I owe my life to you, not Julian."

But I have to.

"So when we met again, when your life was threatened to be taken, about to be sold, I knew what I had to do. I had to save you."

My heart shatters with his words. Because a part of me hoped he was cruel. Hoped I was wrong about him. Pleaded he didn't buy me to protect me.

"Maybe I did it the wrong way. I should have told you the truth sooner. But I bought you to save you, to protect you from the other men."

Zeke is a good person. He's my protector. My savior. I just wish I could say the same thing about myself.

"At first, I couldn't tell you the truth. Julian had everything bugged. He could listen to our conversations, but I removed all the eavesdropping devices."

I close my eyes as tears fall—warm, wet, salty tears.

Zeke being Zeke, the amazing man he is and I always suspected was beneath his shell, wipes my tears away.

"Now, I can complete my promise. Now, I can save you."

There is so much promise in his words—so much genuine affection. I swear I even see a hint of love in his eyes when he looks at me.

And it hurts, god does it hurt.

I swallow back my tears, wiping them on the back of my hand.

Because just like that, my high crashes down.

My world ends.

Whatever we had for a splitting moment is over.

Zeke finally spilled his truth.

Which means it's my turn to spill mine.

Mine is half-truth, half-sin. Mine is going to fucking hurt—leave a permanent scar where our hearts once were.

But I no longer have a choice between truth or sin. Now I must do both.

CHAPTER 28
ZEKE

One second, I'm spilling my heart to her, one word away from saying I love her, and the next Siren has me pinned to the floor.

She's naked still, and I'm only wearing my jeans, but the move isn't sexual. It isn't foreplay. *It fucking hurts.*

She's straddling me at the waist, with one of my arms pinned above my head, and her knife at my throat.

My eyes widen, searching for truth in her tear-stained eyes. If she could pull a move like this the entire time, why didn't she? *How did she let men kidnap her in the first place? Why didn't she fight harder against Julian? Against me before now?*

I breathe heavily, about to move my free hand when she presses the knife deeper into my neck.

"I'm so sorry," Siren whispers as one tear falls.

I frown. "You have nothing to be sorry for."

She shakes her head, barely holding herself together while physically stronger than I've ever seen her. I notice new muscles in her arms. Her thighs clench my waist hard, holding me down.

"Zeke, I—" Siren starts.

Lone, slow clapping cuts her off.

Siren doesn't look, she just closes her eyes tightly and takes a deep breath as if preparing herself.

I cut my eyes toward the sound.

Julian Reed.

What the fuck is he doing here now?

My eyes look up at Siren, who is still pouring herself into me. Whatever she is pissed at me for will have to wait, we have bigger fish to fry.

Apparently, she disagrees or doesn't read my face, because she doesn't release the knife or let me up.

"Good job, Aria," Julian says.

Siren's head drops.

I look from her to Julian.

"What?" I whisper to Siren. "What did he just call you?"

She swallows. "By my name," she says solemnly.

My mouth falls. *Siren isn't her real name—Aria is.*

Julian walks over to us, looking down at the situation.

"So you work for Enzo Black, huh?" he asks.

I don't answer. Instead, I glare back.

He smirks. "You thought you had removed all the bugs from the house." He laughs and pets Aria's head. "You didn't know I had a plant on the inside switching all the bugs back on as soon as you thought you had disconnected them."

What?

Siren drops her head in disgust but doesn't dispute him.

"She works for me," Julian says, finishing the missing pieces of the puzzle.

"And she's gotten me all the information I needed. You would have never told me who you worked for. And it's even better than I imagined. You work for the great Enzo Black." Julian's eyes grow greedy. "And now I have the key to bringing Mr. Black down."

"I will never help you," I growl.

He laughs. "I think you will. I got you to spill all your secrets to my beauty here; I think I can convince you to do just about anything."

I look up at Siren, no Aria, and my passion for her has been swapped for anger. She betrayed me. I trusted her. I could have loved her.

"What does he have over you? Why are you working for him?" I ask, pleading Siren, giving her one more chance to tell me differently.

"Because of what he gives me," she answers.

Julian laughs. "You think I force her? Aria is in complete control of her life. I could never force her to do anything she didn't want to do."

I frown, but I see the truth on her face.

Julian looks to Aria. "Lock him up. We have more work to do taking down Enzo Black."

"Yes, sir," she answers, not moving as Julian leaves the two of us.

"You lied to me," I say.

She shakes her head. "I never lie. I always tell the truth."

"Then explain this! You even lied about your name." I spit back.

"I never said 'siren' was my name, just who I was. You took it to mean what you wanted."

"That's still a lie."

"No, it's lying while telling the truth. I warned you. I'm a siren. I lure men to their deaths. You just didn't heed the warning."

She's right. I didn't.

"You thought I was a monster this whole time?" I ask.

She shakes her head. "I hoped, because then this wouldn't be so bad. But I knew in my heart you weren't. That's why I created this plan. I knew you wouldn't be able to let me be sold to another man."

I frown.

"But you aren't a saint. You sold those women," she spits in my face, her face red and angry, trying to rationalize her actions against me now.

I shake my head. "I didn't sell them. I made sure they were safe. Every. Single. One."

Her eyes widen in pain.

Good, she deserves it.

"I could have saved you too," I whisper.

"Not when I didn't want to be saved."

"Did Julian hurt you? Is that why you work for him?"

She doesn't answer at first. But then she answers with her actions.

I don't know how such a tiny body packs such a big hit. I'm seeing stars before I realize she's punched me. And I'm in handcuffs before I try to strike back.

"How the...?"

Her lips thin into a grimace. "I've trained my entire life for a job like this. I take down men. Usually bad guys. Too bad you aren't as bad as all the rest. Because your fate will be the same."

I realize she has my gun on me. She has all the weapons.

"Head downstairs," she says.

I don't move.

"Go. Downstairs. Or I'll shoot you," she says.

"I don't believe you."

She fires but misses on purpose.

I grunt and decide right now isn't the best time to fight. I'm distracted, and I'm not sure I could hurt her even if I had a clear head. Moments ago, I was giving her the best orgasm of her life, although I'm sure that was a lie too.

When I get to the basement, I see the cage. The cage I could have used on her when I bought her, but didn't. I was good to her, too good.

"Inside," she says.

I walk inside. She slams the barred door shut and locks it. Only then does she drop the gun.

"What did Julian do to you?" I ask, needing this answer. Needing her to be honest. I think back through our history. She's an excellent manipulator, and she's right, I don't think she ever spoke a lie.

She told the truth, I was just too stupid to read between the lines. To realize there was a reason she wasn't like every other woman on that stage—because she wasn't really being sold. She wasn't ever in danger. She was just doing her job—undercover, working for one of the cruelest men I've ever met.

"He saved me," she finally answers.

My eyes shoot up.

"Then why did he hurt you?" I ask. I know that was real. I saw the pain she felt. I nursed her back to health. Those were real bruises and scars. Those were real tears she cried.

"I'm not the one who needs saving, Zeke," she says, backing away.

She walks upstairs and closes the basement door, leaving me alone in the dark.

Siren's right, she doesn't need saving. And even if she does, I won't be the one to rescue her. I need to save myself.

Unfortunately, Siren has had me under her spell since the moment she saved me. Apparently, she goes around saving men who she thinks her boss will want dirt on. She probably got paid for my secrets more than I paid to buy her.

Her words, though, will stay with me forever—her beautiful voice. I close my eyes, and I can hear them again.

"I always tell the truth, even when I lie."

She warned me, and I fell into her trap. *What other lies were hidden in her truths? What other sins?*

It shouldn't matter. I should escape. Run. Return to my old life. Warn my boss about Julian. Forget about Siren.

But I can't stop thinking about her. My cock can't stop wanting her. And my heart, the stupid muscle that it is, still beats for her. *Stupid, stupid heart.*

Siren saved me, only to use me for her own gain. I pull on the bars. They don't budge.

Now I'm the one in need of saving.

TWISTED VOW

CHAPTER 1
SIREN

I'm not the one in need of saving.

I repeat those words over and over to myself.

They are true.

I never speak a lie. Or even think one.

I chose this life.

I was given an option, all those years ago, and this is the life I chose for myself. I chose to work for Julian Reed. I chose to take down dangerous men. I chose to live my life on the edge of right and wrong. I chose to use my body as a weapon.

And I enjoy what I do.

I may hate my boss—Julian Reed.

But I love hurting men more.

Men have done nothing but hurt me. Men promise me the world. They promise me their love. They promise me their fidelity.

Ha.

No man can ever keep his promises. No man's heart is truly pure. No man can keep his dick in his pants when he's faced with a flirty woman, even when he wears a ring around his fourth finger.

Every man deserves exactly what he gets from me. And Zeke is no different.

Zeke Kane—I didn't know his name, not until he spilled his secrets. Not until I learned he works for the infamous Mr. Black. Rumor is the former Mr. Black died a few years back. And there is a war raging for the new heir of the throne of one of the most notorious crime organizations in the world. Mr. Black has his hand in everything. So Julian taking him down would make him one of the most powerful men in the world.

I'm sitting crooked in the chair in Julian's living room as I type on my laptop. And have been for the last few hours.

Ever since I accomplished my mission—getting Zeke to spill his boss to me—I've been searching for everything I can find about Zeke and his former boss.

I click on a grainy picture. Two men of similar age stand next to Zeke. Zeke and a blonde man flank the man in the middle, who must be the new Mr. Black.

My heart thumps in strange patterns as my eyes skim from each man, and lastly, land on Zeke. He's wearing his classic outfit of dark jeans and a black T-shirt. But in this picture, his hair is down. He looks grizzly and bulky and so fucking handsome.

I snap the laptop closed as I feel my cheeks heat.

Nope, not happening. I can't be lusting over the man I just locked up in the basement of his house.

Right now, there are at least three guards watching Zeke. I don't need to be thinking about him. I need to be thinking about the next mission Julian is going to give me.

I've worked with Julian long enough to know what he's going to say before he even says it.

"Good job, pet," Julian says as he enters the living room with two scotches in hand.

He hands me one, then grips my shoulder in a congratulatory way.

I snarl. "I think you can stop calling me 'pet' now."

Julian smirks as he sits down on the couch opposite me and crosses his lower leg over his knee in the way only men do. He sips his scotch, staring me down.

"Why? I like the nickname. It's been years since I called you that.

Since the night you broke into my house and we came to an arrangement."

I sip on the scotch, staring Julian down in equal measure. "My name is Aria; I suggest you use it."

"Well, that's not any fun. You let Zeke call you all sorts of fun names—Siren."

I narrow my eyes.

He chuckles. "Siren was the perfect name for you. What I love even more is that you told him exactly who you were with one word, and he was too stupid to realize his own mistake."

I feel agitation rise in my chest, but I don't take the bait.

I've always felt that breaking into Julian's house was my worst mistake and my strongest moment. That night, years ago, changed my life in ways I can't describe. Ways that are too painful to relive right now...

But what I did to Zeke feels exactly the same—I hurt him. I outsmarted and overpowered a built man. I feel strong, yet everything I did was painful. *What if Zeke is the one man who doesn't deserve what I did to him?*

Sure, he's a man, and he deserves to pay for mankind's sins. *But what if he truly isn't a sinner?*

What if I made a mistake? He said he didn't sell those women. *What did he do with them then? How did Julian get his money if Zeke didn't sell them?*

I down the rest of my drink, needing to forget about Zeke at least for tonight, and alcohol will help me do that.

Julian smiles and downs his scotch. He refills his drink at the bar cart in the corner of the room and brings the remainder of the bottle to fill my glass.

He sets the bottle on the coffee table between us. His eyes blaze as he looks up and down my body. I'm still wearing nothing but a robe. I know how badly Julian wants me, he's made his feelings perfectly clear several times before. But that doesn't mean he will ever get me.

I don't tighten the sash to cover up more of my skin. Julian may be my boss, he may control my life, but I control him too. And I won't relinquish any of my power.

Julian holds up his glass. "To you."

I hold up mine as well, and we clink our glasses together before returning to drinking.

"I mean it. I think this is your best work yet, Aria."

I nod, *it is my best work*. Usually, it doesn't take this much effort to get a man to spill his secrets. A lap dance. A little too much to drink. A slip of my hand on his thigh.

But I knew from the moment I met Zeke that he was different. He would require more. And my suspicions were proven right.

"Your idea to pretend you were being sold to see if Zeke would take the bait and try and save you was incredible. I truly believed that you thought you were being sold," Julian says.

I stare down at the scotch in my glass, those feelings coming back to me. "That's because if my plan failed, if Zeke didn't buy me, I *would* have been sold."

Julian stills.

"You wouldn't have saved me. You would have let a man buy me," I say, my words full of hate.

Julian shrugs. "I would have."

I shake my head, my anger spilling out of me. "You're an asshole."

He chuckles. "You already knew that." He sets his glass down on the table and leans forward. "But, you know why I would have let you be sold to any man?"

"Why?"

"Because you don't need me or any man to save you." He pats my thigh as he says it.

He's right. I don't need a man to save me. I always save myself before any man has a chance to save me.

But his words don't stop me from being mad. Yes, if I had been sold to another man, I would have shot him dead and escaped before he had a chance to touch me, but that doesn't absolve Julian of his other sins.

"Why did you do it?" I ask, my voice trembling as I say it. This time, I wrap my robe tight around my body, ensuring Julian can't see any of my skin.

He falls back in his chair, seeming to choose his words carefully. He doesn't have to ask for clarification on what I'm asking. He knows. Because we had an agreement, and he broke it.

"Zeke needed motivation," he answers.

"No! I was handling him!" I snap back.

"And I was tired of waiting. So I just provided a little push."

I take a deep breath in and out, so I don't kill Julian right now and ruin everything I've been working so hard on for the past four years.

"You had me tied up and dragged in front of a room of strangers," I say calmly with my eyes closed, reliving one of the worst nights of my life.

"You had me manhandled upstairs to your bedroom," I open my eyes, needing Julian to see exactly what he did to me.

My eyes burn red and tears water the corner, ready to spill free.

"You ripped the clothes from my body."

I have to look away for a second as the tears spill, and my body shakes with rage. I exhale deeply, letting it all out before I face Julian again.

"You spit alcohol into my eyes—I could have gone blind.

"You hit me, kicked me—I could have died."

The last part is the hardest. But he needs to hear every fucking word of the pain he caused me. Not that he cares, Julian Reed doesn't have a heart. I learned that a long time ago. It's one of the reasons I'm in this situation to begin with.

"You pulled out your cock. You shoved it between my thighs. And if Zeke hadn't shown up, you would have raped me." My body may tremble, but my voice is strong. I spit every word out. Every drop of pain and fear I felt that night.

I'm a tough, skilled woman. I know how to get out of most situations. I know how to save myself. But I couldn't save myself that night. I signed a contract with Julian years ago. If I had fought back, I would have broken the contract, and I would have lost everything I've worked so hard for.

Julian knew that. He knew I was defenseless, which is why he attacked me. Because he wanted to, not because he wanted to push Zeke into spilling—I was close to doing that on my own. In fact,

Julian's little stunt almost killed me and probably delayed Zeke telling me the truth.

"You made me depend on a man to save me," I growl.

"I did," Julian says, not backing down.

I want to punch him, kick his ass for what he did to me. But like I said, I signed a contract—one that I have no hope of getting out of, at least not like this. If I lay a finger on Julian, I lose—*every-fucking-thing*.

He knows I won't touch him.

"Never again," I say.

Julian shakes his head. "No, you said your peace, now it's my turn. You work for me, Aria. Me! You made your decision, now live with it. And when I decide to deviate from our original plan, you don't fight me on it, and you don't get to lecture me. If you do it again, there will be consequences. Understand?"

Julian's voice is full of threats, but they aren't empty warnings—they are real. And his punishments hurt worse than anything any other man could ever inflict on me, because Julian knows me better than anyone else. He knows my weak points, and he knows where to push to deliver the most pain.

So as much as I want to argue back, as much as I need Julian to promise never to lay a finger on me again—I can't.

Instead, I down more of the scotch. I need it in order to sleep tonight. But it sure as hell won't be under Julian's roof. I'll go take one of the small boats out and sleep on the water. I'll feel safer that way—sleeping out under the stars, rocking along with the waves.

I grab the bottle of scotch and pour myself another glass, while I stare Julian down, letting him know everything I think and feel with my eyes, since I can't say them with my words.

I hate him.

"I'm going to bed," I say, downing the glass of expensive scotch meant to be enjoyed slowly, not chugged like a shot of cheap tequila.

"You know what your next task is?" Julian asks.

I stand and set the glass down on the table. "I already used all the power I have against Zeke. He no longer cares about me. He doesn't even like me. In fact, I'm pretty sure he hates me. There is nothing I can do to convince him to turn on his boss. You are going to have to do that on your own. I did my job."

I turn, intending to walk the fuck out.

"Your job isn't finished until I say it is, Aria."

I stop. I take it back; it's not only 'pet' that I hate him calling me. I also hate it when he calls me Aria, Siren, and any name really. I hate it all.

Julian walks up behind me and runs his hand through my hair, brushing it over one side of my shoulders, exposing my neck so he can stroke it.

"You're right, Zeke hates you. Use his hate then."

I swallow hard, refusing to cry any more in front of Julian. But I can do the task Julian gave me, just like I do every other task.

Use Zeke's hate—that I can do. I strut away from Julian. I know a little something about hate.

CHAPTER 2
ZEKE

It's been a week.

A fucking week.

I've been locked up in this cell under the house I rent from Julian for a week.

The bars hold me in the filthy basement, but they aren't what concern me. With enough willpower and strength, both which I have, I could break the bars within minutes.

But once I escape from my cell, I have guards to take out—three to be exact.

Again, not a problem. Even though they are armed, and I'm not. I could take on a hundred men by myself.

Escaping is the easy part. The hard part is ensuring my friends are safe. Julian knows who my boss is. And he wants him. He wants to use me to get what he wants from Enzo Black; I just don't know what that is exactly. *Does Julian want his power? His empire? His status? Or is there something more about the Black empire that I'm not aware of?*

The bars and guards aren't holding me in this cell, my need to protect my boss and friends is. If I run without killing Julian first, they will never be safe, even if I never return to them. And they're my family. I grew up with Enzo and Langston—I consider them brothers.

Why didn't I kill Julian when I had the chance? I didn't owe him a damn thing.

Because I'm an idiot, that's why.

An idiot who fell for a siren.

No, that can't be true. I didn't fall for her. At least, I didn't fall in love. I just fell under her spell. I let her manipulate me. I let her use her body and my need to protect the innocent against me.

Except Siren isn't innocent.

So I shouldn't want to protect her, except... *Fuck*, I have no idea what I want anymore when it comes to that woman.

Do I want to destroy her like I do Julian?

Do I want to punish her for what she did to me and for putting my family in danger?

Do I want to fuck her hard against a brick wall?

What. Do. I. Want?

I run my hand through my long hair. I really wish I had a scrunchie to tie my hair up with because it's driving me crazy right now.

No—focus. I need to protect my family—Enzo, Kai, Langston, Liesel.

I need to write a letter. I need to send something to warn them while ensuring Julian doesn't find out where they are.

If I call, he could track them.

But a letter that's not even written to them...that could save them.

That's my new goal, to convince the guards to give me a pen and paper to write on. Should be easy enough. The guards have already brought me food, books, a new pillow and blanket, and even whiskey. They don't care what I do as long as I stay locked up in the cell. Apparently, Julian and Siren haven't decided how to get me to break— to give up Mr. Black. They don't realize I'd rather die a thousand times than give them even one shred of information that could cause harm to my family. I've spent my entire life protecting them. I've sacrificed my life before to keep them safe; I'll do it again.

And again and again and again.

I hear the door open to the basement stairs.

My guard, Pete, who is sitting across from me, looks at his watch.

He's been sitting reading a newspaper like it's the 1950s or something. It must be time for a guard change.

He stands up, ready to vacate his seat for his replacement.

My guards have mostly rotated between the same three men. Occasionally, a new guard works into the mix. But it should be Frank who takes over, unless there has been a change or it's his day off.

But when I hear the click, click, click of the footsteps on the stairs, I know there has been a change in the guard schedule, and not a good one.

"Thank you, Pete. I got it from here," Siren says.

I refuse to look at her. I'm lying on the makeshift bed I made on the floor with the pillows and blankets the guards have been bringing me. I have a book opened on my stomach, and I pretend to read.

Ignore her.

She doesn't get to see how angry she's made me. And I sure as hell won't fall for any more of her tricks.

"So that's how it's going to be? You aren't even going to look at me?" she asks in her snarky, annoying voice. I can't believe I didn't realize how annoying her voice was before—*that's because it's not annoying, not even now.*

Focus—read the words in my book. But all I see is blah, blah, blah on the page.

"We tracked down your friends. Their yacht is off the shores of Greece," she says.

I growl and finally look up at her.

She's standing in a tight black dress, sharp heels, and red lipstick. Her dress cuts down in the front, revealing her ample cleavage, and she's not wearing a bra, so her nipples point sharply at me. At least they do until she folds her arms in front of her chest and sways her hips to the side.

"You're lying," I say.

"Am I? I don't lie."

"No, you don't. That is the only honest thing about you. But your words weren't sharp, you're biting your lip, and your heart rate has picked up. You're lying."

She unfolds her arms. "Does it matter if I was lying? I got you to talk to me, so mission accomplished." She smiles and gives me a wink.

I shake my head in annoyance. *How can I keep letting her get under my skin?* I try to go back to my book, but I know it's no use.

"Why are you here?" I ask.

She licks her lips, and then walks back and takes a seat in the chair. She crosses her legs, and as she does, her dress rises higher up her thighs.

She wore the dress to taunt me—*don't fall for it.*

"For you to yell at me," she answers.

I frown. "What?"

I try to figure out her angle. *Why would she come here so I could yell at her? What game is she playing now?*

"You heard me. Now bring it. Yell at me like you want to. You'll feel better," she says, motioning for me to bring it on with a wave of her hand.

I stand up, my anger getting the best of me. "I don't want to get it out. I want to harness my anger into giving you everything you deserve."

She tilts her head. "You sure you don't want to yell at me, Zeke Kane?"

A low rumble of a growl escapes. She knows my last name. Which means she has done her research. She has looked up Enzo and possibly Kai. And every other person who works for Enzo. She could have been telling the truth when she said she knew where their yacht is right now.

I take a step backward, realizing how stupid I was to tell her my secret. Even if I thought we were starting something incredible together. Even if I thought she could turn into the love of my life, I should have never trusted her. I should have never spoken a word about Enzo Black. I should have protected him with my life like I vowed to do all those years ago.

"You weren't lying, were you?" I ask.

She raises an eyebrow. "We don't know Mr. Black's exact location, but we will soon enough."

I frown.

"Now, are you ready to take me up on my offer of yelling at me?" she asks.

No, because who I really want to yell at is myself.

I grab the bars and shake them; the metal of the bars rattles, but otherwise, they don't budge.

She jumps at my outburst.

I'm the strong, quiet type. I don't let my emotions get the best of me. But with her, I'm all emotion.

She takes a deep breath and then leans forward in her chair. "You would have done the same thing if you were in my shoes, Zeke."

I feel like she just slapped me, punched me in the gut, threw me from a moving car. Because if that is what she really thinks, she didn't learn a thing about me in our time together.

"No, I wouldn't have. I'm not a monster!" my voice ricochets off the brick walls, and I watch her heart thump wildly against her chest. I can be terrifying when I want to be. My physical size alone makes me scary, but then when you pair it with my deep, intimidating voice and my bursting muscles, I become a beast. That's what Siren called me—a beast. But it's clear she really thinks of me as a monster.

I pant my breaths in and out, still gripping the bars. Bars I could bend with my bare hands. *But then what? Could I really hurt her?*

Yes.

No.

Fuck.

I study her closer, and I can no longer tell why her body is trembling, her heart speeding, her breath catching. *Why are her lips parting, her tongue resting on the edge of her plump bottom lip, and her eyes growing big? Is she afraid of me? Or is she turned on? Or maybe it's all an act?*

I decide it's option number three. She's a better actor than she initially let on. It has to be. If she works for Julian, then she isn't afraid of any man. Especially one locked behind bars. And there is no way she's turned on by me, not when she thinks I'm a twisted monster. She's just acting so she can learn more secrets from me.

She stands up and flips her hair in that seductive way all women know how to do—tossing it sexily over her shoulder. Her eyes lock with mine.

Don't get drawn into her! Don't let her draw you back under her spell. She's a siren, remember.

She keeps walking, not stopping until her face is inches from mine.

I could reach out and grab her. Strangle her with my bare hands. Or bash her head against the bars. I could knock her out and search her body for a weapon, key, or cell phone—something that would help me get out of here.

But I don't.

I can't.

And my siren, knows it.

It's why she isn't scared of me even though I'm bigger and stronger than she is. Yes, she manipulated me into this cage. Yes, she used her physical skills against me. But the only reason she won is because I was in too much shock to fight back.

Siren grabs the bars, just below where I'm holding them. Our breaths mix together in the space between us. And my body can't decide between choking her and kissing her.

Goddammit, why do I have to be such a man? And why does she have to be so beautifully feminine?

If she were a man, I wouldn't hesitate. I would knock her out in seconds.

No—it's not that she's a woman. It's that she's her—Siren, strong, fierce, and a woman I wanted to protect. My feelings can't change for her in an instant. It takes time. I'm pissed, but it doesn't stop me from lusting after her. Especially when I never got to sink my cock inside her.

I want nothing more than to fuck her hard, fast, and uncontrollably against every rough surface I can find—the wall, the dining room table, the hood of my car, the coarse sand.

"How do we take down Mr. Black?" she asks.

I don't blink; I don't move. If she thinks I will ever answer that question, she's an idiot. I would never betray my boss and friend. Enzo Black is one of only a handful of people I even consider my family.

She sighs, her head dropping slightly.

"You lost, Zeke. Don't make this any harder than it has to be," she whispers.

Our eyes meet again. "I'm not the one making this hard."

Her eyes flutter down; all this talk about making me hard makes her glance at my dick. And yes, it's fucking hard as a rock, but that's not what we are talking about.

I shake the bars again, and she comes back to reality. Her eyes resume her gaze on mine.

"Don't make me hurt you, Zeke."

"You already did."

"Save yourself. For once, put yourself above others."

"No, that's not who I am. I protect my friends, my family. I protect those who are innocent. I protect—that's who I am."

She cocks her head to the side, giving me a disappointed, scared for me look. So I deliver the final blow.

"I just shouldn't have protected *you*," I say.

Siren closes her eyes as my words sting her. But she's not Siren anymore; she's Aria. She's no longer in control. It doesn't matter that I'm in this cage, and she's out in the open. It doesn't matter that she manipulated me. My words hurt her. She's not the fierce woman willing to defy me; she's scared and wearing her heart on her sleeve.

I frown, narrowing my eyes as I study her, trying to remind myself that I thought she needed protecting before. She didn't. Whatever I'm seeing displayed on her body right now is a lie. It's not the truth. The only time she tells the truth is with her words, not her body. And her words are as much a riddle as they are the truth. *Remember that.*

Slowly, Siren walks away. She's a stranger to me now. She stops at the base of the stairs. She turns and looks at me, her hand resting against the wall.

"Saving yourself will protect more than just you, Zeke," she says, and then she's gone.

Just like that, she's back to Siren. And I have no idea what to do with her parting words.

CHAPTER 3
SIREN

I'm beyond frustrated.

It's been weeks, and I've made no progress on getting Zeke to spill his secrets. Julian is growing increasingly impatient with me. I'm running out of time before I have to deal with his wrath, but I'm no closer than I was weeks ago at getting Zeke to tell me anything about how to take down Mr. Black.

And finding Black's location on our own is futile. He travels too quickly in his yachts, going undetected through large spaces of water. By the time we find him, he's already moved on to a different location. And his home base of Miami would be harder to attack than on the ocean.

We could use Zeke as bait, lure him in by threatening Zeke's life. *But what if Mr. Black doesn't care about Zeke like Zeke cares about his boss?* Then all we would be doing is letting Black know that we have Zeke.

I sigh as I pace the main floor of Zeke's home. The furniture and decor are still ruined from when I threw my tantrum weeks ago.

I know what I have to attempt next, but I don't want to do it. But I've tried everything else. I was nice and brought Zeke everything he could desire to keep him comfortable: good food, alcohol, books—I even brought a television down for him to watch. But none of those things got me any secrets. I tried bribing him with everything I brought too. But I just got a grumpy shoulder shrug for all of my troubles.

Bribing isn't the way to go.

I tried seducing him, using my body as bait, hoping he would spill a secret for a kiss, a blowjob, anything.

Nada.

That got me nowhere except my own flush red face when Zeke called me out for dressing like a slut. He looked me dead in the eye and swore he would never touch me again, let alone fuck me.

So today, I'm being myself. I'm wearing jeans and a tight-fitting black V-neck T-shirt. My hair is pulled up into a high ponytail. And I'm wearing makeup that makes me feel fierce, not slutty.

Because today I need all the strength I can get in order to take the next step with Zeke.

Joel, one of the guards, approaches me. "You ready?"

I nod.

"He's all yours then. He's in a foul mood. I doubt you are going to get any information out of him."

I look past Joel to the door to the basement. *Good, I'm glad Zeke is in a foul mood. Because I'm about to put him in a worse mood.*

I don't answer Joel. I just walk past him and descend the stairs.

Zeke is lying in his bed. Sometimes when I come downstairs, he's pacing or doing pushups or pull-ups. The pull-ups are my favorite—watching his biceps tense and curl his body up while he's shirtless is beyond sexy. But today he's lying on his bed staring up at the ceiling as he tosses a small ball up in the air.

I can tell from the creases on his forehead and the lost look in his eyes that he doesn't even notice my presence. He's in his own world. He's just as annoyed with this situation as I am.

I clear my throat. "Ready to talk today? Or are you going to keep wasting your life away in that cell?"

I already know his answer, but it doesn't keep me from asking every damn day, hoping he will answer me with even the smallest piece of information and put us both out of our misery.

Zeke's eyes cut to me. He chuckles to himself.

"What's so funny?" I ask.

"Tired of dressing like a whore, huh? Now you're going to try the tough, badass girl look?"

I look down at my outfit. I guess I wear my emotions on my body, but I'm just trying to prepare us both for what has to happen next.

"I guess so. You made it perfectly clear you don't find me attractive anymore, so why keep trying? Those dresses and heels weren't comfortable. I'd much rather wear jeans and boots."

He stares down at my boots. "Going to kick my ass with those boots? If so, you should make sure they have a metal toe; they will do more damage that way."

I hate how he can read me without saying anything. He knows I'm not here to play nice like I have every other day. Today, I'm here to hurt him. He can sense everything about me, which is why it was so surprising that my original plan worked; that I was able to trick him at all.

I didn't trick him, though. I didn't lie to him. Everything I did, felt, and said was the truth, even if it was the twisted truth.

"I wouldn't risk getting blood on my favorite pair of boots," I say.

He tosses the ball in the air again, ignoring me.

"But I'm done being nice."

Catch, toss, catch, toss...

I bite my lip to keep my frustration in. Spitting harsh words at him has no effect. The pain I inflict has to be physical. Hurting Zeke, spilling his blood, and scarring his body won't get him to talk, but at least I can tell Julian I tried everything.

But the thought of scarring Zeke's beautiful skin, cutting through his tattoos, and penetrating his muscles makes me sick. It will be more torturous for me than him.

I need something quick and effective. Something that will inflict the most pain with the least amount of effort. I've tortured plenty of men before. It's basically my job. But with Zeke—something stops me. Maybe it's knowing he didn't sell all those women—he saved them— that keeps me from wanting to hurt him.

Zeke studies me closely as he keeps tossing that stupid ball in the air. Whichever guard gave them the ball is going to get an ear chewing because it's driving me nuts right now.

"You don't have it in you to hurt me," Zeke says, smirking.

"Oh, really? Don't think I will hurt you? Tell me again how you ended up in that cage," I say.

Zeke stands up, tossing the ball on the bed—*thank god.* And then he walks over to the bars of his cage, his eyes never leaving mine.

"You may be an evil, selfish monster, but you don't enjoy torturing others. If you did, you would have done it by now. You would have hurt me day one, not waited weeks, trying to butter me up to get me to talk. That's how I know you won't hurt me, at least not more than you already did. You played your hand too soon, sweetheart."

I snap.

I grab my gun from the waistband of my jeans. I aim. And fire.

Zeke howls at the impact of the bullet driving into his leg. I'm an excellent shot. Where I hit him will result in a high level of pain without risking him bleeding out too quickly. But from the grimace on Zeke's face, he was more concerned with the fact that the bullet was less than an inch away from hitting his most sensitive of areas.

"You were saying?" I say with a grin on my face. I lower my hand, letting the gun rest next to my leg. I have no intention of shooting Zeke again, but he doesn't know that.

He grabs the metal bars, and I'm not sure if the move is meant to intimidate me or if he's holding on to remain standing on his own two feet.

I see blood ooze out from his inner thigh and spill onto his dark jeans. Beads of sweat form on his forehead as his body heats and fills with adrenaline to deal with the pain. A natural response for the body to try to stop the spread of infection.

"Now, tell me something about your boss. Something we can use to track him down or penetrate his security systems. Just one tiny piece of information, and I'll get you some painkillers, antibiotics, and gauze to deal with that wound."

A half chuckle, half growl rumbles from his body. "You think shooting me in the leg, narrowly missing my crown jewels, hurts me enough to give up even the smallest information about my friends?"

"Nope. I think I could bring you to the edge of death, and you still wouldn't give them up."

"Then why did you shoot me?"

I shrug. "Because I'm tired of being underestimated. The reason I haven't tortured you isn't because I can't handle watching a man in pain. I've tortured plenty of men. I just know you. I know hurting you isn't the way to get you to tell me your secrets.

"That's why I didn't just capture and torture you like I would other men. It's why I didn't just pick you up in a bar and seduce you. You aren't that kind of man. Torture won't work."

I smile, looking at his wound. "But it does make me a little happy to know you won't question me again. Because next time, I won't aim for your leg. I'll see if hurting you in the most intimate of ways will get you to spill."

Zeke's jaw ticks.

I study his face turning white from loss of blood. He's so stubborn that he will literally pass out first before telling me anything. And I don't want to deal with having to call in a medical team to revive him.

But I can't let him know that.

I cross my arms, seeming bored. "Start talking before you pass out."

"I'm not going to pass out. I've been hit worse than this."

I nod. "I'm sure you have. But I doubt you've been hit in the groin like this. It shocks a man's system in a different way."

He shakes his head. "I've been hit worse, trust me."

I frown.

We both stare at each other, neither of us blinking. Whoever blinks first loses. It's the unspoken rule. If I blink, he knows I'll go get him something to take care of that wound. And if he blinks, I know he will spill in order to get the drugs.

We stare.

And dammit, he lets me into his soul. His soft eyes. His big heart. His selflessness. His need to protect, even in death, rather than ever hurt his friends.

I'm going to lose.

I blink.

He smirks triumphantly.

I scrunch my face in annoyance. "Sit your ass down while I go get you a Gatorade and some gauze to stop the bleeding. But if you think you are going to get a painkiller or a drop of alcohol without giving me information, you're crazy."

Zeke doesn't move, not until I've started climbing up the stairs. But as I reach the top, I hear the creak of the mattress as he sits down.

At least he won't pass out while I'm gone.

I return a few minutes later with the supplies: Gatorade, gauze, tweezers, thread, and a needle.

I toss Zeke the Gatorade, which he catches and chugs immediately without argument. He knows he needs to be hydrated so he won't pass out from the blood loss.

Then I slide the bag with the medical supplies to him. I probably shouldn't be giving him a needle, a potential weapon, but he needs it to close up the wound I caused. And having to do it without any numbing medication is another form of torture. I've stitched up myself enough times to know the sharp sting of a needle as it pierces flesh.

I slump down on the floor, feeling defeated.

"Thanks," Zeke says, holding up the bag before he digs through it to pull out the supplies.

God, he's such a gentleman even after I've been an ass to him. What is wrong with him? I know men, and Zeke is so different than any man I've ever met before.

"Don't thank me."

"Sorry, I was taught manners. And I use them, even if you don't deserve them."

I shake my head, my hands falling between my legs. "This can't keep going on like this, Zeke. This has to end. You have to have a weak spot, some way to break you. Being nice, isn't it. Seducing you, isn't it. And torturing you, isn't it. What do I have to do to break you?"

"You had the right idea with the torture," Julian says, startling me as he speaks.

Zeke holds the gauze to his leg but stops rummaging through the bag.

I stand up, not liking being in such a vulnerable position around Julian.

Julian looks from me to Zeke. "You were just torturing the wrong person." Julian looks back at me.

"No," I say so softly that I'm not sure I even spoke the word.

Julian smirks, looking back at Zeke. "It worked before. You spilled your secrets just after I hurt her. Let's see if you still have feelings for her."

"He doesn't. He doesn't care about me that way anymore," I say, looking at Julian, pleading with my eyes for him to not hurt me again.

But I can see from his expression that he's not willing to stop without testing his theory. It worked before; he thinks it will work again. He hasn't spent time with Zeke these last few weeks, though. He doesn't know whatever connection we shared before has been broken. He doesn't know Zeke would rather watch me burn at the stake than ever say a word that could risk his friend's lives.

CHAPTER 4
ZEKE

Julian won't hurt Siren. She works for him. It would be stupid of him to hurt one of his best employees.

He did before, though.

No—whatever happened before wasn't real. It was a trick. A lie. He didn't hurt her.

But it sure felt real to me.

I close my eyes, remembering that night. I remember Siren lying naked and bound on the floor. Blood, gashes, and bruises covered her flawless skin. Her eyes were burning, and her legs were spread with Julian between them.

He didn't rape her. And he probably wouldn't have. He just wanted me to think he was going to.

But everything else was real. I felt the warm blood on her skin with my own hands. I saw the wounds on her flesh with my own eyes. I felt her heart slow in her chest. I watched her pass out from blood loss. I felt how weak she was in my arms. I smelt the alcohol he sprayed in her eyes and hoped that she would still be able to see afterward. I prayed next to her bed when her breathing got so weak I wasn't sure she'd wake up.

That was all real.

Julian really hurt her.

It wasn't fake.

He will hurt her again.

I open my eyes, the pain from that night igniting something inside me. I wince as I shift in place, and the bullet in my legs drills harder into my muscle. Siren hit me good in the leg. She's an excellent shot— to be that confident she would hit my leg and not my balls. *Or she didn't really care if she hit my balls.*

But she knew exactly where to shoot me to inflict the most pain. I don't think a single bullet has ever hurt me so much. My eyes are watering, begging me to let them cry. My teeth are grinding so hard together I'm sure I've broken at least one tooth. And my heart is jackhammering in my chest, trying to spread some pain relief throughout my body. But none of it is working.

I want some damn painkillers, alcohol, something to take this fucking hurt away. If I thought I could get away with lying to her about my boss in order to get the drugs, I would do it.

But the thought of watching Julian hurt Siren drowns out my whining thoughts about wanting painkillers.

Last time, I came into the room after he had already done the damage to her, but now, I'm going to have a front-row seat to the carnage.

Can I really just watch her get hurt without stepping in to save her?

I'm a protector. It's in my blood. *But what do I do when my choices are saving her or saving the only family I've ever known?*

Julian looks at me, and I show indifference. I press on my leg wound to distract me from what Julian is thinking of doing to Siren. *Thank god Julian can't read me as well as Siren can.*

When he turns his attention back to her, my eyes follow. And if I had any doubt about whether or not Julian would hurt her, the look on Siren's face erases it from my mind instantly.

Siren isn't a woman who is easily scared. In fact, the only time I've ever seen her truly petrified is around Julian.

But she's a fighter. She won't back down easily. She took me down even though she's less than half my size. Yes, I was distracted and not focused, but even if I wasn't, I wouldn't give myself the automatic win.

She knows how to use her skills and body in ways I've never had to learn to do. I've always relied on my physical heft to get me through, while she uses her wit.

Last time Julian hurt her, she was tied up. The men who dragged her up there may have even held her down while Julian hurt her. Or she may have agreed to take the punches in order to do the job.

But the way Siren's eyes grow wide, the way her head shakes just a little, and the way she's already inching her hand toward her gun tells me that she didn't consent to Julian hurting her again. She isn't tied up or outnumbered like last time. This time, she will fight.

Good.

I won't have to make a decision. Siren can take care of herself. Yes, I may have to watch her take a punch or two, but that's the worst that will happen. If I just remain indifferent to Julian attacking her, she can hold her own until Julian gives up.

Julian takes a step toward her, and Siren takes a step back.

I frown.

That's not the woman I've come to know. She doesn't back down. But maybe she wants to keep her distance to draw out this tense situation and really sell her fear to me, hoping I'll give in.

Julian steps again; she retreats another step.

They continue like this, both dancing around each other.

I try to focus on the wound I should be dressing, but I can't take my eyes off of them.

I don't understand their relationship. He's her boss. And she clearly gives him her loyalty. *But why, if he hurts her? Even for a good reason?* Enzo Black would never hurt me. He'd never sacrifice my life or my pain to get something he wanted.

Julian slowly inches Siren back, until she's in the corner of the room. Her hands are by her side, ready to attack.

Grab your gun. Shoot the bastard!

But her hands don't move for the gun.

"Let's see how much you mean to the bastard," Julian says.

Punch.

It comes out of nowhere and lands square on her jaw.

I hear the crack.

I can feel it in my own jaw. I've taken enough punches to know exactly how it feels. And I say with certainty, it doesn't feel good. Your eyes immediately want to water, you taste the warm thickness of your own blood on your tongue, and you see stars for a split second.

That's what Siren is going through.

Stop being Aria and turn back into Siren—the woman who calculates everything and would only take a punch if she knew she could deliver something better in return.

I wait for her to fight back.

She doesn't.

I wait for her to reach for her gun.

She doesn't.

Instead, Siren stands strong in the corner of the room, a punching bag as Julian starts attacking.

Punch, kick, jab.

Each time he hits her, more blood spills.

She doesn't beg him to stop.

She doesn't attack.

She doesn't even throw up blocks to protect herself.

She just takes it, all of it.

Fight! Dammit, fight back!

Julian hits her exceptionally hard in the ribcage, and I know he bruised her ribs if not broke some.

That snaps her out of her spell.

This time he lunges, she blocks him, not willing to take anymore. And then she strikes back.

He dodges her hit, as her movements are slow now that she's lost considerable blood.

But she's fighting back. *Yes!* It will take her a second to gather her wits, to get her adrenaline pumping, and for the need to hurt him to push out her own pain. But once it does, she will fight back like a machine.

Instead, her eyes water with fear, and her lips seem to say I'm sorry.

What?

She shouldn't apologize to this monster. He hit her a dozen times.

Her eyes cut to me one last time. And I see everything—her fear, her pain, and her apology.

She won't fight back.

Her eyes break contact and return to her attacker.

Is this her last attempt to break me? To get me to save her over my friends? Or is there another reason she's not fighting back against Julian?

Whatever is happening, I don't understand. I just know that Siren is gone, and in her place is Aria. A beautiful, strong woman in her own right, but unlike Siren, Aria won't fight. She'll sacrifice herself to protect her boss, however misguided her thinking is. She's a lot like me in that way.

I prepared myself to watch her suffer. I can handle watching her in pain. She's choosing this to try and break me. She's letting him hurt her to hurt me. *Don't let them win.*

"You surprise me, Zeke. I never thought you'd be one to enjoy watching a woman get hurt like this. But maybe I was wrong. Maybe you are the same kind of monster I am," Julian says.

He punches her in the face again, breaking her nose. I watch her cough up blood.

Fuck.

I can't sit here and do nothing much longer. *But what choice do I have?*

I feel my own eyes water, but I don't dare let them out. Julian can't see how much pain he's causing me. He has to be close to stopping.

He hits her again, and she stumbles. She's barely standing upright.

This is almost over. *Just hold on for a few more seconds.* But I don't know if I'm telling her that or myself.

Julian's eyes light up watching Siren stumble.

I'm going to kill him. He deserves to die for this moment alone.

Julian looks back to me as Siren falls to her knees, silently pleading for this to be over. She wants him to knock her out so she won't have to feel, or even remember, this pain.

I don't know if I want him to knock her unconscious or not. I just can't watch her in pain anymore.

This next one is the final strike. I know it.

Julian stares at my wound, and then he pulls something from his pocket—a syringe.

"Here," he tosses the needle to me. "For the pain in your leg."

I catch the syringe staring at it cautiously. *Why is he easing my physical pain?*

Julian reaches back and pulls something else out—a gun.

"No!" I scream, but I'm too late.

He shoots her in the leg, in the same spot she shot me.

The syringe falls from my hands onto my crumple of blankets and pillows as I watch Siren writhe on the floor in pain. But unfortunately or fortunately, she doesn't pass out.

"Well—well, I guess I was right. You do have a conscious," Julian says, smiling.

I grab the bars, looking down at Siren covered in blood and pain. She doesn't look at me. She just lies still. She doesn't even grip her gunshot leg.

"Tell me something that can help me locate Mr. Black, or I'll shoot her again. And this time, I won't be so kind with my bullet placement," Julian says.

I stare down at Siren. *Hold on. I'll save you, just hold on.*

"Enzo Black has family in Greece. That is why he was there. Locate his family there, and you'll be able to set a trap for the next time he heads to Greece," I say.

Julian grins. "That wasn't so hard, was it?"

I ignore him and stare at Siren, who still isn't moving or speaking.

Julian looks down at her. "Get yourself cleaned up, and meet me in my office by six. We have work to do."

And then Julian leaves, not bothering to help Siren at all.

I watch her carefully, hoping she won't pass out now because there is nothing I can do to help her if she does. Her eyes close tightly as a single tear rolls down her cheek.

"Why do you work for him?" I ask.

She doesn't answer.

"Why didn't you fight back?" I ask.

No answer.

I sigh.

And then I hobble back to the medical bag and syringe on the floor. One plunge of the needle into my leg would give me incredible relief. But there is only one syringe, and Siren needs it more than I do.

"Here," I say, holding out the medicine.

Siren looks at me finally, her eyes wide as she stares at what I'm offering her—relief from her pain, while I get none.

She shakes her head. "You really don't understand that you need to stop saving me, do you?"

"Saving people is what I do, even undeserving people."

Slowly, she sits up, and I realize Julian's aim isn't as good as hers. He hit an artery. She's going to bleed out within minutes.

"Get the hell over here so I can stitch you up before you bleed to death," I say.

She glances down and then inches over as I crumple onto the ground.

"Hand me the gauze," she says.

I do, and she holds it on her leg to stop the bleeding. She leans against the bars; her breathing slow and weak. She's barely staying awake. But when her eyes look up at me, I know she has something she wants to say.

"Let's hear it," I say.

"Julian will realize you lied. You won't be able to get away with doing that a second time. But..." she moans. "But thank you for saving my life. He wouldn't have stopped until he killed me. So thank you, even though I don't deserve it. Even though, in the end, you'd be better off if I were dead."

She's killing me with her gratitude.

And I can't stand to see her in pain anymore.

So in a moment of weakness, I do what will ultimately stop my own pain. I grab the syringe and plunge it into her leg.

I do what I always do—I save her instead of myself.

CHAPTER 5
SIREN

"You shouldn't have done that," I say, staring down at where Zeke plunged the needle into my leg.

The warmth of the drugs immediately starts spreading, sending new signals of comfort through my nerves—instead of pain.

I take a deep breath in and out. The stabbing, sharp pain leaves my leg and is replaced with a dull ache, matching the rest of my body.

I need to have a word with Julian. It's not okay for him to beat me every time he wants to get Zeke to talk. I'll be dead by the end of the week if he keeps this up.

"Yes, I should have," Zeke's husky voice brings me back to reality. I'll figure out how to deal with Julian later. Right now, I have a bullet in my leg, broken ribs, and a shattered nose. It hurts to breathe, and I don't even want to think about the pain of standing, even with the narcotics soothing me.

I look up at Zeke and see him painfully staring down at me. But not pain from his own wounds. He's not even gripping his leg anymore. He's looking at me in agony. His eyes run over every injury on my body, assessing the damage, trying to pull my pain from my body with his eyes.

I'm still his weakness. He'd rather be in pain than watch me struggle. Julian was right. Even after everything I've done to Zeke, he's still willing to protect me. And it will be his downfall.

"Here," Zeke says, pushing the medic bag through the slits of the bars. He was shot in the same spot I was, but again, he puts my needs above his own. Yes, he doesn't have any other physical injuries, like I do, but we share the most serious wound. And he needs treatment as much as I do.

I push the bag back through the gap.

"You need this," Zeke says, trying to push it back through.

"Stop." I give him a stern look.

He moves to fight me again, but I wince as the bag hits my leg, and he stops. My moan is much louder than necessary to get my point across, but I need him to listen to me.

I scoot my body around to face the door of Zeke's cage. I can feel his gaze on me, but I don't turn to look or stop to explain to him what I'm doing.

Reaching the door is the easy part; the hard part comes next.

I grab one of the bars and start lifting my body up.

"Siren, stop!" Zeke says, running to the door in an instant like he isn't injured at all. He calls me by Siren instead of Aria, like he forgot my real name. And I don't know which name I prefer falling from his lips. *Any name, as long as it isn't 'lying bitch.'*

"No, it's my turn to protect you."

He frowns.

I pull myself up, standing on my good leg as I reach into my back pocket and pull out the key that opens Zeke's cell. A key I haven't used since I first locked him in this cage.

I push the key in the lock and turn; the spring of the lock immediately clicking. I push on the bar door, and it falls open.

I lose my balance as I'm only standing on one leg, and I was leaning too harshly against the bar door.

I'm going to fall to the ground, and it's going to hurt. I don't even have the strength to catch my fall with my outstretched hands.

But instead of hitting the ground, I hit something else. Something equally as strong, but also soft—Zeke. His arms absorb most of my fall, but my head collides with his chest.

A shock of electricity surges through my body at the contact. I feel alive again. The pain shatters. And I want...I want more of this. I just want to be held in his arms, where I feel safe.

"Easy," Zeke says, as he slowly lowers us to the ground. His hands never leave my body.

My head continues to rest against his chest as I sit between his legs.

"We need to fix this," Zeke says, running his hand over my thigh near my wound.

I lean back against his chest and turn so I can see his wound, and then I do the same, my hand feeling his thigh muscles flex. "And this."

Zeke reaches around me to grab the medical bag. He digs in and pulls out a pair of tweezers and rubbing alcohol.

"Don't look," he says.

I bite my lip, smiling. "You numbed my leg, remember? I won't be able to feel anything."

"That's not what I'm worried about."

I tilt my head up and see Zeke look into my eyes. He's afraid I will groan anyway. That I will have pain in my eyes. That it will hurt him too much to cause me any pain.

It's sweet—Zeke is sweet. But I don't like sweet.

I roll my eyes and grab the tweezers from his hand. Then I dig into my wound and pull out the bullet before tossing it on the ground outside of the cage. Then I press a piece of gauze over my leg.

Zeke shakes his head in awe. "You're something else, Siren."

"Aria."

"No, when you are being a badass, you're Siren."

I frown. "Aria is pretty badass too."

Zeke strokes my face. "No, Aria is courageous and sweet. Siren kicks ass."

I smile and then look down at his wound. "Do you want me to do the honors? Or would you like to do it?"

Even though pulling the bullet from my own leg was uncomfortable, it's nothing compared to what Zeke will feel with a pair of tweezers in his leg. He's not numb. I was.

"You do it," he surprises me by saying.

"I wish I had some alcohol or something to offer you for the pain."

He chuckles. "This is nothing, remember? You have no idea what my past life was like. I got shot on a weekly basis."

He places his hand on mine, where I'm holding the blood-soaked gauze to my own wound. I slip my hand out from beneath his, and then he applies pressure, the blood instantly slowing again.

I hold the tweezers in my other hand and then move to examine his would. The bullet looks deep, not near the surface. I use my left hand to gently open the wound so I can get a better look. And then I dive in, knowing the faster I get this done, the faster his pain will stop.

It takes me about ten seconds to find the bullet and pull it out. As I do, one of his arteries starts squirting blood.

Shit.

I grab gauze and apply hard pressure.

Stop, please stop.

Zeke doesn't move. He doesn't moan. He doesn't even flinch at the pain he must be drowning in.

"I need the needle and thread, now," I say calmly, not letting up my pressure.

Zeke doesn't move fast enough. At this rate, he'll bleed to death.

I grab for the bag and find the items I need. But I need Zeke to apply hard pressure while I start stitching.

"Give me your hands," I say.

"But—"

"Now," I snap, not caring about my own wound right now. He needs to apply a lot of pressure or he'll bleed out and die before I can get upstairs to call an ambulance.

I grab Zeke's hands and put them on his leg. I pull off my shirt and tie it around his thigh, making a tourniquet.

Zeke starts moving his hands.

"Don't you dare move. You move, you die."

He stills, immediately.

I start pushing the needle through his flesh, not caring how gentle I'm being or that he doesn't have any painkillers to numb his agony. I work quickly and efficiently, mending the artery and closing up the wound in his leg. Every second that passes feels like an hour.

Finally, I finish. Zeke removes my shirt from around his leg, and he carefully moves his hands away.

I look up at him. He looks pale, but he's still breathing. He's going to make it.

"My turn," he says, lifting my leg up onto his lap.

I don't argue with him.

He finds a new needle and thread and goes to work on my wound. His fingers are slow and gentle, unlike my furious stitch job. My bleeding isn't as bad as his, and my pain is numbed, so I can barely feel a thing. But for a moment, I wish that I could feel, even the pain. Because then it would be easier to feel the brush of Zeke's fingers against my skin.

Finally, he finishes the last loop.

And then we are left staring at each other. I'm in nothing but my bra and jeans. I'm still bloodied and bruised, but I can barely feel anything other than my need to say so much, and yet not being able to say anything, to Zeke.

And from the look on Zeke's face, he wants to speak to me too.

But neither of us say a word.

Zeke digs through the bag and finds a fresh cloth. Then he grabs my chin gently and begins wiping my face with it. It's only then that I realize how much blood and sweat are covering my body. He starts with my face, neck, then shoulders. His hand trails over my breasts and then eases over my badly bruised ribs. He stops when he gets to my blood-caked jeans.

His eyes look up at mine, asking for permission.

I nod.

His coarse fingers unbutton my jeans, then unzip the zipper, and finally, he begins pushing the jeans off my hips. It's not meant to be sexual. He moves more like a caretaker undressing me. But the heat from his fingers, the lust in his eyes, and his teeth biting his lip tell me that this could turn sexual in a moment.

Once my jeans are gone, he wipes the blood from my legs until I'm clean.

Then I turn and face him. He's just as bloody, even though his leg is the only damaged part of him. But I gaze at the hem of his shirt, wanting to do the same thing he did to me.

He nods, as I did.

And then I lift it, exposing his rippling muscles and tattoo-covered body. I dig out a clean cloth and begin cleaning his body of any remnants of blood. As I do, I notice things I didn't before—scars and healed bullet wounds. Someone did a number on his body. He's right in saying that the pain from one bullet is nothing compared to what he's used to handling.

I move to his jeans. I unbutton them, then unzip, ignoring the erection pressing against the zipper. And then I slowly start pulling the jeans down off his hips, trying to limit the pain I'm causing him. Eventually, his pants are free.

I clean away the blood on his legs, forcing myself to focus on his wound, his pain, and not on his enormous package I never got to explore. That might be my biggest regret: not letting him fuck me before I betrayed him. At least I would have that memory. Not that the memory of him licking me, bringing me to orgasm, is a bad memory—it's one of my favorites.

"Let me go see what alcohol or narcotics I can find for you," I say, moving to stand up.

But between my leg throbbing and Zeke grabbing my arm, I don't get far. I fall back against Zeke's warm chest and immediately close my eyes.

This—this is what I need.

Zeke drapes his arm around me, holding me to him.

"This is all I need—stay. The pain hurts less when you're here," Zeke says.

Zeke takes away my pain too.

I close my eyes and decide not to argue with him. It's probably not a smart move. The door to the cell is unlocked. Zeke could run if he wanted to. He could overpower me, hurt me.

But he won't.

Because unlike every other man in my life, Zeke is a good guy.

He saved me.

He protected all those women who Julian wanted him to sell.

And then he saved me again.

He put me first.

No other man has ever done that.

Slowly, I feel the pull of sleep overtake me. And I welcome it. Being in Zeke's arms will force me to dream of him. I'll dream of something I will never have.

Sleep pulls me under.

Sometime in the middle of the night, I wake. We are no longer sitting in the middle of the cell. We are lying on Zeke's bed. My head lies on his chest, and his arms are wrapped around me tightly. We are both practically naked, wearing only our underwear.

I shouldn't have stayed. I've stirred up feelings in both of us we can't act on.

But I feel safe in his arms, even though I shouldn't. Zeke could betray me as easily as I did him. Julian will encourage it. And I'll end up hurt again.

These feelings aren't real. It's just the drugs and pain talking.

I move to slip out from under Zeke's arm.

"Stay," Zeke says.

He doesn't open an eye, but I feel his arm constrict around me.

"Why? This won't end well. We shouldn't feel anything but hatred for each other."

He smiles with his eyes still closed. "I never was one for feeling what I should."

"What do you feel?"

He opens his eyes. "Safe."

I exhale a breath I didn't realize I was holding. *Safe*—I don't know what I was hoping he would feel, but safe wasn't the word I wanted. I wanted more, even though I don't deserve it. Although, what I should hope is that Zeke feels nothing, or better yet, feels hatred for me.

"Promise me, Zeke," I whisper against his neck so the cameras Julian placed won't be able to see.

"Promise what?"

"Promise me that when the time comes, you'll choose yourself."

He frowns.

"Don't choose to protect Mr. Black, or your friends, or your family, or me. Don't choose the innocent lives. Choose to save yourself."

It should be an easy promise. If he truly hates me, he'd make it easily.

Instead, he grunts, and then moments later, he's asleep as if it were all a dream. *Maybe it was.*

I should go.

But I don't, because I too feel safe.

So instead, I drift back to sleep in Zeke's arms and know that no matter what, I won't regret this moment tomorrow. Not for a second.

CHAPTER 6
ZEKE

Choose you.

Her words haunt me all night. I dream about them, have nightmares about them. But every time I awoke and saw that Siren was still in my arms, I calmed.

I told her I felt safe with her here, and I do.

But I also feel so much more.

Lust.

Want.

Need.

My cock is fucking painful as it presses into her ass. I want her so badly. My one regret about how we spent our time together was never fucking her. I should have seduced her that first night. Then, we could have spent our entire time fucking instead of dancing around the issue.

Now it's too late.

My leg feels stiff and painful, but I won't move, not until she's awake. I'll cherish every moment of her in my arms. Because in my heart, I know this will be the last time. The last time I feel her warm skin against my bare chest. The last time I'll smell her sweet scent. The last time my heart will beat in sync with hers.

It will also be the last time I feel like this—like I want her. I want to kiss her.

The only reason I feel any of those things now is because Julian discovered my weakness. I can't stand to see others hurt—especially those who can't or won't fight back.

I don't know why Siren didn't fight back against Julian, but it killed me watching it happen. It stung every time I drove the needle through her body, closing her wound. And when she painfully whimpered out in her sleep, it was like my heart was being stabbed over and over.

Watching her suffer hurt me worse than getting shot.

But it doesn't change the fact that she betrayed me. She chose herself over me. And she will do it again.

I kiss her hair, taking a deep breath. Siren is beautiful and strong and incredible, but she's not mine. Her heart doesn't belong to me. She doesn't love me. I suspect she isn't even capable of love.

We have that in common. We will never love. But that is where we diverge. Because she will always choose herself, while I will always choose others.

I feel her stirring in my arms, and our time together is over. In the daylight, with our wounds closed, our hearts will shut too. But it was nice to imagine, even for a moment, that we could be something more.

Siren doesn't say anything as she slowly sits up, and this time, I let her. I don't pull her back into my empty arms.

She turns and looks at me, while I study her flawless skin. Yes, her skin is marked with scars, bruises, and injuries, but to me, it's flawless. Because it's her, and it represents how tough she is, like body armor.

I can tell she feels like she should put some clothes on, but the only clothes for her to wear are covered in blood, sweat, and dirt on the floor.

I open my mouth to speak, but she puts a finger to my lips.

"I'll be right back," she says.

I frown, but let her go. It takes her a while to stand, her body adjusting to the pain in her leg, ribs, and face. The narcotics from last night have clearly worn off, but she doesn't make a sound or grimace as the pain consumes her body. She's focused and determined on her task.

Eventually, she starts walking. Magically, she makes it up the stairs. She doesn't bother locking the door. *I could make a run for it.*

But I don't. I want her to come back. And I can't leave until I have a plan to kill Julian.

A few minutes later, she returns with a bottle of whiskey and clothes in her hands.

She stumbles, and I jump up intending to catch her, but my leg gives out, and I fall back into the bed. Apparently, taking it slow like Siren did is the way to go.

She recovers from her stumble and shakes her head. "You will never put yourself first, will you?"

She holds out the whiskey bottle to me. I take it and take a swift drink. Alcohol isn't always the best for healing, but it sure helps with the pain. And I'm tired of acting like my own suffering means nothing.

I hold it back to her, but she shakes her head.

"Siren," I say sternly.

She takes the whiskey bottle and takes a long drink.

I smile.

But then she holds out clothes, and I frown.

She laughs.

"Get dressed, I'm tired of looking at your scrawny, ugly ass body," she teases.

"Ugly? And scrawny? Huh?"

She nods playfully.

I snatch all the clothes from her hands. "Fine, but I'll need all of these clothes to cover my body then. I wouldn't want you to have to look at an inch of my ugly ass."

She tries to grab back one of the T-shirts she intended to wear. But I hold it high out of reach. But then she jumps, and the impact of her hitting the ground again brings us both back to reality.

"Fuck, Siren!"

I grab her and pull her back into my arms as I study her leg.

"You popped a stitch," I say.

She looks down at the trail of blood trickling down her inner thigh. I wipe the blood away with my thumb, and then I suck it.

Her eyes grow big, and she bites her bottom lip. "I'm not sure if that was the sexiest thing I've ever seen, or the grossest."

I laugh. "Let me fix you up."

I pull her into my lap, and then she leans back to grab the medical kit. I pull out the items I need and then get to work stitching her up. I'm very aware she doesn't have any narcotics numbing her skin his time. So I hesitate.

"Just stab me already. Take out your anger on my skin," she says with a smile.

I roll my eyes and then do as she says.

She moans dramatically, like I've just shot her again.

I stop. *Did I really hurt her?*

She laughs. "God, you're gullible. If I was a better actress, I could get you to do anything I wanted."

"I thought you didn't lie?"

"I don't."

"What was that, then?"

"Acting, and very bad acting at that."

I want to ask her the next question—*why can't she lie?*

But I don't. I have a million questions, but none of them I ask.

I push the needle through her skin again, carefully this time, but she doesn't move or moan or make any sound to indicate that I hurt her. I've stitched up buddies before, but never a woman. And never my enemy.

She's my enemy—I have to remember that.

I finish the stitch, and then I look up. Siren is staring into my eyes with such emotion that I can't read her expression.

She's two women—Aria and Siren. My enemy and a woman I could love with everything I have.

My hand strokes her thigh automatically; her skin warms under my touch. Her skin isn't the only thing that warms—her eyes soften and her lips part.

I want her.

She wants me.

She's still not wearing a shirt or pants, and I'm dying to explore all of her body—her breasts, her stomach, and I need to get reacquainted with her pussy. The way she's staring at my chest, abs, and biceps; the way she avoids looking down to see my growing erection, all tell me she wants to get to know my body too, even though she won't admit it.

I lean close, so close that a heavy breath could push our lips together. So close that kissing her seems inevitable instead of just something I want.

My siren doesn't move away. But she doesn't close the gap. I won't close the gap either. I won't make the first move, not after what she did to me. But I won't stop this from happening either.

I *need* this to happen. I need to finish the physical connection we started—fuck Siren out of my system. Use her and then hurt her like she did me. Have my one moment with Siren and then turn her into Aria, the sweet girl I want nothing to do with.

The moment stretches into infinity. Both of us too stubborn to move the final inch, both too needy to move away.

My gaze falls down to her bra. *Maybe it will just snap open?* The straps look pretty thin and worn after all.

Jesus, I can't keep this up much longer. I need to move. I need to taste her.

Her breath heats against my mouth. *Yes, just give in, Siren.*

She closes her eyes. She's going to falter. She's going to kiss me.

"Truth or sin?" she says, her eyes opening in pain.

"What?" I ask, shocked that she spoke instead of kissing me.

She stands up and grabs the clothes I dropped on the floor next to us. She grabs an oversized shirt and slips it over her body, wearing it like a dress. Then she picks up another shirt and sweatpants and hands them to me.

The moment has passed, so I don't argue, taking the clothes from her and putting them on. With us dressed, our hormones won't get the best of us again. I will never kiss Siren again. I may never even have an excuse to touch her skin.

I nod. She wants to play this game, so she goes first.

Siren sits down, crossing her legs in front of her like a child, instead of the serpent she is. I wait for her question. A question I won't answer—about my former boss, about my friends. *Not going to happen.* But it means she will get to commit a sin if I don't answer her question with the truth.

Her eyes read my thoughts, and she smiles—such a beautiful genuine smile.

Don't fall for it.

"Why did you plunge that syringe into my leg instead of your own?" she asks.

I frown. She gave me an easy question she already knows the answer to. *Does she think me answering is going to make me feel weak?* Because being who I am will never make me feel anything but strong.

My eyes sear into hers, as I shift my weight forward and sit on the edge of the mattress on the floor, leaning as close to her as possible. "You already know my answer, but since you don't trust actions, only words—the truth is I couldn't handle seeing you in pain. Watching you thrash in pain was worse than my own pain. To stop my own torment, I had to stop yours. You are still my weakness," I say, admitting every-thing. It's the truth, and she knows it. It's why I told Julian a lie to protect her. She may think she's the only special one, but she isn't. I save and protect people. Put any other woman in Siren's place, and I would have done the same thing.

"But don't think for a second that just because I don't like seeing you suffer, it means that I will always protect you. That ship sailed the second you sold me out to Julian."

Her smile brightens. "Good, because I don't want you to save me, Zeke. I never have."

I growl and attack her without thinking. She's on her back, and I'm sprawled on top of her. My leg spreads hers, my breath coats her face, and my arms have her pinned beneath me.

She's not scared though, nor pissed. In fact, she's turned on seeing this side of me, the side that takes instead of asking.

Her eyes light up, looking at me. "Your turn."

Dammit, this is probably part of her game. Get me so turned on I can't think straight to get me to ask an easy, softball question instead of one where I get to sin. I take a deep breath, trying to clear Siren from my thoughts. *Like that's going to happen.* I need to fuck her, then I can get her out of my head, and my cock can stop begging for her. It will realize she's just like any other woman I've ever fucked. My brain will realize that even though she has boobs and a pussy, she is basically an extension of Julian—my enemy, a person I need to take out, not protect.

I open my mouth to speak but stop. I debate which question I want the answer to before finally deciding. "Why didn't you fight back against Julian?"

She doesn't break eye contact, not even to bat her eyelashes at me. "Sin."

She arches her back, her pointed nipples poking through her bra and T-shirt and stabbing me in the chest. I push my groin higher up against her soaked panties. Her eyes darken, and she licks her luscious lips—lips I haven't tasted in far too long.

"Screw it," I say and do both what I want and shouldn't do, which makes this a sin—I kiss her.

Our lips crash together in a sexy ambush. She can't move beneath me, and I grip her wrists to keep myself from exploring too much of her body too quickly. I just focus on her lips. Her fucking swollen lips know exactly how to kiss me. Her lips part just enough to allow plenty of tongue, and what a magnificent tongue she has. It has so many more talents than just lying to me and pretending to only speak the truth. Her tongue teases and taunts mine, before finally surrendering.

But God, her moans are intoxicating. I could live off her sweet moans. They penetrate every ounce of my body and shoot straight to my cock. I'm desperate for her. My cock is throbbing between her legs, and I could easily rip the clothes that separate us and drive through until I'm buried deep inside her.

She tries to move her wrists, desperate to tangle her hands in my hair as much as I am to tangle my hands in hers. We both want this sin with everything we have.

We want this kiss to never end.

We want this kiss to turn to more.

We want this kiss to become fucking.

I slowly let go of her wrist, needing to feel more of her soft flesh, but not wanting her to have too much power. I don't even want to give her the ability to control her own hand, but needing to feel her skin wins out.

I run my hand up her thigh as I continue to taste her mouth.

Slowing my kisses as I feel more of her, taking my time, so I get to experience all of her.

My hand slides up her side, pushing the T-shirt she is wearing up her smooth skin.

"I wish I could enjoy my sin without you enjoying it as well." I bite her lip, sucking it furiously, and I instantly feel her soak my sweatpants between her legs. "But I know that you are going to enjoy this sin as much as I will."

The sound of footsteps startles me. I instantly jerk Siren up and into my arms and away from whatever danger is approaching. But from the slow, careful descent of the steps, I know who is approaching. And I don't know who he is more dangerous to—Siren or me.

Julian appears at the bottom of the stairs in a full suit, like he's attending a formal dinner instead of creeping on us in the basement.

I look around the room searching for cameras, and I spot a dozen places where there are likely some hidden. That means he can see and hear every word Siren and I have said.

I shoot Siren a glare as I think back to everything we said or did. *What did Julian hear?* And he almost got to see what was mine—Siren, her body at least.

"Oh, don't stop on my account," Julian says, smiling.

"What do you want?" I ask.

"Just to say that your little tip was fake, a lie. It's something I wouldn't usually put up with, but after listening in on your little conversation, I got an idea."

I loosen my grip on Siren, who doesn't seem in any hurry to get out of my arms. It doesn't surprise me considering what Julian did to her, but he's still her boss, and I'm her enemy, why is she still in my arms?

"What is your brilliant idea? Releasing me and giving me a boat to leave on?"

Julian laughs. "I can see what the ladies see in you; you are a funny one." He walks further into the room, before leaning against the open door of the cell and crossing his arms as he looks from Siren to me.

"This truth or sin game seems intriguing. Have room for a third player?"

CHAPTER 7
SIREN

I should have been more careful. I shouldn't have played our truth or sin game, knowing Julian had cameras hidden in the basement. I shouldn't have let Zeke kiss me...

But God, what a kiss.

Zeke's kisses are like nothing I've ever felt before. They are toe-curling, fireworks shooting, and every other cliché in the book. His kisses wreck my soul and make me wish I could kidnap Zeke and travel far away from here—start my life over with just him and me.

But that can never happen.

I've been careless, selfish even. I wanted Zeke to kiss me again. I wanted so much more than just a kiss. I wanted every physical thing Zeke was offering.

And I would have gotten it, if Julian hadn't interrupted. Some small part of me is thankful Julian did interrupt before I let things go too far. Because once I fuck Zeke, there is no going back. I can keep protecting my heart from falling for a man like Zeke, but my lady bits —that's another story.

I already know from the way Zeke kisses, from the way he licked me like I was his favorite flavor of ice cream, that if he fucked me, he would ruin me for any other man. No man would ever compare to him, and I would always crave Zeke. He would have the upper hand again, and I can't let that happen. I need to be in control. I need to manipulate him into giving up Enzo Black.

"The truth or sin game is invite-only, and I don't remember inviting you," Zeke answers, his voice deep and throaty.

Every word the man speaks is sexy and makes me constantly on edge and soaked with need.

Julian stares at me, like I'm his. *I guess I am.*

I'm usually comfortable wearing very little clothes. My body is fit and curvy, most men's dream body. And I flaunt it often. It's how I get information for Julian from men. But the only man in the world whose gaze scares me is Julian's.

I should have put pants on. And a baggy sweatshirt. Anything to cover every inch of my skin, because the way Julian is looking at me scares the hell out of me. I can't tell if he wants to taste me, fuck me, or beat me.

Julian laughs. "I think you are forgetting one important detail. You don't get a say in your life anymore. You are locked in that cell, and I'm out here, so I suggest you hear my proposal."

Zeke raises an eyebrow as he runs his hand up my ass and over my smooth stomach like he owns me. I love the feeling of his hand on my skin. I love him taking charge over my body, demanding me to surrender to him. But I don't like him doing it with Julian in the room.

Zeke nods to the cell door. "Seems I've already figured out how to get the door open. I don't think I'm the one whose trapped or should be worried. I would sleep with one eye open if I were you."

"Cockiness doesn't suit you, Zeke." Julian looks at me and snaps his fingers.

I hate being called like a dog, but I'd rather not get beaten or shot again. So I comply. I reluctantly climb out from under Zeke. The ache in my heart is worse than the ache in my leg as I stand, and Zeke's hands fall from my body. He is no longer willing to protect me, not when I'm following Julian's orders. And I don't blame him.

It's better this way.

Knowing it's right doesn't temper the pain from walking away from Zeke, again. And from knowing that this time might be really goodbye. This time will put us squarely on different sides of the line. Enemy versus enemy. There will be no going back. We won't be able to protect each other anymore. I have to protect myself, and Zeke is insistent on protecting Enzo Black and his family.

I pull the T-shirt I'm wearing down until it's covering my ass again, and then I walk proudly over to Julian, like I'd prefer to be by his side instead of Zeke's.

Julian strokes my hair in the way I wish Zeke had the chance to do.

"You are just as trapped as ever, Zeke. You just fell for Aria's beauty and spell again," Julian says.

Zeke doesn't look at me. He doesn't change his expression at all, like the comment didn't even hurt him. Like I mean nothing to him. Not like he didn't just have me trapped and writhing under his body, as his erection pushed between my legs. He can pretend all he wants that I mean nothing to him, but I know the truth. His body can't lie to me.

Julian smirks. "Now, as I was saying. I would like to make you an offer."

"There is nothing you can say to make me turn on my friends," Zeke says.

Julian plays with the ends of my hair as he looks from me to Zeke. His eyes eventually land on the wound Zeke stitched up, more evidence of Zeke's lust for me.

"I'm sure I can find some reason that you might reconsider giving up your friends for," Julian says, referring to me. He doesn't realize Zeke only wants me for my body. He doesn't care about me. He doesn't love me. He doesn't even like me.

"Never," Zeke says.

Julian lets go of my hair, and my stomach settles just a little.

"I thought you'd say that, which is why my deal includes an option other than spilling your friends' secrets," Julian says.

Zeke narrows his gaze, his teeth snarling like a wolf about to attack.

I stand still, watching the two men threaten each other with their bodies.

"As I said before, I'd like to play the truth or sin game with you," Julian says.

Zeke turns up his nose and makes a disgusted look. "You do understand that when I say truth or sin, that sin means something sexual. You may be into men, but I have no desire to fuck you, Julian."

"I think you'd very much like to fuck me, and that's why you'll say yes to my arrangement."

Zeke doesn't spit a comeback. He just waits to hear what sneaky deal Julian has come up with that will more than likely be a win-win for Julian and a lose-lose for Zeke.

"I don't care how you play the game with Aria. With me, the rules are simple. We will play five rounds. Well—you will play five rounds. I won't be offering up any truths or sins of my own," Julian says.

There it is. Julian will play the game by not having to risk anything in the first place.

"Each round, I will offer you a chance to answer a simple question with the truth. If you refuse, you will complete a sin. Any sin that I choose."

"And what's in it for me?" Zeke asks.

Nothing, nothing is in it for you. The sooner you figure that out, Zeke, the sooner you will figure out how to get free.

"Once you complete all five rounds, I'll set you free. I'll even throw in a boat."

"That's not good enough," Zeke answers.

"I figured it wouldn't be." Julian cuts his eyes to me and winks, like he and I are in cahoots. The truth is, I'm on nobody's side but my own. "I also promise not to harm Mr. Black until you have completed all five rounds."

Zeke's pupils dilate. *Julian's got him.* Zeke could protect his boss for as long as the five rounds go on, and as soon as the game is over, he could run to his friends' rescue. All Zeke ever wants is to protect those he loves. I don't know exactly how many people that includes, but I know it's Mr. Black and the immediate people around him. Zeke will take the deal.

I try to catch Zeke's attention, to warn him with my eyes, my tight lips, my clenched jaw. But he doesn't glance my way. And even if he did, I doubt he would listen to me.

Julian, on the other hand, is practically giddy. He knows that Zeke will accept his offer. He knows Zeke's weakness.

"I'll throw in one more sweetener," Julian says.

I still—I don't like the sound of that. Julian never offers something for nothing.

Zeke practically growls in response. He, too, knows that Julian isn't going to offer something without asking for more in return.

Julian wraps his arm around my waist and pulls me tightly to his side, stroking my hip over my shirt. If he so much as slips his hand beneath my shirt, I'm going to kill him. I put my hand on top of Julian's, not even pretending to enjoy his touch. I dig my nails into his hand so hard that I'm sure I'm making him bleed.

Julian, to his credit, doesn't wince, hiss, or pull his hand away. He just takes the pain like he deserves it.

Zeke's lip curls up the tiniest bit, and I know he sees my nails digging into Julian's hand.

"To give you a little more incentive to complete the sins or tell the truth, you'll be playing with Aria's life," Julian says.

I frown, my hand pushing Julian's off my body as I stare at him incredulously. He can't bargain with my life. He has no right. I'm his employee. His best employee, in fact. He can't just decide that he can offer up my life if Zeke fails.

"You complete the five rounds by either telling the truth or completing the sins, and Aria lives. If you lie, or fail to complete a single one of the sins, then Aria dies," Julian says.

I narrow my gaze and tighten my lips. I can't call out Julian's bluff for what it is—a lie. Julian would never kill me. But the bullet in my leg would feel like a scratch if I outed Julian to Zeke.

"And if I decline your offer entirely?" Zeke asks.

Julian grins, thinking he's won. He knows exactly how to take out Zeke.

"Then I'll kill Aria and go after Mr. Black on my own."

I swallow hard.

Lies.

They're all lies!

Don't make the deal, Zeke. It will destroy you.

But some tiny part of me wants Zeke to agree. I want to know that he is still willing to put my life before his own. I still want to be under Zeke's protection. I want him to save me, even at the expense of himself.

Now, it's Zeke's turn to laugh. "Really? That's your offer? Take your deal, or you'll kill Aria?" Zeke's beautiful eyes look to me, taunting me with his disgust for me. "I've wanted Aria dead since the moment I learned she was working for you. So the fact that you'll do it for me if I refuse just incentivizes me to turn down your offer."

"So is that your decision? You are refusing my offer?" Julian asks, with a smile.

Fuck, this is all part of Julian's plan. There is no way for Zeke to win.

"Yes, I decline your offer. I'd rather stay in this cell for the rest of my life than take your deal."

Julian chuckles and then links his arm through mine. "Well, that answers that question. I guess he doesn't love you, after all, Aria. He doesn't care if you live or die, which means you are of no more use to me. Tomorrow, you die."

My eyes cut to Zeke. I know that Julian is bluffing, but Zeke doesn't. I study Zeke's reaction; his face is unmoved. His eyes don't widen with worry; his lips don't tense with fret; his heart doesn't thump wildly begging Julian to reconsider.

Zeke truly doesn't care if I live or die.

Even though I know Julian won't kill me tomorrow, it still hurts knowing that Zeke will no longer protect me.

CHAPTER 8
ZEKE

I should have said yes. I should have accepted Julian's offer, but I couldn't let Siren have the upper hand again. I couldn't let her know that I care about her, even the tiniest bit. She can't have control over me, not again.

I stare at the floor as Siren walks to the cell door, closes it, and then locks it. I can feel her eyes on me, even though I refuse to return her gaze. But I hear the clink of the door and the clank of the lock as the door closes, and I feel her stare on me.

She takes a heavy breath, sighing before following Julian up the stairs.

And then I'm alone. Except for the security cameras, I'm truly alone for the first time in weeks. No guard. No Julian. And no Siren.

Just me with my thoughts and regret.

I made my decision to save myself instead of Siren, but only because I don't truly think she is in any danger. Julian won't kill her. He'll hurt her, torture her, but not kill her. She's too valuable to him.

But what if I'm wrong?

What if he kills her?

What if I chose myself over her?

I shake the thought from my head. I have more important things to worry about right now—like how to get out of here and protect my friends from Julian.

I walk back to the bed and sit down; my leg is sore and achy. But then I spot the bottle of whiskey Siren brought in. She didn't take it with her. I grab the bottle and take a long swig, quickly feeling the sting of pain reducing.

At least I have this bottle to keep me comfortable.

I move my legs to swing them onto the mattress, but my leg bumps into something. I look down—the medical bag. Siren left it.

I grab the bag and quickly rummage through it to find something to use to unlock the door. I keep my ears open, listening carefully in case a guard comes downstairs, so I can hide the bag quickly if one does. This bag holds the key to my escape; I can't let anyone know I have it.

I find a needle.

And then look to the door. *Should I try it now or wait?*

I can't wait. There aren't any guards watching me, at least none in the basement. This might be my only chance. Even if a guard is watching me on the security cameras, it could take a minute or two for them to get down here. This is my only chance.

I run to the door, quickly loop my arms through the bars, and press the needle inside the lock.

One...

Two...

Three...I feel the rattle of the lock turning over, and then I gently push the door open.

I'm free of my cage.

Now, I need to save my friends. I need to escape. But most of all, I need to kill Julian.

I creep carefully up the stairs, completely silent, so if a guard is waiting upstairs, they won't hear me.

I open the door to the main floor of the house I stayed in for months. A house that was just as much a cage as the bars holding me in the basement, even though it might have been a bit more comfortable.

I squint as the sunlight hits my eyes for the first time in months. I blink several times, trying to adjust. And right now, I can't decide if I missed the sun or want it to go away again.

Finally refocused, I look around my house and find no guards.

My heart lightens with hope. I might really be able to get free. Or at the very least, protect my friends by killing Julian.

But if I fail, I at least need to warn them.

I move through the shadows of the house until I find one of the guns I hid in the floorboard of the pantry. I pull it out and put it in the back of my pants. Outside the pantry, I find paper, an envelope, and a pen. I stick them all in my pocket.

My time is running out to stay undetected in this house. I need to leave and hide until darkness falls, then I can carry out the second part of my plan.

So that's exactly what I do. I run outside and down the beach, away from Julian's property, until I reach a neighbor's backyard filled with enough bushes and trees for me to hide in until nightfall.

If I only wanted to save myself, then I should be in search of a boat. But as usual, I'm at the bottom of my own priority list. I need to save my friends, and the only way to do that is to kill Julian and...Siren, if I have the strength to do it.

Siren may follow orders now, but if I kill Julian, she will be the one in charge. He may not have announced her as her second, but since he put her on the most important task he had—*me*, I know that she would take over. And she would continue her boss's mission.

I can't let that happen.

I shouldn't distract myself with thinking about Siren. Right now, I need to warn my friends, and I need to kill Julian.

I take out the pen and paper to write to them in warning. I put my pen to the paper to write to Enzo, but at the last second change my mind, and instead write to Kai.

I smile as I think about Kai's future. About how strong she is and how she will one day rule—either by Enzo's side or on her own. She will claim the Black kingdom; I have no doubt.

Thinking of Kai reminds me of who Siren really is—how strong she is. I can't leave Siren alone. Because she will claim her power, the same as Kai.

♡

Darkness falls hours later. My feet have fallen asleep, my leg has swollen, and my back aches from leaning against a palm tree and squatting behind a bush all afternoon.

I'm thirsty, hungry, and exhausted.

But I'm more determined than ever.

I move through the night, silent as the gentle wind, barely making a whisper for anyone to discover me.

I know enough about Julian Reed's property and routine to know I'll be faced with a high tech security system and dozens of guards when I reach his property. But nothing and no one is going to stop me from completing my mission.

I move across the property, crouching below windows, as I make my way to Julian's house. I need to get into the garage, that's where the power is. I won't be able to disable the security system junction box, since he has it locked up in a vault, but I can disable the power, which should shut off the security system for a few minutes.

I pop the garage side door open, find the power, and disable it. The hiss of the electricity immediately dies. Then I hear the shuffle of men inside. I draw my gun, careful to know exactly how many bullets I have left—six—and that I need to preserve at least one for Julian.

I wait in the shadows as the men throw the house door open and start flowing into the garage.

Pop.

Pop.

Pop.

I take out the three men that ran inside the garage. I run to the first man and take his gun, then quickly make my way over the dead bodies and up the stairs into the house.

The house is silent, but that doesn't shock me. The first men attacked loudly and wildly, but the rest of the men will hide and wait to attack me unannounced.

Behind each corner and each wall is a possible threat. But I take my time. I have all fucking night. And this is where I thrive. Even with a bum leg, I love the adrenaline of hunting men down and making them suffer.

I hear the creak of a floorboard in the silence.

Mistake number one.

I turn the corner and fire before the man even has a chance to aim his gun in my direction. I watch the man fall and hit the floor loudly. If the gunfire didn't already, it draws every man's attention to my location.

But I'm ready for them. Bring it on.

Fire.

Fire.

Fire.

And then...

Fall.

Fall.

Fall.

I take out every guard until I hear silence in the house. Not even the sound of another man breathing leaks into the tranquility. I've disabled the security system. I've taken out his guards. Now it's time to kill Julian Reed.

Even with my wounded leg, I run up the stairs of Julian's house. Ready to complete my mission. Ready for Julian to be dead.

I'm sure Julian has heard the commotion downstairs and is awake now, but when I get to his bedroom door, I hear snoring—loud and thunderous. I creak the door open enough for me to see him lying in the middle of his bed with a face mask and earplugs.

I grin.

He won't even see death coming.

Maybe I should torture him, but I'm not going to. I just want him dead. Torture won't protect my friends; only death will.

I push the door open. Then I aim my gun. I don't even need to go into his bedroom to kill him. I have excellent aim. I could have shot him from across the entire length of the property if all the buildings weren't blocking my way.

I begin to squeeze the trigger and then...

Bang.

My body slams into a wall, my hand barely gripping my gun as it smashes between my large frame and the drywall in the hallway. My head spins for a second from the abrupt impact, and I know that I just busted open the stitches holding my wound together.

But that's all I allow myself—one second of pain before I begin to attack back.

I spin, throwing the body off mine. Before I even look at my attacker, my instinct tells me who thwarted me.

Siren.

Still, my body automatically aims the gun in her direction. I can't pull the trigger, even if I should.

She smiles back at me. "Finally got the balls to aim that gun at me?"

I frown. "Still giving your loyalty to the wrong man?"

She glares, putting her hands up like she's about to enter a boxing match with me. "I'm loyal to no one but myself."

I raise an eyebrow, keeping the gun on her body. "You just saved your boss's life; I think you're loyal to him."

"You and your loyalty, Zeke. Sometimes people do things not out of loyalty but because they want to."

I cock my head to the side. "You and I don't." I don't know how I know her so well, but deep down, she's doing this out of loyalty. I just don't understand why she gives her loyalty to that monster.

Siren stares at the gun. "You going to shoot me? Or are we going to fight fair?"

"Fair? I don't think there is anything fair when it comes to us."

"You're right; we don't fight fair." And just like that, a knife flies at my hand and jabs into my palm, causing me to drop the gun.

I growl as blood pours out of the gash in my right hand.

And then we both run full speed toward each other—full of anger, frustration, lust, need. Everything fuses together. We both fuel it all into this one outburst of emotion about to collide.

And collide we do. Siren's legs wrap around my body as she tries to climb me like a spider. Her hands grip my hair and pull hard, her other fist plummeting into my neck.

In return, I slam her back hard against the wall, my arms dancing with hers, unable to decide if I'm trying to fling her off or pull her tighter.

Our bodies flush, full of blood and nerves, hopelessly in need of a release. But we aren't going to get it, at least not in the sexual way.

Siren digs her nails into my back, trying to get me to free her, but it's not going to happen.

"You're willing to fight me? Why don't you fight him?" I say into her hair, taking a deep breath of the flowery scent of her shampoo. The scent calms most of my body and hardens other parts.

Pain springs into my vision as she head-butts me, and we fall backward. I'm barely able to stay on my feet with Siren tangling her limbs around my body like she's trying to suffocate me.

"Is that the best you got?" I taunt her. "Because if so, this is going to be a quick fight."

She smirks. "Men and their cockiness. Just because I'm a woman, doesn't mean that I'm not capable of taking you down."

"You and what muscles?"

She laughs. "Fighting isn't about strength. Fighting is about knowing your enemy, knowing his weaknesses, and exploiting them."

"You may know my weakness, but there is nothing you can do to exploit it, when the people I care about aren't here."

She jumps back, "Maybe not, but the people you care about aren't your only weakness."

I feel like I've been stabbed as she presses her thumb into my wound. *Holy fucking hell!* That shouldn't hurt that bad, but it does.

I've never punched a woman. Never fought against one. Never had to hurt one. Maybe that's sexist to think that women are any less deserving of being fought than men are. But over the years, I've started to learn differently. Siren is the one who will finally correct my outdated thoughts.

Women are just as capable as men.

Siren lets go of me, and I grunt in pain, griping my leg like she just cut it off. She's walking toward the gun on the floor, and I have no doubt if she gets it, she'll shoot me. And I don't plan on getting shot again.

I run at her, letting go of the pain in my leg as I throw her over my shoulder. She yells, punching my back. "Put me down."

I slap her ass. "Not a chance."

I point the toe of my shoe under the gun, flick it up, and catch it in my left hand. I start walking to Julian's bedroom. I'm not going to let Siren stop me from killing him, not this time.

I'm sure Julian is awake after the commotion we made. And when I enter the dark bedroom, I no longer find him in the bed. My eyes scan the room, searching, but I don't find him. The snake is most likely hiding in his bathroom.

I start toward the bathroom, when Siren flips her body up, her legs throwing themselves around my neck and face, tightening hard, making it almost impossible to breathe.

"Drop the gun, sweetie," she says.

"Sweetie? Really?"

I can feel her smile even though I can't see it. "I'm sure you've already called me every endearment in the book: sweetie, baby, lovely. That's what every man I fight usually does to try to make me feel inferior. You're no different."

I try to pull at her legs with my wounded hand, but her legs are much stronger than my bleeding hand.

"I. Would. Never. Call. You. Sweet," I say each word slowly, gasping for oxygen.

She bites down on the top of my ear, in both a harsh and seductive way.

Jesus, she's going to kill me while my dick is hard and begging for her. I'm not sure which is worse. Worse that she is strong enough to kill me, or that I'm going to die wanting her and never having her?

"Good, because I'm your siren. I'm not sweet; I'm not innocent. And I don't need a man to protect me."

Why are her words so sexy?

I can't pry her legs off me, but I can spin her around, so that's what I do—spin her until her pussy is at my face. I grin, knowing exactly how I'm going to get her to let go of my neck. Or she'll tighten her legs, and I'll die with her taste on my lips.

Either outcome is a win.

She's wearing tight jeans, but that isn't going to stop me. I may not be able to get to her skin, pussy, or clit directly, but I'll tease her enough through her jeans.

I open my mouth and groan into her pussy, biting down over her clit beneath her jeans.

She moans for a second before composing herself. "What are you doing?"

"Exactly what you want me to do."

She gasps when I lick and bite harder, slowly pulling all of her sex from her body as her pleasure soaks her jeans. Until I can taste the one part of her that is sweet.

I wait for her to release me. For her to jump off my face, with the need to attack and not let me control any part of her. But my tongue is magical when it comes to pussy, and she is a woman after all. She may not need a man for protection, but she needs a man for this.

When was the last time she was touched by a man before me?

From the way she's moaning and tightening her legs like a vice grip around my face, she at least wants my mouth and tongue.

And god do I want her too. But my teasing her is having the opposite effect to what I really need. I need to get her off of me so I can go kill Julian.

But when she moans, she makes it impossible to think of anything else. I want to rip her pants off and devour her properly. Then I want to throw her on the bed and fuck her slow and gentle, rocking her world in a way that she's not expecting, before I tie her up and fuck her hard against the wall like the seductress she is.

She pulls the scrunchie from my hair and runs her hand through my long locks. She refuses to let my head free as she pulls me tightly between her legs.

I bite down harder.

"Zeke!" she cries out.

Fuck me. Let me fuck you.

I don't think anymore as I pull at her shirt, needing skin, needing access to some uncovered part of her body.

I need her. It might have been a long time since Siren has been with a man, but it's been even longer since I've been with a woman —*too fucking long.* I've forgotten what it feels like to hear a woman scream my name.

Siren squirms against my legs, and I know she's getting close. I'm torn between denying her an orgasm and giving it to her just to hear her moan my name again.

But right now, all I can focus on is getting her to stop squirming. So I push her hard against a wall, trying to pin her body against my face.

Shattering glass corrects my perception of reality—I threw her against a window, rather than a wall. The window is too fragile to hold up against the force of our bodies slamming into it. I try to pull us back, to keep us inside, but my determination to fuck her with my mouth pushes our momentum forward.

We fall—our skin brushes harshly against broken glass as we fly through the window. Her legs automatically release my neck, and for a second, I feel free before I realize what is happening.

We are falling. Through a second-story window. We might not die if we hit the ground, but we will end up with many broken bones.

I drop the gun and grab onto the window sill with one hand. I reach for Siren's with the other, bloodied hand. Siren grabs on at the last second before our bodies slam into the side of the brick building.

We both breathe heavily as we realize how close to death we just came. How one moment of weakness together almost ended us both. We don't belong together. We just keep hurting each other.

"You okay?" I ask.

"No," she says.

But when I look down, I realize she's physically unharmed, but I can't get a good look at her face to tell what she's feeling.

"Climb up me," I say.

She hesitates for a second but then does as I say. I should climb up first and then pull her up. I don't trust her. As soon as she gets to the top, she could fling me to my death if she wanted to. But for some reason, I don't believe she will.

Siren climbs up my body, and then immediately turns around to extend her hand to me. I take it, and together we heave my giant body up. We both collapse onto the floor, exhausted. We're out of breath from the fighting, almost fucking, and then the almost tumbling to our deaths.

My hand reaches out automatically, needing to touch her to ensure that she is okay. Our fingers touch for the briefest of seconds; I can feel her pulse through her fingers. Rapid, quick, and in sync with mine.

His voice though breaks through any connection we have.

"Well done. Well done, pet," Julian says, using the nickname that he often calls her. He doesn't even show her enough respect to use her actual name—Aria. A name I can't bring myself to call her either. She'll always be Siren to me.

We both scramble to our feet, immediately sensing the danger.

"You can't beat my best asset. I pay Aria well to protect me," Julian says, standing by her side.

I fucking hate it. Moments ago, I was eating her out. I saved her life even when she was trying to destroy mine. And still, she chooses him instead of me.

"You only snuck out because she let you. It was all part of the plan. To seduce you and manipulate you into playing our game. The only way you leave is to play the game. Five rounds, and you can leave. Five rounds, and you are free."

I glare at Siren. I should have known she was manipulating me.

"Don't you get it? I will never play your game. I will never give up any information about my boss," I say.

Julian looks from me to Siren. "I think I can persuade you."

It happens so quickly that I don't even realize what he's doing. He grabs a piece of glass and then holds it to Siren's throat.

I take a step forward automatically but then stop. I need to stop showing how much I care about her. I shouldn't care.

"Play or I'll kill her," Julian says.

I shake my head. "You've already tried that. I don't care about her. Kill her."

"You lied to me before. And you're lying now. You care for her."

"So do you, which is how I know you won't actually kill her."

"I'll kill her if it gets you to play."

My heart beats wildly in my chest at the sight of a drop of blood that has formed on her neck. She told me not to save her. To save myself. *But can I really just stand here and watch her die?*

CHAPTER 9
SIREN

I've never felt this afraid.

I've been through horrible things. I've faced death before, but every time I did, I was in control of my own body. I could fight back. I could save myself.

Julian has threatened to kill me before with the gun. But deep down, I didn't think he would actually do it.

This time, I can feel the sharp blade of glass in my neck. I can feel the blood beginning to spill. I can feel how just one slip would cause the edge of the glass to penetrate my artery instead of just my flesh.

But more importantly, I can feel Julian's heart beating against my back. I can feel the energy flowing through his body. And I know how much he's always wanted to do this. He's just been waiting for an excuse. Zeke is giving him that excuse.

But can I really just stand by and let Julian hold my fate in his hands? Let Zeke's answer decide if I live or die? All because of a contract I signed years ago?

No, I won't let these men hold my fate in their hands.

I always keep a weapon in my pocket. And while Julian is distracted with Zeke, I grab the sharp knife in my back pocket, hidden from Zeke's view, and I silently move it against Julian's balls. He tenses as he realizes what I'm doing. I won't let him kill me, at least not without me castrating him first.

Julian tries to hold the glass tighter against my neck, but I press the end of the knife into his slacks. He loosens immediately until the glass is barely grazing my skin.

I stare at Zeke, trying to tell him not to play. Not to save me. I can save myself. Even though I know the consequences. I'll deal with them later.

From the glare Zeke is sending me, I don't think he plans on saving me. He thinks I planned this. That I seduced him and manipulated him into this very situation, forcing his hand to play the game.

I didn't.

But it makes no difference to Zeke. He will never trust me again.

"So what will it be? Play, or shall I kill Aria here?" Julian says, his voice surprisingly calm, considering where my knife is.

Zeke doesn't tear his gaze from me, and I wish he would. I've never seen him this angry before. My eyes drop to his bleeding hand—another injury I caused. I look at his leg, where his wound ripped open and is gushing blood. He's bleeding because of me. We both almost died because of me.

But god, does he have a magnificent tongue. I would have gladly died and gone through that window all over again just to feel his mouth between my legs.

I doubt Zeke feels the same way, though. He can't be mad for manipulating me when obviously he used my weakness, his mouth and tongue, against me.

"Last chance—are you playing my game or am I killing Aria?"

"I'll play. Not to save her. She deserves to die," Zeke says. His words cut through me worse than the glass against my neck. I didn't realize how much him wanting to protect me mattered to me. It stings to hear him say I deserve to die.

"I'll play because I want to be the one to kill you both. I'm tired of being manipulated. I'll play your game. I'll win. And before I get off this island, I'll kill you both," Zeke says.

Julian nods and drops the glass. I take a beat before I return the knife to my back pocket. I hear Julian breathe again for the first time in minutes.

"Aria will watch you then. We will play the first round tonight at dinner," Julian says, giving me a pointed look. A look instructing me to ensure Zeke's presence tonight, and warning me that he will deal with punishing me later for my little transgression with my knife.

"Why you aren't locking me back up in my cell?" Zeke asks.

"No, Aria is very capable of watching you. She'll do a better job than any bars. Dinner is at nine-thirty," Julian says, dismissing us before he pulls out his phone and yells at one of his maids to come clean up the glass.

Zeke turns and walks out without another word. I follow after.

For a man who is bleeding and injured, he's walking very quickly—not that I blame him. I want to get out of the house and as far away from Julian as possible too. Zeke didn't drive over, so we both walk the ten minutes back to Zeke's house. Neither of us talk or look at each other as we walk.

When we get to Zeke's house, I expect him to talk. Yell. *Something.*

Instead, he walks straight to his bedroom.

I sigh. I know he doesn't have any medical supplies to fix his wounds in there, so I run down to the basement to fetch the medical bag before heading to his bedroom. I pause in the doorway.

Zeke has his shirt off and has undone his pants, ready to remove them as well.

My mouth waters at his rippling muscles. And then I remember how soaked I still feel through my jeans where his mouth was devouring me only minutes before.

"Here—give me your hand and I'll stitch it up for you," I say, walking into his bedroom with the medical supplies.

Zeke growls, his body turning toward me with the force of a brick wall.

I stop dead in my tracks.

He snatches the bag from my hands with his uninjured hand. He doesn't speak, but he doesn't have to. It's obvious he doesn't want me to help him. Not only does he not want my help, but he won't allow it, even though it would be much easier for me to stitch him up than him trying with just one hand.

He's a stubborn man, so I'll let him try on his own first before doing it myself.

I take a deep breath and feel a sting at my neck. I look down and see blood flowing down onto my shirt. I need the medical kit too. But I won't beg for it. And if he won't accept my help, I won't accept his either. I can be just as stubborn. He once told me that seeing my pain hurts him as much as the physical pain hurts me. So I know he's hurting looking at me in pain.

At least, I hope he still is. Because I can't read any emotion in his eyes except anger.

"Out," Zeke commands.

I want to argue. I want to fight. But I'm tired of fighting. So instead, I turn and walk out.

"Truth or sin?" I hear Zeke ask as I get to the door.

I turn, afraid of what is going to come next.

"I should have let you die?" Zeke asks.

And for once, it's not a choice between giving him a sin or telling the truth. The truth is easy enough. "Yes."

He licks his lips. Drawing me to his mouth. Wanting a kiss. A whisper of his lips against my skin. A full-on attack of his lips and teeth on my body. *Anything*.

He smirks when he notices my reaction to the gesture. He's realized the power he has over me now. *Fuck*.

I open my mouth to ask my own truth or sin question. But before I can speak, he slams the door in my face. Leaving me bleeding, needy, and so god damned frustrated with him.

What do I do about Siren?

That's what keeps going through my head as I sit on the edge of the bed and pull out the supplies need to tend to my right hand. I try to work on stitching my hand, but I'm right-handed and struggle to get the needle to cooperate.

I drop the needle.

"Shit," I curse as I reach down on the floor, trying to find the needle. But it seems to have rolled under the bed.

My leg is throbbing.

My hand is burning.

And my chest is tight, exhausted from my near-death experience, and having conflicted feelings as I watched Julian hold the glass to Siren's neck.

I reach into the bag and pull out another needle. I drop it too.

"Fuck, fuck, fuck!" I scream as I kick the bag with my good leg.

The door to my bedroom flies open, and Siren runs in with determination and anger on her face. She may manipulate me with her feelings—pretending to want to fuck me—sometimes even liking me, but there is no doubt now that she hates me. She's not manipulating me; it's the truth.

"Stop being such a stubborn oaf and let me help you." She marches in and grabs the medical bag I flung across the room.

She picks it up and stomps over before kneeling in front of me; she grabs my hand without waiting for me to offer it up.

"Why would I ever let someone who manipulates and betrays me stitch me up?"

"Because you don't have any other option."

I try to pull my hand away, but she digs her fingers into my wound, and I wince and stop. Before she'd have been gentle—offered me drugs, taken care of me kindly. This time, I know she's going to enjoy every pierce of the needle.

And she does.

"That fucking hurts," I yell, as she digs into the palm of my hand.

"I know," she grins. "But that doesn't mean you can move. Stop wiggling."

"But it hurts!" I growl.

"Stop being a baby."

"I'm not being a baby. Do you have any idea how badly this hurts?"

She pushes the needle through my hand two more times, each eliciting a curse from me, before she finally finishes the stitching phase of caring for my wound.

"Yes, I do." She holds out her left hand, and I see a similar size scar to the one that will eventually form in my hand.

"How?" I ask, hating to see her in pain.

"It doesn't matter."

I sigh. *So many secrets, so many lies.* So many things I will never know about her.

She swallows, and the force of the movement pushes a few drops of blood out of her neck. Before, I thought the wound had stopped bleeding. It just looked like dry blood, but now, I can't focus on anything but the blood. On the pain Siren must be in.

She almost died today. Julian almost killed her to get to me. And I could have let him. Then he would have had nothing to hold over me. Nothing to get me to talk. Because everyone I love is safe as long as I don't talk.

I use my left hand to brush her hair off her neck and study the wound closer, but I can't see how deep it is while the blood is still flowing, and she's still working on cleaning my hand.

"Will you sit still so I can finish?" she demands.

"No," I growl back, ripping my hand from Siren's so I can examine her neck more closely.

She gasps at my movement and tries to fight to grab my hand again, but I'm determined now. I dig through the bag for some gauze and alcohol to clean the wound and dab the gauze with alcohol.

I grip her wrists in one of my hands as I clean her wound with the other. She hisses when the alcohol touches her skin.

My mouth moves to apologize for the pain she's in, but I stop myself. Instead, I just give her a glance to do the talking for me. My gaze must tell her everything my mouth wants to because she stops struggling enough for me to get a closer look at her neck.

I exhale a breath when I finally get a look at it.

"You don't need stitches. You'll have a nasty scar, but it's just a flesh wound," I say as I reach into the bag, pull out a bandage, and place it over her cut to stop the bleeding.

Siren doesn't say thank you; she just blinks her response. Finally, I release her, and she sits up, silently finishing bandaging up my hand.

The silence stretches until she is finished. And then she stands. "Be ready at nine-thirty," she says, as she walks to the door.

"Shouldn't I be ready before then if we are supposed to be at Julian's by nine-thirty?"

"No, arriving a few minutes late will allow you some control."

Or get me a bullet in my leg again. But I don't argue.

"You aren't going to stay and babysit me?"

She smiles, weakly. "No, I'm going to go take a bath. You won't run off. You protect those you love. Running would be selfish." And then she removes her shirt, tossing it on the floor as she starts heading toward the bathroom, no doubt leaving a trail of clothes behind her as she goes.

Leaving me hard, desperate, and feeling like I'm going to die if I keep spending time with her. Either from a lack of sex or a gunshot. Right now, I'd rather take the sex with the bullet than be alive and never get to fuck her.

AT NINE-THIRTY SHARP, SIREN REAPPEARS AT MY BEDROOM DOOR. We haven't spoken or seen each other all evening, and the sight of her would knock me on my ass if I wasn't already sitting. She's wearing a simple black dress, with a high slit up the side and heels that make her legs look a million miles long. Her hair is down in long, wavy curls. Her makeup is simple yet striking. It's almost as if she isn't wearing any makeup except on her lips, drawing me to them so I can't think of anything but kissing her.

She's dressed for a night out, while I'm dressed as I always am—jeans and a T-shirt.

"I think I'm underdressed," I say.

She bats her eyes as a sultry smile spreads across her face. "No, you are wearing what is comfortable, same as me."

"That dress and those heels look anything but comfortable."

She shrugs. "You wear jeans as your armor, to be ready for a fight. I wear a dress when I need to feel more in control of the men around me."

Fuck, she's wearing the dress because she knows the reaction she will get from Julian and me. She's right. I won't be able to resist her all night. And neither will Julian. It gives her power. The cost is her being uncomfortable all night and not being able to run and escape in heels as easily.

Although, I'm sure she has plenty of weapons tucked away in various places in that dress. I can't imagine where she could fit any, though, with how tight and revealing that dress is.

"Well, I guess we are driving then," I say as I stand and look down at her heels.

She chuckles. "You don't think I'm as capable of walking in these heels as I am in flats?"

"Your skills constantly shock and surprise me, so I wouldn't put anything past you. But walking in those heels seems impossible."

"Just drive," she says, as we walk out of the bedroom and out to my truck.

The second I pull in front of Julian's house, the air between us changes. There is no more joking—no more appreciative glances. We will return to being enemies as soon as we walk in the door. Even if I don't understand why yet, Siren will stand by Julian's side.

We both walk up to the front door, which opens before we knock. One of Julian's men greets us.

"Mr. Reed is waiting for you in the dining room. Right this way, please," he says.

Siren no longer looks at me as we walk. She's all business. When we get to the dining room, and I see Julian sitting at the end of the table, I get flashbacks to the last time I was here. When Siren was tied up, when the men tried to touch her, when she fought back, only to be dragged up the stairs and...

I growl—the deepest, most ferocious sound I've ever made in greeting to Julian.

He just smiles and folds his hands across his lap.

"You're late," he says.

"I knew you'd wait," I say, not waiting for him to greet me and taking a seat next to him. Siren takes a seat across from me at the table, still not meeting my eyes.

Julian stares at Siren's neck, and then his gaze cuts down to her breasts. She does look incredible tonight. And I don't know what she did to cover the cut on her neck, but it's barely visible when she turns her head.

"Should we get to business then?" I say, wanting to get out of here as soon as possible.

Julian snaps his fingers, and a pair of servants strut in. One brings a bottle of wine and starts pouring, while the other carries soup.

Fuck, this is going to end up being a seven-course meal.

Julian starts talking, but it has nothing to do with our arrangement. I tune him out, trying to focus on the food in front of me when all of my attention is on how Julian looks at Siren and how he finds every excuse to touch her wrist. *And she fucking lets him.*

But when she laughs and leans in at one of Julian's jokes, I lose it.

I slam my glass of wine down on the table, causing the stem to break and red wine to spill onto the white table cloth. He should have served me whiskey, not wine to begin with, and maybe it wouldn't have happened.

All eyes turn to me.

"Ask your damn question already. I sat here and ate your food. If you want me to continue to sit here, then you will get on with why I'm here," I say.

Julian snaps his fingers again, and a servant enters, cleans up the broken glass, and then pours me a new one like nothing happened. But I notice that Julian is no longer touching Siren, so my outburst was worth it.

Julian takes his time drinking his wine like he's still working out how to play this.

"Really? You've had all evening and still haven't come up with the question you would like to ask me? You already know I won't give you any information, so the question is moot," I say.

"What is Enzo's Black main source of income?" Julian asks, narrowing his eyes as he studies me.

The question isn't that difficult. It wouldn't put Enzo in too much danger. With a little digging, Julian could figure out the answer anyway. But as I said, I will do nothing that harms my friends.

"I will never tell you the truth. I choose sin," I say, hoping like hell whatever he wants me to do won't destroy me. But I'm guessing whoever he wants me to hurt or attack is most likely his enemy. And if they are mixed up in this world, then they probably deserve whatever is coming their way.

Julian's eyes cut to Siren, and they exchange a silent conversation.

I try to study their relationship. *What are they saying? What are they thinking? How can they go from almost killing each other to quiet glances and conversations?*

Siren takes a deep breath, then she stands up and walks out of the dining room. Both Julian and I watch her ass as she walks away. She returns a moment later, holding a tablet. She flicks it on and then hands it to me.

I stare down at the screen filled with a picture of a man.

"I'll start you off with a simple task. One so simple that my Aria here could do it in her sleep," Julian says.

My eyes flick to Siren. I have no doubt she could do anything with ease. She is an expert temptress.

"He's a new player in the islands here. He's been buying up large stocks of weapons and persuading men I've worked with for years to change loyalty and work for him. I want him dealt with," Julian says.

Dealt with. I don't have to ask what he means by that. He wants me to find out who he is and then kill him. I don't know who this man is. I don't know if he is a good or bad man. But he's in this world. He knows the risks he takes every day. So if killing five men is the price I have to pay for ensuring Enzo and his family are safe, then I'll do it.

I stare down at the grainy picture. It's not a lot to go off of, so I hope Julian or Siren has more information to give me.

"What is his name?" I ask.

"Eli Beckett," Siren answers. "But that is all the information we have so far. Are you able to handle research, or do I need to find out more about him for you?"

I click off the image and give her a smirk. She has no idea what my life was like before I came here. Langston, my best friend, may have been better at discovering people who don't want to be found, but I have more skills than most. I'm sure Siren is capable, but so am I.

I stand up, not bothering to finish the steak or the rest of the food Julian had prepared.

"No, I think I can handle finding everything I need about Eli Beckett on my own."

I walk out without saying goodbye but pause when I hear Julian's voice. "Aria will ensure you stick to the task, instead of running away."

"I never run away from a deal," I say, glaring at Julian.

Siren gets up to follow me out, but Julian's voice impedes her. "I need a word with you first, Aria."

I storm back to the truck, intent on getting the fuck out of here and spending my night searching for Beckett. The sooner I can complete the five sins, the sooner I can leave this fucking island.

I don't bother waiting for Siren. "Siren can prove me wrong and walk back in her damn heels," I grumble under my breath, not wanting to deal with her right now.

But when I get back to the house, I don't storm to my laptop to search for Beckett. Instead, I find myself in the kitchen, drinking a glass of whiskey, waiting for her.

About thirty minutes later, I hear the front door open. She doesn't even bother to knock. I plan on reaming her out and then spending my night alone.

But as soon as I catch a glance at Siren's thigh from her dress hiking up her leg when she walks into my kitchen, I decide on a very different way to spend my night.

"I'm going to sleep. Let me know if you need any help with your research," Siren says, starting to walk through the house.

I grab her hand, stopping her in her tracks as our hands' touch. And then I spin her around, electricity blasting through us.

"I never got to finish my sin."

"Didn't you?"

"No, our kiss was only the beginning."

CHAPTER 11
SIREN

I shudder as Zeke whispers in my ear, his voice bringing me back from where my mind has gone. I've been locked on my conversation with Julian after our drawn out dinner.

I exhale deeply, trying to push Julian out of my head and body. I just want to go to bed. Tomorrow I can face Julian, Zeke, and whatever else tomorrow brings.

"I need to sleep, Zeke. I'm tired," I say. Before dinner, I would have jumped his bones. I would have done anything for him to fuck me. To steal another kiss or two. And connect our bodies in a tangled dance of sweat and desire to release an explosion inside both of us.

But now, after Julian—well, I just can't.

Julian might have realized we would come back and fuck. He probably said what he said, and did what he did, because he knew I wouldn't be able to after...

"Siren?" Zeke says.

I blink rapidly and look at him.

"Yes?"

He studies me a moment, in the careful way he does, which feels like he's glimpsing into my soul. But of course, he can't. He doesn't know my truth any more than I know his.

"Whiskey or wine?" he asks. He doesn't give me the option to turn him down.

I sigh. "Whiskey." I've had enough wine after our dinner. I follow Zeke to the kitchen, where I've restocked the fridge and liquor cabinet. He goes to work pouring us both a glass. All I want to do is kick off my blister-forming shoes and unpeel myself from this dress.

"Thanks," I say as I take the offered glass. I'm very careful not to let our fingers brush as I take it.

Zeke's lip twitches as he notices how cautious my movement was. If his plan was to slowly seduce me, it's not going to work.

We both slowly sip our whiskey.

"I should get to bed. It's been a long day," I say.

"I agree we should go to bed," he says.

My heart stops at his voice, and a jolt hits me between my legs. *Why does his voice have to be so sexy?*

"Separate beds," I clarify.

He frowns. "There is only one bed in this house, unless you count the one in the basement, but I doubt you'll want to sleep there."

"Care to be a gentleman and sleep on the couch?"

He downs his drink. "I'm no gentleman, Siren."

Siren, I love it when he calls me that. I know he means it as an insult, but when he says it, it never comes across that way. He doesn't say it in the same harsh way he says Julian's name. Zeke calls me Siren like it's a term of endearment.

Zeke places his glass on the counter, and then he starts walking toward the bedroom, but I can still feel his heated eyes on me. His words still reverberate through my core. I remember how his lips felt against mine, kissing me like I am the only thing in his world he cares about.

I want that again.

But I can't have it.

It's not mine to take.

I rub my neck; the fresh scar there clearly reminding me who I really am—a siren. Not Zeke's Siren; I'm a real monster. And I won't mix business with pleasure. At least, not again.

I shouldn't follow Zeke to the bedroom. I should stay out here and surrender to sleeping on the couch. But I never do what I *should* do. I'm a slow learner.

I walk into the bedroom and watch as Zeke kicks off his shoes, preparing for bed like he didn't just promise to commit a sin with me. *Why did I think of that stupid game anyway?* I could have gotten the same number of answers out of Zeke without having to play a game that causes me to lose every time.

I stare at the big bed. We've slept in it plenty of times before; we can sleep in it again without fucking each other's brains out.

Yes, that's all we are going to do—sleep.

Zeke grabs the back of his shirt and begins pulling it one-handed over his head in the way all men know how to do. As it inches higher, my eyes zoom in on every muscle I will never get to feel, every tattoo I will never get to explore, every piece of skin I won't get to add my own mark to.

And then he starts unzipping his pants, and I force my eyes away. I can't look at him. I won't fuck him. Not tonight, not *ever*.

I turn around and start messing with the zipper on the back of my dress, just needing out of these tight clothes and into bed as soon as possible. I don't even care about grabbing a shirt to slip on first; I just want to get in that bed where I can pretend to sleep.

"Here, let me help you," Zeke says when I fidget with the zipper again. I can't get it to move even an inch down.

I relent wordlessly. *He's helping you unzip; he's not undressing you,* I tell myself.

I feel his fingers against my back, and then he moves to my hair to sweep it off my neck.

I still, afraid he's going to discover one of my secrets, but if he does, he doesn't say anything. And if Zeke found my secret, he most definitely would speak up.

I hold my breath, feeling his tantalizing fingers brush against the skin on my back as he works my zipper down, down, down...

Down past the point where I can easily finish the job myself. Past the point where he's simply being a helpful gentleman. But then again, he's already told me he isn't a gentleman. I feel him stop just above the curve of my ass, and I have no doubt he would have continued if the zipper went lower.

He doesn't speak.

I finally exhale when his hands are no longer on my body. I don't dare turn around.

I grab the straps of the dress and lower them before shimming the dress down over my hips until it falls to the floor. I'm not wearing a bra; there was no way to wear one with this dress. So just my thong underwear keeps me decent. I'm still wearing my heels, needing to feel powerful and strong up until the last moment before hitting the bed.

The bed is behind me, and Zeke is standing between it and me. I could walk backward to the bed, and he wouldn't see my naked breasts. Although, he's seen them before and I'm not a shy woman. I should prance over like I know how much my body affects him. But I can't because the problem isn't him—*it's me*.

I can't turn around and strut to the bed without looking at him. Him shirtless, possibly pantless. No matter what happened before, I'm still a woman. A woman with needs that haven't been met in a very long time.

I can't.

I shouldn't.

It's wrong.

But I know what's going to happen before I even turn around. It was inevitable. Everything has been leading to this. And we can't move on until it happens.

Then we can move on...

We can have one electric, passionate moment together. Like a storm blowing through town. Something that can never be repeated because the same storm conditions literally can't converge again.

I close my eyes, trying to steady my breath and heart. My heart is what I'm most worried about. I don't fall in love easily, or anything close to it. But Zeke isn't a typical man. He's capable of tricking my heart into confusing lust with love. And I need to constantly remind my heart that Zeke feels no such love for me.

He hates me. He can never love me. My heart needs to stay steady, strong, and unswayed by his body.

I brush my hair back around my neck with my hands and wince at the feeling. I hated what happened with Julian before I left dinner, but right now, it's the perfect reminder. A reminder that is going to get me to walk into the bed without letting Zeke's naked body tempt me.

I turn.

I walk.

I stop.

Fucking Zeke.

He's standing, in just his boxers, with a damn smirk on his lips and heat in his eyes. The kind of cocky arrogance that says he's about to get what he wants.

I want to deny him just to wipe the smugness from his face.

But his arrogance is earned.

I stand taller, pushing my breasts out as I do, my nipples hardening under his appreciative stare. He rakes over my body, and it's like he's telling each part of my body exactly what he plans on doing. How he will kiss, lick, nibble on my body. How he plans to pull scream after scream from my throat. How he plans to give me orgasm after orgasm.

He won't beg. He won't ask. And he won't force me.

He's making it clear that this is my choice. That if I say yes, he will take control. And I'll have no control left. No power. I will give it all to him. And I don't know in the morning light if I'll be able to get it back.

He thinks he's gaining control in this moment. But I know the trick to retaining power. And it's giving it up willingly. Because you are confident in getting it back. Or you don't care about power in the first place.

"Yes," I say, my voice soft yet strong.

A switch changes in Zeke, and it takes everything in him not to attack me at full speed.

I move to kick my heels off, needing something to do—one last moment of self-possession.

"Leave them on," Zeke says in his deep husky voice.

I do. And I know right here, right now that I want Zeke to have complete dominance over me. I know that if I surrender to him, if I do exactly what he says, I will have one of the best nights of my life.

And I need a night where I don't have to think. I can let someone else do that for me. I can let someone else worry about pleasure and pain, right and wrong.

Zeke smiles when I leave my heels on.

"So you can obey," he says.

"Only when I want to."

"And what do you want right now, Siren?"

"You."

That's all it takes—one word. He grabs my neck, pulling me to his hard chest and exquisite lips, the pain he's causing my neck is undeniable, but I don't care the second our lips crash and our tongues tangle. All I feel is Zeke. And it's more than enough to spin my entire world on its axis.

I kiss back hard, my tongue pushing and pulling and begging for everything I need tonight to be. I don't think about all the harm I'm doing. I only think about how good this feels.

I don't think I've ever been so selfish as I'm going to be with Zeke. But I want to be selfish. Tomorrow I'll deal with the consequences.

"Don't think this is going to be anything but a sin," Zeke says against my lips as his hand runs down the side of my body, feeling every curve.

"A euphoric sin—I can live with that," I say.

More hot, breathy kisses follow. The kind that push us so close to the edge of reason that we could come under attack by burglars, a tornado could rip through the room, and a hurricane could breeze through—none of it would stop us because we are incapable of stopping. The animalistic need we have for each other has taken over. Nothing will get in the way—not this time.

Zeke growls, and I prepare for the storm. But nothing can prepare me for anything this man does.

He grabs my body and flips me over the bed, until my face is on the bedspread and my ass in the air. He kicks my legs apart and leans over my back until I can feel his hot breath on my neck.

"This is my sin, not yours. If I could enjoy you without you feeling anything, I would. But it's impossible for me to fuck you without you feeling pleasure."

I gasp as his teeth bite down on my ear; it's both too gentle and too hard.

I squirm underneath him at the intoxicating way his body gets mine ready for everything he has planned. I already know I'm dripping and more than ready for him, even though I know he's huge from the outline in his underwear. My body wants it all—now. It demands it.

"Where is it?" he asks, panting but no longer kissing or teasing me. For a split second, he's found a way to be back in the real world instead of the storm we've created.

"Where's what?" I ask, forcing the words out.

"Your weapon. You always have one on you."

I smirk, biting my lip. *Smart man.*

"The only place it could be when I'm only wearing a thong."

He kisses my neck, tormenting me as he reaches into my underwear between my butt cheeks and pulls out the knife I forgot I tucked away there. It's why I hate wearing dresses, the places to hide weapons are so much more inconvenient than when wearing jeans.

I hear the sound of the knife hitting the floor. "I don't know how you're able to walk around knowing one wrong move could mean the knife will slice into your body."

I smile and then turn my head, giving him a small wink. "I get off on pain."

And then I get the reward I was looking for. His eyes widen to extraordinary heights. His mouth drops open. And for a moment, I have power again.

But then he slaps my ass, blurring the lines between rough and blissful. And I know I'm about to pay for my split second of control.

"Cameras?" he asks, his ability to speak becoming less and less.

"Door, light fixture, dresser."

He stands up, giving me a moment to breathe. "Dresser?"

"Mmm-hmm," is all I can get out. The door and light fixture are obvious. I always hide one camera in an unlikely place even if it doesn't get the best audio or visuals, it's least likely to be found.

I hear him moving quickly to destroy each of the cameras, but I don't move even though the position is an uncomfortable one. I want to be ready as soon as he finishes to continue on right where we left off.

Zeke moves a little too fast with the light fixture, and instead of just pulling the camera off, I hear a loud crash, and I know the fixture is coming down, right on top of me.

I scramble to climb up the bed, but I won't make it. Gravity moves faster than I do when I'm needy and under Zeke's intoxication.

But instead of the sharp glass, I feel Zeke's heavy body land on top of mine.

We both breathe hard. This isn't the first time we've ended up in a position like this.

"Stop saving me," I say, my voice angry, and my desire slowly departing my body.

"I didn't."

"Then why are you lying on top of me, your back most likely scratched with glass, while I'm uninjured?"

He yanks mercilessly on my hair, and I hear sparks of electricity fly overhead. *Or is it us?* I can't tell anymore.

"Because if you got hurt, then I couldn't do this." He kisses me savagely. And this time, I know a falling chandelier won't stop us. Not even if it caught the room on fire.

I moan as his kisses turn carnal, and I feel his erection press against my ass. I'm sure he's bleeding, but I don't care. I want this. *I need this.* And he does too.

We might both be injured, but we are fucking.

Now.

I need more.

I start turning underneath him. Needing to feel his skin, touch his cock, rake my eyes over my body.

"You aren't in control, Siren," Zeke says into my ear. "Not tonight."

The room has gone dark without the light fixture. So I can barely make him out as he digs through his dresser, I assume to get a condom. A second later, I see the flicker of light as he turns the lamp on.

He wants to see me when he fucks me, not remain in the dark.

I smile. *I want to see him too.*

But then I see what he grabbed—two ties. I won't be seeing much of Zeke after all. He's going to ensure I get as little pleasure out of this as possible, just like he said.

"Wrists," Zeke says, all business-like.

I extend my arms out in front of me. He takes one of the ties and binds my wrists together. I've been with men who are into kinky shit before, but I don't think that's what it is with Zeke. He just wants me to not be able to touch him. He wants to deny me the pleasure of running my hands through his hair or across his chest.

And then he does the thing that hurts even worse. He wraps the second tie around my eyes so I won't be able to see him.

Sure, my other senses will be heightened. I'll be able to feel more than I would have before. But I won't be able to see Zeke's body. Won't be able to see his cock when he enters me. Won't be able to see the expressions he makes when he comes. I deserve to only get one part of him, not the whole package.

I swallow hard, waiting for Zeke to make his move.

And what a move it is.

In one movement, he's ripped my panties from my body, and his face his buried between my ass cheeks, his tongue lapping between my legs.

I get flashbacks to the last time his tongue licked my clit, bringing me one of the best orgasms of my life. But tonight isn't about my pleasure, so I don't expect him to give a repeat performance.

"What are you doing?" I ask, because I can't help myself.

"Making you wet."

"I'm already wet." I may want his tongue, but I'm desperate for his cock. As soon as he slides in, I'll come; I'm that close to coming.

Zeke's tongue flicks, finding my clit even though my ass and folds should be blocking his way. He finds it, knowing exactly what I want.

I moan as my teeth dig into the sheets to keep from screaming. He shouldn't affect my body this quickly. But god, a few more seconds, and I'll be screaming, crying, and exploding all at the same time. *Man, does he know how to work his tongue.*

"Zeke, stop I'm going to—"

"Come, Siren," Zeke commands.

"But...I want..." *I want to come on his dick.* If I come now, I'm not sure I'll be able to come a second time so quickly.

"Come now, Siren. I want you drenched and ready for my cock."

Damn, if I wasn't about to come before, I'm ready now.

I come.

I try to keep from screaming his name. I try to keep some dignity, some control. But he pushes one of his fingers in, expertly curling it against my G spot. And I've lost all control.

"Zeke Kane," I scream, as my arms buck and throb needing to touch him. My eyes yearn to see him. I don't get either, though. But his grin between my legs is enough.

I pant heavily as I come down off my high. It was exhilarating, but my throbbing pussy is clearly more than ready for round two.

Zeke kisses up my ass, then up my lower back.

I smile, content and excited about what comes next. I'm so lost in my bliss that I don't even realize what Zeke is doing until it's too late.

He grabs my hair, fisting it into a ponytail as his cock presses against my ass. He may have made me come with his tongue, but he's going to take me from behind, making it all about sex and nothing else.

But the second his hand grabs onto my hair, he stops. And I know exactly what's stopping him.

Fuck.

Thank god I can't see Zeke because I'd probably lose it. I'd get angry or go right back to what Julian did to me before I left his house. I haven't seen the mark he left on my neck, but I doubt it's a pretty sight.

Zeke releases my hair with a curse, and then I feel him leave the bed.

What the?

I wait for a second. Then another.

What's happening? Is he really not going to fuck me? Is he going to let Julian win again?

"Zeke?" I whisper, feeling more alone than I've felt in a while.

He doesn't answer.

But then I feel the bed sink. I feel my hair being pulled high in a ponytail as he ties it up with a scrunchie. The burn of my neck eases as it does. And then I feel him press a bandage over the scars, covering the mark.

"Does it hurt anymore?" Zeke asks.

"No," I answer. "I don't feel anything when I'm with you." And now that Zeke's removed my hair from my neck and bandaged the scar, it feels numb. But I'm not sure it's enough to get Zeke to fuck me. Not after he saw what Julian did.

My fears are proven right when I feel Zeke loosening the tie around my eyes. It drops away, and I try to hide my disappointment.

He flips me over. He's still naked, still between my legs, but I know this isn't happening anymore. And I won't beg.

My eyes slowly climb up his body until I see his pupils.

"You may be loyal to Julian, but tonight you're mine. I don't want you to forget that," Zeke says.

I don't belong to anyone. But I don't say the words out loud. Because they would be a lie. For the first time, I want to belong to a man. At least, I want to belong in his bed. I want him to know exactly how to get me off, exactly what I need without me having to ask for it.

"Don't close your eyes, not for a second," he commands.

I nod, unable to speak.

This is still happening.

I let my eyes devour all of his body. *Remember this forever. It won't ever happen again.*

I stop at his cock, now on full display, and my lips part in shock. It's huge, just like the man kneeling over me.

He smirks at my expression. "You said you got off on pain. Let's test that theory."

I bite my lip, trying not to worry. *No wonder he made sure I came first.* There was no way he was fitting without me completely turned on and soaked.

He spreads my legs as he moves closer.

"Pill?" he grunts as he moves in, resting his cock over my slit.

I nod. "Clean?"

He nods.

We are going to fuck without a condom. *Reckless?* Definitely. *Worth it?* Abso-fucking-lutely.

He pushes my still tied arms back over my head, causing my back to arch and my breasts to move closer to him.

He leans over, blowing on my nipples gently until they are pointed into sharp peaks just for him. His tongue touches one, teasing and tasting until all I can think about is his tongue.

I'm lost in his tongue, until I feel the unfamiliar stretch as he pushes deep inside me.

Oh, my god.

I can't breathe.

My heart has stopped.

All I can do is stretch as I adjust to him inside me.

It's everything I expected it to be, feeling his intrusion: wrong, painful, and jolting. And it's everything I didn't expect: right, delicious, and intoxicating.

"You with me?" he asks, his voice strained.

"Yes," I pant.

"Good, because I'm not even half-way in, baby."

Holy fuck.

He moves, somehow getting deeper. My eyes water a second as he hits deeper than any man has ever reached inside me. As long as he comes nowhere near my heart, I know I'll be okay. I'll recover from this.

And then he tenderly kisses me. So softy compared to how hard the rest of his body is.

I melt.

Into goo.

My body opens, allowing him all the way in.

And then his hand caresses my neck. *Mine*—his eyes say.

I don't argue. He's right. *I'm his*. At least for tonight.

Then he grips my ponytail.

"Ready?" he asks.

I nod, although I know I'll never be ready for what he has to give.

He pulls out almost completely, and then he thrusts. His pelvis, that part that forms a perfect V, rubs against my clit as he dips all the way inside me. He somehow hits every nerve ending in my body as he thrusts.

All pain leaves. My body is his to do what he wants with.

He thrusts over me, pounding into my body with everything he has. Each thrust more beautiful and delicious than the previous.

And I get to see it all. The way his body moves expertly over mine like he already knows exactly what my body wants and needs. The way his brow furrows with sexy determination. The ways his lips curl. The way his muscles flex with each movement.

We are both getting close to the explosive end. The release we have both been chasing. And then this will all be over. Every sexually charged conversation will be over. The intensity between us will leave when our orgasms hit, and this will all become a faint memory.

My arms twitch above my head. I got my sight back, but Zeke won't let me feel him. No matter how desperate I am to be as connected to him as possible. I want to feel him and kiss him when we both come.

Zeke leans down again as he keeps pumping into me. Until his lips are kissing mine again, giving in to one of my wishes.

"Dig your heels into my back," he says.

I do, and god the movement pushes him deeper inside me. I'm going to come, I'm so close.

"Wrap your arms around my neck," he says.

Shock.

I did not expect that kindness.

But I don't question it. I loop my arms around his neck, allowing me to feel his long hair with my fingers as he gives me everything— kisses, connection, and the most earth-shattering orgasm known to man.

"Zeke!" I scream.

"Siren!"

Our voices tangle together, just like our bodies. I feel the warmth of his cum as it fills me. I've never been fucked without a condom before. I've also never fucked a man who wasn't just a man, but my enemy as well.

Slowly, our bodies come back to earth, but Zeke doesn't pull out of my body. And I don't move or squirm beneath him. I want this to last as long as possible.

"Tomorrow, we return to enemies. This was my last sin when it comes to you. But I promise you this; I will kill Julian. So if I were you, I'd reconsider who you're loyal to. He's a dead man for what he did to your neck alone. Choose who you are loyal to carefully. Because if you choose Julian, I'll ruin you too."

And then he pulls out, leaving me empty and alone.

He doesn't realize it doesn't matter who I'm loyal to. Zeke already ruined me. He may not have left a physical mark on my body like Julian did, but Zeke left a different kind of scar. A mark that no amount of time will ever heal. A permanent stain on my soul.

CHAPTER 12
ZEKE

ucking Siren was everything I always imagined it would be.

Pulling out of her broke me.

Because it was the first time and the last time.

It should be the first of a million times, but I meant what I said. We are enemies. This was a momentary slip in judgment. It was sin in every meaning of the word. I shouldn't have fucked her. I'll never be able to fuck a woman again without thinking about her. But I couldn't *not* fuck her. Even when I saw what Julian did to her.

Why the hell is she still loyal to him? He hurt her, so many times. I may not be able to make Siren loyal to me, but I've decided one thing—my mission now includes making her see that Julian Reed does not deserve her allegiance. I might even convince her to be the one to put a bullet in his head.

I get off the bed, and the second my feet hit the floor, I know this moment is over. I walk over to the dresser and pull out a T-shirt and boxers. I slip the boxers on and carry the T-shirt to Siren, who still lays on the bed with her wrists tied together. It's clear from her expression that she is no longer present. Her mind is somewhere else.

I grab her wrists and pull her into a sitting position, forcing her to look at me. Then I remove the tie and slip the shirt over her head and arms. I pull her feet into my lap and remove the shoes she dug into my back. Finally, I grab the remnants of the fallen light fixture and toss it off the bed.

"Let me see your back," she says.

I turn, letting her see that I'm not hurt before I sit down on the edge of the bed next to her.

"Why? Why are you loyal to Julian? Why did he brand your neck?"

She swallows hard. I don't expect her to answer. But she does. And I realize it's because there are no cameras for Julian to hear her.

"I'm not loyal to him. I'm loyal to myself. Trust me when I say that the only reason I do what Julian asks is for my own selfish reasons. And the second following him no longer serves my interests, I'll kill him myself."

I blink rapidly, not believing her words.

"It's the truth. I don't lie, remember? At least not with my words."

"Why do you put up with him hurting you?"

"I don't."

I frown. "Your neck, leg, and every other scar on your body prove otherwise."

She sighs and pulls her legs up to her chest and wraps her arms around them.

"You didn't deserve to have him carve a JR into your neck."

"Is that what he did?" she asks, her eyes bulging for a second.

Maybe if she sees what he did, realizes how bad of a man he is, she'll change her loyalty. I jump off the bed and then grab her hand, pulling her with me. I take her to the bathroom, remove the bandage I placed on her neck, and hand her a small mirror. She takes her time holding up the handheld mirror and positioning it so she can see the back of her neck where Julian carved his initials—initials she will never be able to remove.

"Help me kill him," I say.

She frowns, blinking rapidly. And I realize there are cameras in this room. She won't speak against him here.

"Look what he did to you," I snarl.

She does, and I see the pain in her eyes. I don't know if I've ever met a stronger woman—Kai maybe, a woman who flipped my boss's world upside down. But Siren has something that Kai doesn't have—skills. She knows how to shoot a gun. She knows how to fight. She could easily fight her way out of this situation. She doesn't need me to save her.

But it's clear from her eyes that she won't fight Julian. I just don't know why.

"You think he got away without me hurting him?"

"Yes."

She shakes her head and then looks past me, I assume to a camera. "I've hurt Julian worse than he will ever hurt me. I'm not faithful to him. And one day, when I no longer need him, I'll kill Julian Reed." Her eyes go back to me. "Until then, my job is to ensure you complete your five sins since I know you will never tell him a truth. Get some sleep, Zeke. Tomorrow we go hunt down a man."

And then she walks out, leaving me more confused than ever. She's the most confusing, irritating, strong, fragile, infuriating woman I've ever met.

But at least I learned one thing—she hates Julian Reed as much as I do. She may not have told me the complete truth yet. Julian has something on her; that's why she follows his orders. And someday, he will hurt her badly enough that she will flip. She'll stop doing his bidding.

I'm close to figuring out what that breaking point is. And when I do, she'll be mine.

CHAPTER 13
SIREN

I*'ll kill Julian Reed.*

I shouldn't have said it. I shouldn't have spoken such truths out loud. Not when I knew Julian was listening. It was reckless of me.

But who am I kidding? Julian already knew I want him dead. I may never have spoken the words out loud, but I've spoken them enough in my mind. If Julian Reed ever stops being useful to me, I'll kill him.

There is only one little problem with that truth—Julian Reed will never stop being useful to me. He will never stop holding my life in his hands. I will never kill Julian; he knows that. Zeke doesn't. But Zeke deserved to learn how I felt. He deserved to know that he isn't the only person who hates Julian.

I pull the throw blanket up, tight under my chin as I curl up on the couch. I should be sleeping in Zeke's bed. Possibly even tucked against his naked body, praying that when he wakes up, we would get a round two.

Instead, I'm alone lying on the couch in Zeke's living room, trying to forget about how swollen my lips are from his kisses and how sore my body is in all the right places. Even though I finally got my wish, I got to fuck Zeke, I'm still horny and turned on and feel like I could explode from his touch. Fucking Zeke didn't get him out of my system; it just made me crave him more.

I close my eyes, forcing Zeke out of my head. Tomorrow I have a job to do. And the faster Zeke completes the five sins he owes Julian, the faster he will be out of my life for good, and my life can return to the way it was before.

Sleep pulls me under quickly, but even sleep can't protect me from my demons...

"A WORD, SIREN," JULIAN SAYS AS ZEKE WALKS OUT OF THE DINING room.

I stay.

I pick up my glass of wine and take a long sip, watching Zeke walk away from me.

"Come here," Julian says as he continues to sit at the end of the table.

I hate being summoned, being treated like a dog. But I choose my battles when it comes to Julian. And this isn't one I want to fight. *Just get this over with so I can go after Zeke.*

I doubt he waited for me, though. I'm going to have to walk back to his house in these damn heels. Zeke was right, heels suck and are almost impossible to walk in, even if they make me feel powerful for a few minutes.

I slide my chair out, keeping my wine glass in my hand as I walk over to Julian.

He pats his lap, telling me to sit there.

I frown. "Really?"

He raises his eyebrows. "Are you going to defy me, again?"

The way Julian says 'again' tells me everything I need to know. He's pissed, and I don't have to think too hard to know why—he's angry I put a knife to his balls, when I swore I'd never hurt him, never use my skills against him.

That stupid vow.

"Sit, Aria," Julian says.

Everything inside of me falls heavily as I sit on his lap, completely defeated. I don't know why I fight against Julian. He always wins. *He will always win.*

I'm surprised to not feel his erection poking me in the ass when I sit. At least I have that to be thankful for.

Julian continues to glare at me, and it's clear my punishment won't stop at just sitting on his lap.

"You broke your vow," he says.

I nod, not defending myself.

"You know the consequences of breaking the vow."

Pain stings my heart. *No, please no.*

"I do. I'm sorry," I say, hating that I'm apologizing to this man.

"Are you? Because I don't think you are sorry at all, Aria."

I'm not. He knows I'm not. I wish I had the guts to slice his balls clean off. But I couldn't...I can't.

"You beat me up, you shot me, threatened to kill me. What was I supposed to do? Let you kill me?"

"Yes."

I scowl. "Well, you should have known I would never let you do that without putting up a fight."

His lips curl just a little. *That was his plan.* He knew I couldn't not fight back. He goaded me.

I slap him.

I watch his face turn shocked. I watch the redness spread across his face. And it's worth every punishment he's about to deal out.

But when his head turns back to me, I realize I've just made a horrible mistake.

"You broke your vow, again," he says.

"Consider my vow over. I quit," I say, moving to get up off his lap.

"Really? You might want to reconsider."

I gasp when I see the glint of evil in his eyes. I want to take it all back. *Everything.* Because I know exactly what Julian is thinking and I can't—I just can't. I can't do this again...

"I'm sorry," I whisper, trying to hold back my tears. And I am truly sorry. He has no idea how sorry I am.

"Prove it," he says.

I close my eyes, taking a deep breath as I try to think of something that will make Julian trust me again. Something that will prove I'm still on his side. That I will always be on his side. Because I can't live with the consequences.

I feel Julian's excitement grow in his slacks. I could fuck him...*No, I couldn't.*

There is only one option—*make another vow.*

I grab the steak knife on the table and hand it to him.

He smiles as I do.

Then I lift my hair, exposing my neck to him. "I vow—"

And then I feel the slice of the blade through my neck. And no matter what words leave my mouth, I promise myself that someday I'll be free of Julian Reed. Even if it's only in death.

♡

My eyes flutter open as I'm soaked in sweat and fear. *Julian's not here. It was just a nightmare.*

But I feel eyes on me. I look up and see Zeke watching me with a frown on his face. He's leaning against the doorframe, shirtless, and wearing gray sweatpants that are somehow sexier than if he were wearing nothing at all. *What is it about gray sweatpants?* I ignore the bulge in his pants and focus on the scowl.

"What are you doing here?" I ask.

"You were talking and screaming in your sleep. It woke me up."

"Sorry, I didn't mean to wake you." I sit up, tucking my knees to my chest. I'm wearing Zeke's T-shirt, and the smell of him alone comforts me. But what I really want is for Zeke to wrap his big, tattooed arms around me. Tell me everything is going to be okay. That he'll protect me. But I've lost Zeke's protection. I'm not his friend; I'm his enemy.

I replay the nightmare in my head. Zeke said I was talking.

"What did I say?" I ask, not sure if I hope he heard everything or nothing at all.

"The truth."

"Which is?"

Zeke doesn't answer. But the unnerving frown on his face tells me enough. Whatever he heard made him furious. At me. At Julian. At the world.

"I'll try not to wake you again," I say, moving to pull the throw blanket back over me and attempt to sleep again. *Like that's going to happen.*

"Come to bed," he says. It's a command. I hate commands, except maybe when Zeke commands me. There is something sexy and protective about how he orders me to do something. And right now, I don't want to sleep alone, even if sleeping in Zeke's bed complicates things.

So I follow Zeke to the bedroom. I climb under the covers, as does Zeke, and then I close my eyes, hoping I will be able to sleep better with Zeke nearby to chase my nightmares away.

I feel the dip of the bed as Zeke moves closer. And then I feel his arms wrap around me tightly. I smile, knowing I won't have another nightmare. But I also know I'm completely fucked as my heart flutters in my chest.

Zeke isn't mine. And I can't be his.

Fucking him might have been enjoyable, and telling him I want to kill Julian may have proven to Zeke that we are closer to being on the same side than he realizes, but in the end, I know my fate—and it will require me to betray Zeke, again.

"I vow..."

Those were the words that Siren said in her sleep, trembling, and lost in a nightmare. It took everything in me just to listen and not wake her up. I couldn't stand to just stand by when I could do something to stop her suffering. But Siren is a closed book when it comes to her relationship with Julian. There is something big I'm missing, something she's not telling me. So I forced my legs to stay still, to not move toward her.

But I'm not sure it was worth it because I got so little for my effort —*I vow*.

Two words with so much meaning.

The only people who typically say vows are brides and grooms getting married.

Are Siren and Julian married?

My heart beats erratically at that thought. Siren is currently using my shoulder as a pillow. Her leg is draped over mine, and her heart rests against my chest beating in sync with my own. I'm afraid my beating heart will be enough to wake her up, but she doesn't move.

I stare down at her left hand. No ring, no tan line, no sign she's married to that monster. *She's not married to Julian.* He wouldn't let her fuck me if she was. He wouldn't let her be sold to me knowing what most men would do to her once they bought her. And the kicker is that I've asked Siren before if she was married and she said no. *She always tells the truth.* And so far, she has.

Except when she's convincing me of a lie, I think. But I heard her say the words; she's not married to Julian Reed. I just don't know what vow she promised him. *What loyalty does he demand of her?*

I run my hand through Siren's hair. *What would I give to make her mine?*

I know the answer, but I won't even allow myself to think it. She's not mine. She will never be mine. She's my enemy. She betrayed me, and she'll do it again if it pleases her. When I've finished my five sins, I'll be gone, and she'll stay here by Julian's side. She might as well be married to him.

I can't keep lying here in this bed dreaming about what a life with Siren could be. There is no could be, might be, or even currently is with us. Because there is no us. It was just sex. Breathtaking, fantastic sex that can never be repeated. I shouldn't even have let her into my bed except I knew I wouldn't be able to sleep if I didn't fuck her.

But there is no reason I still need to be in bed now.

I jump out, not caring if she wakes up, and head to the shower. In the shower, I can wash away all thoughts of last night. I can wash away Siren's scent on my body. I can wash away *her*.

So that's what I do. I force my mind to change from thoughts of Siren to this Eli Beckett guy I'm supposed to hunt down and kill. I've done countless tasks like this for Enzo Black before. I can do this in my sleep. I decide to take a boat over to St. John, the neighboring island where Beckett was last spotted and start there. On my way over, I'll do an extensive background check on our Eli Beckett, but I can't use any of my usual resources. I don't want any of my friends to know where I am; it would put their lives in danger. And it would be easier for Julian to track them down. I'll have to use backchannels.

I start rinsing the shampoo from my hair when the bathroom door pops open and Siren struts in. She's changed, no longer wearing just my T-shirt. She's now wearing jeans with flats, and she's tied my T-shirt up so it stops just below her breasts and exposes her stomach. Her hair is pulled in a high ponytail, and she's wearing a modest amount of makeup. She's dressed for comfort, but my cock doesn't understand the difference between when she dresses for him or for the world; my cock always thinks she dresses just for him.

And there is no hiding my reaction to seeing her stomach in the glass shower. She can see exactly what I think of her outfit.

She smiles, raising an eyebrow when she spots my growing erection.

"What do you want, Siren?" I ask, exhausted. *How can she already exhaust me and it's only seven in the morning?* I got a good night's sleep, I shouldn't be tired, but I am. Siren demands everything from me.

"Just to tell you to stop touching yourself and get ready. We have twenty minutes before our plane leaves."

"I'm not touching myself."

"Maybe you should if you aren't going to be able to control yourself with that *thing* all day," she says with a smirk.

I stiffen in annoyance. "You seemed to like my cock just fine last night."

"Twenty-minutes, plane, St. John," she says and then darts out.

I sigh. It seems that all of my planning doesn't matter. We are taking a plane, not a boat. And I don't have the energy to fight with her. I'm surprised she's willing to help me. I thought she might enjoy seeing me struggle with a task she does on a daily basis. But I remember she wants these stupid games with Julian over as much as I do. The faster they're completed, the faster she can return to her life before me.

I finish showering and get dressed. I quickly throw some extra clothes in a bag and pack up my gun and bullets. If we are flying commercial, I'll have to leave them in my truck, but I'd rather have them if at all possible, which is why I'd rather take the boat. I'm sure Siren knows where to buy weapons once we arrive.

"God, you're such a diva. Thirty minutes in the only bathroom in this house is excessive. I had to do my hair and makeup without a mirror," Siren gripes from the hallway, but there is a smile in her eyes. She's happy. And I'd like to think the sex last night had something to do with it.

"Just enjoying my last few minutes away from you."

She pats my arm like I'm a child, but the second her hand touches mine, the sparks have returned. She jumps back suddenly, not expecting the connection to still be there. We both hoped that after we fucked, the constant throbbing for each other would stop. But nope—if anything, it just got worse.

I clear my throat. "Did you pack a bag?"

She shakes her head.

"Do you want to?"

"Nope, we should be able to get this done in a night, two, tops. I'll buy whatever clothes and things I need when we get there."

My eyes widen. I'm not used to traveling with a woman who is so low-maintenance. But that's Siren. The most demanding, needy woman one minute and easy-going and independent the next.

"Let's go then," I say, throwing my overnight bag over my shoulder and starting to walk to my truck.

Siren follows, jumping into the passenger seat. She flicks the radio on, apparently not okay with any silence. I'm not a talker as it is, and I'm especially not a talker at seven in the morning when I haven't had coffee. More quiet still after I made a huge mistake in fucking Siren last night.

It was great, a night I will never forget. But now, anytime I'm around her, my cock gets rock hard like he expects a repeat. *Not going to happen, bro.* But my self-talk does nothing to talk him down.

I start driving down the gravel road, hoping I'll be able to think about something else to make my jeans a little less tight, but Siren starts singing along to a Beyonce song, and I'm lost.

Her voice is intoxicating and alluring. It could convince any man into jumping over a cliff after hearing it. It's not just that her voice is beautiful; it's haunting and magical. It's different than any other voice I've heard. It's not flawless; she doesn't hit every note perfectly like Beyonce does on the radio; she changes her voice to fit her mood and her feelings. I don't even think she realizes that she's singing, that her voice isn't perfectly in tune with the melody, or that she's now changed several of the lyrics to suit her. When she sings, it's because she loves to sing. And there is nothing more captivating than that.

"Zeke! Watch out!" Siren screams all of a sudden.

I realize I've been watching her instead of paying attention to the road. I slam on the brakes just short of the edge of a cliff with only palm trees to break our fall.

"Shit," I curse under my breath. I realize the truck is most likely stuck in the sand on the side of the road.

We both breathe heavily.

"I think I should drive from now on; I'm tired of almost dying any time I get in the car with you. Or really, any time I'm around you," Siren says with a tiny smile, trying to lighten the tension.

"Know anything about how to get a truck unstuck in the sand?" I ask.

She laughs. "Even if I did, you're the one who got us into this predicament; you get us out. I'm not a mechanic or car person, though, no. My skills stop at being able to fire a gun, a little Krav Maga, and using my body to seduce men."

My heart clenches. She just had to mention seducing other men. *How many men have fallen for her? How many men have slept in her bed?* I'm just one of many. Last night meant nothing to her. I'm sure she's had her fill of men worshipping at her feet.

"Good, I plan on using your seduction skills to get to this Beckett guy," I say, leaning in close to her so she can feel my angry breath as I say it.

She frowns. "Sure."

My eyes flicker between hers. She's pissed. And turned on from the pink flush of her cheeks. *Maybe I have more of an effect on her than I think? Maybe she doesn't fuck men every night?* She was awfully tight for a woman who I assume has fucked every man she's ruined.

Stop thinking about sex.

Ugh.

I jump out of the car, and confirm our predicament—we are stuck in the sand. I find a piece of driftwood to stick under the wheel to give the truck some traction. And then I signal for Siren to step on the gas. She's already moved over to the driver's seat, and I know she won't let me drive anymore. Although, I wouldn't get us into such predicaments if she wouldn't distract me with her singing. Or her body. Or her presence, sitting next to me.

God, I'm so screwed.

She pulls back onto the road, and I jump in the passenger side— I'm a little sandier than when I jumped out, but otherwise, I'm good. She takes off toward the airport, turning the radio up in excitement at the next song.

I flick it off immediately.

"Why'd you do that?"

"Because your voice is what caused me to lose my dignity in the first place."

"Damn right, I won't let you drive when you almost got us killed, again." But she's smiling. She likes that I'm not arguing with her about me needing to drive my own truck.

Honestly, I prefer the passenger seat. It gives me more time to study her body without worrying about killing us. But her singing takes things too far. I'll jump her if she starts singing again. And then she'd be the one to crash us.

So instead, we ride in silence—something I'm used to and thrive in, giving me time to think clearly. Siren, on the other hand, seems irritable as we pull onto the airport's main road. I assume it's because she's still mad about the almost cliff dive we had, or maybe it's because she hasn't had her morning coffee yet either.

She doesn't talk to me yet as we head toward the private side of the airport. *Good, we aren't flying commercial, so I can bring my gun.*

"I'm going to talk to the pilot. We should be ready to leave in five minutes," Siren says after we enter the small terminal.

I nod and watch her walk away. I decide I should do something nice and get us both coffees for the flight. It's the right thing to do after fucking her last night. If I was being myself, I would have made her breakfast in bed, offered her a long soak in the tub, pampered her all morning, and then sent her flowers after she left. But this isn't a normal situation. We aren't dating. She hates my guts.

So I'll just settle on coffee.

While I'm standing in line for coffee, I notice a small stand with flowers. Flowers can't hurt either. Might get her to stop scowling at me all the time and like me enough for us to work together in peace. And honestly, I like being the nice guy everyone likes.

I buy two coffees and decide on a single red rose.

I walk in the direction I last saw Siren and find her standing next to a cute black woman. Siren is wearing her familiar scowl that only deepens the closer I get.

"Coffee black, like you like it," I say, holding out the coffee. And then I lean in so only she can hear. "And a flower because you saved my life back there."

She frowns and picks up a coffee from the table behind her. "I can get my own." She turns and starts walking out toward the tarmac.

I sigh, now I'm holding two coffees and a flower like an idiot.

The woman she was talking to smiles brightly.

"I'm Nora," she says.

"Zeke," I say.

"I like coffee and flowers."

"Oh, here, sure." I hand her the coffee and flower. She tucks the flower behind her ear, just like I imagined Siren doing and then sips the coffee.

"Aria will come around. She's not the romantic type, if you know what I mean."

"A coffee and flower is romantic?"

"To most women, yes." Nora looks toward where Siren is already climbing up the stairs of a small propeller plane. "She's used to being independent and having to take care of herself. Don't take it personally."

"I don't. We aren't together."

"I know. But you should be," she says with a playful smile before heading toward the plane herself.

I jog after her. "Why do you say that? We're enemies stuck working together. Don't put ideas in Siren's head."

She stops. "Siren?"

"I mean, Aria."

This only makes her eyes brighten more, like she can understand our entire relationship from just one conversation.

"Well, I can't put any ideas into Siren's head. It's not possible. I've known the woman for years, and she does what she wants when she wants. But then you know that already."

"I do."

"I think you are just the kind of man she needs."

"And what kind of man is that?"

She sips her coffee, still smiling brightly in the way I wish Siren would every time she looks at me. "You seem like a smart man; you'll figure it out."

"You coming with us to St. John?"

"Better than that. I'm the one flying you."

I look her up and down. She's wearing jeans and a T-shirt. This woman is tiny. Can't be bigger than five foot two. She's not dressed like any pilot I've ever seen, but I would trust this woman with my life and children.

"Lead the way then," I say, carrying my bag and coffee as I follow Nora up the stairs to the plane.

I don't spot Siren anywhere in the back of the plane. I even check the bathroom.

"Need anything before takeoff?" Nora asks, nodding toward the front where I see Siren sitting in one of the pilot seats.

I follow Nora up as she takes her seat and starts going through her checks.

"You a pilot now, too?" I ask Siren.

"Nope, just thought I'd keep my best friend company."

Best friend, huh? Finally, I've learned a fact about Siren.

"I think your best friend would prefer you ride in the back with me. That way, we can make a plan while your best friend focuses on flying the plane."

Siren looks from me to Nora, and I can tell they exchange a silent conversation. Nora may be on my side, but as she said earlier, no one persuades Siren to do anything unless she wants to.

Which is why her relationship with Julian is so weird. The only reason I can think of that Siren does as Julian says is because she wants to. Which means I have no hope of changing her mind.

"My friend would prefer if I keep her company," Siren says.

Nora gives me a look as if to say, *I'm sorry, I tried.*

I sigh and relent myself to sitting in the back of the plane, alone.

CHAPTER 15
SIREN

"So, who's the guy?" Nora asks with knowing eyes as she starts up the plane's engines.

"He's just a guy who works for Julian," I answer, keeping to the truth, mostly. Zeke does work for Julian, so it's not a lie, he's just not working for him by choice. But what Nora doesn't know won't kill her.

She sighs. "Ugh, I thought he was one of the good guys, but if he's working for Julian, there must be something wrong with him."

I take a sip of the coffee I got for myself. "Plenty."

"What? He's rude? Heartless? A bully? Sexist? Racist? An asshole?"

Nope, he's none of those things.

"Have a small dick?"

I shoot her a look.

She grins proudly. "Fine, what's wrong with him then?"

"He's insufferable, thinks he's better than everyone else, arrogant, noble, loyal—"

"Those all seem like positives to me," Nora frowns.

"Trust me, they're not." *Except sometimes that protective streak in him is mighty sexy.* As is his loyalty and nobility. I even enjoy his arrogance.

We are silent as we take off. I glance over at her, waiting for more questions, and I notice her fidgeting with the flower Zeke bought for me but gave to her.

I grind my teeth together at the sight. *Why does he have to also be so fucking sweet?* We are enemies, and he bought me a damn coffee and flower. *Why?* Because he's a nice guy, that's why. When he dates women, he probably takes them on real dates, holds doors open, and sends them daily chocolates or flowers.

I'm not that type of woman—the type who wants him to be all romantic and cheesy. Even if we were dating, I don't want flowers. I don't want a man to buy me shit. *I just want...*

"Have you fucked him yet? Or is that why there is so much pent up frustration in this plane right now?" Nora asks. The way she wiggles her eyebrows and takes the flower from her ear and strokes my arm with it, I know she isn't into Zeke. But she thinks I am.

She's my best friend in the whole world. We met when I first came to the island at eighteen. She knows me better than anyone else. She's a rich princess who flies planes for fun, to have something to do, and to have the ability to travel at a moment's notice without having to coordinate with anyone else. She knows I will only ever tell her the truth. She knows my problem with being able to lie—I can't lie. So she waits for me to answer.

I sigh, I should have stayed in the back with Zeke. I may not be able to lie, but I can evade. "I'm going to check on Zeke."

She smirks triumphantly. I know she wanted me to go sit with him the whole time, but I really don't want to be anywhere near him. Not when I know there will be no more fucking. This trip might even be the last time we are alone together. For all I know, the rest of Julian's sins will be completed with someone else watching guard over him. We need to get back to a business relationship and stop undressing each other with our eyes.

But the sight in front of me when I step into the back of a plane makes me drool with need.

Zeke is sitting in his chair, his biceps and shoulders overflowing into the seat next to him. Good thing we are the only ones on this plane. If he had to sit next to someone, I'm not sure there would be room. Unless it was a woman, then she'd be more than happy to sit on his lap.

The heated look in his eyes when he spots me tells me exactly what's on his mind, but the way he's gripping the seat tells me he's nervous as hell about my friend's flying.

Nora makes a hard turn, and as I'm slung against the doorway, I remember my first time flying with her. She's more than capable of flying perfectly. She passed all her exams to fly a commercial flight with ease. But she prefers to live on the dangerous side of life and enjoys making her passengers push the limits too.

"Nervous flyer?" I ask, enjoying getting to tease Zeke.

"Not usually, but your friend has a death wish. I'm surprised you haven't taken over; her flying is far worse than my driving."

I fold my arms over my chest as I eat up the sight in front of me. "First, it's not possible to be worse at flying than you are at driving. Second, I would if I knew how to fly."

He scoffs. "Like you don't know how to fly."

I frown. "I don't. I don't know how to do everything."

"You sure act like it."

I'm just about to tell him off and go back to sitting up front with Nora when the plane dips, and I stumble forward—right onto Zeke's lap.

His hands go to my hips, steadying me in his lap, as his eyes go to my face inspecting me for any sign of injury.

"Stop saving me," I whisper, out of breath and needy.

"Stop needing saving," he breathes back.

Another turn of the plane and my lips fall forward, so fucking close to his. His lips are beyond tempting for me to kiss. I want them. On my mouth. Sucking on my nipples. Tantalizing my pussy. Instead, his lips are parted, waiting for me to make the final move.

And the space between us is enough to remind me why I can't kiss him. Why fucking him was a one-time thing. Never again. *Never, never, never.*

My heart already hurts after one night. A second would leave me ruined.

I glare up front at Nora, who is purposefully flying like a maniac to ensure I landed in Zeke's lap. *Damn Nora and her matchmaking.*

"Ever joined the mile-high club?" Zeke asks, with desperation in his voice. He's not just asking me if I have, but if I want to.

"Been a member since 2015."

He frowns, the moment over as soon as I speak.

"Who? How? When?" he asks, perturbed to hear stories of me with another man.

But the angry expression on his face tells me everything he's thinking. He thinks I'm a whore. That because of my job, I sleep with any man who I or Julian want something from. That's not how this works. That's not who I am. Sure, I like sex, and I don't mind using it to get what I want on occasion. But I don't like Zeke thinking so little of me.

"We should be landing in about thirty minutes," I answer.

"It's just sex, Siren." He strokes my cheek.

"No, sex is never *just* sex. There is always something more. Sometimes romance, sometimes love, sometimes money, sometimes secrets. But there is always *something*."

"There is nothing more between us. Just two people who hate each other, are mortal enemies, and who happen to enjoy having sex with each other. With us, there are no emotions."

"I thought last night was a one-time thing."

"I've changed my mind."

My eyes flick to the front where Nora sits with a cup of coffee and flower meant for me. I turn back. "Flowers and coffee scream romance, Zeke."

He smirks. "I'm a nice guy, Siren. I'm not going to change who I am just because it makes you uncomfortable."

"I'm not going to change who I am, either."

And that's the problem. We need to change who we are to be together. As lovers. As friends. As *more*.

Neither of us will. Neither of us can.

"Truth or sin," Zeke starts, getting desperate. It's not even been twenty-four hours, and he's already begging for sex. Already wanting more.

My body warms, my body is hungry for his. I understand why he's doing this. It's taking all of my self-control not to kiss him and rip his clothes off right now.

"Zeke, we can't..."

"Can't or won't? You're a strong independent woman. You make your own decisions. You don't let me, or any other man, make your choices for you. What do you want?"

You.

In any capacity I can get you, for as long as I can get you. My lover. My friend. My boyfriend.

But it's not fair. To either of us. We got our moment together. *Never again.*

He must read my decision in my eyes.

"Fine, then what's the harm in playing our game?"

"When I refuse to answer, you'll get what you want."

"I'll add a new rule then. I can't repeat a sin. Which means I can't fuck you again as my sin."

Hearing Zeke say he can't fuck me again hurts when every nerve in my body is shouting for him to do just that. *Would fucking him one more time really be the worst thing?*

"And I promise, no matter what, to never bring you coffee or flowers again. Nothing remotely considered romantic, regardless of what you decide."

"Good," I say. I hate the romantic stuff, and I hate being taken care of.

"Truth or sin? What vow did you promise Julian?" Zeke dips me back so he can look me dead in the eyes as I answer. Even if I was capable of lying, my body screams my honest secrets to him daily. *It's not my fault he doesn't realize the truth.*

"Sin." I bite my lip, waiting for him to do his best to tempt me. Kiss me, torment my breasts, undress me.

Instead, his eyes turn dark before he sits me back up and looks up to Nora.

"Hey, Nora," he shouts.

My mouth falls open. *What is he doing?*

"Yes, handsome?" Nora answers.

"What are you doing tonight? Want to grab dinner with me?" he asks.

I can practically feel Nora's eyes on me, trying to decide if she'll piss me off by going.

"Only if you take me to a steakhouse," she flirts back.

"Deal," Zeke shouts.

I hate him. He fucked me last night. Made it clear that he wanted to fuck me now. And then asked my best friend out right in front of me.

Fuck him.

And I want to. *Literally.*

Damn, why am I more attracted to this asshole version of Zeke instead of the gentleman version? What's wrong with me?

"Your turn," he says, daring me to say something to stop their date.

"Do you want to fuck Nora?" I ask, the question slipping out before I think.

Zeke raises an eyebrow as if he can't believe I just asked that question. And then his hand slides down my bare arm, then over my hip, teasing my skin and making chills run up and down my body. His hands tell me what his words won't—he doesn't want to sleep with Nora, he wants to fuck me.

"Yes," he breathes against my neck, sending the worst kind of chills through my body. They feel delicious, like I'm the only woman he could ever crave, while simultaneously feeling like death to my heart when he says he wants to fuck Nora.

Zeke may be able to tell a lie, but he won't during the game. It's our one rule he will never break. Because if I catch him in a lie, then I get to kill him. *Or maybe he thinks even if I can kill him, I never will?*

I'm so ridiculous thinking that he would lie to me just to get back at me when he knows the consequence of lying is death.

My teeth grind together so hard, I'm surprised my jaw hasn't broken yet. *I hate him. I hate him. I hate him,* I whine to myself.

I'm not the type of woman to complain. I'm the type of woman who goes after what she wants. And right now, I want Zeke to fuck me. To want me. Not Nora. Not any other woman.

Jesus, when did I get this jealous? Just let it go. I gave him up; he moved on. He was never mine anyway. *But damn, why did he have to move on with my best friend hours after he fucked me?*

Because that's not who Zeke is. He's loyal. He's sweet. He's kind. *So is he really falling for Nora in a matter of minutes, or I'm missing something?*

I'm not going to sit around waiting to see what the hell I'm missing. I'm going to kiss him. Fuck him. Remind him why he wants me and pull any secret he's not sharing out of his body.

I put my hand on Zeke's chest, intent on grabbing his shirt and pulling him to me roughly for a kiss to end all future kisses for him. I thought last night was incredible. I thought it easily topped all other nights. *But what if Zeke didn't feel that way?*

Just as my fingers curl around the fabric of his shirt, Nora hollers, "We're about to hit some turbulence. Buckle up back there; we land in five."

Zeke cocks his head in a challenging way. My chance has passed. I got my one night with Zeke; now it's over.

I climb off his lap and into the chair next to him, next to the window, and buckle my seatbelt. But it's impossible to escape him. His shoulder and thigh rub up against me. My stomach tightens, my pussy aches remembering how he felt inside me last night—something I gave up, all to guard my heart and his.

I know it's for the best. If it hurts now, I can't imagine how it would feel to fuck him a dozen times and still have to let him go. Still, when faced with the fact that Zeke will end up in Nora's bed tonight, it all feels like a giant mistake.

CHAPTER 16
ZEKE

What am I doing?

Playing with fire, that's what.

Everything changed on that death trap of a plane. While I was fearing for my life, I realized what I want—Siren.

Whatever I can get from her—sex, friendship, love. Even just the snarky conversation. I want her. All of her ideally, but I'll take what I can get.

I know our time together is limited. That this thing between us isn't going to last forever. But I have a new mission.

And my mission is to fuck Siren in every position and place imaginable. Fuck her until she either falls for me or until I finish my sins for Julian. And keep myself from falling for Siren in the process.

Easy—I hate her. But there is a fine line between love and hate. One that I've never crossed before, and won't with Siren. I could never fall for a woman so heartless.

We decide to setup a base of operations at a local hotel first. Siren gives me a dirty look as she checks us into our rooms. I let her book my room too even though I'm guessing she's going to find the only room with a twin bed to try and keep me from fucking Nora, who I'm sure is staying in the same room as Siren.

Siren hands me a keycard. "Sorry, they only had one king bed left. So Nora and I took it since we are sharing. Gave you a twin bed."

I snatch the keycard from her hand with a grin. "As long as I don't have to listen to you snore all night, I'm good."

She pouts. It's adorable, so I smile. If Nora weren't standing next to her with an even bigger grin on her face, Siren would let me have it. Instead, she turns and stomps off.

"You're really getting under her skin," Nora says with a wink before following her friend toward the elevator banks.

"I'll stop by your room at eight to take you to dinner," I shout after Nora, loudly enough so Siren can easily hear. Siren just pushes the elevator button a hundred times, like that will make the elevator arrive any faster.

"Great, it will give me time to go shopping for the perfect dress," Nora responds with a wink, knowing exactly what she's doing—driving Siren mad, so she'll fling herself back into my arms.

I start walking toward the elevators as one opens, and Siren and Nora step on. But Siren presses the button for the doors to close just as I reach them. I could stick my arm between the gap to keep them from closing, but I decide not to.

But there is no denying the heat in her eyes and the want in her belly, as her lips part like she's dying for water, when really she's dying to taste me.

I make it up to my hotel room a few minutes later. My room includes two twin beds that would be perfect for Siren and Nora to use, but I won't complain. I have no intention of fucking Nora tonight, even if that's what I told Siren during our game.

It wasn't a lie, per se. I'm a man after all, and men like sex with hot women. Nora is attractive; I'd love to fuck her. But nowhere near as much as I'd love to fuck Siren. If given the choice, I'd always choose Siren. But it was fun to tease Siren and know I'm driving her mad all night. Almost as mad as when I do nice things for her like bring her coffee.

I don't know what I want more—to be nice to her and watch her squirm, or flirt with another woman and get her evil eye and snarky mouth. It's a win-win for me. Although, I know which version of Siren is at the top of my list. The one naked on my bed, willing to let me do anything to her body.

I grab my laptop out of my bag, knowing I can't spend the day thinking about Siren. I have a job to do—hunt down Eli Beckett and kill him after getting every piece of information I can from him.

Nora is just part of my plan. It's easier to get to a man like Beckett with a hot woman on my arm. If he thinks we're random newlyweds on our honeymoon, as opposed to the assassins we are, he will let his guard down. And if he doesn't buy that, then I can use her to distract him.

A quick search of all the bars and clubs in the area gives me a very good idea where a man in the underground would most likely conduct business. I recognize several of the clubs from my time with Enzo.

I toss my laptop onto the bed, planning on spending the rest of the day meeting with anyone who might know Eli Beckett. I just have to be careful no one who knows me notices me and reports back to Enzo that I'm alive. He's better off thinking I'm dead.

I KNOCK ON THE HOTEL BEDROOM DOOR AT FIVE TILL EIGHT; showing up early to a date shows how excited I am. Showing up with a large bouquet of expensive flowers is romantic. Showing up early with expensive flowers, chocolates, and champagne is probably overdoing it. But I don't ever get to go out on dates. And I know the sappier I am to Nora, the more I will drive Siren insane.

I attached a sappy love note to each item I brought. I really hope after we leave, and Siren is left alone in the hotel room, that Siren will read every note and realize I wrote each one for her. If she would just tell me her truth, I would save her.

If she opened her heart, I would claim it.

And if she decided to only open her legs for me again, and not her heart, then I'd give her the best sex of her life.

The door opens, and Nora steps out in a smoking hot red dress that brings out the highlights in her black hair. She's left her hair natural in a pile of springy curls on top of her head, and the dress hugs her petite curves, clinging to her black skin.

Beautiful.

But not mine.

I don't get any ache to kiss her. I don't get an animalistic desire to push her against the wall and devour her. I don't feel anything other than respect for her beauty. I'd settle for her any night, but not when I know Siren is the other option.

"These are for you," I say, holding out the items to her.

"Wow, Zeke, these are beautiful. And oh my god! Dom! I haven't had that in forever. We will have to drink this when we get back tonight."

I step into their suite and put the bouquet of flowers in the small kitchenette area, while she puts the Dom in the fridge.

And then I spot her—the only woman my heart bleeds for.

She's flicking through her phone wearing sweatpants and my T-shirt, completely ignoring me, and somehow she's still the most appealing thing in the room. I love that she is still wearing my T-shirt. I never want her to take my T-shirt off again. *That is unless she's undressing for me.*

"Have any plans tonight, Siren?" I ask.

She ignores me.

"I love that nickname for you, Aria, how did you come up with it? I know there's a story I'm missing?" Nora asks.

"There is. Siren here saved me. Pulled me from the sea like she was a mermaid, and I was a drowning sailor."

"Like *The Little Mermaid*," Nora squeals, liking this story a lot.

"Exactly like *The Little Mermaid*," I say, even though I've never seen the movie. I see Siren tense because clearly, she understands the reference. "But unlike the fairytale, Siren here wasn't actually saving me. She was using me so she could serve me to her boss. Hence the name Siren. She lures men to their deaths. And I was one of the stupid men who fell for her games."

Siren frowns but doesn't look up from her phone. I swear it looks like my words wounded her, though. And I hate it. I hate hurting her.

This was a mistake. I can't flirt with Nora; it will hurt Siren too much.

But then, Siren snaps her head in my direction. Whatever hurt was there a moment ago is gone now. "Don't act like you are some prince I hurt. You aren't the prince in this story, Zeke. You are just the damn errand boy, the guy who sacrifices himself for the prince he serves. Someday, I'll find my prince, but he sure as hell isn't you." And with that, she gets up and slams the bedroom door in my face.

My stomach twists, I'm not even going to be able to enjoy dinner knowing that Siren is hurting this badly. Nora, on the other hand, seems extremely happy. She claps her hands together in excitement.

"What are you doing?" I ask.

"Cheering you two on. I wish I had a video camera right now to tape you. This is good stuff, and I know I'm only getting half the story."

"I thought you were her friend. Why are you happy she's in pain?"

Nora takes my arm. "Best friend. And I'm happy because it means she actually feels something for a man. She wouldn't act jealous or vengeful if she didn't like you."

"Maybe I should talk to her instead of going?"

"No, we are going to enjoy a dinner. Trust me, by the time we get back, Siren will be throwing herself at you, and you'll be spending your night in this bed while I sleep in the twin bed downstairs."

"That or she'll have her gun out to shoot me," I mumble under my breath.

Nora giggles. "You know her well. You'll either get the best sex of your life, or you'll end up shot."

I nod.

"Would getting shot be worth it?" she asks, not hiding the hope in her voice.

"Yes, I've already gotten shot by the woman. And trust me, it was worth it."

Nora is giddy with excitement. But it's only because she doesn't know the rest. She doesn't know Siren betrayed me. She doesn't know my only goal is to kill Siren's boss, and maybe even Siren if I can't get her to promise not to go after my friends. My only goal is to get back to my family—Enzo, Kai, Langston, Liesel...

Nora studies me closely. "You're going to break my friend's heart, aren't you?"

I chuckle. "Your friend doesn't have a heart to break."

And then Nora slaps me.

"What was that for?"

She frowns. "For when you inevitably break her. I just hope you are one of the good guys who's able to pick the pieces back up after the damage is done."

I sigh, I don't know what I'm getting myself into. These women are going to kill me. If Nora doesn't kill me on this date, Siren will when we get back.

We go to dinner, have a nice meal, and hop around a few bars looking for Beckett. And when we show up at the third bar, it turns out I won't have to wait until the end of the night to see Siren again after all.

CHAPTER 17
SIREN

Zeke and his perfect date with Nora.

Fuck them and their nice steak dinner.

Fuck Zeke in his suit pants and jacket. *Who does he think he's fooling anyway?* He looks ridiculous in that suit, with this hair pulled up in a man bun, and his clean-shaven look. His smooth, sculpted jawline I want to rub my face all over.

Screw him. I don't care that he dressed up for Nora, when I've never seen him in anything other than jeans and a T-shirt. *Nora can have him.*

And fuck his flowers, his chocolates, his champagne. *Who does he think he's impressing with that shit?*

Nobody. That's who. Definitely not me.

But then I had to be an idiot after Zeke and Nora left on their 'date.' I read the damn notes attached to each gift. I expected them to be impersonal and stupid. Something like:

To: Nora

Enjoy these flowers. I'm excited about our date.

—Zeke

. . .

BUT THAT'S NOT WHAT ANY OF THE NOTES SAID. I GRABBED THE note attached to the flowers first. Flowers I'm sure will give me allergies. *That's just what I need—a stuffy nose to deal with the rest of the trip.*

TO THE WOMAN WHO IS BEAUTY AND STRENGTH ITSELF. THESE flowers are both to honor and prove that I have hope for *more*.

WHAT THE HELL DOES THAT MEAN? MORE?
I snatched the second note, the one attached to the champagne next.

TO THE WOMAN WHO IS AS UNPREDICTABLE, EXPLOSIVE, AND SEXY AS this champagne, I can't wait to watch you explode *again*.

FUCK, THESE NOTES AREN'T MEANT FOR NORA. THEY ARE FOR ME. ZEKE knew I'd snoop as soon as they left. *Damn him. I'm not reading the last note. I'm not...*But of course, I did.

TO THE WOMAN WHO TASTED MORE DELICIOUS THAN THESE chocolates. These are to remind you how incredible we were in bed together and how I can't wait to do it *again*.

I POPPED ONE OF THE CHOCOLATES IN MY MOUTH—ANNOYED, angry, and needy. *Does he really think these gifts are supposed to change my mind?* I'm not fucking him, and I sure as hell am not giving him a chance at *more* or doing anything *again*. These notes were so damn cheesy and romantic—not the way to win my heart or a second night together.

But then I saw another note sticking out of one of the chocolates.

Don't do it.

I snagged it and read it.

I KNOW YOU THINK THESE ARE ALL CHEESY AND NOT REMOTELY romantic. Don't worry, they aren't for you, snoopy. They are for Nora.

—ZEKE

P.S. DON'T EAT THE CHOCOLATE OR DRINK THE CHAMPAGNE. THEY are for Nora, my date, who is not you.

I DROPPED THE SECOND PIECE OF CHOCOLATE I WAS ABOUT TO EAT.

No, he doesn't control me.

I grabbed two and popped them in my mouth.

After that, I knew I wasn't sitting in the hotel room all night waiting for them to get back from their date. Nora asked me if I liked him. I didn't answer, which was my way of avoiding lying to her. But she knows the truth anyway.

Yes, I like him.

No, I don't plan on breaking any more hearts—mine, especially.

So she went on the date. And she won't fuck him. But if I know Nora, she'll do some torturing of her own. Serves Zeke right for trying to make me jealous.

That leads me here to a bar, sipping a martini while I wait for them to realize Beckett is here. It's almost eleven, I expected them sooner. I know Zeke didn't just bring Nora on this date to taunt me. He also brought her because he knows the best way to get to Beckett is through a woman. But I thought Zeke's skills were better than this. That or he is really enjoying his date.

Beckett's been sitting at this bar for the past hour, sipping a bourbon on ice. While I've been trying to keep my distance, keep him from noticing me, so that when Zeke and Nora do show up, I can make my move.

Finally, at a quarter past eleven, they show up. Zeke spots me instantly, but it's not surprising since I immediately spot them too.

Nora is giggling at something he said. It's not a fake laugh, and it puts me on edge because Zeke seldom makes a joke. *But he did for her.*

No matter how attentive Zeke is to Nora, there is no denying that my connection to Zeke is stronger. He can't not notice me, just as I can't not notice him as he walks into the room. I just feel him, deep to my bones, like his presence is sending out alarm bells directed only at me. And I still can't figure out why it happens. Other than it's biological. Science says we should be together even if my brain knows better. Zeke is the kind of man I avoid.

No, I avoid all men. Men destroy my life.

Zeke moves his hand down Nora's back, and he guides her over to where I'm sitting at the end of the bar.

"What are you doing here?" Zeke asks.

"I thought I'd help you out locating Beckett and taking him down. That way, you wouldn't have to stop your date," I answer.

Zeke scowls. "Beckett's here?"

"Yep, at your five o'clock. The man in flannel and missing his right arm."

"Flannel? Really? On an island like this? He must run really cold," Nora asks, surprised.

Or he's not from around here, which is why Julian wants him dead before he takes over any more of Julian's business.

Zeke doesn't seem at all surprised by any of the information I just told him about the man. Which means he's done his research and found out everything I have.

"So, what's your plan?" Zeke sighs.

"What makes you think I have a plan? This is your mission. I'm just here to babysit and make sure you don't hurt my best friend in the process."

Nora smiles at me.

"Because you have a plan. And as you said, I don't want to hurt

Nora. You've been watching him all night. How do you think we should play it?"

I grin. *I win.* Although, when Zeke tightens his grip around Nora's waist, I feel like I lost—big time.

"I go flirt with him and get him somewhere alone. I better move quickly because there is a bachelorette party with their eyes on him," I say.

"But—" Zeke starts.

I don't let him finish, but I can hear the pain in his voice. And I glance back for a second and see the flash of worry in his eyes.

Don't fuck him, he mouths to me.

I glare back. *Really? He's going to try and give me orders? And orders to not fuck him. Does he really think I'd do that? Fuck a horrible man like Beckett, who is about to die by Zeke's hands? Not likely.*

But then Zeke thinks I just whore my body out to anyone. It almost makes me want to fuck the guy. Beckett is good looking after all, if you are into flannel.

I decide to play on his gentlemanly charms. I stumble up to the bar, almost falling in my stiletto heels I'm quite adept in walking in.

And right on cue, Beckett catches me.

I feel Zeke's eyes on me, and I give him a wink as I play the damsel in distress role that worked so well on Zeke.

"Are you okay, ma'am?" Beckett asks.

Ugh, ma'am. "Oh, excuse me. It's just a bit slippery there," I say, slurring my words just enough to sound tipsy, not drunk.

He smiles back. "Let me order you a drink. What are you having?"

"Martini," I say, even though I hate the drink. On nights like this, I drink it because it's sexy and sophisticated, and the olive that comes with it is great for flirting.

Beckett flags the bartender down and orders me a martini and him another bourbon. *This was easy, too easy.*

My suspicions are up, but when Beckett checks out my cleavage that I may have bronzed and used makeup to make extra voluptuous tonight, I know I'm just having an exceptionally good night.

"You here alone?" he asks, looking behind me.

He saw me here with Zeke and Nora. *Observant man. He must be good at what he does.*

"No, but then you already know that," I say, keeping eye contact with him as I sip my drink. I consider touching his arm to see if we get that little zing that sometimes happens with Zeke, but it feels like too much too fast. And I don't want him to get suspicious.

"I did. Do your friends want to join us?" he asks.

"Do you want them to?"

"No," he says with a smile.

I push my breasts out as I take another drink. "I'm Aria."

"Beckett."

Interesting, he goes by his last name.

"And what do you do, Beckett?"

"I'm a cattle farmer."

I raise an eyebrow. His shirt does seem to scream that, so it's not a bad lie, but I know it's not the truth.

"And what do you do?"

I opened myself up for that question. I can seduce and lie with my body, but I can't with my words. I fucking can't. So I make my move. I grab the toothpick with the olive on the end and put the olive in my mouth. Sucking slowly and seductively on the olive as I pull the toothpick out.

His eyes are entranced on my lips. *I've got him.*

I go in for the closer. I brush my fingers over his arm.

"Right now...I want to *do* you."

His body tenses and heats at my words.

I smile. "Sorry, was that too forward of me."

He clears his throat. "No, not at all. I'd—"

But he doesn't finish that thought, because Zeke and Nora are standing behind me.

"Introduce us to your friend, Aria," Zeke says with a commanding voice. All I can focus on is the fact that he called me Aria.

I grit my teeth, forcing myself to continue smiling as I turn toward Zeke and Nora. Zeke has his arm thrown casually over Nora's shoulder, and he's lightly stroking her neck half-mindedly like he doesn't even realize he's doing it.

But Nora does, because she has a delirious look on her face, and her eyes close every other second as she makes small cooing sounds. That is, until her eyes open and she sees Beckett. Her eyes go wide as she realizes the man has lost an arm, but then they quickly turn soft when she takes in his tight body and bright smile.

I sigh. This is why I don't bring Nora with me when I meet dangerous men. She gets all googly-eyed and then gets mad when I kill them.

"Zeke, Nora, this is my friend Beckett. Beckett, these are my annoying friends who were just leaving, Zeke and Nora."

Zeke holds his left hand out, and Beckett shakes it. "Zeke, huh? I think I know a Zeke."

Zeke frowns, obviously not recognizing this man, but annoyed that Beckett seems to recognize him.

"I don't get out much, never been to St. John. You're probably remembering a different man," Zeke says.

Beckett nods slowly, and I'm not sure he's convinced. *Fuck, did Zeke just screw everything up by coming over here and getting recognized?*

"I'm Nora." She holds her left hand out to Beckett, who is smiling cautiously at the woman, like he's afraid she's going to bite him. Knowing Nora, she might.

I grin at the interaction. Nora seems to have distracted Beckett long enough for me to scowl at Zeke.

Really? Was this necessary? I had him.

He raises a scowling eyebrow. *Yea, you had him about to jump into your bed.*

So?

He stiffens and turns his attention back to Beckett. Conversation over.

I grab my drink, needing more alcohol, but when I lift my drink to my lips, I realize that I already finished it when I thought I was going home with Beckett.

I raise my hand to flag down the bartender. I'm going to need a lot more alcohol and something stronger than a martini to get me through tonight.

The bartender smiles as he stops in front of me. "What can I get you, gorgeous?" He winks at me as he says it.

And in an instant, both Zeke and Beckett surround me, ready to defend my honor against the friendly bartender. Both men try to put their arms around my shoulder but only end up bumping arms awkwardly in the process.

"She'll have a martini," Beckett says at the same time Zeke says, "Another."

I lean forward, trying to escape both men. "Actually, your most expensive scotch, neat."

The bartender's eyes light up at that, like I'm telling him a secret the two bozos next to me don't know.

"I'll have that right up," the man says, not even bothering to ask if anyone else wants a drink.

But with the bartender gone, the tension is high. I give Nora a *please help me control Zeke* look, but she's still fawning all over Beckett, touching his arm, and batting her eyelashes. She may have enjoyed Zeke's attention before when she thought she was making me jealous and matchmaking Zeke and me, but now that there is an actual man in the picture who she could take home to her bed, she's changed course. I would support her completely, if I didn't think Beckett was a dangerous man who might drug, rape, or kill her.

Nora, I implore with my eyes to help me out by getting Zeke's attention. She doesn't. Instead, she keeps talking Beckett's head off.

I sigh—deciding I'll just have to wait until she's done talking to get Beckett's attention again.

"What are you doing? I was just about to close the deal," I hiss so that only Zeke can hear me.

He glares, his eyes burning into mine like he can't believe I found what I was about to do acceptable. "And I couldn't let you."

"I don't need you to protect my honor, Zeke. I'm a woman fully capable of making her own decisions. If I wanted to sleep with him, I would. If I didn't, I wouldn't."

"Well, I—"

Zeke is interrupted when the bartender returns and hands me my drink. "It's on the house," he says, winking at me.

That snaps both Zeke and Beckett's attention his way, earning a united scowl from both men.

"Thank you," I say sweetly, taking the drink and sipping on it, the liquid giving me life and enough energy to deal with both of these men. I make sure to brush my hand against the bartender's after I take my drink. If Zeke and Beckett weren't standing next to me, I'd be getting his number right now.

"So, Beckett, do you dance?" I ask, needing to get him away from Zeke and Nora.

He winces and looks down at his missing arm. "I wasn't very good before I lost my arm, and I'm not any better now."

"How did you lose your arm?" Nora asks, always the nosy one and not gentle in how she asks her questions.

"Car accident," Beckett says, taking a slow sip of his drink, his eyes on me. I can read through the lie. He didn't lose it in a car accident. He lost it doing something dangerous. Which is why I don't want him anywhere near my friend. And it's why I have to make sure he ends up dead.

I finish my drink in one large gulp, and I can feel both Zeke and Beckett's eyes on me as I swallow. I lean forward to grab Beckett's hand to pull him on the dance floor and not take no for an answer, but Zeke can apparently read my mind and knows my next move.

He grabs my arm before I have the chance, pulling me sharply toward the dance floor.

"Dance with me," he commands.

And then I'm in his strong arms, feeling like this is where I've belonged the whole time, and knowing I'm so fucking screwed.

CHAPTER 18
ZEKE

I've never felt so much rage in my entire life as I did watching Siren flirt with that man. It was so easy for her. Within seconds she had Beckett dopey-eyed, drooling, and ready to do whatever she asked of him. She is very good. *Too good.*

But then I knew that. She had me falling for her within a few seconds of meeting her, even with me delirious, drowning, and half-dead. I knew she was special. Every man who meets her knows that. It's why she has some deal with Julian. It's why she got me here, doing Julian's bidding. It's why Beckett almost walked right into her death trap.

I'm not special. Siren has treated me like every other man she's ever encountered. Like I'm a mark she's going after. And when she squeezes everything she can get from me, she'll get rid of me, just like she plans on doing with Beckett.

But with Siren in my arms, our bodies moving together on the dance floor, I forget about all of that. I may hate her, but she's hard not to fall for all the same.

"How do you do that?" I whisper into her hair, breathing in everything that makes Siren, Siren. Her intoxicating smell that's a mix of sweet and spice, just like her.

"Do what?"

"Make me like you."

She gives me an *are you absurd* look.

I laugh. Maybe I am, because she's done nothing to make me fall for her. In fact, I'd say she's tried to get me to hate her.

"You are the one trying to get me to fall for you with your chocolates and flowers and stupid notes."

I grin. *She read the notes.*

I turn her toward me, smelling her breath.

"What are you doing?" she asks.

"Looking for evidence." Then I brush my thumb over her bottom lip. "Yep, right there. You had chocolate still on your lip. I told you I bought those for Nora, not you."

She frowns. "I don't have chocolate on my lip."

I suck my thumb that was just over her lip, watching her eyes dilate, wanting me to suck something of hers. "Not anymore, you don't."

She sighs, and it's part desperation, part exhaustion, part need.

"What are we doing, Zeke? We are supposed to be figuring out a way to get Beckett on his own, not pretending we like each other when we both just want more sex."

"Then, we should talk about the sex."

"No, we shouldn't."

I spin her and then pull her tight to my body. "Why not?"

She opens her mouth and then closes it quickly. She's seldom at a loss for words, and I'm not sure I like waiting for her witty comeback. "Because sex will complicate things."

I chuckle. "Not possible. We fucked, we still hate each other. We are both still doing the job required of us. Sex did nothing but make our relationship more enjoyable."

"I just...can't."

Can't—I hate that word. Especially falling from her lips.

"I'm not giving up," I say.

And with a heavy smile, she says, "I never expected you to."

A challenge—I like a challenge. I just have no idea how to win when it comes to Siren.

By killing Julian and her.

But that's not the way I want to win. I want to win her over. I want her to want me in the same way I want her. I want her to fall for me like I stupidly fell for her.

And then what? I'll hurt her? I could never. But at least I would know I have the power too, just like she does. But unlike her, I won't rip out her heart and set it on fire just because I can. I would take care of her heart, even if I never loved her back.

The song turns slow, and I think Siren is going to use it as an excuse to stop dancing with me. She doesn't. She rests her head on my chest, and her arms go around my waist like she's hugging me, like she never wants to let me go.

I drape my arms over her shoulders, and we sway—slowly and carefully, like we are just dancing to the music, but we are dancing on each other's hearts. One wrong move could destroy us both.

I glance over at Beckett, who is listening to Nora ramble but is watching us.

I smirk. *She's mine, you asshole.*

I close my eyes and just live in the moment. This moment where Siren doesn't hate me and I don't want her dead. This moment where it doesn't matter that we are enemies or lovers or even friends. We are just together, dancing to a song neither of us will remember tomorrow. But this peaceful moment, we will remember forever.

The song stops too quickly. And I feel her dip out of my arms, mumbling something about having to go to the bathroom. I let her go because I'm stupid.

And when I glance back over where Beckett was sitting, he's gone. And so is Siren. Nora just gives me a shrug.

Fuck.

CHAPTER 19
SIREN

If my life were a soundtrack, it would be a shitty one. The kind that on first listen sounds great. The music is catchy, and there is just the right amount of emotional, slow songs to fill the track. But listening a second or third time makes you realize it's far too dramatic, has far too few happy endings, and the romance is just one sad depression into despair.

That's my life. From the outside, my life looks good. But once you dig in, you realize how complicated and shitty it really is.

Music is my life. Every important moment in my life had its own song to go with it—even if I was only playing the song in my head.

And dancing with Zeke to Never Give Up by Sia was the perfect song to describe how I feel. Dancing with a man who in another life would be the man I gave up everything for and never stopped fighting for. The man I would marry tomorrow because he's the rare good man in a sea of evil. But I don't live in a different life; I live in this life. I live in a bad soundtrack.

My life isn't Sia or Ariana Grande. My life is like a Taylor Swift love song, filled with regrets and unhappy endings.

"So you and Zeke?" Beckett asks as I walk with him out of the nightclub.

"Old flames. He's dating again, but I don't think he's fully moved on," I say, leaning into Beckett's chest as we walk to his car.

"And you? Have you moved on?" Beckett asks.

No, but then we haven't really had a chance to just 'be' in the first place.

"Do you really care if I've moved on? I'm going home with you," I say.

He smirks and then strokes my face. "By the end of the night, I'll make sure I'm the only man you think about."

I nod, but I doubt it. He could be the most amazing man in bed, and it wouldn't matter. Because I'm stupidly hung up on the oaf, who is still back at the bar about to take Nora back to his hotel room to fuck her as revenge for what he thinks I'm about to do.

I'm on the wrong side of Beckett to hold his hand, so he nudges me over until I'm on his left side and then takes my hand in his.

"Where'd you come from, Aria?"

"I'm a world traveler. But I love it here on the sand, on the beach, near the ocean. And you? Flannel? You obviously aren't from around here."

He smiles at that. "No, I'm from the arctic, the cold, the wilderness."

I tug on his beard. "I like the wilderness."

He leans his head to my side, closing our gap. "I like you."

I scrape my teeth over my bottom lip. "Yea? What do you like?"

I wait for the answer I always get when I ask a drunk man that question. You're beautiful, striking, sexy—something about my physical features.

"I like that you danced with an ex while flirting with me."

I stop walking. "You like that I'm a tease and a whore?"

He looks like I just slapped him. "No, I just meant you know your own value. You are more than just a pretty face. You aren't coming home with me because I'm your only option to get laid tonight. You weighed all of your options. I saw you sitting at the bar all night. You judged every man who walked in, deciding if he was worthy. Even worthy of just one night with you. You narrowed it down between me and your ex. And even then, you made it clear going home was also an option. You are an independent woman who doesn't need a man. I like that."

He puts his hand in his pocket, waiting for me to make the next move since I'm a strong, independent woman and all that. I like that he's letting me make the next move. But sometimes, I want a man I can depend on. A man who will take care of me. A man who does things for me in spite of the fact that I can do it for myself—make my own money, get myself off, and fight my own battles. Sometimes, I want a man to do all those things.

Beckett smiles, shaking his head at me.

"What?" I ask, knowing he can read me well. I still don't know what he does exactly, but he's skilled at reading people.

"You'll find that man someday; I'm just not him."

"How did you read my mind?"

He shrugs. "People are easy to read."

"Is that why you stick to herding cattle?"

He laughs. "Yes, cattle are way more interesting."

I grab the collar of his shirt and pull him to me. "I think you're interesting."

And then I kiss him, because I need to make the first move. If he tried to kiss me, I'd probably slap him or something. He's worried about that too, which is why he's been keeping his distance. But now that our lips are pressed together, he's not being so cautious.

His hand runs down my back over my ass, and then he squeezes as our lips press hard together, urgently. Our lips part and our tongues tangle in a familiar dance. It's a great fucking kiss. Beckett knows how to part his lips, move his tongue, dip his head to deepen the kiss. He knows how to use his one hand to press our bodies together and send little chills down my back. I even get little butterflies in my stomach when he kisses me because I know what happens next. It's exciting and new, but it's not Zeke.

Fuck, it's not Zeke.

I thought fucking him once was enough. But it's clear now that once wasn't enough to rid my feelings of him. I need to fuck Zeke until it's boring, no longer new. Until we've done all the usual positions. Until there is nothing new to explore with each other. Until we crave someone else.

Beckett ends the kiss. "My place or yours?"

"Yours," I say with a smile.

He wiggles his eyebrows behind him. Turns out, Beckett's hotel is right behind us.

I grin as he pulls on my hand, but I feel familiar chills run down my body. The intense kind that only comes from one man—Zeke.

I turn my head and see him walking down the sidewalk alone. He saw the kiss, and he looks like Godzilla about to destroy an entire village.

Maybe it's for the best. Zeke won't want me after he saw me kiss another man. And even though my body craves Zeke, no one will get hurt this way.

Beckett pulls me through the lobby's glass doors and then to the elevator bay. He's a gentleman, holding my hand as we wait for the elevator doors to open, but once inside, he's an animal.

He fists my ponytail as he pulls my head back to kiss me hard.

Focus on this kiss. Let the tingles I feel on my lips ignite a new fire— for any man other than Zeke.

Nothing. The tingles go nowhere. It's nice, but not holy-fucking-hot. It's just pleasant.

But when I look at Beckett, I know he's feeling a lot more than just nice. He's excited and happy about what comes next, and I play along with him.

We stumble back, groping each other, and stopping to kiss as we make our way to his hotel room. I take everything in as we walk. The escape route through the emergency stairs. The fire alarm. Then ten other rooms on this floor. The security camera in the corner. Even the stain two feet from Beckett's room I purposefully step over because, ew.

And once we are in Beckett's room, I realize one thing right away. He's messy as hell.

"Sorry about the mess," Beckett says.

"Ever hear of a hamper?" I ask against his lips, noticing all his clothes piled everywhere.

"Nope." He kisses back, already grabbing at my shirt, trying to pull it up.

I laugh when he yanks my shirt up, but it gets stuck around my ears, and we both have to slow down. Finally, he gets my shirt off, and his eyes devour my black lace bra and cleavage.

"Damn," he says.

I blush, biting my lip, liking the attention, even though I know how this night ends.

"Your turn," I say, grabbing his shirt and unbuttoning the flannel. I'm not sure what I expect when I undress him, but I wasn't expecting abs. *So many abs.*

"Impressive," I say, kissing the first ab. Zeke is big, thick, bulk muscle. While Beckett has thin, sleek muscles. The two men couldn't be more different.

I grab the hair tie holding my hair up in a sleek ponytail and let my hair down. He watches my hair fall with large eyes.

And then I push his bare chest, and he walks back until he hits the bed. He scoots up the bed, leaning back against the headboard while I climb up his body, putting one leg on each side of his, straddling him. His hand rests on my hip as I lean forward and kiss him, forcefully and deliciously. I kiss him to distract him, to make him forget with hopes that if I kiss him hard enough, I'll forget too. Not him, but Zeke.

But no amount of kissing can erase Zeke's kisses from my mind.

I reach into my back pocket, pull out a syringe, and then jab it into Beckett's neck.

"Sorry," I say as he slumps down. The drugs will knock him out for a bit until Zeke gets here and we can go through his stuff and decide what to do with him. I grab a shirt from the floor and tie his arm to the headboard. It won't hold him for long if he wakes up, but it will be one more obstacle to keep him from attacking us straight away.

I glance around the room that is going to take us hours to go through. There is way too much crap. I could start now, but I decide to help myself to Beckett's whiskey while I wait for Zeke.

But I don't have to wait long because a pound on the door tells me Zeke is here, and he isn't happy.

CHAPTER 20
ZEKE

I should have turned around. I should have walked to my own hotel and forgot what I saw. Maybe drank my misery away? Or fucked Nora after all?

But I couldn't.

When I saw Siren kiss Beckett, my world ended. At first, I thought I was dreaming. It was all a nightmare. But soon I realized that it was real. I was standing on the sidewalk watching Siren kiss a man who is most likely the devil—a man who deserves to be killed, not fucked by an angel like Siren.

And in that moment, watching her kiss another man, I know that my life will forever be intertwined with hers. I will never be able to kiss another woman without thinking about Siren. I will never be able to watch a woman who looks like Siren kiss a man without needing a drink to wash her memory from my mind. I will never be able to kiss enough women to rid my brain of her kisses.

Why?

I don't know.

It's not love I'm feeling. Even though I've never loved a woman before, I know that isn't what this is. If I was in love with her, I wouldn't have been able to watch her walk into that hotel room with him. I wouldn't have been able to pause outside for even a minute without chasing after and shooting him dead.

If it's not love, then what is it?

Lust?

Desire?

My claim that Siren is mine?

Fuck, I don't know.

I don't want love. I don't want some romantic fairytale that will never exist between us. The romantic gestures are just that—gestures. I'm a nice guy who likes taking care of others. I like flowering Siren with pretty things and then watching her squirm in discomfort, just like she likes kissing other men and watching the turmoil on my face.

I try to force myself to turn around. Let her fuck Beckett and kill him. Then I don't have to worry about him. I'll have accomplished Julian's sin without having to do anything.

I turn away.

I take a step.

And then I spin on a dime and run in the other direction.

I head into the hotel lobby, knowing it's too late to find out which room they are in by stalking them. My choices are to ask the hotel receptionist or hack the security system.

I stare at the hotel receptionist—a woman in her mid-twenties, already eating me up in my suit.

Flirting with the hotel receptionist it is.

"May I help you?" she asks in a too-sweet voice.

"Yes," I walk over and give her my best worried, puppy dog eyes. "My sister is diabetic. She left the bar with a date. She texted me this address and told me to bring her medicine, but her phone's dead, so I don't know which room to bring it to."

She smiles. "You are such a good big brother."

I lean on the counter until my hand just touches hers. She shivers like a thrill just shot through her. "I am."

"What's her last name?" she asks.

"I think the hotel is listed under her date's name, but I don't know his name. She probably got here five, maybe ten minutes before I did," I ask, hopeful she saw them enter together and knows who I'm talking about. I don't bother giving his name since I doubt he rented a room under it.

She frowns, trying to rack her brain.

"She was wearing tight jeans and a black shirt. He was in flannel and only has one arm."

"Oh, yes. I think he's on the eighth floor. But I'm not sure which room. Without his last name, I can't look him up."

I sigh. "Thanks."

I knock on five doors before I find the right one.

Siren answers the door, holding a glass of whiskey in her hand. Her pants are still on, but her shirt is off, giving me a perfect view of her black lace bra, pushing her boobs up.

"Going to accuse me of being a whore?" she asks, putting her hand on her hip clearly annoyed with me, when I should be the one annoyed with her.

I push past her and go inside; I'm not going to argue with her with the door open and Beckett inside.

I don't know what I expected when I walked inside, but what I find isn't it. Beckett is lying on the bed, slumped over, with his arm tied to the bedpost. His flannel shirt is open, but otherwise, he's completely dressed.

"Or accuse me of being into BDSM?" she asks, slamming the hotel room door.

I turn, and Siren runs into my body, the glass swaying in her hands.

"No, I was just going to say I was wrong."

She blinks rapidly, her mouth falling open slightly. "What do you mean, you were wrong?"

I take the glass from her hands, down it, and set it on the nightstand.

She frowns, crossing her arms, which only pushes her boobs up higher, distracting me.

"I'm waiting," she says when I don't answer.

"I was wrong when I said I don't want to be with you. When I said you were a whore. Or at least, implied it. I don't care who you are. I don't care what you've done. Or what the consequences are. I need to fuck you again."

Her tongue sticks out between her teeth at my words. And I can see so much happening behind her long eyelashes. Emotions I can't even begin to understand.

"You don't get to fuck me again. You had your one time."

"Liar," I say, stepping forward into her space.

She doesn't yield. She holds her ground and stares at Beckett instead of me.

I grab her chin, forcing her to look at me. "Don't look at him; look at me."

She exhales slowly as she looks at me.

"You've had us both. Tasted us both with your lips."

She nods.

"Who was better?"

"You," she whispers.

Heaven, it sounds like heaven hearing her confirm what I already know. Because she can't fake a kiss like ours. I know how incredibly rare it is. She doesn't kiss every man like that. I saw how she kissed Beckett. It was nothing compared to our kisses.

"You tasted his abs. Whose are better?" I ask, after I saw her red lipstick smeared on his chest.

She bites her teeth, holding back a sassy grin. "His."

I step further into her space. "I'm going to make you pay for that. Was that the first lie you ever told?"

She laughs gently, still on edge about what is happening between us. "It wasn't a lie; he has clearly spent more time on his abs than you have. But your arms..."

I growl, my arms definitely win as does another body part.

"Truth or sin? Who do you want to fuck? Him or me?"

She holds her breath, trying to figure a way out of this mess. The only way she ends this is to choose him. But that would be a lie, and she doesn't have it in her to lie, not with her words.

"You first. Truth or sin? Did you lie in our game earlier when you said you want to fuck Nora?"

I grab her wrists, and then I slam them high over her head as I push her body against the wall until she's trapped by my body. She can deny not liking giving up control all she wants, but I can read the signs. When it comes to sex, she wants to be controlled, dominated. She doesn't want nice. And good thing, because in the bedroom, I'm anything but nice.

"I didn't lie," I say.

Her eyes fall closed, and I can feel the pain emanating off her.

"But I didn't tell the complete truth either," I say.

Her eyes fly open.

"Yes, my cock would love to fuck Nora in the same way it wants to fuck any good looking woman. But not nearly as bad as I want to fuck you. If given the choice between fucking a hundred women or only you, I'd always choose you."

Her eyes heat, and her thoughts swirl in her head. She doesn't speak. She pants as she takes in every word I say.

"Truth or sin? Who do you want to fuck? Beckett or me?"

"Sin," she answers.

And I push up against her until she can feel every part of my hardness pushed up against her softness. Until I already know what sin she is planning on committing. She may not have chosen me with her words, but she's going to choose me with every other fiber of her being.

I lower my lips to hers, needing to taste her more than I need to breathe. Her lips part, ready for the kiss, wanting it desperately. But just before our lips touch, she says, "You, I don't want to fuck anyone but you."

Together we close the gap between us. Fuck, this kiss is better than I remember. The softness of her lips, the slickness of her tongue, the way she demands everything from me. I've never felt anything like her. I can't control my body, my thoughts, my wicked desires. She consumes everything within my body when she kisses me.

I trail my kisses down her neck, needing to taste every inch of her. She arches her back as I kiss, moaning as I continue to hold her against the wall. I can't let her go. I'll take her right here against the wall.

I grab her leg, pulling it up as I press between her.

"If you keep that up, I'm going to come before we get undressed," she moans.

"Good, I want to hear you scream my name a hundred times tonight."

My cock pushes up against her again, telling her exactly what I want from her, and what I plan on giving her.

"Fuck," she moans.

I smirk, pushing her bra down and finding her nipple to devour in my mouth. I'm rewarded with a delicious moan, and her twisting in my grasp, needing to get free and feel more of me.

"Are you going to fuck me against this wall?" Siren asks, raising an eyebrow at me.

"No, I want to fuck you in a bed." I grab her around the waist, pulling her from the wall and moving toward the bed when I suddenly remember Beckett is on the bed.

I howl.

She whimpers. "Zeke, I need—"

I devour her mouth again; I can't fuck her on the bed or even in this room, not with Beckett passed out on the bed. I should be focused on him. I should be searching his room and interrogating him before killing him and figuring out how to dispose of his body. Instead, all I can think about is Siren.

"Should we sneak into another hotel room?" I ask, not able to wait until after we get rid of Beckett to have her.

She gasps. "I can't wait that long."

Our hands move all over each other's bodies. Our tongues continue dancing and exploring each other's mouths, but it's not enough. We both want more. And I'm not going to let the fact that Beckett is lying on the only bed in the room stop us.

We both get the idea at the same time. We push through the bathroom door—my desire burning in my eyes, and Siren's need looming on her face.

I sweep the contents off the sink and counter in one swoop, and then I grab Siren and sit her up on the ledge.

My head dips back to her breasts, finding her nipple and teasing each peak as she unbuttons her pants. I grab them and yank them off her body before I kneel down and kiss the folds between her legs, pushing her panties aside. She's so wet, so sweet, so everything I want but have denied myself for too long. Once was never going to be enough when it came to Siren.

She grabs onto my hair, like she needs to hold onto me for balance, to stay grounded here in this moment as I bring her closer to the brink of her orgasm. Just as I know she's about to explode, she yanks my hair hard. And my lips fall away from Siren's body.

"What?" I growl, needing to hear her come, to taste her sweetness spill onto my tongue.

"I don't want to come until you're inside me. I want to save all my orgasms for when I can feel you, all of you."

Fuck. Yes.

She grins, her eyes heavy and seductive as she grabs onto the collar of my shirt. "Now, it's time I get you out of these ridiculous clothes."

"Ridiculous?" I nibble on her bottom lip as she starts undoing the buttons of my shirt. "Because from the attention you have been giving me all night, I figured you quite liked me in a suit."

She pushes the jacket off, then rips the rest of the buttons off as she tears my shirt open.

"I like you every way, but my preferred way is naked," she says before she sinks her nails into my chest, feeling every ripple of muscle on my chest and stomach.

I grab her hand, kissing her palm gently. "I thought you didn't like my abs? My abs aren't good enough?"

She bites her lip. "I just haven't gotten as acquainted with them as I want. I don't know them well enough." She leans forward and runs her tongue over each ripple, moving down further and further until her tongue dips just below the waistband of my pants.

"Jesus Christ," I curse, and then I come undone.

I'm tired of games. I'm tired of pretending we don't want each other when we do. Most of all, I'm tired of not having her when my entire body would give up food, water, and even its ability to breathe in order to have her.

"Fuck me, Zeke. Please, I can't wait."

I grab her off the counter and spin her around, pushing her down until she's hugging the sink with her arms, and her ass is in the air. She's still wearing her bra, and I'm still wearing my shirt ripped open and my pants. But neither of us can wait any longer to get fully undressed. Our need is too great.

I undo my pants, and my cock springs free already pushing at her entrance, knowing it's exactly where he belongs.

Our eyes lock in the mirror, and she spreads her legs wider for me. Her lips part, and her eyes darken, more than prepared for me. I want to take my time, knowing that each time I have her could be my last. But I can't control myself. Not with her.

I grab her hips and sink inside her as she pushes back against me.

"Tell me you want me," I say as I thrust in her.

"I want you. I want this."

"Tell me this isn't your sin? That this won't be the last time we fuck."

She gasps as I push deeper inside her, and then her eyelashes flutter up. "This won't be the last time."

Yes.

She said it, so it will be true.

Because this can't be the last time, I need so much more. I need her on all fours, on top of me, spread on my bed. I need her slow and fast. I need her on the counter, in the shower, on the bed, against the wall, and every other surface I can find. I need her tied up and in control.

I need Siren in every way before I can let her go.

Fucking her now is only the start.

"Harder, Zeke," Siren cries out.

I fuck her slower, not ready to let her come just yet. I know that her pulsing around me, combined with her screaming my name, will make me come far faster than I want.

"Zeke!" Her cries beg me to move faster, to give her what she needs—an explosive orgasm.

I take my time, drawing everything out. "Not yet, my siren. Not yet."

She claws at the sink, and from the dirty look she's giving me, she wishes her nails were driving into my flesh, telling me exactly how desperately she wants me to stop teasing her and let her come.

But when I thrust inside her again, my patience evaporates. I need to come as badly as she does.

So I move harder, faster, gripping her hips as I thrust in and out of her. Her pussy throbs on my cock, telling me how close she is. Her little whimpers push me forward. She whips her hair from her back to shoulder and flashes me a look that reads sin. I reach around her body, finding her clit with my fingers. She shudders at the touch and then...

She sings my name at the top of her lungs.

And I'm hers in an instant. I want a repeat of this moment, now and forever. I don't know about forever, but I can settle on now.

CHAPTER 21

SIREN

When Zeke fucks me, it feels like he belongs in me. Like he's the missing piece of my puzzle.

And the second he stops, I feel alone and desperate. I feel empty—not just physically, but like he takes all of the life inside me with him when he stops.

I stand gripping the sink, my legs weak, and my body trembling. Zeke is standing behind me, staring at me like he can't believe what just happened, and he's not sure what to do next.

I'm not sure either. This wasn't supposed to happen. We were only supposed to fuck once. Now that we've fucked a second time, what is going to stop us from doing it over and over again? Even if I know how this ends—us hating each other even more than we already do.

I take a deep, steadying breath as I look at Zeke in the mirror. He's looking at me with hungry, determined eyes. We fucked so quickly, neither of us is even fully undressed. He's still wearing his pants and shirt. I'm still wearing my bra and panties he pushed to the side when we fucked.

But neither of us look more satiated than we did before we started.

"We should go check on Beckett," I say between heavy breaths crashing through my entire body.

"Should we?" Zeke asks, running his fingers down my back.

I nod.

I watch as he shrugs off his shirt and then steps out of his pants until he's naked. My tongue flicks to the roof of my mouth, trying desperately to not show him how his naked body affects me.

He steps back, keeping his eyes on me, he opens the glass door and flicks on the shower.

"Or?" he cocks his head to the side, with a devious twinkle in his eyes, telling me what he wants without saying it.

So I respond the same way. I unhook my bra, letting it fall down my arms. Then I slide my black panties down before stepping out of my heels.

I take a step toward him, feeling seductive, but my legs are weakened. I grip the sink, keeping myself standing as the effects of my early orgasm roll through me. Zeke took everything from me when he fucked me.

He smirks at my reaction.

He steps forward and grabs my arm, tugging me to him. And then he pulls me into the shower.

"I can never get enough of you," he says, before his lips claim mine again.

And when he kisses me, that's exactly how I feel—claimed. Like he's demanding me to say I'm his with each kiss. Say I belong to him.

I don't want to belong to anyone. I don't want to be claimed. Even if a tiny part of my heart aches to be his. I won't let that part of me win. I will never belong to anyone but myself. Not again.

Zeke kisses me again, and I falter. I stop the kiss, letting my face fall as the water hits my face, smacking me with reality. I need a moment to think, to clear my head.

But Zeke doesn't let me pause. He tilts my head up, until our eyes meet again, and he presses a soft kiss. "It's only sex."

It's only sex. It's what I want to hear and also the same words that will destroy me. His words should be exactly what I want to hear. Instead, they rip me down to my soul.

He deepens his kisses, reminding my body of how badly I want him. And I forget about his words. I forget about everything else except Zeke. My body stirs, needing him again.

He's gentle with me this time. He holds me up against the wall as my legs continue to tremble from exhaustion, but not willing to give up having him again. I want him. I need him. And shaky legs will not stop me from having him.

I pull his hair free from the man bun, and he shakes his hair as the water runs over us both. My back shivers against the cool tile, and Zeke kisses every inch of my body he can find—my neck, my breasts, my stomach. He stops between my thighs when I gasp from a single kiss there.

After our first round, I'm so sensitive that I could burst from a single touch.

But then he lowers his mouth, kissing over the wound that has only started to heal on my leg. And I can read his pain in his eyes.

"This is just sex, remember?" I say to him, not able to handle his pity.

"Just sex," he says back before kissing my scar again.

I gasp at the sensitive brush of his lips over my thigh. He continues over all of my body, trying to kiss every scar he can find like he's kissing away the memory of each pain inflicted. He doesn't realize the only scar on my body that needs healing is the one over my heart. But that scar is unhealable.

I start to shiver again, and Zeke holds me tight to his body, warming me. I feel the hardness of his chest against my cheek, I feel his heart beating against my ear, and I belong here, in his arms.

Zeke kisses down my face, and then without speaking, he lifts one of my legs, and he enters me in one long stroke.

I gasp as he fills me.

It's a feeling I'm not sure I'll ever get used to when it comes to Zeke, or want to ever give up.

I wrap my hands around his neck, and we kiss lazily like we've been kissing each other our entire lives as Zeke slides in and out of me. He moves like he knows every curve of my body and what every whimper escaping my throat means. And he does.

He shouldn't be able to make me feel so good, not when he's being so casual. He shouldn't know my body so well. But it seems he's discovered all of my secrets, at least my physical ones.

We move together in unison, both taking our time, building to the inevitable moment this ends.

I gasp and pant and feel my nerves tingling with excitement. And I know I'm about to come. I bite down on Zeke's shoulder, causing a tiny droplet of his blood to flee as I pierce his flesh.

The roar he gives me in return hits me right in the gut.

When he comes, I feel his warm seed inside me. When he pulls out, I feel it flow down my leg. And for a moment, I feel so incredibly content. If I keep fucking him, I could chase this feeling for much longer.

Slowly, Zeke puts my leg down, making sure I'm steady on my feet. *This was just sex.*

He reaches behind him and grabs the shampoo bottle. I put my hand out to take it from him when he's finished. Instead, he squirts the shampoo on my head and massages it into my scalp with his magical fingers.

I close my eyes, getting lost in how good his hands make me feel. I've never been pampered before, but I guess this is how it feels. Zeke washes my hair, then my body.

When I open my eyes, he has a fluffy towel wrapped around me. I realize this is more than just sex. I don't know what it is. I don't know when Zeke stopped hating me entirely for my betrayal. I don't know when I stopped thinking about him as only my enemy. But it happened.

And now this is happening. Zeke is taking care of me, and I didn't immediately fight him off. This new relationship we have entered into is going to fuck up everything, because it sure as hell isn't just sex. It's definitely not love, we aren't dating, but it's more than just sex.

I wrap the towel around my body and step out without speaking a word to Zeke. There are no words to say. Everything has changed, and although the sex is out of this world amazing, the consequences are going to be equally damaging.

I pick up my bra and ruined panties off the floor. Then find my jeans and shoes. I put everything on except for the panties, while Zeke dries off and wraps the towel around his waist, in no hurry to get dressed.

I wring my hair out, knowing it's going to be a frizzy mess in an hour when it air dries, but I don't want to stay in the bathroom with Zeke just so I can dry my hair.

I run out of the bathroom to find my shirt and wait for Zeke to get dressed. Hopefully, we will get back to business. We will figure out what to do with Beckett, and then when we return to St. Kitts, we will continue to hate each other.

I bend down and pick up my shirt off the floor of the bedroom. And I pause.

"Zeke!" I shout.

He runs out, still only wearing the towel. His eyes are wide, and his teeth clenched.

I run my hand through my hair in frustration.

Beckett is gone. He snuck out while we were fucking.

"We need to start going through his things, see if we can find any clues to where he's gone," Zeke snaps.

I nod.

But as I look around the room, I realize we didn't just make one mistake; we made two. Clothes hang off every piece of furniture in the room. But there is no flannel, no jeans, no men's clothes at all. The room is filled with women's clothes. And before we fucked on it, the bathroom vanity was covered in makeup.

"This isn't Beckett's room," I say to Zeke as he opens a drawer in the nightstand.

Zeke stands up, examining the room closely, and realizing I've spoken the truth.

"Dammit," he says, kicking the nightstand so hard it falls over. He's glaring at me like this is all my fault. Like I tricked him somehow by forcing him to fuck me.

I glare back. I won't let him blame me.

I pull on my shirt and untuck my hair out from my neckline, flipping it to one side.

"I'm going to find Beckett. When you stop glaring, come find me."

I throw the door open. "Or don't." I stomp outside and slam the door in Zeke's face, knowing that fucking Zeke just became an even bigger mistake.

It could cost Zeke everything, if we don't find Beckett.

CHAPTER 22
ZEKE

I'm such a fool. That's how I feel every time I let Siren back into my life. *I'm a fucking fool.*

I should have been focused on Beckett. Instead, I was tempted by Siren. And once I was under her spell, there was nothing to break me free of her. Fucking her again made me realize that with one kiss, she can manipulate me into doing anything. One fuck, and I would risk my life for her.

It was a mistake.

Kissing her.

Fucking her.

All of it.

And now I'm alone in a hotel room, with only a towel around my waist. Siren has run off, and I'm not sure if it's to bail me out of this mess by finding Beckett or to abandon me and make me figure it out by myself.

I head back to the bathroom to retrieve my clothes, and all the memories and emotions of just a few minutes ago come flooding back. The way Siren looked at me, the way she moaned for me, the way she felt around my cock.

Fucking her might have been a mistake, but it was worth it.

I throw my clothes on, not even bothering to button my shirt up as I chase after Siren. I run through the hotel and take the stairs instead of the elevator, hoping Siren didn't get very far in the time it took me to get my head together.

But I don't find her in the lobby or on the street.

I run my hand through my long hair in frustration. A burst of thunder rolls overhead, and I shudder as rain pours down on me, matching my mood. I'm wet, half-dressed, and bewildered as to the locations of either Beckett or Siren.

It doesn't get much worse.

I feel a buzz in my pocket, and I yank my phone out to a text message from Siren.

GOT A CAR. MEET ME AT THE CORNER OF 10TH AND CUMMINGS.

I SIGH AND RUB MY NECK. SIREN IS ALWAYS TWO STEPS AHEAD OF ME. I need to think faster if I'm ever going to keep up with her.

I jog the three blocks to the corner she described. Two seconds later, a Toyota pulls up next to me.

I move to grab the passenger door when the driver's side door opens, and Siren pops out, flicking me the keys. I catch them with a puzzled look.

"You're letting me drive?" I ask.

She sighs. "Just drive. I'll explain when we aren't both getting soaked."

We both run around the car until I'm on the driver's side, and she's on the passenger's side. We climb in, and I start driving, even though I don't have a clue where I'm going.

"Where am I driving?"

"Straight. I'm tracking him on my phone," Siren says.

I glance over at her. "You're tracking Beckett?"

"Yes, I put a tracker on his phone while he was out. But if he's smart, he'll ditch his phone soon. So we need to hurry."

I nod and step on it, making her grip her seat and inhale a deep breath. I'm surprised she's riding in the car with me driving again.

"He's at the docks," Siren says.

I take a sharp turn and head toward the docks.

An awkward silence passes now that we have nothing to talk about until we get there.

"I'm not going to apologize," Siren says.

I stiffen.

"I did nothing wrong," she says.

I pull the car over to the side of the road as we reach the docks.

"You never do."

I don't know if I meant it honestly or sarcastically, but by the scowl on her face, I know the words came out wrong.

I'm a stupid fool. But right now, I can't apologize for it or convince Siren I didn't mean anything by it. Right now, I need to find Beckett.

I pull my gun out as I jump out of the car.

Siren does the same next to me.

"You don't need to come. I got this," I say.

"Sexist," she murmurs under her breath.

"No, you are more than capable of defending yourself. This just isn't your fight. It's mine. And as you don't want me to protect you, I don't want to be protected either."

She frowns. "I can help."

"I know. But don't."

She follows me for another second toward the docks and then stops.

I continue on my own, not looking back at Siren. She's safe, that's all that matters.

The sky is dark, well past midnight. There are no lamp posts on the long pier I'm walking down. The only light is from the moon overhead and the lights from the town behind me. But the darkness doesn't stop me from walking. I need to find Beckett. I need to complete the first sin.

And I need to get Siren out of my fucking head.

I don't see any movement or hear sounds of other men as I walk. I feel completely alone. It's how I like it when I go into battle. Alone, so I have no one to protect except myself.

I keep walking into the darkness, hoping Siren is right, and Beckett is here. Hoping he didn't just throw his phone out the window and keep driving.

A red light blinds me and gives me my answer.

I freeze, as the red light trains on my forehead.

"Put your hands up," Beckett says from the darkness.

I don't know how good of a shot he is, but I do as he says while he has his gun aimed at my forehead. I'm guessing he can at least hit me when I'm out in the wide open, and there is little to no pressure on him.

"Drop the gun," Beckett says, as he steps out of the shadows.

I reluctantly do as he says again. He's several feet away from me. Too far for me to disarm him. And he'd shoot me dead before I was able to aim my gun in his direction. I could try to jump over the side into the water, but my chances of him not hitting me are slim. My only shot is talking him down.

"We should talk," I say.

Beckett laughs. "You want to talk, huh? Right, now that you are the one about to be shot, you want to talk. But when your girlfriend drugged me and tied me up, you didn't seem to be in much of a talking mood."

I take a deep breath, trying to figure out how to get out of here alive. At least if Beckett kills me, Julian will never get any information about Enzo Black. He will never learn how to take him down. He will remain safe.

"Where is your girlfriend?" Beckett asks.

"She's not my girlfriend. And she's not involved in this life at all."

"Maybe not, but she's clearly a pro."

I shrug. "Who cares if she is? She's working for me. I'm the one who wants you dead, not her."

"Who do you work for?" Beckett asks.

"Myself."

Beckett frowns. "And who are you? You say you work for yourself, then who are you?"

"I'm Zeke Kane."

He blinks rapidly. "Zeke Kane is dead. You're an imposter. Trying to use his connections and likeness. Tell me who you really are, or I'll kill you."

I narrow my eyes, my hands still in the air, and his gun still aimed at my head. This man knows who I am. He knows my name. He knows I'm supposed to be dead. But I have no clue who he is. I don't remember him from my life before.

"Three..." Beckett starts.

"Really? Going to countdown like I'm a child? You think that's going to work?" I joke, hoping it will get him to stop long enough so I can think about what to do next. *How do I find out who he is? How do I keep him from shooting me first?*

"Two."

Fuck.

"One."

I close my eyes, readying myself for death. I've already escaped death so many times before. Fate is finally going to win.

"Wait!" I hear a desperate voice scream from the darkness—Siren's wail.

I open my eyes and find her standing next to me, completely out of breath, her body trembling, and her eyes wild with pain.

She doesn't care about me. She's just acting.

"Don't kill him. I'll tell you everything you need to know," Siren says.

Beckett's eyes go between Siren and me, but he keeps the gun pointed at me. *Good.*

"And why should I listen to you?" Beckett asks.

"Because I'm Aria Torres." *Wait...she told me before her last name was Martinez? Did she lie to me then? Or is she lying now?*

Beckett immediately aims his gun at Aria instead of me.

She smirks with her hands on her hips, and I see the relief on her face now that the gun is no longer pointed at me.

"Zeke works for me. Take me, not him," she says.

"Done," Beckett says.

Siren starts walking forward, but I grab her arm. "No," I say.

She rips her wrist from my grasp. "Save yourself, don't come after me. Swear it?"

I don't swear. And then she walks over to Beckett while he continues to aim the gun at her.

"Follow me, and I'll kill her," Beckett says.

She saved me when I didn't deserve saving.

But if she thinks I can just let Beckett take her without fighting back, then she doesn't know me at all. I will never make that vow.

CHAPTER 23
SIREN

Beckett keeps the gun aimed at me as I step onto a small dingy boat, and we speed off. And I resist the urge to look back to the pier to see if Zeke heeded my warning and left, or if he's still standing there, trying to figure out how to save me.

I don't want to know which he chose. Either option would gut me.

"Put your hands up," Beckett says.

I do.

He stops the boat after we've traveled at least a mile away from shore. He pats me down, finding my gun and knife, before tying my arms behind my back with rope. He does quite a good job for a man with only one arm.

With us a mile from shore, I finally glance back at the pier. I can no longer make out people. I can barely make out the pier jutting out into the water. So I have no idea what Zeke decided to do.

But at least in this moment, he's safe. Watching him stand on the pier, defending those he loved, was astonishing. It was an incredible sight of courageousness. *And it fucking terrified me.*

Once Zeke started down the pier, I tried to stay back and do what he asked. But I couldn't stand by and watch him die. I just couldn't. Even if we are enemies. Even if he's destined to kill me one day.

I've never felt so terrified. My body shook with fear, thinking I might not run down the pier fast enough in my heels to stop Beckett from shooting him dead.

And when I saved him, it was like the sun came out again for the first time. I wasn't going to have to live a life cast in darkness, a life without Zeke.

Once Beckett has my arms tied and my weapons taken, he sits back, staring at me. "So you're the famous Aria Torres, man-eater."

I nod. "I'm surprised you didn't figure it out when I told you my first name."

He rests his gun in his lap as he studies me. "I fell for your charm, same as every other man you've encountered. But you're getting soft. You should have shot and killed me in that hotel room, not tied me up and fucked another man. That was careless of you."

"It was."

"So why didn't you kill me then?"

"Because I wanted to question you first, with Zeke's help."

"What questions could you possibly have?"

I smile. "None anymore. You already answered my question."

"And what question was that?"

"Who are you?"

He stills.

"You're Eli Beckett. You work for the Black empire."

His jaw tenses, and his shoulders flex, ready to fight. I thought my comment might get me shot on the spot, but Beckett knows he needs to find out who I work for, or who I've passed that information along to first.

Beckett made it very hard for me to find out who his boss is, which means Mr. Black uses Beckett for secret operations. So knowing his identity would put his job at risk.

"How do you know that?" Beckett finally asks. He doesn't raise his gun. He knows I'll answer without threatening him. Because only one of us is going to survive this boat ride. So there is no danger in us both spilling our secrets.

"Because you know Zeke Kane."

"I don't actually."

Now it's my turn to raise an eyebrow. "You sure seemed like it back there."

"I know the name. I know Zeke Kane used to work for my boss. I also know that he died. But I never met the man. Just heard great things about him."

Ah, there it is. "So you have no idea if the man you almost killed was the actual Zeke Kane or an imposter?"

He nods slowly.

I laugh and lean forward. "Well, let me let you in on a secret. That man back there, is the real Zeke Kane. He survived. I was the one who saved him. I pulled him from the water. You almost shot the wrong guy."

"Fuck," Beckett says, leaning back in his chair in complete shock.

He rubs his temple. "But if that is really Zeke, the infamous man who laid down his life to save people time and time again, then why is he working for you?"

Because I have the ability to control his heart. "Why do you think?"

"Because he's trying to protect the Black family. Same as always."

Bingo.

"Jesus, I guess I should thank you," he says.

"For what?"

"For keeping me from making the biggest mistake of my life. If I killed Zeke, no one would ever forgive me."

Least of all me.

"So are the rumors true? Can you really kill a man with just one look?" he asks.

"You tell me." I swing my still damp hair over my shoulder and push out my breasts as I carefully move my fingers down, where I dropped a weapon into the darkness of the boat before Beckett searched me.

He frowns. "I don't know what to make of you, Aria. But I think you are worthy of every rumor that has ever been told about you."

I smile. "Thanks for the compliment."

"Do you work alone or for someone?" he asks.

"I work for myself." And that statement has never been more true. I work for myself. Everything I do is selfish. Even if Julian Reed likes to claim the title of boss. There is so much more to the truth than that.

"What's your plan now? What do you want with me?" I ask, licking my lip, teasing him with my tongue, and reminding him of our kiss, even though I know that moment has passed. *Sex won't save me this time.*

"You already know what I have to do. I have to kill you. You're a threat to me, my boss, and even Zeke. I have to kill you and go rescue Zeke."

I take a deep breath. "That's my move."

My words are a warning. My eyes flick wide with urgency. And then I jump at the same time Beckett does. We both dive in opposite directions, moments before the bomb goes off. Water sprays my face as I dive under the water. I kick hard to get as far away from the explosion.

And when the explosion hits, I'm deep below the water. But I still feel the explosion vibrate through me. I don't look for Beckett under the water, but I have no doubt he survived.

I warned him; I shouldn't have. I should have killed him. It's what Julian wanted. But then again, I don't always do what Julian wants. I just pay when I refuse to follow his commands.

I watched Siren get on a boat with Beckett pointing a gun at her head, and I did nothing. I didn't have a choice; he would have shot her if I made a move. But it was still almost impossible to stand there, instead of sprint after her.

As soon as the boat got far enough away, I jumped into the nearest speed boat and hot-wired it. Then I took off.

Siren told me to save myself. I should. I should turn around and drive this boat as far away from here as possible.

Beckett told me if I followed him, he'd kill Siren. But his words don't stop me either.

I'm tired of not knowing the truth. I'm tired of Siren confusing the heck out of me. She shouldn't have saved me. She should have let Beckett kill me. Then she could have killed Beckett and gone back to Julian as a hero. And she would no longer have to deal with me.

But she didn't let me die. She saved me.

And as I speed out into the ocean, I guess that's what I'm doing —saving her.

I lose sight of them as they round the corner of a small island.

But a few minutes later, I hear a loud boom before they come into view. There is no way to miss them. The small boat is on fire, smoke billowing out of it. Neither of them is still on the boat, if they survived. They would have burned to ash in the explosion.

I turn off the engine as I watch the flames slowly burn out. My heart stops, my breath extinguishes. And my eyes water at the sight.

Siren's dead.

She died instead of me.

It should have been me!

I wipe the tears on the back of my hand as I start the engine again. *No, she can't be dead.* I start the engine up and am about to speed off again when I hear the most incredible voice.

"You trying to save me again? I told you I don't need saving," Siren says.

I let out a stifled laugh that's half cry and half pure joy, as tears fall down my face. I wipe them quickly before I turn, hoping she won't see how much emotion she pulled out of me.

I clear my throat to prevent some high pitched squeak before I speak. "I wasn't coming to save you. I came to finish the job." I nod in the direction of the fire. "But it seems like you took care of Beckett yourself."

Her eyes glisten, and I wonder if she's teared up as well. But it's impossible to tell in the night.

"Zeke, I—"

But I stop her from speaking when I yank her out of the water and pull her into the deepest hug. She's soaking wet, and I swear I hear sobs into my shoulder as I hold her.

I may have questions I need answered, and she may have truths she needs to tell. But right now, I need a moment just to celebrate the fact that she's not dead.

Holding her in my arms isn't enough, though. And apparently, it isn't enough for her either.

"Zeke, I need—" she lets out a deep breath instead of finishing that sentence.

And man, do I want her to finish that sentence. But I want to feel connected to her even more. And if physically is the only way she will let me connect with her, then so be it.

"Kiss me," I demand.

And she does. She tilts her head up, stands on her tiptoes, and kisses me with everything she has. Her tongue pushes into my mouth with great efficiency. She knows exactly what she wants from me. And she's not afraid to take it. I guess almost dying makes things clearer in one's head. At least, it does me.

I run my hands down her arms, realizing that the reason her hands aren't all over my body is because they are tied behind her back. My hands fist in anger at the thought of another man tying her up. Trying to control her. She's mine.

But my conscience is laughing at me for thinking a woman like Siren could ever be claimed, or could ever belong to a man. She's the kind of woman who will only ever belong to herself.

I slowly spin Siren around, who whimpers when I force her to break the kiss. I have fantasies of tying Siren up every which way in my bed. But I'm not going to fulfill any of them with her arms tied by another man.

I pull a knife from my pocket and slice through the ropes, freeing her hands.

"I'm the only one allowed to tie you up," I whisper into her ear. "You're mine."

And the beautiful exhale that escapes her lips tells me she agrees.

She shivers, cold, and soaked in her clothes.

I wrap my arms around her, needing her warm.

"There are better ways to keep me warm," she pants.

I nuzzle her neck and then press a sweet kiss to her neck. "Yea? What are you thinking?"

She turns her head and kisses me, hard like she needs the kiss in order to stay alive. "Fuck me, Zeke."

God, how I'll never tire of hearing her say that. But I want answers.

"Truth or sin?" I ask.

She nods.

But then she kisses me again, and I forget about our game. It's not a game either of us need in order to fuck anymore. We are going to need to change the rules to get each other to spill truths, since we'd both rather commit a sin together.

She shoves me back onto the bench in the middle of the boat, and I sit as she straddles me.

I grab the hem of her shirt and peel it off, watching as the goosebumps spring up all over her delicate skin. She wastes no time unhooking her bra. I'm sure it's uncomfortable being soaking wet, but it's not the only reason she's removing it. She wants assurance that I fuck her no matter what questions I ask or truths she answers. And sitting naked on my lap is definitely a guarantee.

"You're incredible. You saved yourself from an explosion. You swam with your arms tied up. I've never met a woman quite like you."

She leans down, grabbing my head as she kisses me. "I caused the explosion. That's how I saved myself."

And then she kisses me, and I feel every bit of that explosion in my mouth, against my tongue. Her hands dip beneath my shirt, shoving it open, ripping the remaining buttons from our last romp off my shirt. Her hands feel amazing, but I'm not going to let her avoid answering my questions.

"Why can't you lie?" I ask, holding her back, refusing to let her kiss me without answering.

She opens her mouth, probably to say sin. "If you choose sin, trust me—you won't like it."

The only way she is going to get me to fuck her is by answering my question. When it's her turn to ask a question, I will answer it truthfully no matter what she asks, refusing her a sin.

She realizes it in my eyes. *But does she want to fuck me badly enough to tell me a truth?*

"It started when I was a girl."

I feel the pain in her voice when she speaks.

"My parents hated it when I lied. So they made sure I was appropriately punished every time they caught me in a lie."

"Your scars?"

"Some of them were caused by my parents."

"And the others?"

"That's not part of your question."

I sigh.

"What keeps you from lying now?"

She runs her nail over my chest. "Most of the reason is I can't. Part of the emotional trauma from my childhood of literally getting beaten every time I lied."

"And the other part?"

"A vow I made to a man never to lie."

"To who?"

"You already know the answer."

Julian Reed.

I want to ask more, but I've pushed enough. She answered my question, and I got another piece of her puzzle. I know what my next question will be, and I just hope that I can get her to answer and not choose sin.

She exhales a breath when she realizes I'm done asking my question. *Your turn, Siren.*

"Where is Enzo Black?"

Her question isn't a fair one. It makes me hate her. It makes me distrust her. And it makes me think the only way to save Enzo and my friends is to eventually kill her.

But she's also asking because she wants a sin. She doesn't realize that after her spilling her truth, I'll fuck her without needing her to earn a sin.

"Sin," I answer.

And with that, she steps back. She removes her pants, now naked in front of me. Her skin shimmers in the moonlight, still damp from the ocean water.

She steps forward, grabbing my jeans. She undoes the button and zipper and yanks them down.

My eyes roam her body as she stands in front of me. My cock is hard and straining to be inside her.

She grins seductively as she straddles me again, taking full control. This must be her sin, fucking me without letting me demand anything from her. She's going to take what she needs from my body without thinking about me, and I've never seen anything sexier.

When she sinks down on top of my cock, all my feelings come flooding back. Feelings I have no right to. I shouldn't fall for her in any single way. Not as friends or lovers. This is all a trick, just like before.

She wants something from me, and she using my emotions to get it. *Not going to happen.*

But my cock gets lost in her pussy, thrusting in and out as our eyes lock wide open, while kissing each other. My heart flutters in my chest feeling her heart so close to mine. My brain may know who Siren is, but right now, it's having trouble explaining to my cock and heart how to feel.

Siren moves on top of me in careful, practiced movements. She doesn't let me do any of the work. She takes it all herself, pumping up and down over me. Her boobs bob up and down in front of my chest. Her hands grip my shoulders, and she moves herself up and down in a beautiful rhythm. The boat rocks as we do, and I get completely lost in her.

"Jesus, Siren, you're incredible. And you're mine."

She takes my pleasure for her own. And then we both crash, our bodies explode with each other, and it feels bigger than the explosion that happened moments before.

Slowly, Siren stops rocking over me. She climbs off, picking up my shirt off the floor. She puts it on, along with her jeans.

"What am I supposed to wear?" I ask.

She grins, tossing me my slacks. I guess I'm going shirtless. And it's worth it to see her wear my shirt.

I come up behind her and pull her to my chest. "That was one hell of a sin."

"That wasn't my sin."

"Oh?"

She reaches down and grabs the knife I used to untie her ropes with. She hands it to me. I take it looking at it in confusion.

Then she sits down on the bench and motions for me to sit behind her. I do.

She lifts her hair up in a ponytail.

"Carve your initials below Julian's," she says.

"What? Why would I do that?" I ask in disgust.

"Because I earned a sin."

I stare at her in disbelief. "No."

"You don't get to say no. I earned a sin. I get to choose anything. Now, do it."

Her voice shakes me. I've never seen her so determined. "Why?" And I know as soon as I ask it, it's the wrong question. And her answer is going to break me.

She looks me dead in the eyes. "Because I'm tired of men thinking they can own me. Tell me what to do. Or even save me. You think you can own me? Then mark me as yours, just like Julian."

I growl. "I'm nothing like Julian."

"You're exactly like him," she snaps.

"Not possible! I tried to save you, Julian would never do that! I've seen how he treats you. He hurts you over and over again. All I've ever done is try to be nice to you!"

"No! You try to save me, even when I tell you not to. Even when I plead for you not to. You have no idea the damage you've done. You have no idea I now belong to you as much as I belong to Julian."

I blink rapidly, not understanding. "What are you saying?"

"I'm telling you to carve your initials below Julian's. You already think of me as yours. You tell me I'm yours whenever we fuck. I'm telling you that you saved me one too many times. I'm telling you that you ruined my life! That you've taken from me too many times. So carve your damn initials into my neck, so I can remember you are not my friend, you're just trying to control me the same as Julian."

"No."

I drop the knife.

She picks it up with tears in her eyes I don't understand. Tears that say she's feeling more, but she's afraid, so damn afraid. "Carve your initials, or we are done. There will be no more truths. No more sins."

No more us.

Whatever that means. I don't know what *us* is.

Reluctantly, I take the knife.

She turns, holding her hair up for me. I see Julian's hastily carved initials and a faint outline of a different mark just above his, buried in her hair. I have a feeling carving my initials is more than what she is asking. There is more truth she isn't speaking—a reason she wants me to do this.

One reason is she knows hurting her will hurt me.

A second reason is she's scared of her own feelings for me. And this is a way she can stay angry instead of letting her feelings for me out.

And the third reason is yet to be discovered.

I press the knife carefully to her flesh, and then I carve my initials —ZK.

I watch myself hurt her. I watch the blood flow. I watch the pain I cause, and tears roll down my cheek.

When I've finished, she releases her hair. "That's what it feels like every time you try to save me. Every time you claim I'm yours. Every time you don't trust me. Like you are laying claim to something you have no right to earn." Her tears spring free until we are both crying in the back of the boat.

I open my mouth to say I'm sorry, but then I stop. Because I'm not sorry for saving her, or at least trying to. Just like she's not sorry she saved me. And I'm sure as hell not sorry for saying she's mine, even when I know she can never be.

Instead, I grab her and pull her tight to my chest, comforting her.

I look out at the sea and the wreckage of the boat. She survived. *Could Beckett have survived too?*

CHAPTER 25
SIREN

I let Zeke drive me back to the hotel. We don't speak after the sin I made him carry out, but it was an intense moment. A moment where I felt all my power return. I'm tired of men controlling my life.

Zeke parks the stolen car a block from the hotel. We step out, and I start walking up to the hotel in his shirt and my damp jeans. Zeke chases after me, still shirtless, only wearing his slacks and carrying his suit jacket.

He grabs my hand as we walk.

I try to pull my hand free.

But he only tightens his grip. "You can fight me all you want. But I'm bigger than you and as you made me carve into your neck, you're mine."

He's pissed I made him hurt me. But maybe he'll think twice now before playing that stupid game again or using it to get what he wants from me.

I'm exhausted, so I stop resisting, and we walk hand in hand through the lobby of the hotel and into the elevator. Once inside, I try to pull my hand away again, but he continues gripping it.

"You aren't in control anymore. I committed your sin," he growls.

The doors open on my floor, and Zeke drags me down the hallway. For a second I think, he's bringing me back to my hotel room to fuck me again, and my heart speeds up at the thought. But when he knocks on the door, and Nora opens it with her eyebrows raised, I realize he's just delivering me to my hotel room to ensure I don't get into any more trouble.

Zeke gives Nora a curt nod and pulls me inside.

"Nora, can you give us a minute?" Zeke mumbles, barely looking at her.

"Sure," she grabs her purse and then heads out the door.

Finally, I yank my hand free. "You can go, too. I don't need a babysitter."

He huffs. "You've run off on me enough times; it seems to be exactly what you need." He heads toward the bathroom. "Sit," he commands. The look on his face telling me that if I don't sit on the bed, he's going to return and spank me so hard I will no longer be able to sit.

So I sit.

I hear him rummage through drawers and cabinets in the bathroom, mumbling and cursing. Finally, he returns, carrying a small bandaid and washcloth.

"This is all I could find," he grumbles, holding the items up.

I sigh. Zeke can't stand not to help me.

"I don't need your help."

"I don't care what you need. You're going to take my help so I can sleep tonight."

"No, I'm not." I fold my arms across my chest.

"Yes, you are." His voice booms so loud I'm sure everyone in the hotel heard.

"If I let you, will you leave?"

"Yes."

I lift my hair and turn so he can see my neck. And then I feel him press the cool washcloth to his initials. It feels like heaven against my warm skin.

I melt just a little, sinking into the bed and into his hand pressing against my neck.

"You are the most stubborn woman I've ever met."

"And you are the most arrogant man."

He moves the washcloth, and I let out a low hiss as the sting jolts me.

"I'm sorry," he says softly, meaning every word.

But I don't want him to be sorry. For anything.

"I think the bleeding has stopped," he says a few minutes later.

I nod.

And then I hear him unwrapping the bandaid before he presses it to my skin.

"It's not big enough to cover the entire area, but at least your hair won't rub against it and irritate it."

I drop my hair back down.

"You should get out of those wet clothes," he commands.

"Turn around," I say, even though he just saw my naked body before. Right now, I'm angry at him, and he doesn't get to see me naked when I'm angry.

He turns, and I slip out of my wet jeans and heels. But I leave his T-shirt on.

"Okay," I say, when I've done as he said.

He turns. I expect him to tell me to give him his shirt back, but he doesn't. He acts like his shirt belongs on my body.

"Now get under the covers. You need to rest."

I don't want to be ordered around, but he's right. I need sleep. So I crawl into bed.

Zeke sits on the side of the bed, pulling the covers up tightly around me and tucking me in. He hesitates for a second and then asks, "Is Beckett dead?"

I knew he would ask. If I'm alive, Beckett could have survived the blast too. And I have to be careful with how I answer. Because when we return home, I'll be the proof Julian needs to know that Zeke did his job. I need to believe that Beckett is dead, whether he is or not.

And right now, I don't know.

"Beckett was on the boat when the bomb went off. What do you think?" I answer.

Zeke nods, accepting my answer. That answer won't fly with Julian.

Julian knows all my tricks. He knows how I can answer without truly answering the question to avoid lying. He will want a yes or no. I need Zeke to get me to believe that he found evidence of Beckett's death in order to pass that information along to Julian. Whether Beckett actually died or not.

Zeke tucks my hair behind my ear. "Get some rest. Tomorrow we will head back to St. Kitts."

Zeke stands as Nora opens the door to the hotel room.

"Take care of her, Nora," Zeke says as he leaves.

Nora sets her purse down and then climbs up the bed next to me. "Want to talk about it?"

"No."

She sighs. "So you're telling me I can't have Zeke or Beckett?"

I throw a pillow at her.

"I was just asking," she says back. She stands up, pulls her dress off, and climbs under the covers, wrapping her arms around me. "I'm always here if you need a friend to talk to."

I nod and kiss her hand because Nora is a good friend. But I need more than someone to talk to if I'm going to fix the predicament I'm in. I need a way to stop letting men into my life.

CHAPTER 26
ZEKE

I pull on a shirt in my hotel room while thinking about Siren. She better stay in that damn bed tonight. I hope Nora will make sure she does.

Beckett is dead. I will never know who he worked for. *Did he work for Enzo Black? Was he an ally? Or was he an enemy?*

I toss my wallet on the nightstand and start kicking my shoes off.

Wait...Siren didn't actually answer my question. She never said if Beckett is alive or dead.

Beckett could be alive.

I snatch my wallet back up and race out of the hotel, back to the docks, and into a boat to search the water for him.

It takes me an hour of searching before I spot a man, gripping onto a piece of the boat floating in the water.

I kill the engine and pull him onto the boat with one hand. He collapses onto the floor of the boat. He coughs a few times, trying to rid his body of the saltwater. It brings back memories of before, of the last time I was in the water, and Siren saved my life.

"Who do you work for?" I ask, as I sit on a bench, waiting for him to compose himself. If I were smart or more weary, I would aim a gun

407

at him until I got my answer. But I already suspect the truth. And he's in no condition to fight anyway.

He doesn't answer; he just coughs again. And I'm impatient.

"Do you work for Enzo Black?" I growl.

He smirks. "I work for the Black empire, yes. I'm Enzo's half brother, actually."

I exhale a deep breath, realizing that we are on the same side. And he almost killed me. He almost killed Siren, although she got her revenge for that.

"And who are you?" he asks.

"I'm Zeke Kane."

"Zeke Kane was supposed to be dead."

"I survived. I mean, Aria saved me."

"Is that why you work for her?"

"No, I work for her because I have to to protect the Black empire."

"Enzo and Kai are going to so happy to know you are alive. And Langston..."

My eyes water thinking about them. "They can't know. Not yet."

Beckett frowns, sitting up. "They have to know. They're still devastated by your death. They've been living with it for so long."

"And someday, I hope to be able to tell them I'm safe. But for now, they need to think I'm dead. It's the only way to protect them."

Beckett runs his hand through his hair.

"You have to pretend to be dead, too," I say.

He sighs. "Enzo's my half-brother. And I've learned to love Kai like a sister. I know they trust you. If you're telling me I need to pretend to be dead in order to keep them safe, then I will."

"Thank you," I nod, feeling the pain of not knowing what has happened to my friends and of making someone else they love pretend to be dead. To make them mourn another person they love.

He studies me a moment. "I don't understand your relationship with Aria. I don't know what you feel for her or if what I saw was all just an act on your part. But Aria tried to kill me. She knows who I am, that I work for the Black empire. You can't trust her; she's not on our side."

"Don't worry, I don't." I can never trust Siren, no matter how my heart aches to.

CHAPTER 27
SIREN

The next morning is exhausting, but not because of a lack of sleep. I slept hard with my best friend holding me, reminding me I have someone on my side.

The morning is exhausting because Zeke is completely ignoring me, while giving Nora his undivided attention. They both talk to each other like I'm not even here. In the hotel lobby, Zeke even offers to carry her bags.

I drive us to the airport, and the happy couple decide to sit in the back seat. Nora even rests her head on Zeke's chest.

So by the time we get to our plane, I'm exhausted from watching them together. I board the plane immediately, not speaking to either of them and taking a seat in the far back of the plane.

Nora boards next and looks over at me. "You okay?"

"Yep, just tired."

She nods and then heads to the cockpit.

Zeke boards last, carrying two coffees. He heads to the front and hands one to Nora, who takes it happily. And then he takes a seat across the aisle and ahead of me. He sips on his own coffee, continuing to ignore me.

Finally, we take off, and I try leaning my head back and sleeping.

But Nora is back to her antics, and the plane dips side to side. This is her way of keeping us both awake and trying to force us to talk.

"Here," Zeke says, holding out the coffee cup to me.

"What are you doing?"

"Offering you a sip of my coffee. But it's my coffee, so don't drink it all. You are going to need to stay alert if we are going to survive this ride back."

I take the coffee and drink a couple of sips, accepting his peace offering before I return the cup.

"I would move back there to talk to you, but I'm afraid of getting tossed out a window with the way Nora is flying," Zeke says.

I don't laugh, but his comment earns him a smile.

"We need to talk," I say.

He frowns.

"Truth or sins?" I ask, hopeful that he'll play if he thinks there is a chance he'll get to fuck me on the plane.

"Who did you fuck to earn you a mile-high club membership?" he asks.

I smirk, I wasn't expecting that question. "Pete Miller."

"Pete Miller? That's such a boring name. And who was this Pete Miller? Someone you needed information from?"

His comment is like a jab to the heart.

"No, I fucked him because I wanted to. Because I thought it would be fun to have sex on a plane. And Pete was hot, despite having a boring name."

Zeke relaxes his shoulders.

"Is Beckett dead?" I ask, taking my own turn. I don't know if Zeke will tell me. He might take the easy way out and say sin; that way, he can pay me back for what I made him do last night and hide the truth about Beckett.

The sexual tension between us has heightened. All I want to do is to race over to Zeke and make him a member of the mile-high club too. If he chooses sin, then I'll get to. I need this.

But I also need his answer.

I wait for Zeke to make his decision. And the two choices flash before his eyes as well. He licks his lips, and I know what he's going to choose—sin. Even if it gets us both killed.

"Beckett's dead," he answers, surprising us both. He decides to give me what I need in order to tell Julian the truth, whether it is actually the truth or not.

CHAPTER 28
ZEKE

We left Nora at the airport. She said she was meeting a friend in the Bahamas, but would check in on Siren soon. Siren and I headed straight to Julian's, both wanting credit for the first sin being over with.

We walk up the driveway to Julian's house. Siren doesn't bother knocking; she just walks in like this is her home. I guess it sort of is.

I follow behind. Siren seems to know exactly where Julian is, so I let her lead me through the house to a study. She's right, Julian is sitting in a lounge chair with a cigar in his mouth.

"I expected that task to be completed faster," Julian says with a grin.

We both ignore his remarks. Siren walks over to the bar cart in the corner and pours herself a drink. I decide to stay sober until I can celebrate my victory.

I take a seat in the remaining chair, and Siren leans against the wall with her drink in her hand.

"Is the job done?" Julian asks me.

"Yes. We found Eli Beckett."

Julian nods for me to continue as he puffs on his cigar.

"We found out he works for Mr. Black."

Julian grins, and I realize he already knew who Beckett worked for. This was a test to see what I would do.

"And we killed him," I finish.

Julian's eyebrows go up in surprise. It's then I realize the sins he will have me complete will be as devastating as the truths he wants me to spill. This time I got away easy. But next time? It could be a choice between killing two people I love, either physically or by spilling a truth.

"Interesting," Julian says, studying me closely, trying to determine if I'm telling the truth or lying. But then he turns his attention to Siren, not caring about my answer at all. He only cares about Siren's.

That's why he sent her with me—not to babysit. He knows I won't run as long as he threatens the lives of the people I love. He needs Siren to report to him if I completed the tasks or not. Because Siren can't lie, I can. And Julian knows that.

"Is Beckett dead?" Julian asks Siren.

Siren has been ignoring us so far, staring down at her drink. I have no idea what her answer will be. All I know is that to her, it will be the truth. But does she think Beckett is alive or dead? Or will she finally learn how to lie?

Her eyes flick up, somehow meeting both Julian's and my gaze at the same time.

"Yes, Eli Beckett is dead," she answers.

Julian grins. "Excellent." And then he turns to me. "Well done. I didn't think you had it in you."

"What's next?" I ask, anxious to get the five sins over with.

He puffs his cigar again. "Patience. I'll have a new game for you soon."

I stare at Julian in frustration. I want these stupid games of his over so I can go. But I also want to put off the next round as long as possible, because I'm not ready to go through that all over again so soon.

I stand up and leave, not sure if Siren is staying or coming. When I arrive at the truck, she hops into the passenger seat.

I drive us the minute up to my house and then kill the engine.

"Did you lie back there? To Julian?" I ask.

She opens her door, ignoring me. I follow, stomping after her into the house.

"Did you lie back there?" I ask again when we are both inside the house.

She spins around on her heels. "No, I told the truth as I know it."

I freeze. She truly thinks Beckett is dead. Or at least my lie let her believe that.

"I want you out of my house. I can't trust you," I say.

"It's really not up to you."

"You killed Beckett! A man who is on my side. A man who is loyal to my boss, to my friends."

She steps into my space. "No, I gave him a chance to live. A chance to save himself. If he's alive, it's because of me." She turns to walk away. But I grab her arm; she doesn't get to give a comment like that and then run off.

"What does that mean?"

"Nothing, I shouldn't have said anything."

"Siren, tell me."

"I warned him, okay? I warned him before the explosion happened."

Beckett didn't tell me the truth. He was just trying to convince me she isn't on our side. But what if she is?

It doesn't matter if she is or isn't, I still feel myself falling for her a little in this moment. A woman who is always selfish, always looking out for herself, did something to save a man she didn't even know when it could have cost her everything.

I want to tell her thank you for saving Beckett. For letting him live and making sure she only knew enough to be able to tell Julian she believes Beckett to be dead. But I can't thank her without telling her the truth that Beckett is alive, which would change her answer if Julian asks her again.

Instead, I do the only thing I can do. I fucking kiss her, giving her the biggest thank you I can offer without saying any words.

The kiss is more like a collision. We both need this kiss, while not wanting to admit it to the other. But as soon as our tongues meld, we lose all pretense of hating each other. My hand fists her hair; hers cling to my neck. Our bodies press together, and our tongues beg to move deeper into each other's mouths.

Siren claws at my shirt, and she shoves it up, needing to feel my chest. I stop the kiss long enough for her to get my shirt off. Then my lips cling to hers again, swearing silently that I will never let them go again.

I grab her shirt and pull it up before I realize I'll have to break the kiss again to remove her shirt.

I growl as I do.

This time, the moment our lips are apart is enough to remind me I don't just want to fuck her. I want answers. I need answers. I need to know whose side she is on. It's the only way to guard my heart. Even as it's already falling.

"Truth or sin?" I start.

"No." She grabs my neck and kisses me again. "We already played today."

She unhooks her bra as she continues to kiss me over my lips, then my jawline, then neck. It feels incredible, but it's not enough to fully distract me. Even when I take her breasts in my hands and hear her moans caress me.

"What is the vow you made to Julian?" I ask her.

She steps back. "I said not tonight."

I step forward. "I need the truth. I need to know whose side you are on. I need to know what keeps you from fighting back against Julian. What makes you save me?"

She opens her mouth, but I know it's to argue back, so I shut her up with a fierce kiss, slamming her into a wall of the hallway.

She shoves me back, refusing to let me deepen the kiss.

"Are you married to Julian?"

Her face falls, and I can't tell if it's truth or anger.

A buzz in her pocket breaks the moment.

"Don't answer it."

"I have to. It could be Julian." She grabs the phone from her pocket and answers. "Yes?"

I watch her eyes widen in fear, I watch the pulse in her neck speed, and her breath catch.

"I'll be right there," she finally says before ending the call.

I step in front of her. "You aren't going anywhere. Not without answering me."

"Let me go, Zeke."

"You aren't running to Julian because he called. Not without answering my questions first."

It's only then that I see the tears in her eyes. The way her hands tremble at her sides. She's scared to death. And I feel like a monster for blocking her path. Is she afraid Julian will punish her if she doesn't get to him quickly?

"I'll answer any damn question you have, but you have to let me go, now."

I pull my keys from my pocket and toss them to her. "Fine, but I'm going with you."

She nods, running toward my truck, picking up her trail of clothes along the way. I jump into the passenger seat, assuming we are headed to Julian's, but when we drive past his house, I'm utterly confused.

CHAPTER 29
SIREN

I squeeze the steering wheel in a death grip as I drive down the road. Maybe I should have had Zeke drive? I'm too distracted. But I figure even my distracted driving is better than Zeke's best driving.

My thoughts are taken over by the phone call. I still can't believe what happened or that I feel it this harshly.

Julian always talks about there being consequences to my actions. If I break my vow, I will pay. But it's been years since he had to inflict any real consequence on me. And he's never inflicted a punishment this bad.

Bu then, I've never done anything this bad. I've never threatened Julian. Never hit him, never hurt him. I knew the moment I did that I crossed a line. And that eventually, Julian would make me pay for it.

I just thought him carving up my neck was the end of my retribution, that he had moved passed it.

Now I know he didn't.

But still, I didn't think it would torture this much. What Julian did shouldn't hurt me. It shouldn't affect me at all. But of course, it did. I'm human, after all. And you can't just turn off feelings, even if those emotions should be long gone.

Zeke studies me for a long time as I drive. He's still shirtless, but at least he's gripping his shirt in his hands so he can get dressed when we arrive.

I threw my shirt on in haste and didn't even bother to put my bra back on. I'm sure Zeke can see my nipples still hard beneath my shirt.

Zeke's hand reaches out, flicking on the radio. I don't pay him any attention. I'm surprised he turned the radio on at all. He usually prefers the silence.

But then I hear him sing. It's horrible. His voice is way off-key.

I bite back a smile. "Your voice is horrible."

"Well, sorry we can't all be pros like you."

He continues singing, and my smile brightens, the ache in my chest getting just bearable enough for me to drive.

And then I find myself humming along to the song too. My right hand loosens on the steering wheel, falling to the side. Our hands find each other. And when Zeke's fingers lock with mine, I feel him take on some of my pain, even though he doesn't know why I'm in such a state.

He doesn't know any of the words, but he keeps singing along. I finally join him when it returns to the chorus of a new Miley Cyrus song I've never heard before. But it feels fitting. The song talks about telling a guy to slide away back to the ocean. And it's the exact words I want to repeat to too many men in my life—all for very different reasons.

CHAPTER 30
ZEKE

Siren stops the car in front of the hospital.

My heart stops.

"Nora?" I ask, assuming she got into an accident. It's the only person I know of in Siren's life that would cause the pain I feel drumming through her body.

She shakes her head. And I exhale in relief for myself and Siren.

"A family member?" I ask, realizing I don't know any of Siren's family, or if any of them are alive.

"No."

She steps out of the truck, and I follow.

I link our fingers again as we walk inside, ready to face whatever heartbreak awaits us as a team.

Siren takes a deep breath and then walks up to the front desk with me still holding onto her. I grip her hand in comfort as much as for me as for her.

"I'm here to see Hugo Martinez."

I frown. *Martinez? That's her last name. But I thought she said it wasn't a family member?*

The nurse smiles sadly at the mention of the man's name. He must be in critical condition for her to give us that sort of response. "Are you a family member?"

My eyes go to Siren's, not sure how she's going to respond. She can't lie, and I'm sure only family members will be allowed to see him.

She closes her eyes for a second, as if this entire situation is painful.

I give her hand a tight squeeze, reassuring her. Even if the nurse won't let us back because we aren't immediate family, I will find a way for her to see Hugo if he means so much to her.

Siren opens her eyes, ignoring me, and says, "I'm his wife."

I forget everything after those words. I forget the look on Siren's face. I forget what the nurse said. I forget how it felt when Siren slipped out of my hand and walked away without me, leaving me rooted to my spot in the waiting room.

And now, I have no idea how long I've been standing here, just that I have been waiting. Waiting to understand how it's possible. Waiting to find out what this means. *Why this man, who Siren says is her husband, in the hospital? Why?*

I pace while I wait, coming up with a hundred different answers, and none of them make sense in my head.

Until I see her—Siren Aria Torres Martinez. So many names and none of them make sense to me.

"How is your dear hubby?" I ask, not hiding the anger in my voice now that she's returned to the waiting room.

She holds out a styrofoam cup of coffee to me. "I got you this."

I laugh. "Is that supposed to make up for you lying to me?"

"I didn't lie."

"Really? Because I seem to remember you saying you weren't married."

She takes a step toward me. "I never said I wasn't married. I held up my ringless finger and implied it. But I never said I wasn't."

She's right, of course. She never actually said she wasn't married.

I run my hand through my hair as I finally sink into a chair. "Is he going to be okay?"

She sits next to me, still gripping the cup of coffee. "I think so. He's in critical condition after a car accident."

My anger takes hold of me again, and I stand up suddenly. "You're married, and you still fucked me!"

"It's not that simple."

"It sure as hell is that simple to me! You are married! You're a cheating whore!"

She stands up. "Call me whatever will make you feel better, but it's not true. Being married is more than just a signature on a legal piece of paper."

"So, you don't love Hugo Martinez?"

She doesn't answer. Because she loves him.

I slump back into the chair. "Explain. Now."

"I met Hugo when I was eighteen. He saved my life. Saved me from going down a path where I would have ended up dead in a ditch somewhere. We fell in love and got married.

"A few years later, Hugo needed saving. And it was my turn to save him. He got mixed up with a drug lord. He owed him a lot of money that he could never pay back.

"I tried everything. I gave the drug lord all the money I had. I sold every possession I owned. It wasn't enough. I even offered my body to him, but he would only take money. So I snuck into Julian Reed's house to try to steal something I could sell. He caught me and offered me a deal."

She takes a deep breath, and I'm entranced by her strength even if I hate her right now.

"So, I made a vow to Julian to save Hugo's life."

I narrow my eyes.

"Julian paid the drug lord and freed Hugo. I paid Julian back with the only thing he wanted—my loyalty. I vowed to work for him for ten years. To never lay a hand on Julian. To never disobey him. To follow his orders. And for the last seven years, I've been doing just that. But then I threatened Julian, so he arranged a car accident to show me what happens when I break my vow to him."

There's more. As painful as her story already is, I know there is more.

"I made a vow to two men. I vowed ten years of service to Julian.

And I vowed my heart to Hugo. But Hugo betrayed me. We've been separated since, but never got around to filing for divorce."

"It's why you don't like people saving you; you don't like owing others anything. They can't betray you that way."

She nods. "Yes. I've been branded by three men. Saved and protected by all. But in the end, they all eventually hurt me."

Except me, I haven't yet. But I'm about to.

"Do you still love Hugo? Even though he hurt you? Even though you are no longer faithful to that marriage?"

She stares down at the cup. "I shouldn't. He doesn't love me. But I'm not sure you just let go of love like that. I wish I could because then maybe I could end my vow to Julian. Even though Hugo betrayed me, I'm still loyal to Julian. I still do everything to keep Hugo safe and protected. I can't let Julian hurt him. If you call that love, then that is what it is. But it feels like Hugo stole a piece of my heart I don't know how to get back."

I understand the feeling. Because right now, as much as I hate Siren, she stole a piece of my heart. Even now, watching her in pain, I feel myself falling for her again. But she's not mine to fall for. She never will be. She'll always choose Hugo or Julian. She doesn't have a choice. And if she ever gets free of those two men, she has no reason to fall for me. She will protect her heart no matter what—it's already cost her too much.

I stand up, knowing where Siren stands in my heart, but not being able to accept it.

"Zeke," she starts, but she never finishes her sentence.

"It's my turn to make a vow."

She sits up taller, and I can see fear in her eyes as she waits.

"I vow to never save you again, Siren. From now on, I'm only saving myself."

And then I turn and walk away, intending to be true to my word.

But is it too late to keep that vow when my heart is already falling?

RECKLESS FALL

PROLOGUE

SIREN

The truth is a strange thing.

I've always been one who valued the truth. I always spoke it even if my actions or behaviors were less than one hundred percent true.

I've tried lying. Time and time again, but I can never get the words out, that's how important the truth is to me.

The day I started working for Julian Reed, the truth started to bend. My entire life became about working for a man I hated. I thought I was doing it for love. I thought I was protecting Hugo Martinez, a man I loved. A man I envisioned forever with.

But is it really love when it's one-sided? If the man you love doesn't love you back?

From the day Hugo betrayed me, I made a vow to myself to never love again. I told myself I didn't need love. I definitely didn't need a man in my life. I told myself I was a strong, independent woman. I owed no loyalty to him but was unable to sentence Hugo to death, which is what I would have done had I ended my vow to Julian. So I kept my promise to Julian to ensure that Hugo stayed alive. I think some small part of me hoped that my sacrifice would make Hugo fall in love with me again, even though I knew I would never accept his love. He didn't deserve to die for his betrayal. It's not Hugo's fault he fell in love with another woman.

Love is, after all, uncontrollable. If we could tame love, we would choose to only fall for those people who would make the best match for us. Ones in the same social circles, the same financial status. Ones our families approve of. We would only fall for the safe ones. Ones who only made us better instead of bringing out the worst in us.

But we don't get to choose who we fall for. We just fall...

Carelessly.

Whole-heartedly.

Recklessly.

For months now, I've told myself I'm not falling. I can't fall. I'm incapable of loving, not after being hurt so many times by men. I told myself that Zeke Kane was just like the rest of the men in my life. That he was as bad as all the rest. But at every turn, he proved me wrong. He saved me time and time again, at the expense of himself. He protected innocent women from being sold. He showed me that he cared—about his boss, his friends, his family, and even me. He could have loved me if I had let him.

But Zeke thinks I betrayed him, even when I didn't. He thinks I hurt him. And that's what I want him to think. It's the only way to save him. The only way for him to eventually get free. And now I have the perfect plan to get him out of this mess with Julian. A way to get him off the island.

I can save Zeke, earn my redemption in his eyes. There is just one problem...I've learned that I *can* lie, at least to one person—myself.

I've been lying for months. Telling myself I can't fall in love, and I sure as hell can't fall for a dangerous man like Zeke. If I was going to fall, I should fall for a teacher or banker, not a man in this crime world.

The truth is, I did fall. My heart fell off a cliff the day I met him, and it's been falling a little more ever since. Until now, I'm so deep in love with him that I can't think straight. I can't breathe without inhaling Zeke's smell. I can't dream without Zeke in my head. I can't exist without him. *But I have to.*

Zeke may think I'm a selfish bastard, someone who has betrayed him time and time again. The truth is, I love him. I've always loved him. I've never betrayed him. I just can't tell him the truth.

431

CHAPTER 1
SIREN

Falling in love is easy; not getting hurt is the hard part. Not destroying the one you love—that's the hardest of all.

I stare down at the man lying in the hospital bed. My first love—Hugo Martinez. He looks so broken and shattered. His face is beaten up. Tubes connect to his arms. Bandages cover his body. And the gentle sound of a beep on the machine next to him is the only indication that he's still alive and not dead.

Hugo made me believe love is real. Sure, I'd thought I'd felt it before with my high school crush. When I fell in love with the stray dog in the neighborhood. When Nora became my best friend. And sure, that was love. But it's not the same as falling in love.

When I fell for Hugo, he became my everything. I couldn't think except of him. I couldn't plan my day without him in it. I couldn't breathe...

I became a little obsessed. *No, obsessed isn't the right word; I became enchanted with him.* Hugo could do no wrong in my eyes. He was it. The elusive one. I knew it from the moment he kept me from putting another needle in my arm and yanked me up off the street where I was planning on offering my body in exchange for money. Hugo saved me from a life of sin. He saved me from myself. If I had slept with a stranger for money, I wouldn't have survived. I would have never forgiven myself.

And then he kept saving me. From the drugs. The depression. The anger. He saved me from it all.

At twenty-one, he felt like a man, while I was barely eighteen and still acted like a child. Hugo helped me find who I was. Taught me self-defense. Bought me my first guitar. But then, he became so much more.

He taught me how to kiss. When his lips touched mine, fireworks exploding was an understatement.

When his fingers explored my body, toe-curling orgasms followed.

Hugo was my match. He made me a better person, and I was in desperate need of becoming a better person. I was desperate to have something to live for. And Hugo filled that void. He gave me more than something to live for; he gave me my life back.

I came alive against his lips.

I thrived in his arms.

And I learned to find purpose even when Hugo was gone.

Which became more and more often. I didn't realize Hugo was fighting his own battles while I was becoming stronger. I didn't realize he was making his own plans even while proposing forever with me.

I didn't realize that falling in love with Hugo meant giving him the ammunition he needed to kill me. He had the ability to wipe me from this earth with one blow—and he did.

After Hugo betrayed me, I became a different person. One incapable of love. I gave it all to him. Married him. Sacrificed ten years of my life vowing to work for Julian in order to save his life.

And Hugo shit all over my love. He showed me not only how little he cared about my feelings, but that he enjoyed hurting me.

I tried to take my heart back. I tried to ease the pain in my chest. But I couldn't. I couldn't re-capture my heart.

It took me a while to get over the disloyalty, to be able to breathe again. And when I did, I wanted to take the vow back. Let Hugo deal with his own mess, even if it meant Julian or the drug lord Hugo owed money to would kill him.

But as much as I act heartless, as much as I want to punish bad men, I couldn't sentence Hugo to death. I tried. I've tried countless times over the last seven years when Julian ordered me to do something I didn't want to do. But I couldn't.

Call it love.

Call it heartbreak.

Call it loyalty.

Call it whatever you want. I feel like a coward every time I can't let Hugo go, but it's not just letting him go that holds me back. If I end my vow to Julian, I have no doubt that he would kill Hugo. Julian is the reason Hugo is in the hospital—to remind me what will happen if I break my vow.

I look at Hugo lying in the bed, lifeless. I could kill him. It would be so easy. Suffocate him with the pillow. Snap his neck. Unhook the tubes providing him life. Push too many narcotics through his IV.

I could end this. I could be free. At least of Hugo.

I stand over his bed, considering how easy it would be to kill the man who both gave me back my life and then ruined it.

But I can't kill him, because I'm not heartless. And Hugo still holds the tiniest piece. A piece that has turned cold, black, and unfeeling.

I look back to the hallway that Zeke escaped through. His words will haunt me forever. He won't protect me anymore. He won't save me; that was his vow.

Those may have been the words he spoke, but I know what he was really saying, *I won't love you anymore. I won't let my heart fall anymore.*

He may have never said I love you. But we were close, even though we shouldn't have been. We both tormented and betrayed each other time and time again. I did everything I could to make Zeke hate me. I claimed it's because I don't want to fall in love again. Thought I pushed him away only for selfish reasons—I don't want to give a man the power to hurt me again.

But it was a lie, maybe the first lie I ever told myself.

Because I didn't push Zeke away to save myself, I pushed Zeke away to save him. And he still fell for Julian's trap. Because Zeke isn't like Hugo, he's a man of honor. A loyal man. A man who loves with everything he has. A man capable of changing the world.

He doesn't deserve to be trapped in this life. He deserves to be free. To return to his friends. His boss. His life.

I'll be trapped here forever. I have three years left of my debt to Julian, but that isn't the only thing keeping me trapped, holding me hostage.

My heart clenches, looking at the empty hallway. Zeke is most likely headed back to Julian now, trying to find a way to get out of his own deal with him or figuring out how to complete it as fast as possible so he can get the hell away from me.

Hugo may hold a tiny piece of my heart I never got back, but Zeke holds the rest of my heart. It belongs to Zeke.

Because I fell...

Hard.

Stupidly.

In love with Zeke.

I fell too fast.

I fell too hard.

Long before I ever admitted it to myself. I tried to protect Zeke from my love by making him hate me. But it backfired on me.

I'm done hiding my love, but it's too late.

Zeke hates me.

Good. That means there is no reason to hide how I feel. He'll lash back and try to hurt me, and I'll let him. Because I deserve it. I failed to protect him from Julian. But I can set him free.

I look back at Hugo. I want him dead. But first, I want the tiny piece of my heart he still holds. It's not his. I want it back. I want to give Zeke Kane everything—my entire heart. Even though I know how much it will hurt when he doesn't love me back. Even though I know the pain when he betrays me. *Wrecks me.*

I want to feel it: the good and the bad. I want to show him how much I love him. I want to fall, screw the consequences. My life is no longer mine. But my heart, my heart is all that I have left to give. And if I'm going to give it up, I'm going to give it to a man like Zeke.

A man who, in a different life, I would have loved from the moment I laid eyes on him. I would have loved out in the open. We would have made each other better, instead of bringing out the worst in each other. Hating Zeke didn't save him, maybe loving him will.

"I hate you," I say.

"You sure about that? Because your puffy eyes and running nose say differently. You came running back to me as soon as you found out I was in the hospital," Hugo answers, without opening his eyes.

Did he really speak? Or am I imagining he did?

Either way, he's right. I did. I shouldn't have come back, though. And Hugo can't read me as well as he used to. Because this isn't love, this is heartbreak. And it's nothing compared to how I felt watching Zeke walk out the door.

CHAPTER 2
ZEKE

Siren's fucking married. She's capable of love. She's not heartless. She can fall in love, just not with me.

She hurt me once, shame on her.

She hurt me twice, shame on me.

I won't let her hurt me a third time.

My heart may have been falling, but seeing her run to another man. Seeing her pain for a man who was hurt, that turned my heart to stone.

I will never let her in again. I will never love her. Never care for her. Never consider her on my side. I will never protect her again.

She betrayed me to Julian, and now she's married to another man. I don't care if she claims she doesn't love him. That he hurt her, and they just haven't gotten around to divorce. I don't care what her excuses are. I'm done.

Done with her. Done with my deal with Julian. I'm done.

I want out of here. I'll make sure Enzo, and Kai, and Langston, and Liesel are safe and protected by killing Julian. Then I'll destroy Siren, so I know she will never come after my family. I won't kill her, I'm not vicious enough to be able to finish the job, but I'll get my message across that if she comes for me, she's a dead woman.

I'm tired of playing games. I want answers. And I don't trust Siren. I want the truth. And the only way I'll get that is from Julian.

I drive fast toward Julian's house. Away from the hospital. Away from her—my siren. She will never be anything but a siren. The devil in disguise. The woman who told me who she was with one word. And I was too stupid to believe that she might be what she claimed—a monster.

I drive, imagining what Siren would say if she were riding next to me. How pissed off she would be that I'm driving too fast. I'm being reckless. I'm going to get into a car accident.

I smirk.

Good, let's see if she would come running to my bedside if I were to get into a car accident. I doubt it.

I press my foot down on the pedal harder as I turn a curve, the truck swerves, but I make the turn, barely avoiding rolling off the edge of the hill and down the cliffside. It doesn't slow me down, though. It only makes me drive faster, trying to outrun my pain.

Somehow I make it to Julian's drive without crashing. I throw my door open and jump out, slamming the door hard behind me—wishing I could hurt Siren the way I just hurt the door. But I can't hurt Siren, because she doesn't care about me. She just likes watching me bleed.

I pull my gun out of my pocket as I storm inside Julian's house. One of his servants spots me and turns on the spot, heading back down the hallway when he sees my gun. I'm going to finish what I should have done months ago. I'm going to kill Julian Reed. And then I'm getting the fuck off this island.

I march down the hallway, to Julian's office, the scent of cigar smoke leading the way. I kick open the door and aim my gun at his head.

I should fire immediately, kill him without questions. But I want answers. I need answers. I need closure, so when I leave, I won't have Siren floating around in my head, fucking with me.

Julian chuckles when he sees me standing in the doorway. Not the reaction I'm used to when I aim a gun at someone's head.

"I've been expecting you," he says, puffing casually on his cigar.

"Then, you know I'm here to get answers and then kill you."

He exhales. "I might be willing to give you some answers. But you won't be killing me."

I step into the room, keeping my gun trained at his head. "I will. Your little guard dog isn't here to protect you this time. You sent her away to take care of the man she loves."

Julian chuckles louder, until he's throwing his head back and his belly jiggles.

I fucking hate him.

"I also think it's hilarious that you are about to die," I say.

His dark eyes snap back to me. "I'm not about to die. But you have to admit, my Aria is good. She got you to fall for her, when she was married to another man the entire time."

"I didn't fall for her."

He lifts his scotch to his lips. "Then why did you save her? Why did you come storming over here threatening to kill me but not actually killing me?"

I don't answer him. I refuse to accept that I fell for her. *Sure, she's strong, independent, sassy, smart, kickass.* But she's also a liar, deceitful, selfish, and in love with another man. I'm better than falling for her tricks.

"Sit," Julian says.

I frown. *I'm not doing a damn thing this man asks again.*

"Sit, and I'll answer your questions."

"I don't—"

"Don't lie; the only reason I'm still breathing is because you have questions. Now fucking sit."

I refuse. I won't let anyone control me, not anymore. I want out of my deal, and as I see it, the best way to do that is by killing the man in front of me.

"You're just like Aria," Julian smiles to himself.

"I'm nothing like her. I'm loyal, honest, a good person."

"Unfortunately, she's all those things, too, even if she refuses to show you that side of herself."

I freeze. *Maybe I don't want Julian's point of view on things? He's just as manipulative as Siren is.*

I turn, planning on walking out and shooting him only as I leave.

"Aria can't divorce Hugo, that's why she hasn't."

His words cause me to stop. Because I want to know the truth. I need to know. I need to know everything. *What makes Siren tick? What makes her do what she does? What makes the strongest woman I know bow to such men?*

Love?

Hate?

I'm tired of being goaded. I'm tired of not fighting back. I turn and run with everything I have, knocking Julian out of the chair until he's on the floor on his back. I grab his neck and push him hard into the ground as I aim the gun at his head.

"Tell me everything, now."

His smile drops, but there is still light behind his eyes. He still doesn't think this is his end. But from where I'm sitting, I know this is when Julian Reed dies.

"Why can't Siren divorce Hugo?" I ask.

"Because of the prenup she signed."

"What does the prenup say?"

"I don't know, but Hugo drunkenly told me one night that she is his forever because she signed a contract without reading it first. She trusted him, and now she's trapped. She would have to give up something she's not prepared to give up. You'll have to ask him or her what the prenup says."

I will.

"Does she still love him?" I ask, even though I know it's a stupid question. Julian doesn't know the answer. And even if he did, he's just going to manipulate me.

"Do you still love her even though she betrayed you?"

No. *Yes.*

"There is no *still*. I never fell for her. I hate her."

"Hate is the opposite of love. You can only truly hate those you once loved."

I push the gun against his head. "No, I hate you, and trust me, I never loved you."

Julian smiles. "You don't hate me like you hate her."

And then I hear her—Siren. She's standing in the doorway.

Fuck, I thought she'd still be at the hospital. What is she doing here?

I should have killed Julian, immediately. Now she's going to try and stop me like last time.

"You here to try and stop me from killing your boss?" I ask, staring at Julian, refusing to look at her.

"No. I'll finish my vow to Julian as long as he's breathing. I'll complete the tasks he's too chicken to carry out on his own. I'll put my life at risk every day facing his biggest enemies. But I'm done being his personal bodyguard. I re-read the contract I signed. There is nothing there saying I have to protect him at risk of my own life." Siren walks over to one of the chairs. She sits down and kicks her legs up on the coffee table and then puts her arms behind her head. "I'm just here for the show."

Siren isn't going to stop me from killing Julian. I'll have to deal with her when this is finished. I can't just let her go free. I don't trust her. She could continue Julian's mission of hunting down Enzo Black and his family. But right now, I'm focused on Julian.

"Any last words?" I ask, done with him.

Julian's eyes cut from me to Siren and then back again. If eyes could kill, his would have killed us both.

Finally, Julian is going to be dead. We are going to be free of him. I will be able to go home.

"If you kill me, my men will kill Lucy," Julian says.

How the hell does he know about Lucy? No one knows. Not even my best friends know.

But Julian's snicker says it all—I won't be killing Julian, at least not until I can ensure Lucy is safe.

CHAPTER 3
SIREN

I turn to follow Zeke out of the room, when I hear Julian's voice. "We have a deal. Don't defy me again, Aria."

His words chill me for so many reasons. For seven years, I've regretted my vow to Julian, but right now, I don't. Because that vow led me here. And that vow kept me alive. And it led me to Zeke. And now I can save him.

I run out of the room without another word. I chase Zeke outside and go to jump into his truck. But when I reach for the handle, the door is locked. He doesn't look at me, but I swear I see a hint of a snicker at the corner of his lip. He knows what he's doing—shutting me out.

It's a short jog to his house, and the weather is abnormally cold, but I'm not worried about the walk. I fear that I'm permanently shut out. That Zeke won't let me in again. That he's locked me out forever.

I start walking down the street toward his house, when the skies open up, and a loud thunder rolls through. Then raindrops start pouring down, and my easy walk turns into an uncomfortable slog. It's like the weather itself is against me now, in addition to Zeke.

Fuck you, rain! All I've ever done is the right, unselfish thing, and it's turned the entire world against me. Everyone hates me—my husband,

445

Zeke, even Julian is pissed. But the only person I care about liking me is Zeke. I need him to like me enough to at least listen to me.

I reach the doorstep of Zeke's house completely soaked, not exactly the look I was going for to tell Zeke the truth. Or at least enough of the truth to set him free.

I knock on the door loudly as the wind picks up and the rain starts blowing sideways. It's the tropics, but when it decides to rain like this, it can turn cold quickly. I shiver, crossing my arms over my body and rubbing my hands up and down my arms, trying to stay warm.

I listen for Zeke's footsteps to come open the door, but I don't hear him move. He can't hide from me; his truck is parked in the drive.

I pound on the door, loud enough that there is no denying he can hear me, even over the howl of the wind trying to knock me into the door. But still, Zeke doesn't answer.

I may have hardly cracked the surface when it comes to understanding Zeke, but I know that if it were up to Zeke, he and I would never speak again.

"Open up! I know you are inside, Zeke."

I pound again.

No answer.

"I'll break the door down!" I yell.

I hear footsteps this time, and I smile—*finally*. I hear the clink of the lock as Zeke turns it. And then nothing.

He doesn't open the door. This is as far as he'll go, unlocking the door so he doesn't have to deal with the hassle of replacing a broken door.

I grab the doorknob and push my way inside.

Zeke is no longer standing on the other side of the door. He isn't waiting for me or greeting me. He's going to ignore me.

I shiver as I step inside, my wet shoes leaving water tracks wherever I walk, and my soaked hair is dripping down my face. I should go try and find some clothes to change into—something to warm myself up, so I don't get pneumonia. But I need to see Zeke first.

It's selfish to see Zeke right now when he's so hurt. I should have told him the truth about Hugo. He shouldn't have found out that way. But there is so much Zeke doesn't know. So much he can never know.

I thought if Zeke thought the worst of me, I could save him easier. But it turns out I can't stand for Zeke to truly hate me, to shut me out, and never protect me even if it's for the best. *I need him to like me, just not save me.*

I march through the house—the kitchen, the bedroom, the sitting room. Zeke isn't in any of the rooms.

What?

Did he immediately run out of the house in this storm to avoid talking to me?

I turn to head to the front of the house to check if his truck is still here, when I spot his dark hair outside.

He's leaning against the side of the house, with a whiskey in his hand, as he stares out at the rain. He's standing close enough to the house that the rain can't touch him. But it still seems like a stupid move when a crack of lighting roars overhead.

I open the door. "Zeke!"

He doesn't turn. Or speak. Or even blink.

Zeke ignores me completely.

I became dead to him as soon as he found out I was married. Which is a fair way for Zeke to respond. But only because he doesn't know the truth. He doesn't know that my marriage isn't a marriage at all. It never was. Not really. I'm trapped into staying, and I can't do anything to get out of the marriage.

I step out next to Zeke, the rain pouring down on half of my body.

"Zeke!" I try again.

He sips his whiskey, deaf to my words.

Maybe it's for the best. I can get my side of the story out without him interrupting. He can pretend he can't hear me all he wants, but try as he might, he won't be able to resist listening.

"I didn't run to Hugo's side because I was worried. I ran to Hugo's side because I needed to know if he was alive or dead. I needed to know—"

"Enough," Zeke says, with one word sinking all of his indignation into me.

I close my eyes, forcing my pain inside. A tear escapes anyway. The rain hitting my face quickly washes it away, hiding my agony at being so close to him, at finally allowing myself to feel my love for Zeke, while accepting his hate.

"You deserve the truth," I say, opening my eyes and discerning the anger on Zeke's face. His eyes are red with passion, his body stiff with rage.

"I deserve more than the truth, but I'm not going to get it from you."

"Let me try," I say firmly. He needs to know the truth. At least part of it. Enough so that his hate softens. It will never go away, I hurt him too much, but maybe he can see that the brief times we spent together were real. The feelings we sparked—real. All of it was real. And I wouldn't take a second of it back.

"No. Go back to your husband," Zeke says, finishing his drink.

I take a deep breath, knowing that he won't listen. That my time is running out.

"I'm sorry," I say, meaning my words more than any others I've spoken to him. If I could pour everything I'm feeling into those two words, we would be standing here all day. But I try in the single moment Zeke gives me.

Zeke turns sideways until he is facing me, half of his body is now getting pounded with rain, same as me.

"What exactly are you sorry for, Siren? Sorry for lying? For cheating on your husband? For betraying me again?" Zeke's voice doesn't need the entire day to express his feelings. It's clear he's only feeling one thing—anger.

"For all of it," I answer, not backing down even though it looks like he's about to hit me. Zeke may be angry, but he'd never hit me. He can pretend he's a vicious man with everyone but me.

Zeke takes another step toward me, blocking some of the rain from my face. I want him to kiss me. To put his hands on me. To touch me. Give me any amount of hope that we will get one more night together if we can't have forever.

He doesn't touch me; his eyes command me—tell me exactly what he wants me to do.

And for once, I do as he commands. I step aside and watch him walk inside. Leaving me for the second time in twenty-four hours without a chance to explain my truth.

I reach out to grab the door, to prevent him from locking me out, but I miss. Instead, our fingers brush. Zeke freezes at our electric touch. I've never felt such a spark with a man before. I thought for sure it would be gone. It would have been easier to let Zeke go if it was. And I know Zeke would have preferred it that way.

The spark isn't gone. In fact, I feel it deeper into my soul than I've ever felt it before. Zeke feels it too. It's why he's frozen in place. We can fight our love for each other all we want, but we can't fight our attraction, our physical connection. It won't go away. Not now. *Not ever.*

Zeke finally snaps out of it, he walks into the house, leaving me standing in the rain. It's what I deserve in his eyes, and what I wanted —for him to shut me out. But it's the most painful thing I can imagine. I'd rather be dead than live in a world where Zeke hates me, and yet, that's exactly the world I created.

CHAPTER 4
ZEKE

Two women keep floating around in my head. Both of them kept me up all night, and not for good reasons. I didn't get to kiss or fuck either of them.

Lucy Greene.

Jesus, I haven't thought that name in years. I never thought I'd think that name again. I thought Lucy was out of my life forever. No one knows about our past. At least, that was what I thought until Julian mentioned her name.

How in the hell does he know about Lucy?

She was my ultimate secret.

The one piece of my life that wasn't tainted with darkness.

But now that Julian knows about her, I have to act. I have to go back to the one light spot in my life. The one woman who I thought would never enter my new life. None of my friends or family knew about her. So I have no idea how Julian knows about her, but I will fight to the death to keep Lucy safe.

Lucy is a true angel. She's innocent. Sweet, kind, a school teacher. She volunteered at animal shelters. She was the perfect woman if one was ever to exist.

I should have spent my entire night coming up with a plan to keep her safe. A way to safely contact her. A plan to find out how Julian found her. Because if he found her, anyone could.

That's what I was doing outside as I looked out at the storm. But then Siren walked outside and consumed my thoughts.

Siren looked hot as sin standing outside in the rain, her clothes clinging to her body, revealing every curve. And then she shivered, and I got the urge to wrap my arms around her. To carry her inside, rip her wet clothes from her body, and warm her up.

But then I remembered—*she's not mine.* She never was. She may not be Hugo's either. But she certainly isn't mine.

The outrage came back, keeping me from touching her. Followed by the resentment, the double-cross, and finally the need to fuck her harder than I ever have before, until I make her mine only to tell her that I don't want her.

All I let her see was the anger.

I did everything right. I ignored her. Yelled at her. Refused to let her tell her side of the story. If she isn't talking and I'm not looking at her, then her lies can't hurt me.

I did everything right and yet...*I made one mistake.* I let our hands touch. It wasn't so much a mistake as an accident. I thought I could control my feelings. I thought any attraction I felt for her left my body the second she said she was married. I don't fuck married women, no matter their circumstances. I don't do cheaters, and backstabbers, and liars.

But what the fuck was with that touch?

How can one touch knock all sense from my head?

I've never felt anything like it. It's like her body is calling to me, and when we touch, it's the only way my body can operate at full power. Without her, I feel like I'm slowly being drained of all my energy, and the second our fingers brushed together, I came alive.

She's just messing with my head again. She doesn't care about me, and I don't care about her. *So what if we have physical attraction?* I can find that again with any girl. It's just been too long since I've been with another woman. I can find the spark again.

I spent the night shutting Siren out of my room. I didn't speak to her. And I didn't let her into my room. But it didn't stop her from speaking.

I tried not to listen, really I did.

But she said everything I was desperate to hear—*I don't love Hugo. I'm not sure I ever did.*

Eventually, I threw a pillow over my head to drown her out. And at some point in the night, she gave up, because when I woke up, Siren was gone.

I may have spent too much time last night thinking about Siren. But this morning, it's clear what my next step is.

I grab my keys, jump in my truck, and head back to the hospital. I know Julian and Siren are my enemies. But I need to know if I have one ally. Julian was the one who put Hugo in the hospital. Siren cheated on him. Maybe Hugo's on my side. Although, when he finds out I'm the one who's been sleeping with his wife, that may change.

Still, I need information, and Hugo might be my best bet to get it. He may be the only one who hates Julian more than I do.

I park in the parking lot and walk inside. I smile at the receptionist who remembers me from the other night and tells me that Hugo has been moved to a regular room.

The hospital is small, and there are only two main hallways, which makes it easy to find Hugo's room.

My temper flares when I see who is occupying his room—*Siren.*

Their conversation stops, and both of their heads snap to me as I step in. I walk in like I own the place. My plan is to ignore Siren and show Hugo just how powerful I am and that he shouldn't mess with me, at least until I figure out if he's on my side or not.

But when I see Siren's hand resting on Hugo's leg, I can't help myself. "You sure do spend a lot of time here for a woman who claims she doesn't love her husband."

Siren rolls her eyes like my jab didn't hurt her, but I know her well enough now—*it does.*

The reaction I care more about is Hugo's. He doesn't seem surprised at all to learn that his supposed wife doesn't love him. He just eats his Jello with a small smile.

Hugo looks horrible. There are bruises and cuts everywhere. Tubes connect into his arm and chest. A cast wraps around his right leg.

But the way he's moving happily and eating without difficulty feels off. I've had full body injuries like him before, and I could barely breathe, let alone eat twenty-four hours after it happened. *How can he move so easily? Even with pain medication?*

And this hospital looks like it's barely standing upright, let alone able to handle his extensive injuries. That was why Siren took me to Julian to get me medical help. This hospital can't handle severe injuries. Something isn't right.

I look from Hugo to Siren. She's an expert at figuring out liars and deceit. Yet, if she realizes something is off, she doesn't let on. *Unless she's in on the deceit?*

Fuck, I can't trust anything when it comes to Siren. This was a mistake; I shouldn't be here. I can't trust Hugo anymore than I can trust Siren.

"And you are?" Hugo asks.

"The man who slept with your wife," I answer. Not really the best way to get this man on my side, but I want everything out in the open. And I want to hurt Siren as much as I can.

Siren glares at me. "This is Zeke Kane. He owes a debt to Julian."

Hugo stops eating his Jello as he looks from Siren to me. And I know immediately that he wants her. He may not love her. And I may not understand what happened in their marriage, but the desire is there. Siren's eyes don't look at Hugo, though. They sink into me, straight to my heart. Like she knows why I'm here, and she thinks I'm stupid to trust Hugo. Her eyes tell me not to trust Hugo. Which gives me even more reason to trust him.

Hugo wants Siren, but what does Siren want? Who does she love? If she loves Hugo, it makes me want to hurt him just to hurt her. And if she loves me...*she doesn't, so it doesn't matter.*

My guess is she loves no one. She's a selfish minx incapable of love.

I turn my attention back to Hugo. It doesn't matter who Siren loves or even who Hugo loves. It matters who Hugo is loyal to.

"I'm Zeke, and I'm looking for an ally. Are you that man, Hugo? Do you hate Julian Reed?"

Hugo throws back the rest of the Jello into his mouth like he's doing a shot, then swallows with a big smile.

"No one hates Julian Reed more than I do," Hugo answers.

I grin. "I do."

CHAPTER 5
SIREN

I look back and forth between the two men. One is my asshole of a husband. The other—a man I wish was my husband.

These men should hate each other's guts. Hugo is my technical husband, who I never told Zeke about. Zeke feels betrayed because I'm married, even if it's only on paper.

And even though Hugo has slept with countless women since we've been married, he should hate that Zeke has been the one warming my bed.

Instead, these two men just made an arrangement. They became allies with a couple of words and a handshake.

What. The. Hell.

This can't be happening. I must be dreaming. I must have lost my mind. I'm sleep deprived from sitting outside Zeke's bedroom door all night, wishing I didn't have to be the devil in disguise for just once. But I don't think I could dream up an entire conversation. *Could I?*

Zeke nods at Hugo. "Rest up and get better. I'll check up on you when your wife isn't here, and we can talk gameplan."

It's happening. Zeke is talking about making a gameplan to take out Julian.

"I look forward to it," Hugo answers.

No, no, no! These two men are supposed to be enemies. Hate, not love each other.

Zeke starts walking out the door as I'm still gaping in shock. That was the last thing I expected to have to worry about.

Hugo raises his eyebrow at me, just as shocked by the turn of events as I am. But unlike me, Hugo just grabs another Jello off his tray and goes back to eating while he flips the TV back on to some baseball game.

Ugh.

I'll deal with Hugo later. He's not going anywhere. Although, he's surprisingly chipper today for someone who was just hit by a car.

Instead, I run after Zeke.

"Zeke," I snap, when I reach the hallway and see him about to round the corner. I don't expect him to stop, to give me any time to talk. *He didn't last night, why should he today?*

Maybe it's the desperation in my voice. Maybe it's the heartbreak he wants to stick around and witness. Maybe he wants to rub his new alliance in my face. Maybe he's just tired of ignoring me and wants to have it out.

Whatever the reason, he stops.

I jog down the hallway to where he's standing in the hallway of the small hospital. I don't want to have this conversation here in public, but I doubt Zeke will follow me somewhere more private.

"What are you doing?" I ask as I stand a foot away from him. So close, yet so far. What I really want to do is throw my arms around him and kiss him. Remind him that he likes me if not loves me.

He puts his hands in the pocket of his jeans as he tilts his head with a smile. He hasn't shaved, and the scruff on his face makes me drool. And he wore his hair down, just how I like it—the bastard. He knows exactly what he's doing—driving me insane with need. He's trying to play me like he thinks I played him. The only difference is, I wasn't playing him for my own enjoyment. I was playing him to protect him.

"Why would I tell you anything, Siren?"

"Don't work with Hugo."

"Hugo is your husband. I would think you would want me to work with him."

"You shouldn't trust Hugo. He only looks out for himself. He's only interested in money."

"I trust him more than I trust you."

I close my eyes at the impact of his words. He has no reason to trust me. *None.* But it still hurts. Like a knife to the chest.

I miss the old Zeke. The Zeke who would protect me with his life. The Zeke who would bring me coffee and flowers for no reason. The Zeke who was a romantic deep down. This Zeke is cold and calculated. This Zeke is closed up.

"Don't, Zeke. Don't trust Hugo. If you want to work with him, fine. But don't let your guard down with him." I can't look at Zeke. Seeing him hurts. Being near him and not touching him hurts. Seeing how pissed he is at me hurts. Because all I want to do is explain. If I could show him my heart, I would. Because my heart holds the truth.

Zeke's fingers go under my chin, tilting up so that I look at him. He looks into my eyes, like he can tell all of my secrets. I wish he could. Then he would know the truth.

His words still hang in the air—I trust him more than I trust you.

Zeke has no idea who Hugo is. He has no idea that on a scale of an angel to devil, Hugo falls second only to the devil himself. I may have once thought of him as an innocent, but now I know that he and Julian are more alike than different. The main difference is that Julian tells you exactly who he is, while Hugo hides his monster better beneath layers of charm and pretty blue eyes.

"You trust Hugo more than this," I say, and then I do something wonderfully stupid.

I grab Zeke's T-shirt and close the gap. He opens his mouth to speak, but it's too late. Our lips have collided in one hungry kiss—his eyes hood and then close. And then I let my eyes fall closed.

He doesn't fight the kiss like I expect, but I keep my grip on his shirt just in case. Zeke may not let me explain with my words, but maybe I can explain with my tongue.

The kiss is open-mouthed. It's the kind of messy kiss that involves teeth clashing and heads tilting the wrong way to make the most of the kiss. It's sloppy; our tongues battle each other in a frenzy.

But the kiss still does things to my heart. It makes it beat harder. It gives me hope. It sets me on fire.

And from the erection poking me in the stomach, I know that it does things to Zeke too.

Someone moans. *Me? Him? Both?*

And then his hands start greedily exploring my body. Over my ass, then under my shirt.

He wants me. He can hate me all he wants, but his hate won't stop him from fucking me.

I should want him to like me before I let him fuck me again, but I need this. And sometimes, fucking can lead to more truths than words can.

A throat clears.

"If you are going to continue on like this, I suggest the hotel up the street."

We both stop, turning our heads to face the surly nurse who is grimacing at us. My leg has somehow wrapped itself around Zeke's hip. His hand is on my ass. My hand still grips his shirt. And I know my hair is completely disheveled.

The nurse walks away, satisfied that we will stop making out in the hallway of the hospital like two unruly teenagers.

Slowly, Zeke lowers my leg, and he removes his hand from my ass. I loosen my grip on his shirt and run my hand through my hair. And then we separate.

I have no words, and yet, I have so much to say. Zeke doesn't give me the time to speak, though.

He clears his throat, and I think for a moment he's going to speak, but it seems he's just clearing his head of his impure thoughts as much as he's readying his throat to speak.

And then he's walking away, leaving me standing in the hallway with no answers.

"Zeke!" I shout again.

He doesn't turn this time.

"Promise me you won't trust Hugo," I yell after him.

He pauses for the briefest of seconds and then continues walking out of the hospital. Zeke doesn't make me any promises.

I stand in the hallway, torn between running after him and returning to Hugo. Right now, the best way to protect Zeke is to keep him away from this idiotic deal. And if Zeke won't listen to me, I know a man who has no choice but to listen to me as he's stuck in a hospital bed.

I storm back to Hugo's room. The look I give him is full of anger and rage. My eyes shoot into him like bladed knives.

Hugo chuckles. "Really? You going to give me that look when you've probably just fucked the guy while still married to me?"

I march over to his bed and yank the remote from his hand before turning off the TV.

Hugo huffs.

"You are not going to work with Zeke, under any circumstances. You are not allies. You are not friends. You are nothing to each other. Understand?"

Hugo smiles. "You don't get to tell me who I can and can't work with."

"Yes, I can."

"No, you can't. We're married; you aren't my boss. You have nothing on me. You're the reason I'm in this hospital bed, in fact. If anything, *you owe me*, not the other way around."

I cross my arms, glaring at him and wishing that car accident had killed him. It might have been on my conscious that Julian killed him because of me, but I'd rather have that than put Zeke at risk.

"You will stay away from Zeke," I say.

"And what will you do for me?" Hugo's smile cuts deep into me. It's not a happy smile; it's a smile that says I own you.

I may not be a slave, but it doesn't stop me from being owned. Three men own me, all in different ways.

Julian owns my actions and loyalty.

Hugo owns my name and past.

And Zeke owns my heart.

Someday, I won't be owned anymore. Someday, I will claim everything back. Everything except my heart.

Today isn't that day, though. Today, I have to save the man I love—a man who, even after one betrayal, continued to protect me—only giving me up after I betrayed him twice, both in unforgivable ways.

"How much?" I ask.

Hugo's smile falters. "You really think my loyalty can be bought?"

"I know it can. All you care about is money."

He shakes his head. "Oh, Aria, my sweet. You really don't know me at all."

"One million, all you have to do is avoid Zeke, stay the hell away from him. It will be the easiest money you've ever earned."

"No."

"Two million."

"No."

"Five million."

"And who exactly will you be stealing this money from, Aria?" He laughs. "You don't have that kind of pocket change."

I glare. "You don't know me that well."

He leans forward. "I do know you that well. And we're married. So if you have five million stashed somewhere, half of it is mine."

I frown. Money apparently isn't the way to go with him.

"What do you want, then?"

His eyes run up and down my body in a slow, seductive way, telling me exactly what he wants—me, on my knees, sucking his cock before I spread my legs for him.

"Not going to happen." I flip my hair. Although, I would. I'd fuck him if it meant saving Zeke. Surely, I can find a better way to convince Hugo just to stay the hell away from him.

I sit down on the edge of his hospital bed, turning up my charm as I take his hand in mine. I rub my thumb across the back of his hand in a slow, teasing way I used to when we were teens. "What else do you want, Hugo?"

"You can play your games on me all you want, Aria, it won't work. I know all your tricks." He grabs my hand with his other hand, forcing me to stop.

I sigh.

"What do you want, Hugo? I know you don't want to work with Zeke. What will it take to get you to stay away?"

He grins, and I know exactly what he's going to say before he says it. And it's the one thing I'm desperate for yet can't have because of what it will mean.

"I want a divorce, Aria."

I suck in a breath. *So do I, but the consequences of getting a divorce are too great.*

I stand up, done with this conversation. My hands falling from his as I walk to the door. I tried with Zeke. I tried with Hugo. But in the end, I lost my fight with both. I have to find a different way to keep them from working with each other.

"Tell me when you're ready for that divorce," Hugo says as I walk out the door.

I stiffen, not letting him get to me. As I round the corner, I spot something on my hand and stop. There's a red substance on my fingers, similar in color to blood. But it's not.

Dammit, Hugo.

And suddenly, I know exactly why Hugo wants to work with Zeke. Not because he hates Julian, but because Julian is paying him to be in that hospital bed. And none of it is real. He's not really hurt. It was all a lie. He never got hit by a car. I don't know when Hugo went from being Julian's enemy to his ally, but I'm going to figure it out. And my vow to Julian to protect Hugo's life just went out the window in my book.

CHAPTER 6
ZEKE

That motherfucking kiss.

Why did she have to go and do that?

Or did I initiate the kiss?

I can't remember. It just happened. Like neither of us had any control over whether we would kiss or not. It was inevitable.

It should have felt like poison to my lips. The kiss should have tasted bitter.

But of course, what my mind thinks and what my body feels is constantly at odds. I can never get my body to feel what my mind tells it to.

Fuck!

I throw my whiskey glass across the room and watch it shatter against the far wall of my kitchen, its contents rolling down a cabinet. It's much too early to be drinking anyway. But the outburst does nothing to tamper my pent up frustration.

When did everything in my life get so fucking complicated?

I used to have an easy life. I worked for my best friend. I was the muscle of the group that got things done. Not the man tied up in drama, women, and complications. But that's my life right now.

I almost want to march over to Julian's and demand he gives me another task just so I have something physical to do. I'd love to kill a man with my bare hands right now.

A soft rattling at my front door stops those thoughts. Because I know exactly who is standing behind that door—Siren.

And instantly, all my thoughts shift to her. I just can't make sense of my feelings. You know that game—fuck, marry, kill? You are supposed to choose one for each person in your life. Who you'd fuck, who you'd marry, and who you'd kill. With Siren, I don't want to choose just one. I want to do all three.

Dammit, why'd I have to go and throw my drink? I'm going to need it to get through this conversation. I need to use it as armor to keep her away from me, so I don't do something stupider than that kiss.

I open the door and find Siren standing on my porch. I glance behind her and spot a red corvette behind her. *Where'd the car come from?* Usually, she takes a cab if I don't drive her. Or that beat-up thing I've seen her drive in the past.

It's Hugo's.

"You can't trust Hugo," Siren says, pushing past me to come inside without waiting to be invited.

I roll my eyes. "Yes, please come in. I don't hate you or anything. You haven't betrayed my trust every chance you get. Shouldn't you be telling me not to trust *you?*"

She ignores me. *Probably smart.*

She throws off her leather jacket, revealing her toned arms and giving me a better view of her tits beneath her thin white shirt.

She notices where my eyes have landed.

"Zeke, this is important," she huffs, putting her hands on her hips, which only makes her boobs look bigger.

I let my eyes drift up lazily. "You have five minutes to talk, and then I want you out of my house forever." I don't add that I want her out of my life as well. But not before I fuck her, then marry her, then kill her.

"Hugo is working with Julian. The car accident wasn't real. He faked it," Siren says.

I walk over to my bar. *Yep, this conversation is definitely going to require a drink.* At least a glass in my hand will keep me sane or give me something to throw at her when she pisses me off.

"Zeke, are you listening? Did you hear what I said? You can't work with Hugo because he's working with Julian."

I pour the scotch three fingers high. *Yep, I'm going to need every drop.*

"Zeke!" Siren grabs my arm, and I spill a couple of drops of the scotch.

"Why the fuck did you do that?"

"Listen to me! You can't work with Hugo. Not because you think it will somehow get under my skin to be working with my ex."

I lift the glass to my lips. "You mean current husband."

She rolls her eyes. "Hugo is an ex, trust me."

"I don't."

She sighs. "You can't work with Hugo because he's working with Julian. Together they faked the accident. Why, I don't know, but I'm guessing to try and manipulate us both."

I take a sip. "Are you finished?"

"That's all you have to say?" She crosses her arms and pouts her adorable lips in the way that says she's not going to let this conversation end until I agree with her. And I do agree with her, but I hate letting her win. I prefer to watch her squirm like she is now. But I said only five minutes, and I'm sure our time is about up.

"I know," I say just as she opens her mouth to spill more info that will convince me of Hugo's loyalty.

"Wait... you know?"

"Yes."

"How?"

"Because it doesn't take Sherlock Holmes to figure out that Hugo wasn't in a major car accident. I've been through enough accidents to know that you don't just sit up in bed and eat Jello the next day. And that hospital doesn't have the capabilities to save a man from major injuries anyway. It's why you took me to Julian to save my life." *Dammit, I forgot she saved my life.* Although after everything that's happened since, I'm not sure if it was a blessing or a curse.

She leans against the counter, her head falling back. "How'd I miss all of that?"

I run my hand through my hair because I know exactly how you miss all the obvious signs that someone is lying to you. "Because you fell for him. You loved him. Even if you don't currently. People become blinded by love."

Our eyes meet, and the unspoken past slides between us—*love*. Neither of us ever said it. I was close to feeling it. The closest I've ever been with a woman. But I never said it. And now, I never will.

It wasn't love. It was attraction, lust, loneliness. I saw a pretty woman who was smart and a fighter, and I fell. That's all; it wasn't love —just me falling out of my orbit.

"So, you won't work with Hugo?"

I take a drink, hoping to avoid this conversation. Because there is no reasonable explanation I can give her as to why I need to work with Hugo. Even knowing the truth, without telling her about Lucy. And enough people already know about her. I can't risk her life by telling Siren about her as well. It's a miracle she didn't hear Julian whisper into my ear. Although, there's a good chance he will eventually tell Siren about Lucy. I won't be the one to be disloyal to Lucy, though.

"Zeke?" Siren's voice is full of hesitation, because she can read me too well. She knows that I'm avoiding.

"How can you still work with him when he isn't on your side? Why?"

Because I need to know everything they know about Lucy. I need someone that I may be able to flip. Someone who is vulnerable. Someone I can use as leverage. And Hugo Martinez seems like the perfect man.

Julian wants me to fall for his tricks. So I'll let him think I fell.

I look at Siren with a raised eyebrow. "I've worked with plenty of people who aren't on my side."

Her face falls when she realizes I mean her.

And then she walks over to my bar and grabs the scotch bottle. She takes a swig straight from the bottle as if she needs the courage to say what she needs to say next.

"We haven't had sex," she says.

My head snaps to her. Whatever I expected her to say that wasn't it. I expected her to try and convince me to not work with Hugo. Not tell me something honest about herself.

"Well, that's not true entirely. Hugo and I haven't had sex since we were married."

My mouth falls open into a huge gape. I don't know what to say to that. She wants it to change things. But I won't let it. She lied to me about being married. No, she never said she was married, but she manipulated me into thinking she wasn't married, which is somehow worse.

Then she used me to cheat on her husband. I don't care how horrible he is. If he's that bad, then divorce his ass. Or at least tell me the truth, so I can decide if I want to participate in her infidelity. So I can at least protect my heart from falling for a married woman.

"Is that supposed to make it better that you cheated on him with me?" I ask.

She takes another sip of the scotch and then puts the bottle back before hopping up on my counter with her hands in her lap. She looks so young sitting there like that. Not like that strong independent traitor of a woman I know she is.

"No, it's just the truth. You want the truth? I'll tell you."

I'm not sure I want the truth, not anymore. Not from her. But apparently, I do because I don't tell her any of that. And I listen like I might fall off a cliff if I don't catch every syllable she speaks.

"We fucked one night in the backseat of my car."

"The same one you rescued me in?"

She nods.

Shit, now I know I really hate that car.

"Hugo was my first. It wasn't perfect. It wasn't magical. It was messy and painful and uncomfortable. But that was my life."

God, I really don't want to hear about how another guy took her virginity. But I don't stop her from talking.

"But I knew afterward that he was the man for me. I didn't want perfect. I didn't want romance. I wanted real. And Hugo was as real as it got. He taught me self-defense. He taught me how to play guitar. Encourage me to write songs, to sing to get through the pain of my childhood instead of turning to drugs. He saved my life. He brought me back to life."

Siren can play guitar? God, I would do anything to hear it. And she writes her own songs. I'm desperate to hear just one of them. *What would she write about me?*

"So when I found out the truth—that the reason Hugo didn't want me doing drugs was because he was already addicted. That he sold drugs to make enough money to buy them. That he was in huge debt and was going to be killed if he couldn't pay it back. I did everything to save him."

How does this story make me wish that I was Hugo? She already saved your ass as well. Hugo isn't special. Tell me more...

"I tried to steal something valuable enough from Julian to pay off Hugo's debt. But Julian caught me. I thought I was going to die, but he offered me a trade. He would pay off Hugo's debt, if I worked for him for ten years. I agreed. I would have done anything."

Anything.

"So I went back to Hugo. We got married. And then I went to Julian to work. I thought Hugo would wait for me. I thought we'd get our happily ever after eventually. We were young, after all. Ten years was nothing. And we could still see each other whenever Julian didn't demand work from me. But the first chance I had to go home, I caught Hugo with another woman in our bed. A woman he'd been fucking our entire relationship."

I can feel her heart breaking. I want to run to her. I want to protect her. Comfort her. But I can't. I can't show her that I care.

"Do you have any idea the pain I felt at having a man I loved betray me like that? I gave up ten years of my life to save him? And he was cheating on me the whole time."

"I have an idea," I say.

And then I see a tear roll down her cheek, and I break. I can't just watch her cry without doing something.

Slowly, I walk over to her. She leans away, thinking I'm going to make fun of her pain.

Maybe a stronger man would have. But if there is one thing I understand better than most, it's pain and heartbreak. And I don't wish that kind of pain on my worst enemy. I'd rather be shot than deal with a broken heart.

Carefully, I reach my thumb up to her cheek and brush away the tear. Careful, not to do more than just touch the tear. *Don't let any feelings in. Don't give her the wrong idea.*

"You've never fucked him since you got married?"

"No."

"Have you fucked other men?"

She nods. "I wanted to hurt him for what he did to me. So for a while there, I fucked every man I could find just to hurt him."

She means she fucked any man she could to numb her own pain. I understand; I feel the same way.

"In some states, you wouldn't be considered married, since you never consummated the marriage," I say.

She smiles, weakly. "Do you consider me married? Because I don't. It's only real on paper."

I lean forward and smell her hair. *Fuck.*

"You aren't getting out of your betrayal on a technicality."

"I'm not trying to," she breathes back. "I just want to know what you think. Am I married or not?"

I take a step back. *Don't fall for it. Don't fall under her spell. It could all be a lie.*

"Why are you still married to him? Why didn't you divorce his ass as soon as you found that whore in bed with him?"

She smiles when I call the woman a whore. "I can't."

Julian said as much. "Does it have something to do with a prenup?"

"Yes."

"Why sign something if you knew it would trap you in a marriage forever?"

"Because I thought it was forever. I loved him. It didn't matter what the prenup said."

"What did it say?"

She shakes her head. Apparently, it's the one truth I won't be getting. "It says that I will be married to Hugo Martinez until one of us dies."

I sigh. One step forward in the truth with her and two steps back.

"Do you still love him?"

"No, seeing him in that hospital bed confirmed it. When I went to the hospital, I wasn't sure what I felt. My feelings were complicated when it comes to Hugo."

I nod. *My feelings are complicated when it comes to you.*

"Divorce him," I say.

Her eyes flutter, shocked.

"Divorce him. Whatever you have to pay him. Whatever you have to give up, it's worth it to be rid of him."

She doesn't answer back, but I have a feeling she will never divorce him. Which means I have to let her the fuck go.

"Can I kill him since you obviously won't divorce him?"

She sucks in a breath but then shakes her head no.

"Why not? You hate him. He's ruined your life. Most women who were cheated like that would want him dead or at least tortured for what he did."

She looks off into the distance past me. "I loved Hugo once. Really loved him. And I think even though he was cheating on me, that for one magical moment, he loved me too. And as much as I want to hurt him for hurting me, for ruining my life, I can't betray those people we once were. I can't denounce that love. Because it was real. And it was special. It was everything. And if I ever have hope of feeling that again, I have to believe in love. That love exists and that it should never be crossed. Even when both people fall out of love. Even when two people fall into hate."

Like us.

But we never fell in love. We came close. But it never happened. She stopped it from happening.

Siren wipes her eyes and then rolls her shoulders. This conversation is over.

"I think my five minutes are up." She jumps down from the counter. "Do what you need to do when it comes to Hugo. But just know that he can manipulate people just like I can. And unlike me, he has no problem lying with his words. So make sure you are the one doing the betraying this time."

She starts walking toward my front door. Leaving me for the first time on her own accord.

And for once, a small part of me doesn't want her to go.

"Siren," I say.

She stops. "Yes?"

"Ask me again."

She narrows her eyes, trying to understand what I want her to repeat. A moment passes, then another.

"Do you consider my marriage to Hugo real?"

"No."

She smiles lightly and then walks out the door. And I know I've fucked up because I just sparked a hope that will never happen. Siren will never be mine, and I'll never fall for her again. She may not be in a real marriage, but she's lied and betrayed me enough that I can never trust her again. I shouldn't give her hope. I shouldn't give myself hope. I should be cold and calculated with her.

But maybe I need to think that in a different universe, we would have a chance. One in which we didn't have other people to be loyal to. One in which we always told each other the truth and always chose the other person over everyone else.

I need hope that in some other universe, we are living together happily ever after. Because in this world, all we are ever going to do is destroy each other.

CHAPTER 7
SIREN

Zeke gave me hope, and somehow that is worse than making sure he ended things between us for good. Because now I have hope. Now my heart flutters in my chest, pretending that I'm about to become Mrs. Zeke Kane, instead of being stuck with a name I hate.

No, I'm not Aria Martinez married to the asshole Hugo Martinez. Zeke said so himself—our marriage isn't real.

But I'm not Siren Kane either.

I'm Aria Torres.

I'm an expert manipulator, man-hater, and slayer of men.

Even after my last three years are up with Julian, this is who I will always be. I don't even know how to hold down a normal job anymore. I've been doing this for Julian for so long. And some part of me likes it. I like making men pay for their crimes. I like traveling. I like the adventure. The control. The power.

I like it all.

The only thing I don't like is having to answer to other men. Men like Julian Reed and Hugo Martinez.

But somehow I'm not sure I'd mind answering to Zeke Kane.

Although, I'd argue back and want him to listen to me as much as I listen to him.

Fuck hope.

I don't get to have hope.

This is my life. And my goal hasn't changed. I need to get Zeke free of this world and back into his. Zeke thinks Hugo can help him do that, but he's wrong.

I've played all the cards I have when it comes to Zeke. But I have one card left to play with Hugo. And I'm going to play it.

I drive recklessly fast back to the hospital, where Hugo is lying with a fake injury.

And as I make the last turn, I spot a familiar-looking truck driving just as recklessly behind me.

Really Zeke? You say you want me out of your life, yet you won't leave me alone for five minutes when I want to do something by myself.

That's okay. He can watch the show and see how weak Hugo is. Zeke can see how he doesn't really want him on his side.

I park my Corvette illegally in a no parking zone. I don't care if it gets towed. It's Hugo's car anyway. I prefer beat-up, older cars. Cars with plenty of muscle, heart, and grit. Just like I like my men.

I strut inside. If this was a bar, I'd be turning heads. I nod at the woman behind the nurses' station, but I'm not stopping. I'm pretty sure it's still visiting hours, but even if it isn't, I'm not letting that stop me.

I throw the door open to Hugo's room; his eyes pop away from the stupid TV he's been watching all day.

Carefully, I close the door behind me, wishing the door had a lock, but it won't take long to do what I need to do.

"You fucking, lying bastard," I say.

Hugo cocks his head to the side as he flicks off the television. "And why would you say that?"

"Because it's fucking true."

I march over to his bed with more fury in my eyes than when I caught him fucking another woman in the bed I bought for him.

And I'm rewarded with him recoiling into his bed like the slime that he is. I love this power that I have in this moment. And I almost don't want to do the next step because once you use your power, it starts fleeting. You can never be as powerful as you are when you make the threat and display. When you enact the threat, your power starts slipping until you earn it again.

I grab Hugo's hospital gown and jerk him out of bed. He stands immediately, his hand holding onto mine.

"Oh, look at that. He can stand," I say, with vengeance in my eyes.

Hugo blinks rapidly. He wasn't expecting this.

Hugo may have taught me self-defense. He may have paid for classes for me to learn Krav Maga. But I've never used the skills I learned on him. Even when he cheated on me. *Today that changes.*

"Only because you're holding me up," he says.

I let go. "Still standing."

I take a step forward, forcing him to take a step back.

"Why are you working with Julian?"

He takes a step back.

"Why would you work for a man who trapped me in this life? I knew you couldn't keep your dick in your pants, but I never thought you were cruel."

"I'm not."

"Then, why?"

"I'm not working with Julian."

I take another step forward, and he takes his last step as the bed prevents him from walking further back.

"Don't lie. You weren't injured in a car accident. You faked it with makeup and the help of the nurses. Julian hired you."

"He thought it would be easier to control you if he controlled me. My choice was to work for him, or he'd actually have me run over by a car or shot. So forgive me for not wanting to get shot."

I laugh. "Forgive you? That's a poor choice of words. I'll never forgive you. And I would have taken the bullet every time rather than stab you in the back."

"No, you wouldn't have."

"I've worked for Julian for seven years because of you! I sure as hell would have taken a bullet for you. I loved you once. That's a mistake I'll never repeat."

I hear the door open, and I know we have an audience. I also know who it is. And it isn't some nurse coming to check on the commotion. I'm sure Julian paid off the nurses to ignore whatever happens in this room.

Julian may think he can manipulate Hugo in order to control me. But today is the last day that works. I will no longer protect Hugo. I'll no longer save him. From today on, he's on his own. We are enemies, not friends, not exes—enemies.

"This is for not taking a bullet for me when you should have," I say.

"Baby, you're not going to hurt me," Hugo says.

My eyes light up at his words. Hugo used to know me. He used to know what I'm capable of. But seven years of working for Julian has changed all of that.

Seven years has turned me bitter. Seven years is too long to go without getting revenge.

I grab his arm and slam him into the wall before he has a chance to react. Seven years has changed Hugo too. He's lived a cushy life with plenty of money since I set him free. Seven years of not having to look over his shoulder. His self-defense skills are weak.

He winces, his head rattling as it hits the wall.

"This is for me," I say, slamming his wrist into the wall until I hear little bones crack.

"And this is for Zeke," I say, head butting Hugo, breaking his nose.

I let go of Hugo and step back. He grabs his wrist, and his eyes water, barely containing his tears as he crumples to the floor in front of me.

"You are such a bitch!" He cries out, not bothering hiding his tears now as he cradles his wrist.

"And you're a cheating, lying cunt who now has the required injuries to warrant a hospital stay." I grin.

"Julian will hear about this."

"Good." I fold my arms across my chest. "He'll be happy to know my skills are still sharp. That I realized this was all a trick and handled the situation. Because Julian Reed doesn't give a shit about you, Hugo. He cares about me. I'm his prized possession. His armor. His secret weapon. And you are nothing but a game to him."

I crack my neck and flip my hair as I turn and look at Zeke, who is leaning against the wall with a smirk on his face. I wasn't sure how he was going to react. If he was going to be pissed that I'd outed Hugo's plan or happy.

But from the look of awe on his face, I think it's the latter.

"He's all yours," I say as I walk over to the chair in the corner of the room and take a seat. I know Zeke came here on business of his own, but I'm not going to let him talk to Hugo alone.

Zeke shakes his head. "I'm never going to get over how you can bring a man to his knees." The way Zeke is looking at me with a wolfish expression makes me wonder what he means—how I brought Hugo to his knees in pain, or Zeke to his knees in lust.

CHAPTER 8
ZEKE

Siren is the most kick-ass woman I've ever met. She doesn't need a man to take care of her. And she's been screwed over by enough men that even if she did need a man to protect her, she wouldn't take a man's help.

It gives me a little perspective on why she doesn't trust me and why she was willing to betray me. It doesn't make me forgive her or envision any future together. But it helps to understand.

To most men, Siren might be intimidating. She just broke her ex's wrist and nose. Sure, I'm bigger than her and could stop her if I really wanted to if she tried that shit on me. But she has the ability. And if she really wanted to break my wrist, she'd find a way.

Intimidating.

And so fucking sexy.

I've always been the romantic type. I enjoy taking care of women. But with Siren, I want to take care of her even more. Because I can see past the armor she wears, I can see that she's just as desperate to be taken care of as any other woman, even if she is more than capable of taking care of herself.

She just broke her ex's wrist. But I don't think she did it for herself. She did it because he tried to mess with me. And that won't go unnoticed. *Why? Why did him possibly hurting me affect her more than when he fucked with her?*

I don't have time to analyze it right now. Siren just changed the plan. When I jumped in my car to come here, I debated continuing to be on his side or breaking his leg. Siren just made that decision easier. And it was the right decision.

I hate him.

I hate him for marrying the most incredible, badass woman and then cheating on her. He's probably the reason Siren is cold as ice and incapable of feelings. He's the reason she was willing to hurt me. He's the reason she's working for Julian. I hate him for letting her be sold like property to another man. I hate that he hurt her. I hate that by hurting her, he threatened any hope Siren and I have of being together.

I hate it all.

Siren got to take her vengeance out on him; now it's my turn.

Hugo is still writhing on the floor in pain. He turns his head and spits blood mixed with his own tears.

God, he's such a baby. How could Siren ever fall for a man like him?

Hugo and I are polar opposites. He's thin and lanky. His hair is light brown. His eyes are bright blue.

While I'm hulk-like, with dark hair, and a scruffy beard.

He's clean-cut.

I'm a broken ship with more scars than perfect skin.

There is no way one woman could love us both. Even at different times in her life.

She likes a man like Hugo, maybe not one that cheats, but the perfect looking man. And I'm not him.

It makes me even angrier.

"Get up," I say.

Hugo wipes the blood from his nose on the back of his hand.

"Get the fuck out, and call a nurse," he demands back.

Tsk, tsk.

He should learn to follow my orders faster. He's not the one in charge here. *I am.*

"Get up," my voice booms with the full force of my anger. Shaking walls and telling every person in this hospital that I'm in charge of everyone and everything.

Hugo immediately scrambles to his feet.

"Sit," I say, calmer this time, knowing when to use my powerful voice and when to hold back.

Hugo sits.

"Good dog," I say.

"I'm not a dog."

"Aren't you? You do whatever Julian says, just like his obedient dog would. You don't have brains of your own."

"Like I told Aria, I didn't have a choice. It was follow his orders or get shot."

"Hmm, that sounds like you made the wrong choice. No one hurts Siren and gets away with it."

"Siren?"

I don't answer him.

Instead, I lean forward and look him in the eyes. "Now, you are going to answer my questions, and I won't break your other arm."

Hugo looks like he wants to hit me, but he won't. His muscles are thin compared to my bulk. He wouldn't have a shot against me. And at the same time, he also looks like he's about to cry at the thought of having his other arm broken.

"I'll tell you whatever you want. I really do hate Julian Reed. You didn't have to send your bitch in to do your dirty work so I was weak before you talked to me," Hugo says, sending dirty looks to Siren, who is still sitting in the corner of the room watching us like a hawk. I have no doubt if Hugo tried to lay a finger on me, she'd jump in to defend me, just like she did with Julian.

With Julian, she was ordered to do it. *With me, though?* I'm not sure why she keeps protecting me and hurting me. She's a conundrum.

"I didn't send her. We aren't working together. She handled her business with you; this is about you and me."

Hugo rolls his eyes. "Get me some pain pills, and I'll tell you whatever you want to know."

"No, tell me what you want to know, and I won't break your other arm, that was the deal."

He huffs. "What do you want to know?"

"What does he want with my boss, Enzo Black?"

"What he always wants, control and money. Mr. Black is the most powerful man in these oceans. He wants to take him down and take over his business."

"How much does he know about me?"

"Just that you used to work for him. He thinks you know everything about Mr. Black and that when he is finished using you, he'll be able to use you to trade you to get what he wants from Mr. Black."

"He thinks he'll get control and money in exchange for me?" That doesn't make sense.

"I guess," Hugo shrugs. "He doesn't tell me his entire plan or why, but I assume he wants a weapon or something from Mr. Black that can help him become more powerful."

"Siren, go get us those pain pills. Hugo's been a good boy."

Siren eyes me suspiciously, but she leaves. Giving me a minute, two at the most, before she returns.

"How does Julian know about Lucy?"

Hugo's eyes light up. It might have been a mistake to ask him when he can use the information to hurt Siren. But I need to ask. I have to protect her. And I vowed to stop protecting Siren. This is me keeping that promise.

"Aria."

My eyes fall. *Siren knows about Lucy? She was the one that found out about her and betrayed her to Julian?*

That can't be?

But when I look at Hugo's happy grin, I know it's true. And he just destroyed all of the relationship I've built with Siren. We are officially over. It's one thing to hurt me. It's another to hurt an innocent woman.

CHAPTER 9
SIREN

I don't know why Zeke sent me out to get pain pills. I know he isn't going to give them to Hugo.

I suspect it's because he wants to ask Hugo something without me there. And I don't know if it's because he's hiding something from me or if he thinks Hugo will answer more honestly without me there.

But loving someone is about trusting them. And the only way I can earn Zeke's trust in return is by showing him that I trust him.

So I go and get the damn pain pills from the nurse.

And when I open the door, I feel the shift in the air. Zeke's pissed, and Hugo is happy as a clam.

Hugo's eyes find mine when I enter the room, as if to say he's won. I just don't know what the fuck he won or what he's talking about. But it doesn't feel good.

I shouldn't have left. Now wasn't the time to prove my loyalty to Zeke. Not when I know what scum Hugo is. Zeke doesn't know all his tricks yet.

"Thank you for answering my questions, Hugo. You've earned your pain pills." Zeke turns to me and motions for me to toss him the pills.

I do.

He catches them with a coldness in his eyes I wasn't expecting to be aimed at me.

What did you tell him, Hugo? Before I left, Zeke and I were basically on the same side. And now, I can't read him at all.

He unscrews the cap and hands two pills to Hugo, who takes them and swallows them dry.

Such a wimp, I barely injured his nose. And his wrist—well, I guess I did some damage there.

"I won't break your other arm," Zeke says.

I hold my breath because I already know what Zeke is going to do. And it's going to be exhilarating to watch.

Hugo grins smugly. *Oh, you idiot.*

Zeke grabs the IV pole and slings it as hard as he can against Hugo's kneecap.

The scream Hugo makes is the most magnificent melody I've ever heard. I'll never forget the sound. It's high-pitched, and agonizing, and everything Hugo deserves. The pain hits him everywhere. His voice, his eyes, his entire body rings with the pain as his kneecap shatters.

"That's for hurting Siren," Zeke says, and I get flutters in my stomach. He hurt Hugo to defend my honor. Just like I hurt Hugo to defend his.

"You said you wouldn't hurt me if I told you the truth, you fucking bastard."

"No, I said I wouldn't break your arm, and I didn't. I keep my word, unlike you." Zeke stands taller. "And I gave you the pain pills even though it wasn't part of our arrangement. Too bad it will take at least half an hour for them to start taking effect. And Tylenol will do nothing to stop the sharp pain in your knee."

Zeke starts walking toward me, but I'm not sure if he's walking toward me or the door.

"Dammit, I should have gone for the kneecap, so much more effective than the wrist," I say, hoping that the joke will lighten the mood.

But Zeke isn't in a playing mood. He's all seriousness. As he passes me, he snaps his fingers, indicating for me to follow.

I want to, but I don't like being treated like his pet. Not by him.

I follow, but I bring my anger with me. Zeke searches the hallway before spotting what he's looking for. He walks to a door that has a janitor's sign on it. He pops the lock with a quick thrust up of the door handle, and then he opens the door, holding it open for me to step inside.

I study him carefully, trying to figure out what happened in the two minutes I was gone to get the pain pills.

"You first," I say, needing to take back a sliver of control.

He growls, but I don't back down. Not until he tells me what's going on.

After a quick staring contest, where neither of us back down, Zeke steps into the dark closet. Only then do I follow.

The door shuts behind me, leaving all light outside the dark closet. I'm sure there is a light switch, but neither of us moves to find it.

The closet is small, so small that we are face to face, and I can feel his breath on my cheek.

I try holding my breath, not willing to give him any pleasure until he talks to me. But he doesn't hold back. He's angry. *With me.*

Well, good, I'm angry with him. For shutting me out. For not letting me talk. For not letting me spend every second kissing his face and riding his cock.

He can be pissed at me and still fuck me. We are too good together not to.

"How many secrets are you hiding from me?" His voice comes out strained and wanting.

I exhale a shaky breath, doing everything I can to not kiss him again. I was the one who initiated our last kiss and that got me nowhere. If he wants to kiss me, he's going to be the one to do it.

"Too many," I answer honestly. "How many are you keeping from me?"

"Not enough."

And then his lips claim mine.

The kiss slams me back against the door. It's hard, taking my breath away, but also demanding so much more. It takes my control, my power, my heart. It demands I spill my secrets in order to get more.

But both of us have our secrets, and neither of us will ever tell the whole truth. Because we need to keep our secrets in order to protect ourselves, and more importantly, each other.

Our secrets can wait, though.

This kiss cannot.

My hands wrap around his neck, as his hand grabs my shirt, flinging it off me before I realize that he's trying to angrily fuck me in the janitor's closet.

I don't care; I want this man too much. And I'll take him any way I can get him. Rough, dirty, in the fucking janitor's closet.

My bra goes next, and then his head dips, nibbling roughly on my nipple, making me gasp and squirm against his lips.

"Zeke, fuck."

He smirks against my nipple.

And then his hand is dipping down to my pants. Undoing the buttons and zippers before shimming them down my hips. Then his fingers plunge into my panties, ripping them from my body before finding the wetness between my legs.

Yes!

More.

His fingers tease between my folds but never find my clit. The longer Zeke goes without touching my most sensitive spot, the faster I realize that he is never going to. He's going to take out his frustrations on my body by denying me the one thing that could bring me the most pleasure.

Two can play at this game.

I lunge forward, grabbing at the waistband of his jeans, but Zeke grabs both of my wrists and has them pinned above my head with one hand, while his other hand continues to torture me by rubbing everywhere except the one spot I want him to.

I could fight him. I've done it before. Sure, Zeke is strong and has muscles for days, but I'm smart. I could get out of his hold.

But the striking gaze of Zeke's eyes, even in the dark, tells me that I'd be smart not to fight.

"What did Hugo say?" I ask.

"Really? You're going to bring up the topic of your ex-husband when I'm currently trying to fuck you?" he hisses against my cheek. His breath like fire and temptation and so damn hot.

"But you're not trying to fuck me; you're trying to torture me."

He grips my wrists harder, the weight of his body pressing against mine. Him clothed, me basically naked.

It's hot.

But it's also the angriest I've ever seen Zeke. Something happened. Something I'm missing the pieces to. Something he thinks I did—the worst thing.

But what?

Worst than betraying him to Julian? Worst than not telling him about my husband?

We are both silent for a beat. Both trying to decide what to do next. How to have the upper hand with the other person. But there is no upper hand when it comes to us because there is no us. There is just tension, frustration, and longing. Secrets, truths, and lies. And stories that aren't ours to tell.

"Truth or sin, Siren?" Zeke asks.

"Ask me," I say, waiting for him to accuse me of something that most likely Hugo or Julian did. Because Zeke doesn't trust me, he'd rather trust either of them than me. Even though he knows they are evil. I'm worse.

"How did you find out about Lucy?" Zeke asks.

I blink—once, twice. Racking my brain for the information he seeks. The information that has caused him to pin me naked in a janitor's closet. The information that has him more pissed than anything I've ever done before.

"I don't know who Lucy is," I answer.

He laughs. "Stop lying! For someone who says they can't lie, you sure do it all the time."

"I'm not lying! I have no clue who you are talking about." Although, I'm desperate to know who he's talking about. *Who is Lucy?*

He growls, low and beast-like. The sound is half-anger and half-need.

"Tell me or I get to commit a sin," Zeke says.

The threat is meant to intimidate me. It's meant to scare me. I'm vulnerable, pinned naked against the door. I'm completely at Zeke's mercy.

Except I'm not. I could escape if I wanted to. And as much as Zeke hates me, he isn't like Hugo or Julian. He won't really hurt me. He can't without hurting himself.

There is nothing Zeke could do to me. But he could do it to someone else. Drag a nurse into the closet to fuck and make me watch. That would be the only torture I couldn't stand.

"Truth or sin, what did Hugo tell you?" I ask, needing to get the complete picture from Zeke.

"Truth—Hugo said that you were the one who told Julian about Lucy. That's three times you betrayed me. And it will be the last."

I swallow, holding back tears. Because there are no words that can make Zeke believe that I not only have no idea who Lucy is, but I didn't find her and turn her over to Julian. And right now, I can't prove to him the truth.

So I only have one option.

"Sin," I say, and I know it's what Zeke wanted me to say. He didn't want me to tell him the truth. He didn't want me to defend myself. He wanted me to give him a reason for him to be cruel. He needed a reason to show me how pissed he is.

"Wrong choice," Zeke says, and then his mouth comes down hard on my neck. Marking my skin with his lips, his teeth, his hungry growls.

The move isn't meant to bring me pleasure; it's meant to treat me like he owns me. He doesn't know that no matter the reason, having his mouth against my skin is hot as hell.

I feel my body come alive again with hope that Zeke will finish what he started. That he'll fuck me. And inadvertently make me come.

But that wouldn't be a sin.

I moan, accidentally letting him know how much I enjoy him kissing my neck hungrily.

"You like that, babe?"

Babe? He never calls me anything but Siren. And I hate any other name falling from his lips.

"What about this?"

His hand reaches between my legs, and if I was wet before, now I'm drenched. Because unlike last time, he finds my clit, confirming that he knows exactly what he's doing when it comes to my body.

"Fuck, Zeke," I moan as I hump his hand. Knowing that at any moment, he could stop and leave me unsatisfied. Leave me wanting, desperate to come without a release.

"Yea, baby? Just like that. You're so close."

I am. I'm so fucking close.

And then he stops. His hand disappears from my body.

So...so close!

Dammit.

My eyes open, and my body ices at the loss of pleasure.

Zeke smirks.

"Last chance, tell me the truth, and this will all be over."

"You wouldn't believe the truth, even if I told you."

"You're right; I wouldn't."

Zeke jerks my hands down and spins me around, before pinning my hands behind my back. Again, he's holding my wrists with just one hand—as if that is enough to contain me. The move might work with most women, but not with me. I could break free.

But Zeke needs to punish me. He needs to hurt me for something he thinks I did. Even though I didn't.

But if letting Zeke take out his pain on me just this once helps him heal, I'll do it. I've destroyed this man enough.

And I can take it. Whatever he has planned can't be as bad as what I've gone through with Hugo and Julian. Or even before as a kid.

"I choose sin, Zeke. So far, all you've given me is mild amusement," I say, goading him a little.

He doesn't take the bait.

"I'm not a cruel man, Siren. So don't twist things around and make me out to be one."

Siren, I'm back to Siren.

"Then stop acting like one," I say, hating that my voice sounds small and scared and timid. It doesn't sound anything like me.

Another lie to myself, because Zeke most definitely can cruelly hurt me. Only he has the power. Saying he doesn't is a lie—one of the biggest.

He doesn't answer. Instead, I hear him unzip his jeans.

And I tense waiting for the intrusion. Waiting for the delicious stretch. Waiting for him to drive inside of me with all of his fury.

Instead, his hands release my wrists. I stand hunched over my ass in the air. Waiting. But I realize, I'm waiting for nothing. Because Zeke isn't going to angrily fuck me.

He moans.

Slowly, I turn and see Zeke jacking off to my naked body. And I realize what his sin is. He's going to come, but I won't. He'll use my body to get off, but he won't touch me. He won't help me come.

I consider touching myself to the sight of Zeke pumping himself. It's a glorious sight. One I know I'm going to have dirty dreams about later. And I want nothing more than to come with him.

But I want to show Zeke that I'm not a monster. I want to show him that I'm on his side. That I would never hurt this Lucy person whoever she is.

So I don't.

Zeke's eyes heat when I turn, and he gets a clear view of my body. My nipples hardening under his heady gaze.

I want him so badly.

But he won't let me have him. Not right now. Maybe never again.

He pumps furiously, taking his anger out on his cock since he can't on my body. He wants to come fast. End this quickly. And I have just the idea to help him.

I kneel in front of him, his eyes gaze at me in a curious way, but he doesn't stop or ask what I'm doing.

My lips are level with his cock. And I know what I want, but I'm not sure Zeke will let me.

But his eyes haven't left mine, and I know he's trying to figure out what I'm doing. This is my chance to touch him, to get to taste him. If I can't have him how I want, then this is the next best thing. Giving him pleasure and stealing some for myself.

I lick my lips and then open my mouth wide. My eyes turn sultry, telling him exactly what I'm willing to do.

He groans, still pumping with his hand, but he can't resist. And he won't deny himself the pleasure of a blowjob.

He glides his hand over his cock one more time; his cock grows another inch in his hand as it somehow hardens more at the prospect of my lips wrapping around him.

And then he inches forward, pushing my lips wider as his cock slides between them.

I smirk around his cock, feeling victorious. And then he starts moving in my mouth, hard and fast, trying to punish my mouth while he chases his orgasm.

He thinks he can hurt me this way. He doesn't know I don't have a gag reflex. He literally can't hurt me this way. *But I can hurt him.*

I let my teeth scrape against the ridge of his thick cock, and he gruffs, his eyes shooting me a warning.

I smile and then wrap my fingers around him in addition to his cock. He stills, letting me do all the work as I pump over him.

Each thrust of my hand and lips earns me another moan. Each deeper, louder, and stronger than the previous. Each telling me that he's seconds away from exploding in my mouth.

He started with all the control here, but I took it. I demanded it.

His body begins to tense as his orgasm nears. I consider dragging it out, making him wait and torture him like he tried to torture me, but I won't. Because I want to taste him. I want to know that I'm the one who made him come.

The only one.

Except I'm not. *Who has made this beast of a man come before? How many others?*

My thoughts made me hesitate, and Zeke shoots me a look as if to say, 'if you stop now, I'm going to kill you.'

It does the job, and I'm quickly back to driving the man crazy with my lips and hands.

My other hand reaches up and strokes his balls as I take Zeke all the way in my mouth and down my throat.

His eyes widen, and his mouth parts as the most wonderful throaty sound pushes from his mouth.

Say my name. Say it.

I push him further over the edge. He's so damn close. I never want this to end, and yet, I want everything. I'm greedy like that.

I swirl my tongue over the tip, before plunging him deep in my mouth again. And this time, the tidal wave that is Zeke explodes in my mouth. He fists my hair as he comes hard into my throat. And then I wait for the sound I've earned after the blow job I just gave him.

Instead, I get...

"Yes, Lucy!" Zeke screams, destroying me.

I didn't think he could hurt me. *I was wrong.*

With one word, he cut me down.

With one word, he punished me more than any man could.

Lucy.

If I didn't know who Lucy was before, I do now. She's the woman in his life. The woman he loves. The woman he'd do anything for.

And I just let him use me while all the time he imagined her.

I swallow and then wipe my mouth on the back of my hand before I gather my clothes, throwing my shirt on quickly and angrily.

Zeke doesn't speak. But he stares, judging my reaction to what he just did.

I grab his T-shirt off the floor and throw it at him.

"Ask Julian," I snap at him.

"Ask Julian what?" he asks.

"Ask him how he found Lucy. Because it sure as hell wasn't me." And then I storm out, leaving him in the damn janitor's closet of the hospital I hate for so many fucking reasons. This moment just added one more. I'm never stepping foot in this fucking hell hole again.

And I'm never thinking about Zeke again. Not as a friend. Not as a lover. I'll protect him only because by protecting him, I'm getting him the fuck away from me.

I storm outside, ignoring the stares at my tears and half-dressed appearance. When I go to jump in the Corvette I drove here in, I remember I illegally parked, and the car has been towed.

So much for a quick getaway.

And then I see Zeke walking out to his truck, and my heart aches. Once again, I lied to myself. I may hate him, but I still love him. And I'm going to make him pay for making me feel both.

CHAPTER 10
ZEKE

I screamed Lucy's name.

Lucy!

A woman I haven't thought about in years.

A woman I haven't envisioned naked in decades.

A woman I haven't dreamed about since I was eighteen.

A woman who would slap me if she knew I had called out her name during sex with another woman.

I'm an asshole.

Worse.

I'm a jackass, a dumbfucker, a cunt. I'm every curse word you can think of.

I'm also a man.

A dumb, stupid, idiotic man.

I had only planned on jacking off to the sight of Siren. I planned on denying her what she wanted—*me*. I planned on coming on her magnificent tits. And then leaving her to clean up her mess.

Instead, Siren kneeled down in front of me with her big eyes and plump lips, offering me what every man in the world wants. And I couldn't say no.

Literally couldn't.

My brain said to tell her no. But my body, *damn, I didn't have a prayer against her*.

The longer she licked, pumped, and tasted me, the more I lost control. All of it. I gave it all to her.

Siren knew exactly what she was doing when she knelt in front of me. It may have looked like she was surrendering to me, but bloody hell, she was taking all of my power.

Thrust after thrust.

Deeper into her throat I sank. Until she completely controlled me, and my sin became more of a surrender than a threat to cause her pain.

We've been locked in this twisted game of truths, lies, and sins since the moment we met. We've been playing even before I came up with the exact rules of the game. We've been playing for a lot longer than that.

And I couldn't lose.

Not when she struck me where it hurts the most—*Lucy*.

So in my moment of haze, the last moment before I gave her everything, I came up with a plan to keep my power—a stupid plan. One I regretted the second her name fell from my lips.

Lucy deserved better.

Even Siren deserved better.

I should have let her won. I should have known that I could win the next round.

But I was beyond pissed. I thought that in the moments we've spent together since Siren told me she was married that we've made progress in our relationship. That we've moved beyond the hate and found our way to somewhere new. Somewhere where we wouldn't lie and hurt each other.

I was wrong. Because it is all part of Siren's plan. To wreck me, destroy me without ever laying a finger on me.

I walk outside the hospital, vowing never to return to this horrible place. A place where I do stupid, cruel things I regret. Although, I don't regret breaking Hugo's kneecap. That was rather fun to hurt the man who married Siren and made it impossible for me to ever claim her.

And then I spot her.

Siren is standing on the sidewalk with her phone in her hand and no Corvette.

It got towed.

Which means she's either waiting for a cab or me.

She hasn't spotted me yet. I could sneak off to my truck and drive home without having to face her. But I figure the least I can do after calling out another woman's name while her lips where wrapped around my cock is to offer her a ride home.

Home.

I don't even know where she considers home.

My house?

Julian's?

Does she have her own house somewhere on the island? Or does she share a place with Hugo?

Just another secret that Siren keeps from me.

I walk over to my truck, still deciding what to do. If she rides back with me, the car ride is going to go one of two ways. Either we will sit in awkward silence the entire time, or we are going to have a fight that's going to lead to me wrecking my truck and us fighting until we both fall off a cliff.

I unlock the truck and get in. And then I'm backing out of the parking spot before I realize what I'm doing.

What am I doing?

I drive to Siren standing on the sidewalk waiting for a cab, that on this island will take a good half hour or more to get here.

I lean over and pop the passenger's side door open without a word, commanding her to get in the truck.

She hesitates for a single second, and I swear her eyes are glistening with moisture.

A sure sign of tears that she's desperately trying to hold back.

Tears I don't understand.

She can be mad, *sure.*

Angry, *absolutely.*

But sad? *No way.*

She can't be sad about what happened. She can't be emotional.

She's the least emotional person I know. She doesn't have a heart. I guarantee when she said yes to marrying Hugo that it was a calculated move. She thought she would get something out of it.

But then she's climbing into the passenger seat and slamming the door shut like she wishes my balls were trapped between the door.

There's the anger I expected.

I nod and wait until she buckles her seatbelt before I take off. More to make sure she's contained to her seat and can't reach over and strangle me than for her safety.

I start driving; neither of us speaks. Apparently, we are going with the awkward silent treatment the whole drive.

Which sounds like the better of the two options.

Until I realize there is a third option.

I flick the radio on. The radio stations are limited here. And there is more Bob Marley on the radio than anything else.

But the song currently playing is the rare non-Bob Marley song. It's 'Before He Cheats' by Carrie Underwood. It's a song about heartbreak and how the woman plans on making the man pay for what he did.

Siren doesn't miss a beat. She starts singing along until her voice overtakes the artist singing. Until she is all I hear. Until I know I won't be getting her voice out of my head. It's beautiful and haunting and so damn mesmerizing.

"Zeke! Watch out!" she screams.

I slam on the breaks just in time to avoid hitting a stray chicken. But the car spins at my sudden stop. I step harder on the breaks, forcing the hunk of metal to stop just inches from the damn chicken that Siren was so worried about saving.

I huff, out of breath.

Siren grips her seatbelt as she stares over the front of the dash. "Is it alive?"

The chicken takes the moment to flap its wings and jump forward out of the road.

You couldn't do that thirty seconds ago?

"Yes, it's alive. But we almost weren't," I growl as the truck is also inches from slamming into a palm tree.

"Because you are the worst driver ever!"

"I was driving just fine until you had to get all noble and try to save a chicken. A fucking chicken! It's a bird you eat for dinner, and you seem to have no problem with that. Yet you were desperate to save the chicken when..." I huff, ending my sentence on mumbled words instead of the truth. That she cares more about a chicken than she does me.

Siren doesn't have to hear the end of my sentence to know what I was about to say. Somehow she seems to know my every thought before I say it.

"Well, if you behaved better than the chicken, then I would want to save you too," she yells.

All hell breaks loose after that.

"You know, for a second, I was going to apologize for what I did, but then I remembered you are an arrogant, manipulative woman who thinks she's better than me, and now I won't," I say.

"Yea, well, you're an ass!"

"Great comeback."

"Speaking of coming, how was your orgasm? Because it will be the last you will be getting for a while."

"Ha, you wish it was the last orgasm. It will be the last orgasm I'll be getting from you. Not the last one I'll be getting. And thank god for that, it was a struggle to come, what with you slobbering all over me." *It was sexy as hell and the best damn blowjob of my life.*

She smirks. "Yea, it looked like you really struggled to come."

"It was very difficult, but it shut you up, so it was worth it. Unlike now."

It's all a lie—every word. But somehow, I can't let her have the upper hand. I just can't.

"Asshole."

"Bitch."

"Bastard."

"Cunt."

"Jackass."

"Siren."

Our eyes lock, and I want to say more. I want to tell her that if she'd just stop lying and trying to ruin my life, I could call her my lover. I could call her my everything. But that will never happen.

A horn honks.

And I realize we've been sitting in the middle of the road blocking the path for far too long.

I turn the wheel and start driving again.

This time, I drive in silence, but it's not awkward. It's horrible really. Because we both keep replaying all the horrible things we've said and done to each other. All the things that ensure we never go anywhere near loving each other again.

There is no love between us, only hate.

Siren's phone rings, and she stares down at it with trepidation, but she answers, which means it can only be one man—Julian.

"Yes," she answers.

There's a short pause, and then she says, "We're on our way." Before she hangs up.

I don't have to ask what Julian said. I know that he summoned Siren and me to his place. And I know why—to discuss the next round of the stupid game. Which means he'll be assigning me another task. The second of five for me to complete. Which means I'll be one step closer to being free. One step closer to returning to my normal life.

Right now, I don't care about the stupid game. I care about getting the answer to one question. *How did Julian find out about Lucy?*

Hugo said it had to do with the sassy brunette sitting next to me. But something feels off. My gut doesn't know who to trust—*Hugo or Siren?*

Julian is the tiebreaker. Not that I can trust him either.

I need to know the answer. I need to know how to protect Lucy. But I have a feeling needing to know how he found out about Lucy has a lot more to do with my feelings for Siren than it does Lucy.

CHAPTER 11
SIREN

Zeke drives straight to Julian's house without asking me what Julian demanded.

He knew.

And he didn't argue with being summoned.

I don't analyze why. My focus is on something else entirely.

When Zeke pulls up in front of Julian's house, I'm out of the truck before he's even put it in park.

I don't wait for Zeke. In fact, I want to get as far away from Zeke as possible. Even if it means running toward Julian.

Julian spots me when I enter his house without knocking. He raises an eyebrow when he spots my angry snarl.

"Don't wait for me to start," I say, running upstairs, not waiting for permission from Julian.

I head down the hallway to what I know is a spare bathroom—a bathroom no one ever uses.

I shut the door carefully and lock it even though I know no one is coming after me. No one is going to check on me. Because no one loves me. No one could ever love me.

I'm too ruthless.

Too cold.

Too heartless.
Too determined.
Too strong.
Too callous.
Too everything.
I don't need a man, or at least that's the persona the world sees. And therefore, no man needs me. No man loves me.
I slump to the floor in front of the door.
And then I cry.
Big ugly tears.
Tears that turn to sobs.
Tears that consume me.
That rattle my entire body.
That shake the door.
Tears that ruin the mascara on my face.
Tears that turn my eyes big and puffy.
Tears that cause snot to run down my face.
Tears that pour out of my eyes until they begin to burn.
I've never cried over a man, not until Zeke Kane.
When I saw Hugo in bed with another woman, I didn't cry. I was angry; boy, was I angry. But I didn't cry. I was strong.
But Zeke is a man worth crying over. I cry so long I'm not even sure why I'm crying anymore.
Sure, him calling out another woman's name hurt. But it was intentional, not an accident. He didn't mistake me for Lucy. He knew exactly what he was doing—*hurting me.*
And he succeeded.
Not because of his stupid game. Not because he said her name. But because I realized who she is to him.
He loves her. Or at least did.
Lucy has what I will never have—the love of Zeke.
I've hurt him too many times to earn his love. And I'm too self-reliant to ever depend on a man, even Zeke.
I don't want a boyfriend, definitely not a husband.
That's what love requires—a commitment.
Something I will never give. Something I will never have.

I will never experience love. Not real love. The kind where the man loves you as much as you love him. The kind that makes you do stupid things like get married and have kids. I will never have that kind of love. Not because I'm not worthy, but because I know what love does. Love destroys. And I refuse to spend the rest of my life crying on the floor because of love.

But when I stand up, clean my face, and try my best to cover up my puffy eyes with the makeup I find in the drawer, I know that I'm lying. Because I still love Zeke. He's the man for me. Even if he doesn't think I'm the woman for him.

Even though we continue to hurt each other, my heart is his. And I'd rather have it shattered by Zeke than loved by another man.

CHAPTER 12
ZEKE

"**S**top playing games," I say as I enter Julian's sitting room. The room he prefers to do his business in. The room that contains more cigar smoke than actual oxygen.

"Hmm, I don't know what you are talking about," he says, pouring three glasses of scotch even though Siren disappeared upstairs and has yet to return.

"Sure, you do." I snatch one of the glasses and take a sip.

He eyes me. "Nope, no idea. I've kept to my side of the deal."

"I'm talking about Hugo Martinez."

"Oh, you mean Aria's husband? Yea, I heard he had a horrible accident and ended up in the hospital."

I glare. "He had an accident all right—took a swing to the nose, a wall to the wrist, and an IV pole to the kneecap. He'll be in the hospital for at least a week while those heal, I suspect."

Julian's eyes widen at my admission. Apparently, Hugo hasn't told him what happened.

"Sounds like my Aria," he says, assuming she was the one to deliver all the blows. I don't correct him. I'm not the kind of man to break a bone and tell.

"About Lucy," I start.

Julian just shakes his head. "Aria will be down soon, and then we can talk."

I frown. Julian just wants Siren here when I ask about Lucy. He's trying to play games. I don't like it.

My ears strain, trying to listen for Siren. Siren disappeared up the stairs on a mission the second she stepped foot in the door. *I have no idea why. Could she not get far enough away from me fast enough?*

Or did it have to do with something else?

Julian and I wait in silence, mostly glaring, trying to intimidate each other.

But with each second that passes, I grow more uncomfortable. *Where is Siren?*

I consider going to look for her, but there is an unspoken rule hovering between Julian and me. Neither of us will go look for Siren. Neither of us will show weakness for a woman that we have both fallen for in different ways. A woman we both despise, while respecting how incredible she is. A woman we both want to be ours.

So we stare, our eyes doing the talking our mouths won't. Each of us confident we are going to win this battle between us and win Siren over to our side.

"What are you two doing?" Siren asks as she struts into the room, instantly warming the room with her heat.

"Waiting for you, my pet," Julian says with a knowing smile.

She shoots him a dirty look before grabbing the glass of scotch he poured for her and sitting in a chair between Julian and me.

"I told you not to wait for me," she says, avoiding my gaze and looking at Julian.

"We didn't think it would be polite to start without you," I say. *Look at me, dammit!*

She doesn't.

"Did you get whatever was so important taken care of?" I ask.

She nods into her glass, still not looking at me, which only piques my curiosity more.

Suddenly, I notice all the changes in Siren—they're subtle. I don't think Julian sees them, but he also hasn't spent all day with her like I have.

Everything is slightly different. Her hair was pulled back, but it's now let down, dangling in front of her face like a shield over her face. Her jeans and shirt have damp spots on them. Her face looks like she's reapplied makeup, as her face is a shade brighter than before.

She takes another sip of her drink, this time, her hair falls back, and her eyes cut to me for the briefest of seconds. And then I see the real difference—her eyes.

Her eyes are red—both of them. Just enough for me to notice something is wrong, but not enough for her to be getting sick. The puffiness around her eyes stands out, even though she's mostly hidden it with her caked-on makeup.

And then she sniffles. Just once, but it's enough.

Enough for me to know what she's been doing upstairs this whole time—crying.

Why?

Because of me?

Because of her situation?

Hugo?

Almost dying in the car?

I've never wanted to read her mind more than I do now. I've never wanted Julian out of the picture so I could scoop her up in my arms like I want to now. I want to know who made her cry for almost an hour upstairs so I can hurt him like I did Hugo. Even if that bastard is me.

Instead, I'm forced to sit in my chair and act like I don't notice her eyes, her sniffles, her heart breaking.

But the way her eyes study me noticing her, she knows that I know. And I swear I see moisture gather in the corner of her eye at that thought.

"Ready for round two?" Julian asks.

"Yes," I hiss impatiently.

He grins. "You don't have to act all impatient about it. You have four rounds left. It can be all over today if you just answer each question honestly instead of choosing sin."

"Ask your question," I say, refusing to acknowledge him. If I was selfish and just wanted off this island, I would answer all of his questions. But I'm not selfish. I protect my friends. I protect Lucy.

"Where is Mr. Black's vault?" Julian asks.

Fuck, he knows everything. Everything I've vowed to protect for so long. Julian Reed knows.

"How the fu..." I start, but Julian's dark glare stops me. I can't make Julian know how secretive the vault is and how impressive it is that he knows about it. He can't know that it's important.

And yet, without me speaking, he already knows. He knows how crucial it is. He probably knows what the vault contains.

Fucking christ. How does he know?

Siren.

She's being incredibly silent during this conversation. Her eyes are buried in her glass, not lifting to look at me.

Because she was the one who found out the information about the vault. She was the one who found out about Lucy. I'm sure of it. She might have even met Enzo Black before.

I don't trust her, but *god, that doesn't stop me from wanting her.*

"Sin," I say, knocking the rest of my drink back, praying like hell that this task he gives me will be easier than the last one.

"Since you won't give me the location of the vault, I want something equally as valuable as what I would find inside," Julian says.

"And what would that be?"

"One billion dollars."

I scoff. "You have plenty of money. What do you need that kind of money for?"

"None of your business," he answers.

"Fine, I agree to the deal, if you stay away from Lucy. She is no longer part of your negotiations."

His smile curls up. "No. Lucy is very much part of our negotiations. You may not love Siren anymore, but you love Lucy. I found your weakness, and I promise to exploit it."

Siren looks at me now. And her eyes say everything. That she had nothing to do with finding Lucy. *Why would she, when the mention of her name slices into her heart as easily as a knife?* Siren wouldn't help Julian find a woman from my past, not when it impeded her ability to control me by being the only woman in my life. I see the pain in Siren's eyes. Pain at the mention of me loving another woman.

I do love Lucy, but not in the way Julian is saying. And definitely not in the way Siren is thinking.

But I don't let either of them think differently. I keep my mask on like a protective armor.

"Lucy stays out of this," I say firmly.

"No, you finish your five tasks or answer your five questions honestly, and I won't touch Lucy. Just like I won't touch Enzo, or Kai, or Langston, or Liesel. Not until the game is over. Afterward, they are all fair game again. But you'll be free to go and protect them."

FUCK!

My choices are to drag this game out into eternity to ensure Julian never goes after my friends, or spend this time learning everything I can about Julian, so when the game is over, I can defeat him.

Or find something he wants more than Enzo Black. Something to keep my friends safe.

"Aria has my bank account information. I don't care how you get the money or who you steal it from. I want that amount deposited to my bank account by the end of the week."

I open my mouth to argue. To yell. To say I would never get him that kind of money.

"Lucy is doing great in Seattle, by the way. The rain and coffee life suits her," Julian says, standing and walking out the door, dropping a bomb to ensure I do exactly as he says.

Enzo Black is strong. His empire is formidable. I've done my best to protect him so far. I never want to bring an enemy to Enzo's doorstep. But if I had to, I would, knowing Enzo would destroy them.

Lucy is different. I can't bring an enemy to her. She doesn't belong in this world. It's like Julian knew I'd grow tired of his games. That I'd grow tired of being away from my friends. That soon, I would give up defending them, and I'd run to their side, preparing them as best I could to defeat Julian. Lucy was his ultimate bomb drop. He knew he could control me as long as he had access to Lucy.

She's in Seattle.

She's probably living a happy, unsuspecting life in the city. Julian mentioned coffee, and I can very much see Lucy loving that town. She loves coffee. I can imagine her being an excellent executive at the newest coffee roasting company. She wouldn't settle for anything less than being an executive.

Siren stares at me while I'm thinking about Lucy. And I finally realize what the tears she cried earlier were about. Because I see the look now on her face. A look that says her heart is shattering right in front of me.

But why?

Siren doesn't love me. She doesn't even care about me.

There is no way she can be feeling anything other than jealousy at me thinking of another woman.

But that's not what my eyes see. And that's not what my heart feels. And whatever Siren is feeling scares the shit out of me.

CHAPTER 13
SIREN

"I'll meet you at your house in an hour, and we can discuss a plan," I say.

Zeke stands, like he can't get out of the room fast enough. It would make sense if it were Julian he was running from. But he's not running from Julian; he's running from me.

"How are you going to get back?" He pauses in the doorway.

I don't look at him. I can't, not without breaking and showing him just how much he means to me. How much I love him. How I know he'll never love me back.

I stretch. "I have two feet. I'll walk."

He doesn't say anything else, but I feel his presence leave the room. And I don't know if it ends up more gloomy with him gone, or if the fog lifts when he leaves.

I wait a moment, trying to decide what I want to do. Trying to figure out what Julian's plan is.

But Julian Reed is a complicated man. He doesn't tell me his thoughts because he doesn't trust me as much as he wants me to be his number two, I'm not there yet. Not in reality.

I could let Julian destroy Lucy, get rid of my competition, so to speak. But I can't stand to watch Zeke shatter. I love him. And that means doing the right thing, even if the right thing means sacrificing myself in order to save the woman Zeke loves.

I stand up and pour myself another glass of scotch, shooting the glass of liquid down my throat for courage to go do something that someday is going to lead to a broken heart.

And then I go in search of Julian, who is, of course, nowhere to be found on the main level. His car is still in the garage, though, which means he's in his bedroom. The one place in this house I feel completely uncomfortable in. Julian knows that.

Fuck.

But I'm not going to let the fact that I have to talk to him in his bedroom stop me. I'm on a mission. A mission to save Zeke's girl.

Zeke's girl—what I wouldn't give to earn that title myself.

The door to Julian's bedroom is closed. So I knock. I'm not about to walk in on him indecent or fucking another woman or touching himself. That's exactly what Julian would want.

But of course, it doesn't stop Julian from opening the door shirtless. He's wearing his dark dress pants and no shirt.

His body is nice. He has abs and hardness in all the right places. He has a slim waist and wide shoulders. But I guess it's the evil heart and wicked eyes that stop me from pining after him in any way. It's hard to be attracted to someone after you've seen them kill someone just because they fucked up and brought you the wrong food. *A big turnoff, trust me.*

"Yes?" Julian says, his eyes telling me to ogle his body like he's doing to me.

"We need to talk."

He holds the door open, and I step inside, ignoring his perfectly unflawed body. Unlike Zeke and I's body that has been marked with bullet wounds, with knives, with scars, Julian's body is perfect. Because he has people like me who do his dirty work, so he never has to.

"You breaking up with me, Aria?" Julian asks at my choice of words.

I wish—I wish I could break up with Julian, but somehow, I keep finding myself more and more in debt to him.

"What will it take to ensure that you never go after Lucy?" I ask. I don't even know her last name. All I know is that Zeke needs her protected. So I'll protect her with my dying breath. I'll do anything. I can't pretend I wouldn't. I need to try to manipulate Julian into trading Lucy for a simple task I can do for him.

But Julian knows me too well. He knows I have a thing for Zeke. Worse—he knows I'm in love with Zeke. He was the first to know, even before I realized it myself.

Julian shakes his head in disappointment. "I thought you were better than that. Are you really going to keep loving a man who will never return your feelings?"

I don't answer that. Because I am better than that. I am stronger. *And no, I don't plan on spending the rest of my life loving Zeke when he's in love with someone else.* But from the outside looking in, I've hurt Zeke so many times. If I can do something to mend the bonds I've broken between us, then I will.

I put my hands on my hips, staring Julian down, refusing to talk to him about my feelings.

"What will it take?" I ask again.

He stretches, and his pants hang lower on his hips. *Gross.*

"Let's see," he rubs his chin, pretending to think. But he already knows what he wants. It's the same thing he's always wanted—me in love with him.

He's never raped me, except for the one time he came close. He's never taken it because he wants me to offer myself to him willingly. The only thing I've offered is my loyalty. My skills are working in his favor. That's the best he's ever going to get.

"Julian," I hiss my warning.

He cocks his head. "Aria Torres."

Chills surge through my body, and not the good kind. If Julian calls me anything other than his pet, he always uses my real name—*Aria Torres.*

No one else calls me that. Not Nora, not Hugo, and not Zeke.

Sometimes I feel like the only person I can truly be myself with is Julian. He's the only one who knows everything about my past. He's the only one who can see my true feelings because he's desperate for me to turn those feelings towards him.

"What will it take for you to leave Lucy alone? For you to tell me where she lives so I can make her disappear? So you can never find her again?"

"Don't you mean so Zeke can never find her again?"

"No." I'll tell Zeke where she is. Even if it will kill me to see him run to her.

"You're getting better at that lying thing, Aria."

I frown; he's noticed. I'm so close to being able to lie out loud that it scares me, the temptation of it. Because if I can lie, I can be in control again. Right now, I've only been able to lie to myself.

"But you aren't there yet." Julian sighs. "You know most people see you as the devil's right-hand woman. But you are every bit an angel."

"An angel that can murder you and sleep peacefully right after."

He grins. "That sounds like the very definition of an angel to me."

"You're stalling."

"Am I? I guess I'm just hoping you seeing me shirtless in my bedroom will give you ideas. Especially since that oaf doesn't know a good thing when he sees it."

"This was a mistake," I say, turning and pretending to walk out. I know the second that I rescind his ability to strike a deal with me, he'll gravel. He likes our arrangements. He likes keeping me close.

"Wait!"

I smirk but then let my expression fall when I turn around. "Yes?"

"Agree to a date."

"What?"

"Go on one date with me, and Lucy is off the table."

My eyes widen—he's serious. I thought I would have to trade years of my life to protect Lucy. I thought I would have to do something big. Something huge to keep her safe. But all he's asking for is one date. One single date.

And somehow, one date seems like the worst thing he could ask for. A date with the devil, not exactly thrilling. But not the worst he could ask for.

"One date. Two hours. No kissing."

He puts his hands in his pockets with a grin. He looks like such an innocent boy, not the horrible serpent he is.

I hold out my hand to make the deal. "And no sex."

He sighs. "No sex, not unless you agree."

"I want her address, now."

He pulls out his phone and types something before handing it to me.

I study the Seattle address until I have it memorized.

I sigh. I don't know who Lucy is, but her life just got a lot more complicated. Even though I trust Julian to keep his promise to me, I know Zeke won't. Which means I have to make her disappear. Get her to a new place, with a new identity. It means I have to tell Zeke where she is and that she's safe.

It means Zeke will be one step closer to realizing I have feelings for him—true feelings.

And it scares the shit out of me.

Because I don't want him to know the truth. The truth will kill me. The heartbreak will end me.

I'd rather pretend I'm a strong, unbreakable woman—the independent, calculated siren.

Instead, I'm just a woman who fell in love with the wrong man. Then I fell in love with the right man, but it was too late. Because the right man hates me. The right man is in love with another woman. The right man will never love me back.

I hold my hand out again until Julian's hand meets mine. I've made deals with him before for love—but this time, I know I got the better end of the deal. One date to save a life is nothing, especially when it means saving Zeke's love.

"When?" Julian asks.

"Tonight, I want to get this over with."

CHAPTER 14
ZEKE

I open the door after the petite knock barely makes me aware of the presence of someone at the door.

I assumed it was Siren, and she was timid after talking with Julian. But when I open the door, it's one of the last people I expected.

"Nora, what brings you to my door?" I ask, hesitantly.

"Aria texted and said you were going to be in need of a plane and wondered if I could help," Nora answers, pushing past me into my house without waiting for an invitation.

I rub my neck, not having a clue what to do with Nora while we wait for Siren. I'm not the best at being friends with women. At least not the kind who wear dresses and makeup and don't have a clue how to hold a gun—women like Nora.

Women like Siren, like one of my closest friends, Kai, who belong in this world and wield a gun as good as the rest of them, that kind of woman I understand.

"Siren isn't here right now," I start, but notice Nora has already made herself at home with a beer in my living room. She's flipped the TV on, something I haven't had time to watch since I've moved here.

I brace myself to watch one of those redecorating shows or reality TV shows, but instead, she flips to a soccer game.

"You like soccer?" I ask.

She nods. "I lived in England for a while, and I fell in love with soccer."

By the way her eyes are following the men's asses on the screen, I'm not sure if she fell in love with the game or the men. Or both.

But I grab a beer and sit on the couch next to her, hoping the game is enough to distract me while I wait for Siren to get here so we can make a plan on how to steal a billion dollars. I'm not bad with security systems, but I've never stolen that kind of cash before. So I'm hoping Siren has a better plan than I do.

Because my plan is to shoot Julian in the head, and hope none of his men kill Lucy before I can get to her. Which is a stupid, idiotic plan. Not one I will be able to risk. I won't risk Lucy's life.

I feel her before I see her. Of course, Siren let herself into my house.

"Don't you have a house of your own?" I ask, my eyes leaving the TV for the first time in an hour.

Nora glares at me, thinking I'm an idiot for asking.

But Siren just sighs. "No, I don't have my own house, actually. I have a room at Hugo's, a room at Julian's, and here. I would sleep at Nora's, but she still lives with her parents in Anguilla, and just sleeps in hotels when she comes here. So no, I don't have a house. And I'm sorry if I prefer your house to Hugo's or Julian's, but I don't have a lot of choices."

I swallow. *I made a mistake.* I realize now that I'm not even sure if Julian pays her with money for the job she does.

I clear my throat. "Do you have a plan?"

"Of course," she responds, but she doesn't look happy. Nora and her exchange a glance, and it looks like they've had an entire conversation I'm not privy too.

"So, where are we going? Who are we stealing from?"

"France," Siren answers.

"Okay? Who's in France?"

Siren walks down the hallway to the bathroom.

"Hugo's parents," Nora answers.

We are stealing from Hugo's parents. "His parents have that kind of money, and Siren had to sell her soul instead of them helping their son out when he got in a bind," I put together.

Nora nods solemnly.

Siren pops her head back in. "Do you have a dress I can borrow?"

"Nope, I'm all out of dresses," I answer.

Siren rolls her eyes.

"Yep, I brought one in my bag," Nora answers.

Siren nods.

I look at her closely. "You really want to steal from your in-laws?"

"Don't you?" she asks.

"Well, yea...but I just thought..."

"Trust me, I've wanted to steal from them for a long time. If Hugo is an ass, they are the hole he came from."

Nora runs off and returns a moment later with her bag. She starts digging through it and tosses Siren a black dress.

"Are we going tonight? Is that why you're getting dressed up? Should I change?" I ask.

"No, we aren't going tonight," Siren grabs the dress and disappears down the hallway.

I follow after her and catch the bathroom door before she closes it.

She bats her eyes at me as if waiting for me to leave so she can change, but I'm not going to. She's hiding something from me. If she's planning on crying in the bathroom again, I want to know about it.

I open my mouth to ask her what happened and why she was crying, when she throws her T-shirt off over her head and starts undoing her pants.

Yep, there goes thinking about anything other than her body.

I should go. I shouldn't keep looking at her when she's undressing. But it's too late. There is no way I can walk away now. Not from a mostly naked Siren.

"Why aren't we going to France tonight? Wouldn't it make more sense to fly overnight so we can sleep on the long flight?" I ask, finding my words somehow, even though I'm sure my mouth is gaping open as I stare at her.

"Nora can't fly us all the way to France in her little propeller plane. She can fly us to Miami, and then we can catch a flight from there."

Miami.

I stare at her, devoid of emotion. She knows Miami is Enzo's base of operations. *Is this a ploy to get me there and then use me as bait for my friends?*

If it is, she's a very good actor, because she gives me nothing.

"So, we can't fly tonight?" I ask.

"We could, but the flights to France usually don't leave until the evening. We wouldn't make it to Miami before the flights leave for the night. We will have to wait until tomorrow."

Her words make sense, so I try not to read too much into them.

And then she unhooks her bra, and I watch with wide eyes as it falls to the floor at her feet. But I'm not looking at her feet. I'm looking at her perky breasts and pointed nipples. She totally knows she has me under her spell. There is no hiding how I feel in response to seeing her naked body. My reaction is immediate and intense. My cock pushes hard in my pants against the zipper, desperate to have my way with her again.

My brain shouts *never*, while my cock screams *aways*. And my heart —that asshole has sped up at the beautiful sight of her, and it wants to give her another chance. We've already given her two! Two chances, and both times she hurt us.

Her breath catches at my response. She grabs the dress off the vanity and slips it over her head in one quick motion like she wasn't just standing in front of me, baring her gorgeous tits to my face.

She reaches behind her and pulls up the zipper in one motion. This is Siren, and she never needs a man's help. I can no longer breathe because Siren is standing in front of me in the tightest fucking black dress. It barely covers the important parts of her. The dress belongs to Nora, who is a good half a foot shorter than Siren.

She flips her hair back, and I realize now why she can't wear a bra with the dress.

I'm drooling, staring at her breasts in the dress that accentuates her curves, and her nipples are just visible enough beneath the fabric to be sexy, but not overtly.

She looks damn good in that dress.

She turns away from me, running her hands through her hair to fluff it. Then she's searching for the drawers of my bathroom until she pulls out a couple of makeup items. Makeup she must have stashed in here earlier.

She starts applying red lipstick, and that's when I come to my senses.

"Siren? Why are you getting all dressed up?" *And why don't you want me to get dressed up?*

Her eyes cut to me out of the corner of her eye, but she finishes applying her lipstick and looks at herself one last time in the mirror before she turns to me, as if she knows that when she answers, she won't be continuing to apply makeup.

"I'm going on a date," she answers.

I take a deep breath as she hasn't said with whom yet. *Hugo? Or me?*

Since Hugo is in the hospital with a broken wrist and kneecap, I doubt it's him.

And since I'm standing here not in date attire, I doubt it's me either.

"Hmm, and who is taking you on a date?"

She bites her lip. "Julian."

I lose it. "Julian? You mean the asshole who has you trapped in a contract for ten years? The asshole who is blackmailing me into turning over my boss to him? The man who is slimy and evil and killed innocent men? That man? The man I thought you hated?"

She nods.

"So let me get this straight. It wasn't enough that you are married and have been fucking me, but now you want to date Julian? How many other men are you sleeping with?"

Her face turns red. "How many men am I fucking? Really? That's the question you care about?"

"Yes," I growl. I care. I want to know just how big of a slut she is. I want to know what number I am on her list among many.

"None! I'm not fucking anyone. You were the last man I fucked, and hell will freeze over before I do that again." She tries to move past me out of the bathroom, but my large frame is blocking the way.

"Move!" she gruffs.

"You really are a slut, Siren. You'll spread your legs for any man if it means you get something in return."

Shit, I may have taken things too far by calling her a slut. But I'm pissed. It was one thing to learn she had a husband. Even one she doesn't love. It's another thing to learn that she also wants to date Julian, the most vile man on the planet.

Her eyes water in anger, sadness, shock. *Yep, I definitely took things too far.*

"You're an ass," she says, shoving me hard against my chest, pushing me back out of her way so she can escape the bathroom. She struts to the living room with me right behind her.

"Yea, and you're a slut," I say, doubling down on my insult. I don't think I've ever used the word against a woman before, but heartbreak will do that to a man. Make you lash out in any way you can to prevent the pain.

"Shoes," Siren says to Nora, who is sitting on the couch watching our exchange wordlessly. Nora reaches into her overnight bag and pulls some strappy black heels out.

Siren snatches them and starts putting them on while still standing. That's how much of a hurry she is to get away from me. Not that I blame her, I want to get away from her. She starts walking toward my front door with her shoes halfway on.

Just as she reaches for the door, I slam it shut, caging her in with my hands.

"Why?" I whisper, taking my anger down a notch. Maybe there's an answer, an explanation. My voice pleads for there to be a good reason for her to be getting all dolled up to go on a date with Julian. But for the life of me, I can't come up with a reason.

She closes her eyes as if to shield herself from me.

"Why are you going on a date with Julian?"

She reaches for the door handle again, and this time, I let her open the door. I'm not going to force her to tell me the truth, not anymore. If she has a good reason she wants to share, she'll tell me.

And then I see them, the glistening tears against her cheek.

"I'm doing this for you. To keep your precious Lucy safe." She walks out the door, slamming the door in my face, leaving me alone with my stunned expression.

"You really are an ass," Nora says from behind me.

I agree, the biggest.

"Come on, let's make some popcorn. I have a feeling we are going to be up all night worrying about our girl," Nora says, taking pity on me.

But I can't turn to follow Nora. Instead, I keep looking at the door and the expression on Siren's face. It was the truth. She's going on a date with Julian to protect Lucy. She's doing it for me.

Why?

The answer is obvious. But I'm not ready to go there again. I'm not ready to risk everything. I'm not ready to be vulnerable. But I do know that I'm going to be staring at the door all night long, desperately waiting for Siren to strut back through it.

It's just a date.

Exactly—it's a date. So I don't know why I expect her to be walking through my door again tonight. She'll be spending the night with Julian. She'll spend the night in his bed. Or at least his house.

I may have gotten Lucy back, but I just lost another woman —Siren.

This date is by far the worse date I've been on, and I've been on some doozies. Dates that ended with a drunk man puking on me, getting left with a two hundred dollar bill, and even an attempted drugging. But my date with Julian Reed tops them all.

And I can't even tell you why exactly, just this strange feeling in my gut that says Julian is up to something. *He's always up to something.*

Because as much as Julian has wanted to control this date, he isn't. *I'm in control.*

At first, he tried to fight back, but I quickly took control, and I haven't let him have it back since the moment he tried to pick me up in his fancy Aston Martin. He opened the passenger door and expected me to sit obediently, but instead, I slid all the way into the driver's seat.

After my little fight with Zeke, I needed the distraction that driving offers. And I couldn't stand for Julian to drive. I needed to feel in control.

It continued when he tried to hold the door open for me; I took it and waited for him to enter first. When he tried to order my drink for me, even though he ordered my favorite, I asked the bartender to bring me a different one. When he ordered my meal, I ordered another.

The date became one big fight for control, one I was definitely winning. However, Julian didn't seem too upset to be losing.

I was winning—until now. I feel the brush of Julian's fingers under the table against my knee.

I freeze. I can't stand to be touched by this man. By any man really, but especially this man. The only man I want touching me is Zeke. And right now, I don't even want him to touch me because his touch reminds me of everything that we will never have.

Julian's hand slides up my thigh.

"What are you doing?" I ask, gritting my teeth to keep from yelling at him in this posh restaurant.

"There was nothing in our rules that said I couldn't touch you."

His hand slides higher, hitting my limit.

I grab his middle finger and twist, getting that instant release of pressure as I dislocate his finger.

Julian's face scrunches in pain for a split second, and then his face goes neutral.

Huh. Maybe he has a higher tolerance for pain than I thought?

"It wasn't part of our agreement because I didn't think it was necessary to state that you weren't allowed to touch me. You are never allowed to touch a woman without her expressed permission."

His eyes darken as he leans forward. "You want me to touch you. I can see it in the way your lips part anytime I talk, hanging onto every word I say. I can see it in the way you keep crossing and uncrossing your legs. The way your eyes grow heavy with lust. You want me."

I take a deep breath, and then I dislocate his ring finger. This time he doesn't even cringe. He was expecting me to hurt him.

"Well, let me clear some things up then. I don't want you. I don't like you. I hate you." I release his hand and fling it back in his direction. "Don't ever touch me again."

"You can say whatever words you want. They are all lies. You may not even realize it yourself. But your body doesn't lie to me. Your body wants me, even if your mind doesn't."

I shake my head. "My body wants Zeke, that's who I've been thinking about all night."

It's true. I've been thinking about Zeke all fucking night! Been thinking about our last kiss. Been thinking about the taste of Zeke's cum between my lips. Been thinking about how great angry fucking against every hard surface in the house would be, but it isn't going to happen. Because Zeke doesn't understand. He will never understand why I make the decisions I do. Why I outwardly betray him, while secretly protecting him from greater evil than he even realizes exists.

Julian shakes his hand and then carefully pops each finger back into place.

Excellent—now I can dislocate them again.

"Zeke will never want you like you want him."

"You don't know that." *Even though I know it's the truth.*

"I do. You want to know how I know for sure?" He leans forward again like he's about to tell me a secret. And I find myself leaning forward as well.

"I know because you will never like me like I like you," he says.

I frown and lean back before taking a sip of my Pina colada. *Yes, I ordered a frozen Pina Colada even though this is a restaurant where you only order wine or scotch.* I also ordered macaroni and cheese off the kid's menu—anything to make this less of a date and more awkward for Julian.

"That's because you are an evil monster who would feed his child to the wolves if it meant you got ahead in this world."

He nods. "Exactly, and Zeke thinks of you in the same way. He thinks you are a selfish cunt who only cares about herself. He doesn't know what you've done for him. He'll never know. Even if you told him, he wouldn't believe you."

I suck on my straw until I get every last drop of the frozen drink that's more sugar than alcohol into my mouth. Julian's right. Zeke will never want me. Never like me. Definitely never love me.

But it doesn't change my feelings for him, at least not right now. Maybe when he's gone, and he takes my heart with him, will I realize that loving him was a mistake. Right now, it feels right. Like I was put on this earth to love Zeke. To protect Zeke.

Zeke may think I'm a siren luring him to his death. But he got it right the first time—I'm his guardian angel watching out for him, he will just never know that I'm an angel in disguise.

"Don't give up hope yet, though," Julian says out of nowhere.

My eyes flicker up hesitantly, unsure what he's saying.

"I thought that was exactly what you were saying, to give up hope. Because it's the same lost cause as you trying to go after me. It's never going to happen."

He drinks down the rest of his scotch. "The odds are against us both. But every once in a while, a man picks the winning lottery numbers, gets struck by lightning, and hits the game-winning three-pointer. It doesn't happen often, and sometimes the results are worse than the current life. But it happens. It can happen. Rarely, and unexpectedly. But our lives aren't about the expected."

I swallow, afraid of the words that are coming next.

"You have three men who want you in different ways. Three men who have carved their names into your neck. Three men who have wanted you. And by the time this is all over, you'll end up with one of us. Hugo, Zeke, or me. You're destined to."

"What if I want to run away and live a normal life with a normal man? A man who is a teacher or lawyer, a man living a sane life, one where I don't have to carry a gun with me everywhere I go."

He smiles gently. "Because you don't want that life, Aria. A teacher's life is boring. And a lawyer can be just as corrupt as I am. And don't for one second pretend that you don't enjoy carrying that gun. It gives you power and control over your life. Something you desperately want."

He's right. I like the gun. I like using my skills. *But what if I want more? What if I want something different? Something that isn't just shooting and killing people? And fighting?* Sometimes I'm tired of fighting.

But I'm not tired of this life. I just want my partner to carry on the fight when I can't. When I'm too tired to fight. When I need a break.

Julian's right that I can only ever be with a man from this world. I can't start over with a plain, normal, and boring man. I need a man who can fight as well as I can.

Hugo, Julian, or Zeke.

But the only man for me is Zeke.

"Have I fulfilled my dately duties? Are we finished?"

"Just about."

Julian stands and motions for me to do the same. He guides me out of the restaurant with his hand on the small of my back.

I'm going to make him pay for the gesture. For the burning touch that I can't do anything about without making a scene in front of all these people. The second we get to the car, all bets are off. The date is over, and I can do whatever I want.

The valet has already pulled the car around without us having to ask. Julian is a regular at this restaurant. It's also why he never handed them his credit card. They already have it on file.

The valet goes to open the passenger side door for me, and this time, I don't fight Julian for the driver's seat. I want a few minutes to be lost in thought before we get back to Julian's compound, and I have to decide between finding a guest room in Julian's house to sleep in or going to Zeke's. Neither seems like a great option right now.

Julian drives wordlessly back to the compound, but he doesn't stop in front of his house. He stops in front of Zeke's. As if he knows that's where I'm headed. Or he wants to make Zeke jealous or angry by him showing up with me.

He put the car in park.

"Deal over? You won't touch Lucy?" I ask.

"I won't touch Lucy. You have her address and information, and I'm guessing you already have a plan to move her elsewhere."

I don't answer, but he knows me well enough to know that it's exactly what I'm doing.

I grab for the door handle, when Julian grabs my face and turns it toward him until our mouths are inches apart.

My eyes fly open, and red warning bells go off everywhere.

And without thinking, I have a gun pointed at his temple.

He grins at my reaction but doesn't release my face. Probably because he knows I won't kill him. If I do, Lucy is dead. And so is Zeke. He has fail-safes in place to ensure Zeke and I don't kill him without losing something we love as well.

"This date is over, Julian. I agreed to one date. No kisses. No sex."

He nods. "The date is over."

"Then, what are you doing?"

"Offering you a second deal."

I close my eyes. *Don't listen. Whatever it is, it's not worth it.*

"I'll trade a kiss for time."

"Time?" I ask, keeping my eyes closed. *Don't fall for his tricks. Don't fall for the devil's schemes.*

"When the game is over. When Zeke has finished his last task or answered his final question, I'll be free to chase down his boss. I'll be free to kill them all, Zeke included. I'm trading one kiss for one day. I'll wait one day, give Zeke a one day head start to return to his friends and try and keep them safe. One kiss for one more day of Zeke getting to live instead of dying. One kiss for one day."

Damn him. He already knows I'm going to accept. I would do anything to keep Zeke alive. I would give Julian anything to ensure Zeke has the best chance of survival. And in this game, one day can mean everything.

"Deal," I say, keeping my eyes closed, keeping the tears at bay. *It's just a kiss.*

A kiss Julian will play in his head over and over. A kiss he will dream about. A kiss his thoughts will stray to when he's masturbating. A kiss he will think means so much more than just a kiss.

I wait, unmoving, for him to kiss me. My heart thuds wildly, not from excitement, but from trepidation. *I can't do this.*

Zeke. *Think about Zeke.*

So I do, and I realize that is what Julian is waiting for—for my mind to go somewhere else. For him to be able to kiss me without the pain, for him to kiss me when I'm most vulnerable.

His lips press against mine, and his hand cradles my head and neck, keeping me from ending the kiss too soon.

We didn't talk rules of the kiss.

How long?

Are tongues allowed, expected?

Nothing.

I'm a passive participant.

I let him kiss me, but I don't kiss him back, even with Zeke flicking in my head.

Julian puts everything into the kiss. He spreads my lips, his tongue dips and swirls in my mouth, and his throat gives off soft moans.

I feel nothing but sticky lips against mine.

Finally, he releases me. And his eyes heat into devious slits.

I've never understood why Julian hasn't just forced me. *Why hasn't he raped me if he wants me?* I'm sure he's raped other women before. But with me, it's his favorite game. To try and convince me to choose him. Only then will he have his way with me.

I don't know why. *Does the man think he loves me?* I doubt Julian Reed is capable of love. But then, most creatures are. They just love in different ways.

Julian shows his love by not raping me.

Zeke shows his love by protecting me.

And I show Zeke my love by betraying him to keep him safe.

I step out of the car wordlessly. I walk up to the front door and knock, unable to push my way into Zeke's house when I was just kissing Julian.

When Zeke opens the door, I know he saw the kiss. If his anger was a ten before, now it's a hundred. The ensuing battle is going to be one of our most intense.

CHAPTER 16
ZEKE

Siren went on a date with the devil to keep Lucy safe—a woman I've led Siren to think I love. A woman who means the world to me, but not in the way Siren thinks. I'm not in love with Lucy; I just love her. She's part of my life, my family, my world. And I will do everything to protect her.

And it seems, Siren will too.

I stare at the door Siren just left through, unable to get passed what just happened. I'm angry. And happy. Confused and blind. I feel warm and cold.

"Here," Nora thrusts a drink into my hand, but I don't register if it's alcohol or not. Or even what kind.

I just sip.

"What is Siren doing?" I ask, needing to understand who Siren is.

"Isn't it obvious?" Nora replies.

No, it's not obvious. Nothing Siren does is obvious. She's manipulative and selfish and unkind. She's the exact opposite of everything I've ever wanted in a woman. And yet, I'm still here standing in front of the door, regretting letting her go on a date with my biggest enemy.

I take a drink and then spit it out. "What the hell is this?"

"Apple juice."

I raise an eyebrow at Nora. "Why the fuck are you giving me apple juice?"

"Because you need a clear head when Siren returns, not be drunk off your ass."

"And apple juice is the way to do it? Why not water?"

She bites her lip. "Because I thought you were too focused on Aria to notice I wasn't serving you wine or alcohol."

I shake my head. "I'm not focused on Siren."

"Then why are you standing in the foyer staring at a door? She's going to be gone a least a couple of hours; you should sit in the living room and finish watching the soccer game with me."

"No," I answer, not giving her more of an explanation.

Nora doesn't push me, though.

"You two are so fucked up that you belong together, you know?"

I frown, still staring at the door, memorizing every dark spot, flaw, and scratch. "No, I don't know. We are so fucked up, we are completely wrong for each other."

She laughs. "Want to make a bet?"

Finally, I look at her. "I don't bet on people's hearts."

"What about your own?"

I turn back to the door.

"I don't want your money. I just want you to realize that you've already fallen. It's all wrong. You are both so wrong for each other. You're both toxic to the other. But you're also the cure."

"That's not possible."

She smiles, knowingly. "I've known Aria for years. At the time, she was with Hugo. In love with him, so to speak. It might have been love, but it's not what you two have. When Hugo and her would walk into a room, they didn't demand attention and change the feel of the air like you two. Depending on how connected you two are, you turn the room cold as ice or hot as fire. The two of you together control more than just each other; you control the whole dammed world. And together you can save it or destroy it. Whatever you two have is that powerful.

"Call it hate. Call it love. Call it fate. You were destined to be together. For a moment in time or forever, I don't know. But together, you can inflict so much pain or save so many. But only together. Apart, you are fated to destroy us all. Your pull is too great. Stop fighting it. You don't have to love her, just be with her. Stop letting your jealousy and pride get in the way."

"What about *her* pride?"

Nora shakes her head. "Aria doesn't have any pride. She's selfless."

I snort. "Then you don't know her very well. Or at least you don't know Siren."

Nora gets in my face, her petite body barely coming up to my chest. But she stands on her tiptoes, demanding my attention. "No! *You* don't know her."

Her words shake me. Her words, combined with Siren's actions, have my head spinning. I realize I don't understand anything. And I'm further from the truth than I've ever been.

Nora goes back to her TV watching until eventually, I hear her snoring on the couch. While I stay in the foyer, watching the damn door, willing Siren to come back. To explain what the hell is happening.

Hours pass or days, no idea which. But I see Julian's Aston Martin in my driveway, and I feel like a protective brother ready to pummel his ass for taking my sister on a date.

But when I see him press his lips against hers, any thoughts of her being my sister vanish. She's so much more. She's nothing like a sister to me. Not even a friend.

She's mine.

I don't know what I want with her yet. *To protect her? To love her?* But I do know one thing I want from her. And one thing I want her to keep from every other man.

I want her. I want to fuck her. And I want her to fuck me and only me. I want Siren. I want to make her mine. And I want her to stop being around other men who complicate things and cause me to want to break through the door in jealousy.

But then Siren is out of the car, knocking on my door. And I think I imagined it. Until I see Julian smirking at me through the window. He kissed her. Probably because of me. To play me and manipulate me.

Fuck him.

He may have gotten the date and the kiss, but *whose door is she knocking on? Whose house is she going to sleep in? Whose bedroom is she going to get fucked in?*

I stare at him darkly, and Julian realizes his mistake. He got the kiss—while charming and delicious and everything. I get the girl. Siren doesn't want him; she wants me.

She can pretend to be impartial to the men in her life. But it's me she keeps coming back to. It's me whose cock she seeks. It's me she wants in her life.

Siren is mine, not his.

As I open the door, I make a plan to demand her fidelity once and for all.

Siren walks in silently. Her eyes avoid mine. Nothing on her body tells me she even sees I'm here at all.

I hear the flicker off of the TV in the other room and assume Nora is coming to greet Siren. But she must be making herself scarce instead of coming to meet her friend, because she never appears.

"Truth or sin?" I ask.

"Sin. I'm tired of talking," she answers, willing to play even though she won't fucking look at me. Won't acknowledge my presence.

"Wrong choice," I say, getting her attention before my mouth claims hers. When I say claim, I mean claim. My mouth devours her lips, demanding everything from her.

At first, she doesn't kiss back. She's stunned. I don't know if she's still turned off from her earlier kiss with Julian or if I surprised her by kissing her. But the tension she left me in for three hours caused this —this explosion of want and need and desire.

I don't think she's going to kiss me back. I don't think I'm going to be able to convince her to sin with me.

But then she kisses me back. Her tongue presses between my open lips, hesitantly asking for what she wants instead of taking it. It's all the opening I need.

I grab her neck and kiss her with everything I have, sweeping my tongue deep into her mouth, telling her how much I want this. Need this. Demand this.

Her tongue doesn't accept mine; it fights back. We battle for control, for space, for air, each of our tongues viciously dancing with each other. And then it's not just our tongues fighting.

It's our entire bodies.

We battle to rip at each other's clothes. My hand is slipping under her dress, hiking it up over her ass.

Hers reach beneath my shirt, pushing it up as her nails trickle over my abs.

The force of which we battle, limb for limb, causes us to stumble into everything. We dent the wall as I crash her body into it. She pays me back when she shoves me into a glass table, shattering it. Next goes a vase, then a lamp.

We continue to dance, unspeaking. The heat of her kisses does strange things to my body. Somehow her breath alone heats my entire body. All of my muscles contract begging to put all of their energy into Siren. It's making her mine.

She rips my shirt open, and then I rip her dress as I push it higher up her body until it's around her waist.

Her body controls me entirely. She put a lot of effort into manipulating me and my feelings, but all Siren had to do to control me was strip naked, and I would have done whatever she wanted. Her body controls me that much.

Then her teeth bite down on my ear hard, and I suspect she drew blood.

I growl, and that one sound is enough for me to find my voice.

"You traded a date for Lucy," I say, it's not a question. I realized what she was doing. Why she went on a date with Julian, what she meant by she's doing this for me. *For Lucy.*

"Yes, she's safe now," she says, her eyes saying *I don't have to work for Julian anymore. I can run. No one will hurt Lucy. I just need to decide on a plan and leave.* There is nothing keeping me here.

My deal with Julian only keeps my friends alive for so long. But the end result will be the same. I'm just helping Julian get more information he needs to kill my friends while simultaneously trying to get information on Julian for my friends to kill him. But in the end, it's all a wash. I should leave, that's what her eyes say.

I should.

I absolutely should. If I trusted Siren, I would. But I don't. I don't trust that Lucy is safe. Not until I hide her away from everyone, including Siren.

Her eyes read what my mouth won't say. There's a glimmer of disappointment in her eyes, before she grabs my face again and kisses me hard, nibbling on my bottom lip to help ease her sorrow from the thought of me doubting her.

I growl and moan as she tugs, hoping it's enough for her to forget that I don't trust her. We don't need to trust each other to fuck each other.

She must agree, because two seconds later, she's grabbing at my jeans trying to get them undone, and I have her dress up around her arms.

She lifts them, and I pull the dress over her head before I slam her into the wall. And then I see the gun she hid beneath her dress around her thigh.

My eyes go big at how she always keeps me on my toes.

I hold her arms against the wall as I kiss down her body. The sweet curve of her neck, the swell of her breasts, the flatness of her stomach, the soft muscle of her thigh. I undo the strap holding her gun to her leg, and unload the gun while I kiss the inside of her thigh, earning a moan from her. Her eyes never leave mine as she watches me remove the bullets and toss the gun away.

"My turn," she says, turning me and slamming me into the wall like I did her.

She unzips my pants roughly and shoves them down, grabs my gun and tosses it aside with a smirk.

She found my weapon, but I've yet to find all of hers.

I only carry one gun unless I know I'll need more, but Siren carries multiple. While I rely on my size as a backup, she relies on multiple hidden weapons. Although it really should be the reverse, because she has something I don't—the ability to manipulate, coerce, and taunt others into doing what she wants them to do.

"Where is your other weapon?" I ask.

"Why would I tell you?"

"Because you want me to fuck you, and I won't as long as you have a weapon on you."

"It hasn't stopped you before."

"Yea, and I about got my balls cut off because of it. I won't make the same mistake again."

She rolls her eyes, but reaches into the sole of her heel and tosses a knife aside.

We stare at each other. Her topless, wearing her black thong and heels. Me in only my boxer briefs.

Both of us breathe hard.

Both with completely fucked up hair.

Our backs bruised from being shoved into objects.

This is the moment we make a decision. *Do we cross the line again? Or do we stop?*

Do we talk instead?

We each have several thoughts going through our heads.

Siren wants to know who Lucy is.

I want to know why Siren saved Lucy.

Neither of us ask our questions. We're both too afraid of the answers.

Instead, I grab her hand and pull her toward my bedroom. Once inside, I lock the door, hoping Nora found a different place to sleep for the night, because what we are about to do can not be unheard.

Siren looks at me with heady eyes.

I look at her with longing.

Neither of us touch. If we do, we won't stop. Touching feels like losing, which neither of us wants.

But I know how I can win.

I walk over to the nightstand, pull out a condom, and toss it on the bed before removing my briefs and lying back on the bed.

"I'm tired of you not being mine. I'm tired of not getting my part of you. Julian gets your loyalty. Hugo gets your last name. What do I get?"

"What do you want, Zeke?"

"I want you. I want your pussy. I want your fidelity. I want you to fuck me and only me." *I want you to be mine.*

She swallows, looking nervous.

"Fuck me, and we are entering our own deal. As long as we fuck, we only fuck each other. We don't fuck other people. We don't kiss other people."

Her eyes widen, but I don't have a clue what she's thinking.

"Do we have a deal?"

CHAPTER 17
SIREN

Zeke is asking for my exclusivity. He wants me to fuck him and only him.

But that's all he wants.

Me to spread my legs for him and no other man.

Easy enough, since I only want to fuck him. But there is just one problem—*I want more. So much more.*

I want to go on dates.

I want to snuggle after we fuck and not worry about whether or not I should leave his bed.

I want breakfast in the morning and long talks in the evening.

I want chocolates and flowers.

I want to go to the shooting range and take Krav Magra together.

I want to go dancing and sing karaoke together.

I want all of Zeke, not just his spectacular cock.

I want him to be mine, and me to be his. But he doesn't talk about making me his. And I can never make him mine.

Zeke still thinks my loyalty is to Julian, and my last name belongs to Hugo. Zeke doesn't realize all he has to do to make me his is ask. Ask for me to be his and then I'd tell him everything. The entire truth, and then he could figure out if my loyalty really belongs to Julian, and if my name really belongs to Hugo.

Zeke isn't offering me any of those things, though. He's only offering one part of him. The part he thinks he can protect from my scheming. The part that I can't hurt.

Well, technically, I can hurt it physically, but he trusts me not to because of the benefits his cock has for me.

Zeke stares at me, studying every expression, every exhale, every everything. When his lips curl up in the corner of his mouth, he knows what my answer will be.

He runs his hand through his long hair that I can't resist, and then he stands...

Fuck me. I run my tongue over my bottom lip. Zeke may not get hurt in this deal, but I sure will. If I wasn't already in love with this man, fucking him constantly, being so close, and yet not getting everything, I will be soon.

I extend my hand like this is a business arrangement.

Zeke holds out his hand.

And we shake.

The sparks fly between our two hands. Zeke feels it too, because we release our hands far too quickly for two people who just agreed to a sex deal.

I watch as Zeke swallows his uncertainty and splays out on his bed again seductively.

I'm so screwed. My mouth waters, staring at his nakedness on his bed. He's waiting for me to take control. *So fucking sexy.*

"Fuck me, Siren. Prove to me you only want my cock."

My panties are soaked at his throaty words. His dark eyes bore into me, challenging me to make this fuck the best fuck of his life. Prove to him that he was right to take another chance on me, even if he isn't risking anything this time. He's kept his heart as far away from me as possible.

He wants this to be memorable. He wants me to give him my best, while he lies back and does none of the work. *Asshole.*

But damn the way he's staring at me, making my body tingle in all the right places, getting me wet with just a look, tells me he's already doing plenty of the work.

I hook my thumbs into my panties and slowly shimmer them down my legs before stepping out of them. I never think undressing with another person's eyes on you is sexy. It's always hard to not look clumsy or ensure something doesn't get caught on a heel or an ear. But the pained exhale I hear from Zeke shows just how sexy me undressing was to him.

I stand tall in my heels and run my hand through my long hair before flipping it over my head to one side. The move earns me another growl.

"You're not acting like a woman who only wants my cock. You're acting like a woman who wants to play with me," he groans.

"I enjoy playing before I claim what I want," I say, strutting over to the dresser, where a glass of water rests. I slowly take a sip, purposefully spilling some onto my chest. Little beads of water run down my breasts over my sharp nipples.

I can't keep this up much longer, or I'll combust. Zeke has me just as needy as I have him.

My eyes flick to Zeke, who has his cock in his fist, stroking himself.

"I guess I'll just have to get myself off," he says, teasing me into giving him what he wants.

I arch my back as I lean against the wall next to his bed. "My fingers work better than yours at getting me off anyway," I tease back.

My fingers circle my clit, while Zeke strokes his long, thick cock.

Somehow we ended up in another battle. The battle to not seem weak. The battle to prove that we don't need the other as much as they need us.

"Our deal was you'd only fuck my cock, Siren."

"I'm not fucking any other dicks."

"I think our deal includes self-pleasure."

I raise my eyebrows. *He's going to play that way, huh? Fine, I can play that way too.*

"Then the same goes for you. If I don't fuck anyone but you, then you don't either. You only fuck me, not your hand."

His face is in inexplicable pain. His jaw tenses, his throat locks, his eyelids still, and his nostrils flare.

"Deal," he says, releasing his hand from himself.

He must really want my pussy. Or he can't stand to see me get myself off when he wants to be the one to do it.

I want him to get me off.

Why are we battling again?

We both surrender at the same time.

I jump on the bed as Zeke catches my hips, and my mouth comes down hungrily on his. My hips position themselves over his rock hard cock until my slit is sliding over him, begging him to be inside me.

He grabs my hair, pulling my head back and arching my back to keep my clit against his cock.

"Condom," he gruffs.

"Pill, remember?"

We've fucked before without a condom, so I don't know why he's asking now.

The anger in his eyes tells me he won't verbalize his concerns.

Did I fuck Julian or Hugo? Am I clean?

His tip presses at my entrance, so close to getting what we both want, but he won't let himself, not until he has the answer.

But when I tell him, will he believe me?

I doubt it.

I should just grab the condom on the bed. It will get me the result I want faster, but I crave Zeke without a barrier between us.

Liar!

What I really want is Zeke to trust me.

This is a step toward trusting me.

"I only fucked Hugo once when I was eighteen. I haven't fucked him our entire marriage," I say, repeating what he already knows, but with truth in my eyes.

He nods, accepting this as fact.

But we aren't done yet, because Zeke has more questions.

"Other men?"

"There haven't been any other men after you. Not in my bed. I don't want any man but you." My words make me vulnerable, but they are the truth. "We didn't need to make a deal to be exclusive because I've been exclusive this entire time."

He growls huskily, pulls harder on my fisted hair, and brushes his lips against mine. His cock slowly moves an inch into my throbbing pussy.

*So, so, close...*if he let go at all, I could slide all the way home, enveloping him. But I won't, no matter how badly I want to. I need him to trust me, and he won't if I'm selfish and take what I want without giving him his answers first.

There is one last question in his eyes, and this question hurts him.

"I saw you kissing Julian."

Of course, he did.

I know the truth. I know why I kissed Julian; I did it for Zeke. But I'm not sure he's going to believe that answer. It's one thing to go on a date with Julian to help Zeke. It's another thing to kiss him for Zeke.

But Zeke isn't going to let me get away with not answering him. Not this time. He wants the truth, no matter what that is.

"I kissed him in exchange for getting you one day."

He blinks at me, not understanding.

"I went on a date to save Lucy. And I kissed him to give you one day headstart when this is all over to run before Julian starts chasing you."

He growls, and this time he has no restraint. He flips me over, his cock still resting at my entrance but not entering me. We are having a serious conversation, and yet, we are both turned on. Nothing will extinguish our flames except fucking.

"Stop offering yourself in exchange for saving me. I can save myself."

I scoff. "You would be dead if it weren't for me."

"I know," his voice is serious, his eyes wide. "But I don't need your help anymore, just like you don't need mine."

I nod.

"Stop saving me," he says.

"I'll stop saving you."

"No more kissing other men."

I nod, agreeing.

"No more going on dates."

I nod.

"No more spreading your legs for anyone but me."

I nod slower, agreeing.

Finally, his mouth devours mine, a sweeping kiss to remind me I'm his even if he never says the words. What he said was close enough. We get the physical part of each other for as long as we are together. Which, in our line of work, could mean only a day. But if it is meant to only be a day, I'll make it the best damn day.

I roll us over again, to be on top and in control.

"Trust me," I say, *trust me with this*. I haven't fucked any man but him. I'm clean. We don't need a condom.

He starts to nod but then stops, his eyes revealing a sliver of pain again.

"You haven't fucked Hugo, but did Julian ever..." he can't finish the sentence, but the pain in his eyes tells me everything. *Did Julian ever force me to have sex with him? Was I ever raped?*

I shake my head.

"Say it," he says, his voice desperate. He's right; I need to say it. I can lie with a head shake, but not with my words.

"I've never been raped. Julian has never forced me into sex. I've never fucked him. Since we've started fucking, it's only been you."

"Thank fuck."

His hips buck as I slide down on top of him, his cock filling me completely in one thrust.

I grip his shoulders as the fullness consumes me.

Zeke stops thrusting, waiting for me to adjust to his girth.

But I don't want this to stop.

I start rocking over him.

He grabs my hips, helping me move, but keeping our rhythm slow and steady.

"Faster," I cry. We've gone so slowly, I'm going to explode before ever getting to the good part.

He laughs low and deep. "Slow down or this is going to be over way too fast."

I nip at his lip. "That's what seconds are for." I move faster, and his pained breath tells me he isn't in control anymore.

His hands on my hips slide me faster over his cock, no longer holding back.

I ride him hard, needing the release more than I need to breathe. It's been too long since I've felt this man. I shouldn't go a single day without him, not weeks like it's been.

I shouldn't ever have to worry I won't get to fuck him again, but that's exactly what's going through my head. Even though we promised each other our fidelity, we didn't promise each other forever. This can all end at any time. While it lasts, we are only with each other.

"Siren," Zeke's voice is deep and breathy. But it does what it was intended. His voice brings me back to him.

I smile timidly as I move back in rhythm with him.

Zeke's hands slide up my hips to my breasts bouncing over him. He flicks each nipple, making it harder to control myself. He's driving me wild, and I'm going to come from him playing with my nipples alone.

Not yet; I'm not ready. I want us to go at the same time, and Zeke is still a bit away from his impending orgasm.

I grab his hands and push them back, pinning his hands to the bed as I ride him.

Our fingers interlock, along with our eyes, and at least my heart. This moment is so much more intimate than a simple romp in the sheets.

Zeke seems to understand the change, but when I try to pull my hands free from his, he holds them tighter, not letting me go.

I'm so screwed.

I blink back the tears at all the intense emotions pulsing through me. *I can do this. Just sex. No emotion.*

The task is impossible, though, with the intensity of Zeke staring back at me.

Focus on the mechanics—hips rolling, legs rocking, lick my lips sexily, rub my clit against his steel core.

But the mechanics all go to hell when his voice strains, his eyes roll back in his head, and his orgasm begins.

The effect my body has on his pushes me to my orgasm as well. We both come in an explosive way. A way that's far too big for emotions to not get tangled in.

But I bury those emotions deep within myself as I cry out from the bang of the orgasm racking my body.

My breath is quick and fast, even after my orgasm rolls through.

Suddenly, I realize Zeke is staring at me calmly. Not like I just rocked his world. But like he's studying for a school test he's not sure how to pass.

I frown. "I can do better..." I start. *What am I doing? Admitting the sex wasn't the greatest of my life?* Just because it wasn't great for Zeke, doesn't mean it wasn't great sex.

Zeke slowly untangles our fingers, and then one hand cups my head, while the other pushes at my hips.

And then I'm lying back on the bed, and Zeke is over me, staring at me like I'm the most impossible woman.

"What?" I ask tentatively.

He smirks. "If you think that wasn't the best sex of my life, you're crazy, Siren."

Then he's spreading my legs with his hands.

"What are you doing?" I ask.

"Showing my appreciation for the sex and giving my cock a moment's rest before I fuck you again."

His head dips between my legs, and he begins licking me sultry and slowly, a complete one-eighty from what just happened.

My gasp takes me by surprise. My hands go to his hair, unable to decide between pushing his head deeper into my folds or pulling him back from the intensity of the pleasure.

Then his fingers are inside me, finding that delicious spot and curling around it. I hate to admit it, but I come hard and fast, letting him know exactly what his lips are capable of doing to me—controlling me completely.

He collapses on top of me, his cock beginning to stir against my thigh, promising more after a quick nap.

I close my eyes and let the gentle pull of sleep drift me away as Zeke's naked body keeps me warm. The difference between lust and love eats at me.

This is just lust, not love. At least it's just lust for Zeke. He loves Lucy. He wants Lucy. This is just sex. Something for him to pass the time until he gets the woman he loves back.

But it's hard to distinguish the difference when he starts playing gently with my hair, doing more to my senses than his cock ever could. For Zeke, this may be lust, but for me, it's all love.

"You're mine, Siren," Zeke says.

I smile and feel settled for the first time all night. It may not be forever, but for now, I'm his. And that's enough.

CHAPTER 18
ZEKE

We fucked two more times last night, but it wasn't enough to satiate either of us. At some point, she fell asleep against my shoulder, and I couldn't stand to wake her up. She needs her rest for what is coming today. I loved how she felt buried in the crook of my arm; our bodies melding together perfectly.

Has any woman's body ever felt so perfect in my arms?

Not that I can remember. Maybe it's just been so long since I've fucked another woman. It will remain that way, though, because I plan on fucking Siren in every position and place I can come up with while I'm in Julian's debt.

I say 'debt' because I refuse to be trapped here. I refuse to be a hostage. I'm here because I decided to be here. I want to know everything about him, so when my deal with him is over, Enzo and I will enjoy squashing him like the cockroach he is.

Julian thinks he outsmarted me by having a man monitor Lucy, but Siren gave me the advantage back. I need to talk to her about the details of keeping Lucy safe. I may trust that Siren thinks she made a deal with Julian, but I don't trust either of them fully. I need to hide Lucy myself.

You trusted Siren last night when you put your dick in her without a condom.

That's different.

How?

I don't know. It just *felt* different.

But when Siren wakes, her coldness makes it feel like nothing has changed. We don't talk to each other; we ice each other out. We move around each other like we aren't sharing the same space. Like we didn't explore every inch of each other last night.

I decide to leave it. Eventually, we will have to talk. I shower. I get dressed. I pack a bag full of the essentials I'll need.

"Did you pack a suit?" Siren asks, leaning against the doorframe of my bedroom.

"Do I look like the type of man who owns a suit? Especially when I live on an island?"

She smiles. "We'll get you one when we get to France."

I nod, I don't know why I'll be needing a suit, but I'm guessing Siren has a plan. Right now doesn't seem like the best time to argue.

"I also thought you'd want this," Siren walks forward and holds out a piece of paper to me.

I take it hesitantly and unfold it to read a Seattle address with a phone number underneath it.

Lucy.

My heart beats quickly. More for Siren than for Lucy, but Siren definitely misinterprets why, and I don't correct her. I'm not letting Siren anywhere near my heart again. This is just sexual tension between us, nothing more.

"Thank you," I say, holding up the note and memorizing it before I shred it into tiny pieces. I have no doubt Siren has already committed everything on the note to memory, and so has Julian, but I want that address in as few people's heads as possible.

"I'm going to need to move her," I say, not saying Lucy's name.

"I know."

"And I can't tell you where I hide her," I say. I can't trust her with someone as precious as Lucy.

"I know," Siren answers sadly.

"It's time to go, you two!" Nora hollers from the hallway, ending the tension between us.

I lift my bag, and Siren starts walking toward the door. "Where did Nora sleep last night, anyway?"

Siren blushes. "Um…"

"Siren, where did Nora sleep?"

"When I first got back, she went out on the back deck to give us some privacy. But it got cold, so she slept on the couch," Siren blushes.

"She heard everything?"

Siren nods.

Fuck, I owe Nora all the coffee at the airport for keeping her up last night.

When I walk into the living room where Nora is waiting with her bags, she drags her eyes over my body.

"So how did everyone sleep?" she winks at me.

Fuck. I run my hand through my hair, ruffling it. I need to put it up in a bun, so I don't keep nervously playing with it.

Fuck it. Everyone already knows what Siren and I did last night. I'm the kind of man that owns his mistakes. Or, in this case, the one fucking thing I did right.

I grab Siren and dip her as I kiss her good morning, surprising the hell out of her.

Nora squeals. "I knew you two would end up together! If only you had actually bet me, I'd be rich right now."

"You're already rich, Nora," Siren says when I release her lips. The smile on her face immediately drops as her brain starts working. "But Zeke and I aren't—"

I kiss her again to shut her up. We aren't together. We are only fucking. But no need to shout it to the world. No need for Nora or anyone else to know our relationship. I'm sure we will have to play the happy couple enough in France. It will be more believable if Nora plays along.

There is no way I'm letting Siren out of my sight. She's mine. Pretending to be a couple is the best way to fend off other men. She won't be flirting with other men to steal the money, if that's her plan. Siren seems to understand because she doesn't bring it up again.

Siren picks up her bag, so I pick up mine and Nora's, and we head to my truck.

I flick Siren the keys to my truck, knowing she will feel safer if she drives. However, I get a scowl in return as I get in the passenger seat.

"What's her problem?" I ask Nora before she climbs in back.

Nora shakes her head. "Men really are clueless, aren't they?"

And women are cryptic.

We all climb in, and Siren drives us to the airport in silence.

When we get to the small airport terminal, I head inside to grab coffees while Siren and Nora head to the plane.

I want to grab a coffee for Siren, but since the last time I ordered one for her, I almost got my head chewed off, I decide against it. I just get one for myself and Nora.

"Here's my sorry for keeping you up all night," I say, handing the coffee to Nora, who is already in the cockpit.

She smiles at me as she takes it. Siren is sitting next to her. I don't look at her. But I can feel her scowl, confusing me even more.

"I can sleep through anything. I only heard the beginning part. And knowing my friend was finally getting properly laid made the lack of sleep worth it." Nora winks at me again.

I nod and then head back to my seat. Siren stays in the cockpit the whole flight. I continue to remain out of the mile-high club.

From the snooty, jealous look Siren gives me when we depart the plane in Miami, I think I played my cards very wrong.

"I screwed up somehow, didn't I?" I ask Nora as she departs next.

"Yep," she says, annoyed with me too.

"You going to clue me in as to what I did wrong or how to fix it?"

"Nope."

Ugh.

But as we walk into the Miami airport, Siren becomes the least of my problems.

We are in Miami. The headquarters of Enzo Black's organization. He, or some of his men, could be here in this very airport. Or this could all be a ruse to use me as bait to get Enzo.

But from the way Siren stalks off inside and Nora chases after, it seems that Siren's focus is on whatever I did wrong and not on an elaborate scheme to take down my best friend.

I let out a calming breath, but nothing more. I need to stay on guard. This could all be a trick. Julian could be here.

I find Siren and Nora sitting at a bar—a whiskey in front of Siren and a margarita in front of Nora.

"Isn't it early to be drinking?"

Siren ignores me and finishes her drink.

Nora gives me side-eye.

Apparently, I can't do anything right.

"When does our flight board?" I ask.

"Twenty-minutes," Nora answers when it's clear that Siren won't be answering me.

"I'll meet you at the gate in twenty then," I say.

Nora nods. Siren acts like I'm the plague.

I rub my neck as I walk away, trying to figure out why Siren is so pissed.

It hits me all at once. *Jealousy*.

Siren can pretend she's not a flowers and chocolates girl all she wants, but she is when I'm the man she's exclusively fucking.

I carried her friend's bag.

I let her drive instead of taking care of her and driving myself.

I got her friend a coffee and didn't get her one.

She wants me to do nice things for her, to court her. To act like she's more than just the woman in my bed, even though that's exactly what she is.

I shouldn't treat her like my girlfriend. She can stew all she wants, but she's told me time and time again—it's not what she wants. And I've told her this is only sex.

But it doesn't stop her jealousy.

It doesn't stop me from wanting to hold her hand and buy her all the damn flowers.

I decide against the flowers. Instead, I get her a coffee, and a grilled cheese sandwich, and a cookie for dessert.

When I get to the gate, I don't spot either of them. Most of the plane has already boarded, so my guess is they are already on the plane.

I board and find Nora and Siren sitting together on one side of the aisle in first class, while there is an empty seat for me on the other side.

I give Nora a glare, demanding her seat.

She stands and gives me a protective snarl.

We dance around each other in the aisle until I'm free to take Nora's spot next to Siren. Siren has put headphones in and is planning on tuning me out.

Not going to happen. I don't plan on spending the flight ignoring each other. I plan on fixing this so the long flight can be much more enjoyable.

I lift her tray out of the armrest. This gets her attention.

Then I place her coffee on it. Then her sandwich. And last the cookie.

I look at her smugly, knowing I did the right thing.

"Wipe that smug smile off your face," she says, reaching for the cookie first.

I smile larger. I wouldn't have guessed she's a dessert first kind of girl. Then again, with our jobs, if you don't eat dessert first, you might never get to taste the best part of the meal before a gunfight breaks out.

"Why? This is what you wanted, right?" I reach out to take a bite from her cookie, and she slaps at my hand.

But she's smiling as she eats, crumbs sticking to her lips, and falling into her lap.

Her eyes cut up to the flight attendant at the front, who has started the safety demonstration. Siren then looks at me with noticeably pink cheeks, and her eyelashes flirting with me.

"Want to finally join the mile-high club?" Siren asks.

I'm instantly hard.

The flight attendant walks by and says, "Seat belt, sir."

My eyes meet hers, and her face is bright red after noticing my erection.

"How long is this flight?" I turn back to Siren.

"Nine hours."

"I think we can handle becoming a member of the mile-high club at least twice on this flight."

Siren licks her lips, teasing me with what I can't have. If I could have her right this second, I would. The moment we are in the air—she's mine. Fuck the fasten your seatbelt sign, or turbulence, or flight attendants. I can't wait much longer than the five minutes it's going to take us to get up in the air to have her.

But then I remember a not so happy thought—this isn't Siren's first time becoming a member. "You ever going to tell me how you got your mile-high membership?"

She cocks her head, giving me a seductive glance as she thinks about the last time she did it on a plane. "Nope."

I growl, but it only makes her smile brighten as she pulls out her phone and pretends to read a book. There is no way she's reading, not when her thighs are clenched together, and her breath is heavy with thoughts about what we are going to do in that bathroom.

I know one thing that's going to happen—I'm going to erase the other guy from her memory so it will feel like the first time all over again.

CHAPTER 19
SIREN

Zeke's legs bounce up and down, and I remember that he's a nervous flyer. At least when Nora is flying us. But I don't think that's what this is about. This is about us having sex in the bathroom.

Something I can't wait for either, but it could still be a while. We have to climb to an appropriate height. Then the pilots have to turn the seatbelt sign off. Then we have to wait for the first group to use the bathroom to be courteous. Then we have to take turns sneaking off to the bathroom without the flight attendants noticing.

"We have reached an altitude of 10,000 feet. It is now safe to use all approved electronic devices...", the flight attendant speaks over the speakers.

Zeke undoes his seatbelt and then mine, before grabbing my hand.

"Zeke, what are you doing?" I laugh at his eagerness.

"If it's safe to use electronic devices, it's safe to go to the bathroom," he grins back, with determination in his eyes.

I roll my eyes. That's not how this works, but I don't argue with him. There is no use. My stomach clenches with need—I don't want to argue either. I can't wait.

The flight attendant is still making announcements on the speaker when Zeke and I pass her on the way to the bathroom. Her eyes are big, and she's about to tell us off when a man in the front row says, "Ma'am, there is a puking infant in the tenth row."

She runs off to take care of the infant. And Zeke and I casually stroll into the bathroom. Zeke latches the door, and we are face to face in the tiny room.

"They really should make these bathrooms bigger," he says.

I smile. "Don't think you have enough space to put on your moves?"

He grabs my hips and pushes his against mine, letting me feel how hard he is. My pussy soaks and throbs, preparing for him, and he doesn't even have a clue.

But the hitch of his eyebrow says he knows exactly what he's doing to my body.

"We have to be fast—" I start, but I'm cut off when Zeke kisses my neck, making me purr.

"Why? I want to enjoy every inch of your body."

"Because...because we have to..." but my mind can't form words anymore. My mind doesn't have a clue why we have to be fast.

Fast?

Slow?

I want it all.

Zeke's hands are working over my jeans, and I know he can feel how wet I am through them. I should make him take them off before the wet spot becomes even more noticeable when we walk back out. But the feel of his hands over my jeans make my purring and groaning louder.

Finally, I get enough oxygen to my brain. "Are you going to fuck me or just tease me like we are in high school or something?"

That gets him moving faster.

His finger dips beneath my jeans so fast I don't even see his fingers move, but I feel them beneath my panties against my hot wetness.

"Holy fuck!" I cry.

Apparently, fucking all last night did nothing to take away my desire for this man. I want him all the time. *All. The. Time.*

And after we fuck this once, I don't know if it will be enough to survive nine hours on this plane without getting to fuck him again.

"You like that?" Zeke growls.

"Yes!"

But it's not fair to be the only one screaming.

I dip my hands beneath his jeans and find his hard cock.

"Siren," he says my name like a curse, which is exactly what I am—a fucking curse.

And then we can't wait. I rip open the button on his jeans as he undoes my zipper. We both push each other's pants and underwear down at the same time, not even bothering to remove our shirts. Somehow seeing Zeke pantless with a shirt is sexy. Everything about Zeke is sexy.

I grab the scrunchie holding his hair up, pull his hair free, and then I put it around my wrist. He looks like the beast at the end of Beauty and the Beast when he's turned back into a man. Just a pantless beast.

God, his hair is gorgeous. I tangle my hands in his hair at the same time he grabs my hips, pushing us together. There isn't much room in this bathroom, so we are both fighting for everything—room, control, oxygen.

The mirror fogs up as our kisses turn to uncontrollable devouring of each other.

We spin, trying to find a way to make the bathroom bigger so we can take each other the way we want to. Our hands sneak between us, rubbing each other furiously, trying to get the other harder, wetter, more turned on, and reveling in the sound of the other screaming our name out.

My back is against the bathroom door, and Zeke lifts my hands up, demanding control as he kisses my neck.

"God, if I had a bed...the things I'd do to you," he says.

I shudder, holding back from coming at the sound of his deep, sexy voice.

His lips curl up as he notices my reaction.

Control—I need control back.

But more importantly, I need Zeke's dick inside me.

I shove him hard, and he stumbles back until he's sitting on the lid covered toilet seat. Not exactly sexy, but neither of us care. We need each other too badly to care about how we are doing it.

I straddle him, and his cock pushes inside me in one stroke.

I grab his hair, holding on for dear life as I ride him up and down, and he thrusts short and hard into me.

Our eyes lock with each other, and this quick romp in the bathroom starts making me think and feel things I shouldn't. Like how I want to find every bathroom, closet, and alleyway in France to fuck him in.

Then he's pushing up my shirt, and his head dips under as he carefully takes a nipple between his teeth. The sharp pain is just enough to alert all my senses.

I come—hard. *Too hard.* I scream his name, completely forgetting that we are in a bathroom on a plane with hundreds of passengers.

Zeke has a devious expression on his face, but then I thrust down on him while yanking on his hair, and he's growling his own orgasm out.

He shakes his head, like he can't believe we just did that.

"How is it that you always end up on top lately?" he asks, kissing me gently. *Too gently.* I like rough, hard, fast Zeke. Not tender, caring, soft Zeke. Not the man who got me coffee and cookies. This version of Zeke is dangerous to my already falling heart.

"I guess I'm just the stronger of the two of us." I wink.

He nips at my bottom lip. "Yep, that's it. It couldn't be that I like watching your tits bounce up and down in front of my face."

I roll my eyes. "Definitely not."

We both stand and take a second to clean ourselves up before dressing.

I reach for the door handle, and then Zeke grabs my face, turning my lips toward him for one final kiss.

"Meet you back here in an hour?" he asks.

I laugh, but I'm desperate to make it happen again.

At least I am until I open the door and die from embarrassment. There is a line of three people waiting for the bathroom. None of them look happy when we exit the bathroom.

"Sorry," I mumble quietly under my breath as we pass them and return to our seats.

"How can three people need to go to the bathroom already? We just took off," Zeke says.

Nora laughs next to us. "You've been in there for an hour."

"No way," I say.

"Yep, the flight attendants knocked on the door twice, trying to get you two out, but you were too occupied to hear."

I'm going to die from embarrassment. I've survived gunfights. Battles. Disgusting men. Julian. Hugo. But this is how I'm going to die —of embarrassment on a nine-hour flight from Miami to Paris.

Nora laughs. "I'm just kidding. You were only in there twenty minutes."

I grab a nut from the container the flight attendant brought around and throw it at her.

Zeke just frowns.

"Why are you upset?" I ask.

"It's not a funny joke. I think we should go back to the bathroom right now and prove that I can last longer than twenty minutes."

I chuckle and realize all the eyes in our cabin are on us. The women are drooling and panting, wishing Zeke would do to them what he did to me. And the men are either scowling or ready to high-five Zeke for his impressive stamina.

"I don't think you need to prove anything to anyone," I say.

Yet Zeke kisses me hard, his tongue sweeping away any doubt that he isn't the most impressive man on the plane.

When he stops, I don't even care that he only kissed me to show off to the rest of the plane. *That's why he kissed me like that, right?* Because his eyes are looking at me like he's afraid he's going to lose me again. As if losing me, not embarrassment, would be the death of him.

"Can I get you two a drink? Maybe something that will keep you in your seats?" the flight attendant says, apparently annoyed with our little show.

Zeke turns to her, flashing his million-dollar smile that rarely comes out because he's usually sulking. "Yes, we'd both love a whiskey."

Suddenly the flight attendant is smiling back at him.

What the fuck?

Isn't she upset with us still? Going to lecture us?

Nope—Zeke smiles, winks, and then she's off to get us drinks like nothing happened.

Isn't there something in the rules about Zeke not smiling at other women if I'm not allowed to fuck other men? It seems like there should be.

I slump into my chair and take the whiskey the flight attendant immediately brings back. I sip on it, hoping it will drown out my jealousy.

Doubtful.

This plane ride is going to feel like forever. I'm not going to survive. And if I do, I'm definitely not going to survive what I have planned in France.

If I can't handle Zeke smiling at another woman, how am I going to survive him pretending to be engaged to another woman? *Me and my stupid plans.*

CHAPTER 20
ZEKE

Siren has a plan, and I don't like it. Not one bit. It's a stupid plan. Not only that, but if she thinks I can actually pull this off, she's insane. She's lost her mind. She knows I'm not a good actor. I don't know why she thinks this is the only way to steal a billion dollars from her in-laws.

Can't we just sneak into the city and hack their bank account or something? Hell, I'd even take robbing a bank at gunpoint over this plan.

Nora seems just as reluctant as she slips a giant engagement ring on her left finger.

"I swore I'd never wear this ring again," Nora says, staring at the sparkler on her finger.

"Why do you still have it if you rejected his offer?" I ask.

"I didn't reject his offer. I said yes, and then I found him cheating on me, so I got to keep the ring," she growls.

"Okay, but why didn't you sell it? Get something useful out of it?" I ask.

"Do I look like the kind of girl that needs a man's money?" she snarks with a sassiness I wasn't expecting.

She doesn't need money any more than Siren needs a man's help.

But I don't respond. Her question seemed rhetorical, and all I'm doing is digging myself into a deeper hole.

The ring on Nora's finger isn't what has me worried. It's the ring Siren is holding in her hand and looking at like it's poison.

I still, staring at it.

It's a gold ring with dozens of tiny diamonds all around it. It's beautiful, simple, and timeless.

She stares at it. "I thought Hugo worked his ass off to be able to pay for this ring. I thought he scrounged together and saved every last penny to be able to buy me this. I thought it cost thousands. I didn't realize I had the million dollars Hugo owed the drug dealer on my left finger. If I did..."

She would have sold it to free Hugo instead of selling herself to Julian.

I walk over to her. "Is it really worth millions?"

She nods and holds out the ring to me.

I take it and study the intricacy of the ring. There are more diamonds than I first realized.

"It doesn't seem like it should be worth that much."

"A family heirloom. And yes, Hugo's mom told me the value of it last time I visited."

She takes the ring back and slowly puts it on her finger. I hold my breath to keep from making a sound, a twitch, or any movement that would reveal my feelings at seeing another man's ring on her finger.

She takes a deep breath. "Ready."

Siren looks to me and then Nora. We all nod in agreement. Ready. At least as ready as we can be.

We stopped at an expensive clothing store on the way to the hotel Hugo's parents own, where we will be meeting them and staying. Apparently, jeans were not going to be appropriate attire to meet them in, so I'm wearing khaki slacks and a buttoned-down gray shirt.

Nora is in a flowery dress that seems too sweet for her.

A soft, flowy pink dress hides Siren's curves, the complete opposite of the Siren I know.

"Stop staring at me, stare at Nora. You're supposed to be in love with her, not me," Siren hisses.

"You sure you want to go with pink?"

She sighs. "Yep, it brings out the softness in my eyes."

It does, but the softness in her eyes isn't her best asset.

We all climb into the back of a black town car. Apparently, a taxi wouldn't be appropriate for us to arrive in.

The ride is short, into the heart of Paris. The hotel we stop in front of is the grandest I've ever seen. Suddenly, I think I should have entered in a suit, not khakis. I'm definitely glad I didn't arrive in ripped jeans.

The hotel doorman opens our car door, and Siren walks out like she belongs here. Her face and posture change completely.

I step out, looking completely lost. My hair is up in a bun, my beard is trimmed, and my clothes are tidy, but I'm as far away from belonging here as possible. You can't cover my tattoos or scars, and I sure as hell wasn't letting Siren cut my hair to help me fit in.

"Hold my hand," Nora whispers, her fingers dancing against my palm.

Reluctantly, I take her hand.

"And don't act like it's killing you to be my fiancé. You didn't have such a hard job pretending I was your girlfriend in that bar."

"That's because it was one night, and I was trying to make Siren jealous."

"Well, pretend you're trying to make her jealous again. It worked that night. It can work again."

I lead Nora inside, following Siren. Siren barely waits for us to enter before she's wrapping an extravagantly dressed older woman and a suited, graying haired man in a hug and quick kiss on the cheek.

Yep, should have gone with the suit.

"Aria, it's so good of you to visit," the older woman says.

"It's been too long, but my best friend is getting married, and she wanted the best wedding. So I thought this was just the place and the people to help her get ready for her big day."

"Of course, we are the best," the woman says, looking past Siren to us. A frown immediately appears on her face. Apparently, she doesn't approve of Nora, nor me.

"Let me introduce you to the happy couple," Siren says, ignoring the woman's glare.

"Mrs. Bisset, this is my best friend, Nora Taylor," Siren says.

Mrs. Bisset, who apparently didn't take her husband's last name, holds out a snooty hand to Nora.

"Mrs. Bisset, it's so nice to meet you," Nora says.

The woman just nods as they shake, not offering for Nora to call her by her first name. But then Mrs. Bisset spots Nora's engagement ring.

"Well done, that is an exquisite diamond," Mrs. Bisset says.

Nora nods hesitantly but then grabs my arm. "I snagged a good husband to be."

From the way Mrs. Bisset is looking at me, the only thing she approves of is the expensive ring I supposedly bought my fiancé. She stares down her nose at me, doubting I could afford it. She doesn't realize if I was getting married for real, I could afford a ring three times as expensive.

"Zeke Kane," I say, introducing myself and not holding out my hand, because I know the woman doesn't want to shake it anyway.

"Hmm," she says.

Siren gives me a quick roll of the eyes only I see.

"And this is Mr. Martinez, he owns a string of hotels here," Siren says.

The man looks up from the phone he has been busy typing on. He nods in our direction, apparently not caring who the new guests are.

"The courtyard out back is the ultimate dream location to get married. The flowers are blooming and beautiful this time of year, but of course, I'll have more flowers brought in for your special day. However, the location and my services do come with a hefty price tag," Mrs. Bisset says, looking at me like I couldn't afford to get married in a barn, much less in a swanky hotel in Paris.

I stare around like this place is nothing more than a Marriot. "It's not up to my tastes, but if my baby here wants it, then I guess this place will do."

Nora smiles, annoyingly, and leans into my chest. I stiffen at how wrong it feels to have any woman leaning against me that isn't Siren.

I'm beginning to think we should have stolen the money from anyone else on the planet. Once we get the money, it's going to feel incredible, but I'm not sure it's worth playing pretend fiancé to a woman who isn't Siren for an entire weekend with these people.

"Oh, look at the time! Dinner will be served in two hours. You will want to get showered and changed before dinner, I'm sure. You'll want to know how the dining room can be transformed, so of course, you'll want to try it out tonight and see it in all its slender."

I sigh. Apparently, what I'm wearing isn't appropriate for dinner with these people. But if I have two hours to change, then at least I'll have two hours away from them. Two hours with Siren—I can think of plenty of things we can do with that time. *She needs, what, thirty minutes to get ready?*

"Ms. Taylor and Mr. Kane, I reserved a suite for you," Mrs. Bisset says.

She snaps her fingers, and a butler appears with our bags to take us up to our room.

My eyes land on Siren. *What room will she be staying in? Where will I need to sneak off to?*

"And Aria dear, you'll be staying in the princess suite as usual. Now, where is your sweet husband?" Mrs. Bisset says.

I stop dead.

Hugo? He's here?

No way! Last time I saw him, I'd broken his kneecap, and Siren had broken his nose and wrist. He should be in a hospital or with Julian doing his bidding. Not here. Not in France. Not with us.

But then I spot him, rounding the corner.

He has crutches, his wrist is in a splint, and he's wearing more makeup than a stage performer to cover the bruises covering his face. But he's here. In a gray suit, somehow looking more refined than I do, even with the crutches.

"Oh, there you are, dear," Mrs. Bisset says, kissing her son on the cheek. "I'm just so happy you two were both able to come. It's been so long since everyone has seen you together. And now that Aria is here, I'm sure you'll heal from that horrible car accident so much faster."

Siren is glaring at Hugo, while I swear there's fear behind his eyes.

Yea, Mrs. Bisset, Hugo will heal a lot faster with Siren here. That, or she'll break his other wrist.

CHAPTER 21
SIREN

Hugo is here.

I knew he would be. Mrs. Bisset told me when I called to make the arrangements, but seeing him in person makes me angrier than I expected. He's the only one who could ruin our plans. He knows we aren't here because Zeke and Nora are getting married.

However, he won't rat us out to his parents. Not unless he wants a broken dick to go with his broken wrist and kneecap.

I see the fear in his eyes, but there's also a need for revenge. He wants to stop whatever mission Julian sent me here on. He doesn't know what my mission is, though, or he would have put a stop to this back on the island.

Instead, he goads me. "Come here and give me a kiss, baby."

I hate being called baby, but I walk over and put on a show for his parents. Parents I can't wait to steal everything from. They stole my life by not paying for their son's debt.

The kiss is chaste, our lips barely touch, but I can feel the jealous glare from Zeke on the back of my head.

This is all an act. Stay cool or this won't work. You're supposed to be in love with Nora, not me.

When I pull back from the kiss, Hugo has a smug expression on his face. He knew exactly what he was doing and enjoyed it thoroughly.

"You kids better go upstairs and get ready. Less than two hours until the ball tonight," Mrs. Bisset says.

"We won't be late. But you don't need to throw a party on our account," I say.

"Of course, I do. The world loves seeing the two of you together. And we have a new couple to celebrate," she answers.

I nod.

Zeke and Nora are pushed into one elevator, while Hugo and I are pushed into another, probably headed to different floors and different ends of the hotel. The butlers take our luggage to be delivered and unpacked in our rooms, escaping via servants hallways.

Hugo and I are left alone on the elevator, headed to our usual room.

"So kind of you to stop by France and see how I'm doing. You haven't been here since I dragged your ass here in our early twenties," he says.

"You know me—just wanted to check on my husband after such a horrible car accident and all."

The elevator doors open on the top floor, and I step out, not waiting for Hugo to stumble along with his crutches.

I walk to the door of our suite. It's always the same suite every time we come—only the best for their precious son.

A waiting butler opens the door for me and then holds it open for Hugo.

"Thank you, Travers." Hugo hands him cash. "Could you give us a moment alone please before you start unpacking?"

"Of course, sir. The hairstylists will be up shortly."

Hugo nods at the exiting butler, and we are alone in the gorgeous suite. The suite has three bedrooms, a dining room, a living room, and a dressing room bigger than most bedrooms for us to get ready in. But even though there are three bedrooms, I won't be able to get away with not sleeping in the same bed as Hugo. The maids work for Mrs. Bisset. They will inform her if we don't share a bed.

Hugo leans his crutches against the wall and hops gingerly toward me. I consider walking further into the suite just to make him have to walk further, but I want whatever he has to say over with.

Surprise takes over as he presses a knife against my stomach and shoves me hard against the wall. He drew some blood, although, the pain doesn't register.

I let him think he has me cornered, but even without his broken leg, I can outmaneuver him. He's not a threat.

"What do you want, Hugo?"

"What are you doing here?"

"Working for Julian, same thing I'm always doing. You have yourself to thank for that. Couldn't use Mommy's money to bail yourself out."

He snarls. "Last time I'll ask—what are you doing?" I feel the knife press deeper into my stomach. Even if I couldn't defend myself, he wouldn't really hurt me. At least not in any visible place, he couldn't explain it to his parents.

"Julian sent us. We have someone we need to woo tonight at the party. Someone with lots of money. Don't worry, we will be gone and out of your life again before the weekend is over."

Slice.

I feel it this time. The knife rips through my stomach, making a decent cut. For a second, I can't breathe; the slash hurts me deep and makes my eyes water. I wasn't prepared for him. But breaking a man's wrist and nose will him seek revenge.

It only takes me a second to recover before I punch him in the nose again, making it bleed.

"Fucking bitch! How the hell am I going to explain this?"

I hold my hand over my stomach. "Don't worry, I'm sure your mother hired the best makeup team. They can cover up the bruising. You can just say your nose started bleeding again."

He shoves me hard this time against my wound, making me lose my breath again.

"I'm warning you, Aria. Don't mess with my parents. Don't mess with me. Or I'll make you wish you were dead."

"There is nothing more you can do to me. I've been through too much."

His eyes turn golden with the evilness I didn't realize Hugo possessed until it was too late.

"I'm going to enjoy sleeping with you tonight, Aria. It's been too long."

He releases me. I take a deep breath as the door to our suite opens. I need to take care of my wound before any of the servants see it.

He pockets his knife, wiping the blood from his nose on the back of his hand.

"Unless you're ready to give me that divorce," he says under his breath, threatening more than a knife ever will.

No way in hell I am.

I duck into the bathroom to change my shirt and dress my wound before I spend the next two hours getting ready for the ball tonight.

I get a text from Zeke.

I open it. *Meet me in my room.*

I text back—*Can't. Two hours of hair and makeup.*

He doesn't respond, and my heart aches to be anywhere but here.

I don't want to spend the night with my ex while the man I love pretends to be engaged to another woman. I don't want to spend time with any of these people. But it's the only way to get back at them for what they did to me years ago. And it's the easiest way to steal a billion dollars.

CHAPTER 22
ZEKE

I'm wearing a damn tux.

A tux!

I've never worn a tux in my life. I never thought I was going to either. I've never been anywhere fancy enough to need one. A suit is as far as I've ever gone.

"Stop squirming," Nora says as she applies another layer of lipstick in our hotel suite.

The room is fucking huge—plenty big enough for the two of us to share.

"I'm not squirming," I pull at the bowtie at my neck.

Nora just glares at me in the mirror.

I sigh and stop messing with the tie. My hair is slicked back in a bun. My face is cleanshaven. I have enough cologne on that you can probably smell me coming from a hallway away.

Nora stands in her light blue dress. She seems to shimmer as she walks in the slinky dress.

"You look nice," I say.

She raises an eyebrow. "Just nice? This is Gucci. These are Cartier diamonds. This is better than nice."

I rub my neck. "Fine, you look beautiful. Better?"

575

She nods. "You look handsome as well."

I stare down at my tux. "Really? I feel like a penguin."

She laughs and loops her arm around my elbow.

I stiffen.

She notices. "You've got it bad, huh?"

"Yes," there is no reason not to tell her the truth.

"You're making Aria jealous, remember? Flirt with me and pretend it's her. Every time she looks at you, it will only make her want you more. Trust me."

I nod. I don't really have a choice. We've chosen Hugo's parents as our target. And they think Siren and Hugo are in a loving marriage. I can't walk in with her on my arm. This is the only way to get close enough to steal the money.

"Let's go. We wouldn't want to be late," Nora says.

"Of course not. We wouldn't want to be late to meeting all of Mrs. Bisset's rich, snooty, stuck up friends."

We head down the elevator and walk through the lobby toward the ballroom, looking very much the couple as Nora keeps her hand in the crook of my elbow and tells me funny stories about Siren to distract me and keep me smiling.

"Names?" a man asks when we reach the ballroom.

"Zeke Kane and soon to be Mrs. Kane," I smile, acting completely ridiculous and out of character as I kiss Nora on the cheek.

Nora smiles back, happy with my act.

The servant is pleased as well, because we're quickly allowed to enter.

"Holy fuck," I curse as I stare wide-eyed at the room.

Nora smirks. "Welcome to the world of the rich and famous." She snags us two champagne flutes off a tray and hands one to me.

"I'm going to need something stronger than this," I say.

She shakes her head. "First champagne, then wine at dinner. The hard stuff doesn't come out until later."

I moan.

"Come on, let's go find our table," Nora says, navigating me through the room like this is where she belongs.

"So I take it this isn't your first time in a room like this?" I ask as we find our seats at a table in the corner of the room.

"Nope, I was brought up in society life like this. But don't act like you don't have money or designer clothes. Just because you prefer a nice pair of jeans over a tux doesn't mean you don't have money."

"I do have money. I just would never spend it on things like this."

And then everyone's attention in the room turns toward a grand staircase at the far side of the room that no one has been on. A man has a microphone and is announcing the arrival of our hosts—Mrs. Bisset and Mr. Martinez.

Mr. Martinez escorts his wife effortlessly down the stairs as everyone cheers and thanks them. It feels like such a ridiculous show.

Then the announcer asks the room to stand and welcome back Mr. and Mrs. Martinez.

I hold my breath and wait as the double doors open, and Siren and Hugo step out.

He isn't using his crutches. Instead, he grips Siren's arm tightly, using her as his crutch, taking baby steps. It makes no sense for them to enter down the stairs. They should be entering through the regular entrance and take the elevator. But nothing about this world makes much sense to me.

Not the gold plated dinnerware, the real silver silverware, the crystal glasses, or the chandelier that's bigger than a car. Nor the thousands of dollars worth of flowers that are only going to be used a single night.

But when I turn my attention to Siren, finally taking her in, everything about this world suddenly makes sense. Siren is wearing a rose gold gown. A gown that hugs every curve. She shines brighter than anything in this room. The dress is sexy as hell—it has a long train on the back, and she wears heels that make her six feet tall.

Her makeup intensifies every feature on her face—her catlike eyes, plump lips, and pink cheeks. Her hair is curled and pinned up on her head, with only a few strands hanging down.

Siren is why a room like this exists. Without it, Siren would never wear a dress like that, and that would be a shame. She was born to be dressed in beautiful clothes and jewels.

Siren is beautiful in jeans and no makeup. She's beautiful in rags, but this version of Siren demands everyone's attention. No one speaks like they did for Hugo's parents. Everyone just stares, showing their appreciation for the couple with their silence.

Finally, the couple makes it down the stairs to Hugo's parents. Mrs. Bisset starts speaking into a microphone, welcoming everyone, introducing her son and beautiful daughter-in-law, and gushing about how excited she is to host a party in their honor.

It's clear she threw this ball not so Nora and I could see her event planning skills and what she could do for our fake wedding, but because she wants to show off her son and daughter-in-law.

Mrs. Bisset ends her speech, and everyone begins to scatter. I lose sight of Siren.

I stand, intending to go find her, when Nora touches my arm, telling me to stay.

I realize then that everyone is taking their seats to eat.

The dinner lasts two hours. A dinner where I had to listen to a lawyer talk about divorce settlements, and a wine connoisseur talk about how a different wine would have been better with the duck.

"These people are so boring," I say to Nora.

She chuckles. "Why do you think I learned to fly? So I could leave whenever I wanted."

I clink my wine glass with hers and drink to that.

Finally, our dessert plates are removed, and the dancing portion of the night starts. I swear this night is right out of the 1920s. I didn't know people still behaved like this.

"Dance with me," I say to Nora.

She smiles. "You only want to get closer to Siren."

I shrug. "We can also be in search of finding you a man for the night."

"How scandalous." Nora puts her hand over her mouth and fakes outrage.

I roll my eyes but smile as I lead her to the dance floor.

Hugo may have been able to hobble down the stairs and hide his injuries, but there is no way he can dance. This is my chance to get closer to Siren.

I lead Nora onto the dance floor even though I don't know how to dance to this classical music.

Nora laughs. "I'll lead."

She does a fine job, and I'm a fast learner, so we glide across the floor.

As expected, I don't see Siren on the dance floor. But after a few minutes, I do feel her gaze on the back of my head.

It lights my eyes up.

Nora, of course, notices as the song ends. "Go get our girl. Now's your chance. I need a moment to freshen up in the bathroom anyway."

I give her a little bow I've seen the other men do like she's a princess or something.

"Not bad, you're catching on. A few more hours in this world, and you'd be a pro."

"Nope, I'd have to chop off the hair. And that's not happening."

She laughs and then leaves the dance floor. I head in the direction of the intense feeling I have behind me, knowing it's Siren.

But I'm too focused on her that I don't see him.

"Zeke, a word," Hugo says in a crowd of people, ensuring I can't say no without making a scene. I nod angrily and follow Hugo away from the ballroom and out into a small balcony.

"Stay away from Aria," Hugo says.

So that's why he's so pissy.

I fold my arms looking bored. "No."

"It wasn't a request. You are in my world. Aria will be sleeping in my bed tonight. Do as I say, or she'll pay the consequences."

I notice he's wearing even more makeup than before, but it does nothing to hide the new bruising around his eye.

I smile. "Looks like Siren can take care of herself just fine."

He growls, but then it turns dangerous. "And I can take care of myself."

His words stun me. *What did he do?* I didn't see any physical mark on Siren, but if he raped her, I wouldn't see anything.

I grab the asshole by the neck and push him until he's dangling over the edge of the railing.

He grabs onto my wrist. "Don't threaten Siren. I swear if you touched her—"

"You'll what? You're up to something. Something Julian ordered. If you fail, he'll kill your friend—Lucy, was it?"

Fuck, I still haven't had time to move her and make sure she's safe.

I pull him back just a little.

"If I find out you touched her, or if you hurt her in any way, I'll kill you. That's a promise." And then I punch him hard in the gut and pull him back over the balcony.

I head back inside the ballroom just in time to see a ghost.

Kai Miller.

My boss, Enzo's Black's girl. The last person I wanted to see here. She stands taller than the last time I saw her. Her hair is twisted up, similar to Siren's. She demands attention and respect. I look around for Enzo but don't find him anywhere. *Why would she be here? And without him?*

He's here. He wouldn't let her out of his sight. *Unless...*

Nope, not going there.

Kai's eyes seem sad. But then her eyes cut to me. They land on me for less than a second. But in that second, I see everything—surprise, concern, hope. And then her face returns to vagueness, like she's unfazed by seeing me here.

She got my note.

I see the black scrunchie around her arm—a scrunchie I gave to her just before I was shot and lost to the sea.

I smile.

For a second, I wonder if I should run to Kai and go find Enzo with her. My heart hurts at seeing one of my closest friends again and not being able to hug her.

Our worlds will cross again. But tonight isn't that night. I'm here on a mission, not to reminisce with old friends. I'm doing this to prevent them from having one more enemy when I get back.

Just a little longer. Make sure Lucy is safe. Finish this job, learn about Julian's bank accounts, and then leave. If I can liquidate Julian's bank accounts until he has nothing, then he won't be able to come after me. Siren will have no money to chase me with. No army. I would have protected my friends.

CHAPTER 23
KAI

Watching one of my best friends die shook me to my very core, but finding his note in our vault telling me he was alive was one of the happiest moments of my life. Every day since, I've wanted to find him. I've wanted to chase after him. Hunt him down and bring him home to Enzo and me.

But I had to trust that Zeke had a good reason to not return to the living. That he needed to remain dead to those who loved him.

I honored that. *Really, I did.*

It was just coincidence that we are both in the same ballroom in Paris. I'm here to meet a man who has new technology to improve the security system on our yachts. It's an easy meeting, and Enzo decided to stay back with the kids instead of mingling with snooty, rich snobs. *He got the better job.*

Until I saw Zeke.

My heart stopped when I saw him in the flesh.

I knew he was alive all this time.

But seeing him, my heart lept. It came alive in a way it hasn't since falling in love with the man of my dreams and getting my own happily ever after.

I wanted to run to Zeke. I wanted to hug him and drag him home with me. Tell him whatever trouble he is in, whatever enemies he's made, we don't care. We are a family, and we fight our battles together.

But when I looked into Zeke's eyes, I knew today isn't the day to bring him home. That he still has battles he needs to face, alone.

I still don't understand why. And it's taking everything in me not to send my men after him.

But then I see her. The most beautiful woman is staring at me with complete fascination. As she looks from me and then searches for Zeke in the crowd, I make the connection. I know who this woman is. I may not know her name. I may not know her life story. But I know who she is. She's the reason Zeke hasn't come home.

He's in love with her.

She could be his happily ever after.

Or she could break his heart.

He needs more time. I'll give it to him, even though it kills me to keep his secret. To know he's alive while everyone else mourns his death.

Only a little longer, Zeke. I can't wait forever for you to come home.

CHAPTER 24
SIREN

This entire night has been horrible. I hate having to talk to rich people who don't give a shit about me. They just want to judge what I'm wearing and the fact that I haven't visited my in-laws in years.

If they only knew the truth, that I was here to steal a billion dollars from them, then they'd really have something to judge.

I spot Hugo and Zeke head out on the balcony to talk or fight; I'm not sure. I want to go with them, but I know Zeke doesn't need me to fight his battles. He can handle Hugo just fine. And this gives me a chance to enact the plan without Hugo noticing.

I need to find Mr. Martinez. The goal is simple. Steal his phone and hope it has the security information we need to hack their bank account. I'm a bit rusty when it comes to hacking, but Zeke says he has the skills if we can get the phone. Or that he knows someone he can contact to hack it if he can't handle it.

So tonight's job is simple. Get the damn phone from Mr. Martinez. Should be easy enough since he always has his phone on him. But he's always surrounded by people, and he's not exactly my biggest fan, so getting close to him has been difficult without Mrs. Bisset stepping in and wanting to introduce me to another couple.

I spot Mr. Martinez ordering a whiskey from the bar.

Now's my chance. I make my way through the crowd of people toward him, but something odd catches my attention as I walk—a woman wearing a black scrunchie around her wrist.

Very odd for such a formal night.

I can't stop looking at her. I take in everything about her—dark hair, olive skin, sparkly skin-hugging dress, high heels, diamonds, and a black scrunchie on her wrist.

A scrunchie completely out of place. I can't take my eyes off the scrunchie. I have this weird feeling I've seen it before. A sense of déjà vu washes over me; I'm suspended in time.

Who is this woman?

Finally, I let my eyes drift up. She's deep in a conversation with two men, completely controlling them with her words and body language. She's here on business.

But she must feel me staring because she turns her head in my direction. Our exchange of glances is the most bizarre thing I've ever felt, and yet, it's the most peaceful.

She gives me a tight-lipped smile, nodding at me as if she knows a secret I don't and approves.

I look at her in confusion, which makes her smile kindly at me.

Then all at once, it hits me who she is. She's from Zeke's world before. She thought he was dead, which is why she carries the scrunchie with her everywhere.

My heart breaks for her and for me. It's clear she loves Zeke as much as I do. *Has Zeke seen her? Does he know she's here?*

The woman shakes her head, as if to say, 'No, don't tell him.'

Apparently, she's a mind reader too.

I frown. This woman is beautiful and strong. She's probably not a liar like me. She's probably always told Zeke the truth.

How many women in Zeke's life do I have to compete with? Lucy? This woman? How many more?

Zeke is easy to fall in love with, so it wouldn't surprise me if he had hoards of women in love with him.

I see Mr. Martinez moving out of the corner of my eye toward the stairs. He's leaving for the night.

This is my last chance. I have to go now. But I want to ask this woman so many questions. I want to know how to protect Zeke. I want to know how to return him to the world he belongs in.

Choose now.

Stick to the plan.

So instead of questioning the woman who holds all the answers to Zeke, I head after Mr. Martinez.

There isn't much time for a plan on how to get the phone, so I do the only thing I can think of. I bump into him. I retrieve the phone easily from his pocket and hold it begin my back.

"I'm so sorry, Mr. Martinez," I say.

He huffs and then continues up the stairs.

When I turn back, the woman I saw before was gone. It was almost like I'd seen a ghost.

I turn toward the balcony and see Hugo and Zeke re-entering the ballroom.

Both men spot me.

I sigh. And then plaster a fake smile on my face as I make my way over to them.

I nod at Zeke as I pass him, slipping the phone into his jacket pocket. But that's all the interaction I give him. He needs to go find Nora and spend the night hacking into the phone and bank account.

"Ready to leave?" I ask Hugo.

He holds his hand against his stomach like he's in pain.

I grin. *What did Zeke do to you?*

He slips his hand around my arm, using me like a crutch. We walk slowly to the elevator. I consider calling for a wheelchair, but I know he wouldn't allow it. So instead of a five-minute walk to the suite, it takes us twenty.

Finally, we get to the door, I unlock it, and once Hugo is inside, I release his hold on me. I don't care if he never makes it to the bedroom.

I walk straight to the dressing room to remove my dress and caked-on makeup. I spend a long time scrubbing my face clean. I put on pajama pants and T-shirt before heading to bed. Somehow, Hugo has found his way to the bed and is rolled over on his side, facing away from me. And from what I can tell, he's shirtless.

Please let him be wearing pants.

I walk around to the far side of the bed and pull the covers back that have already been turned down by the maids.

I can't tell what Hugo is wearing, but I see the waistband of something, so he isn't naked.

"Touch me, and I'll kill you," I say, pulling the covers up.

Hugo doesn't respond. Maybe he's asleep.

I close my eyes and immediately feel the pull of sleep. Tonight exhausted me. I need to shut my brain off. I can't think about Hugo, or stealing Mr. Martinez's phone, or the woman with the scrunchie, or Zeke. I just need to shut the world out and decompress for a few hours; then I can face the world tomorrow.

Sleep pulls me hard. When I drink too much, like tonight, sleep comes easily and hard.

Sleep.

HE'S HERE. HE CAME FOR ME—ZEKE.

I feel his presence. I feel him pressed up against me, his erection at my ass begging for entrance.

I smile and lift my legs to allow him better access.

He pushes his cock between my legs but doesn't enter me yet.

I feel his rough hands at my breasts. *Yes, tease me.*

His hands are rougher than I remember. He's not gentle, but then he never really is. But this is different—frantic, almost angry.

Something's not right.

Stop.

Wake up.

Tell him to stop.

"Stop," I whisper.

But he doesn't stop touching me, pushing himself on me.

I start fighting back, but my eyes are too heavy to open. *Wake up! Don't let this happen!*

I fight harder.

My tears are stinging my eyes.

"Stop," I say louder.

He doesn't listen. Zeke always listens. This isn't Zeke. The man hurting me is someone much worse...

Hugo.

His name on my tongue wakes me up, jolting me awake. He's on top of me, using the pull of sleep to try and have his way with me.

Fucking bastard.

My arms are pinned, tied together, and pushed over my head. My shirt is pushed up; my pants are ripped and barely hang onto my waist.

"Stop," I say calmly, hoping my calm will end this frenzy.

It doesn't.

"Hugo," I say, and my voice catches his attention. He looks at me, past the anger, and really looks at me.

"Stop, please. This isn't you. You aren't this person."

He shakes his head. "You don't know who I am or what I've become. Not anymore."

"Yes, I do. I fell in love with you. I know the depths of your heart. I could even love you again. But I won't if you do this. There is no way to ask forgiveness for this. If you do this, there is no going back."

He pauses as if deciding, but I don't trust Hugo to make the right decision. I've been manipulating him this whole time, distracting him until I could get my hands free. And finally, I did. I'm not going to wait to see if he has a heart. I protect myself at all costs.

I snap his neck, immediately putting him into a deep sleep. He won't wake up for several hours.

I pant heavily, and then I push him off me onto the other side of the bed.

I need air. I can't breathe.

I get up from the bed, realizing how close I came to being raped. If he was better at tying my hands or if he had managed to tie up my legs before I woke up, I wouldn't have been able to protect myself. He would have raped me. He could have killed me if he wanted.

I head to the bathroom and splash some water on my face. And then I stare at myself in the mirror.

That was close. Too close. I'm better than this. I don't let anyone get close. I don't let myself be vulnerable. I protect myself. I save myself. Because no other man will.

Zeke—his name floats into my head. Zeke would have saved me.

I shake my head. He would have wanted to. But he wasn't here. He didn't save me. I saved myself. I can't rely on Zeke. I can't rely on any man. I'm my only protector. And I almost failed.

CHAPTER 25
ZEKE

Nora wanted me to stay in our hotel room all night and work on breaking into the phone. But I was able to break into the phone within five minutes. The phone had a simple password, and his bank account was accessible right on the app.

Siren was right, Hugo's parents are loaded. We can steal the billion dollars from them. We have everything we need.

Tomorrow, we can leave. But tonight, we are stuck here.

"Just sleep, Zeke. Time will go by faster if you sleep. Tomorrow we have a long day of flying back. Sleep, you'll see Siren tomorrow," Nora says before yawning.

"I can't sleep. Not with that fucker sleeping in the bed next to her."

"They won't share a bed. Their suite is bigger than ours."

I raise an eyebrow. "They will share a bed, or the maids will know they are fighting."

"Oh."

"Yea...oh."

Suddenly, I get the strangest feeling. A feeling that disturbs me to the bones.

"Something isn't right," I say, running my hand through my hair as I grab the room key.

"Where are you going?" Nora asks, jumping up like her tiny frame is going to stop me.

"I need to make sure Siren is alright."

"Zeke, you can't. She's fine. She's a big girl. She can protect herself. Just try to sleep or watch TV or something. We can check on her in the morning."

I look at Nora. She doesn't get it, but Siren and I share a connection I don't understand. I can feel when she's in pain or happy. I just know when she's experiencing the worst emotions.

"This can't wait until morning. She's in trouble," I say.

"Zeke..." Nora starts again.

I open the door and stop.

"Be careful, please. And let me know when you find her, and she's alright. Or I'll worry."

I smile. "Will do."

I don't know which room Siren and Hugo are staying in. I just know the room is the best.

So I head to the elevator bank and hit the top floor, hoping that when I get there, it will be obvious which room is theirs. If not, I'll be sneaking into a lot of suites until I find the right one. Nothing is stopping me right now; something is wrong. And if Hugo touched her, I'm going to kill him.

The elevator doors open to the top floor, and there are almost as many rooms up here as there are on my floor. That is until you walk to the far corner. There is only one door for most of this corridor. It's by far the biggest room in the hotel.

This is their room.

I lean my ear against the door, trying to hear if they are awake, but it's silent. They have top-level security here, so if I don't seem like I belong, a guard will be here in minutes to escort me away.

I lift my card to the door for the cameras, as I slip the small screwdriver below the keycard to unlock the door. But the cameras only see me flash my keycard, and the light turns green.

I carefully step inside, putting the tool and card back into my pocket as I step into the darkness. From what I can make out, the suite seems a few rooms bigger than mine but is otherwise decorated the same. With gold and art, and a lot of breakable shit.

I head through the living quarters toward the bedrooms. I poke my head in the first two, but as I knew, Siren isn't in either. That leaves the master bedroom, where they both are.

The door is cracked, but not closed.

I stand next to it, listening carefully, but I only hear the gentle sound of them breathing.

Hmm. That's weird? I thought for sure something was wrong.

Slowly, I open the door, thankful the door doesn't creak, and then I walk into the dark room.

Hugo is sleeping on one side, and Siren is sleeping on the other.

I walk over to her side to study her closer and make sure she's okay. She seems to be sleeping deeply, her breathing deep and heavy.

I pull out my phone and text Nora that Siren is fine, asleep in her bed.

I should leave her to sleep. I should head back, but I can't stand being so close to Siren and not having her. Not tasting her. Not making definitively sure she's okay.

So I lean down, and then I put my hand over her mouth to keep her from screaming and waking Hugo up.

She immediately bucks and punches me hard in the nose, fighting for her life, not realizing it's me.

Yea, I made a mistake with the hand over the mouth move.

"Siren, it's me, Zeke," I whisper.

But she keeps trying to fight me, even as I pull her out of the bed and carry her to the bathroom. I lock the door and turn on the lights so she can see me.

Her eyes open when the lights flicker on, and I remove my hand from her mouth and step back.

"It's me," I say again.

She takes a second to catch her breath, her eyes blinking, assuring herself that I'm standing here in her bathroom, and this isn't a dream.

Then she runs to me and collapses against my chest, her arms wrapping around my waist tightly.

I grab her, holding me hard against me.

I was right. Something is clearly wrong.

But I don't ask her about it. If she wants to talk, she will, when she's ready.

"How did you know to come?" she finally asks.

"I don't know. I just knew something was wrong."

She nods into my chest.

And then her hands are working their way up my body to my chest, then neck. She pulls me down, and my head dips to meet her for a perfect kiss.

A kiss that tells me everything I need to know. She's scared. Me being here is everything. *Thank you. Don't ever leave.*

I push my tongue into her mouth, fisting her hair, keeping her lips against mine. They say my reply for me. *I'm here. I'm not leaving.*

I want to add—*ever*. But that's a promise I can't keep. A promise I shouldn't want to keep.

I grab her ass and lift her up until she's sitting on the vanity. We need a different kind of connection right now.

"God, I love fucking you everywhere, but someday I'd really like to fuck you in a bed again. Nothing beats a bed."

She laughs nervously. "Agreed."

Nervous? Why?

I step between her spread legs studying her for a second, but she just pulls my face back to hers to kiss me harder, not wanting me to see her anxiety.

So I ignore it for now. Fucking her is the best medicine to reduce the nerves she's feeling at whatever Hugo threatened her with.

I put everything I have into the kiss. On her lips, her neck, the perfect spot at the base of her neck before her skin disappears in her shirt.

But I'm greedy. I want all of her.

I grab her shirt and lift it up over her head before I take her nipple in my mouth.

She stiffens.

I stop.

What's wrong? Did I bite down too roughly? What's going on?

And then I see it.

The bandage over her stomach.

Siren tries to push my hands away, but I have to know. I need to know what happened to her.

I put my hand on the bandage, wishing my hands alone would be enough to take away her pain. I look into her eyes, desperate to see what's beneath the bandage, but I won't remove it without her permission.

She sucks in a breath for just a second and then nods.

Carefully, I peel back the bandage, keeping my eyes on her. Trying to reassure her that whatever lies beneath, I will get revenge for. I will find a way to fix it.

When I see the gash on her smooth stomach, my heart hardens. I'm pissed. Beyond pissed. All I see is red. I want to murder whoever did this, and I don't have to ask who.

But this wound isn't fresh. This happened earlier. This is what Hugo was referring to on the balcony.

"What else?" I ask, my voice softer than I feel. I need to know what else Hugo did. *What had her so scared tonight?* Because this injury didn't cause her fear. She fought back and hurt Hugo as badly as he hurt her. A gash on the stomach, while looking bad, is only skin deep. He didn't really hurt her. I'm not even sure it will scar long term.

But he did something. Said something. Did something that scared her in a way this didn't.

"Truth or si—" I start, hoping the game we play will convince her to talk. Or at least give her a way out if she doesn't want to talk where I can't get angry with her.

But she presses her fingers to my lips, silencing me.

She bites her lip, then opens her mouth. "I want both. To talk and to sin. Don't make me choose."

"You can have both."

She nods. "When I was asleep..." her voice catches, and she takes a deep breath before starting again. "When I was asleep, Hugo tried to rape me."

Her words hurt worse than a bullet to the heart. The snake tried to hurt her. *Tried, she said tried, right?* I'm not just hoping that he didn't do more than attempt.

I wait. She has more to say.

"I woke up, and he had my arms tied up. He was on top of me, ripping my clothes off."

I stare down at her pants for the first time, realizing her pants are ripped.

"Fuck," I exhale, needing to get rid of some of my anger before I explode.

"I was able to keep him talking until my hands got free."

Thank god.

"And then I snapped his neck."

I look at the door. *The bastard deserved worse.*

"He's not dead; he's just passed out."

I nod. But he won't live for much longer.

Siren grabs my cheeks and turns my face back to her. Hesitantly, she leans down until our lips are close, but not touching. Her eyes are watery. Her hands tremble. Her throat is tight.

But she takes a deep breath over my lips, and I know I'm easing her pain. Just being with me does that to her. Just like it's easing my anger.

"Make me forget, Zeke. Make me yours."

There is an unspoken sentence she's not saying—make love to me Zeke. She's not asking me to fuck her. She's asking for gentle, for slow. For something that feels like love and not lust. She wants to be taken care of. The only thing I could possibly want more at the moment is to destroy the man who made her feel this vulnerable.

I hear a man stirring outside the bathroom door. But Siren doesn't. She's focused on me.

I can kill two birds with one stone. I can make love to her, and let Hugo know he will never touch her again. That his time is limited. That Siren is mine, not his.

I had hoped to fuck her quietly in the bathroom, but now, I'm going to make sure Hugo and every other person in this hotel know exactly who Siren belongs to—me.

I kneel down in front of her, kissing over her stomach wound. Her eyes light up—big, gorgeous dark eyes that reveal how good my lips feel on her stomach.

I hook my fingers around the waistband of her pants and slowly bring them down, keeping an eye on her the whole time and letting her feel in control. In control enough to keep any memories of what Hugo tried to do out of her memory.

Carefully, I spread her legs as I kiss every spot of skin from her toes to her thighs, taking my time as I worship her body with my mouth.

She grips the edge of the counter, lets her head fall back, but keeps her eyes locked on me. I can't break eye contact with her. She needs to know it's me doing the wonderful things to her body.

This is as intimate as it gets. She's trusting me with her pain, her heart. I make love to her without falling myself.

I can do this. I can make love without being in love.

A soft, throaty cry escapes her lips. It's beautiful and painful and tells me everything she's not saying. *Stop the pain, ease the pain. You're the only man who can.*

Dammit—if that doesn't make me fall a little, nothing will.

"I got you," I say, gently opening her legs for my mouth to find her delicious pussy. I'm slower than I've ever been with her. Taking my time as I tenderly kiss over her. Not yet using my tongue, just lighting up every nerve and bringing all the blood south, so her head doesn't have to think anymore.

I want Siren to come.

I want her to explode on my lips, on my hand, on my cock. As I finally let my tongue out to flick over her clit, I realize the main difference between fucking and making love, and it's not how fast you go. The difference is sex is about mutual pleasure. It's about chasing your own orgasm as well as hers. Making love is selfless. It's putting her needs above my own until her needs are all that matter. Siren is all that matters.

Looking at her now, naked and spread for me, sharing a vulnerable secret to show me she isn't always strong. She was inches away from failing to protect herself. She isn't a seductive manipulative monster like I thought. She's a woman doing her best to survive in very much a man's world.

Every man in this world is a danger to her. Every man is bigger. Stronger. More powerful.

And every man in the underworld is capable of rape and murder.

Siren is always vulnerable.

But not anymore.

Because whether she likes it or not, I'm here to protect her.

I lick her slow, finding every button to push between her legs. Exploring her like I've never explored her before. Always keeping my eyes on her. Watching to ensure she's enjoying every second.

I see it the moment she's mine completely. Her eyes widen, she bites down on her lip to hold in her moan, and she grips the counter like she's holding onto a bucking horse.

I put my hand over hers, squeezing gently, reminding her I'm in this with her. That I'm not letting go.

Her teeth rake over her bottom lip as her body tries to contain her impending orgasm, but I've built her so slowly for so long that the explosion is going to greater than any we've experienced.

"Zeke! Yes, fuck Zeke! Yes!" she screams as my tongue dips inside her just in time to feel her contracting around me, her sweet taste filling my mouth. A taste I can never get enough of.

I give her a minute to come down from her high. I continue to kneel in front of her, watching her, worshipping her.

Finally, she touches my face as her cheeks flush. "More." Her eyes light up with what she wants to do next.

Thank fuck, because I'm going to die if I don't get to fuck her soon.

CHAPTER 26
SIREN

Zeke found me. He would have been too late to protect me from Hugo if Hugo had succeeded in raping me, but he would have been here to comfort me and kill Hugo for what he did.

I don't care about any of that. I care about Zeke kneeling in front of me like he would give me the world if I asked.

Zeke came to find me without even changing out of the tuxedo he hates but looking hot as fuck in. The pants show off the curve of his ass, and the jacket bulges around his biggest muscles—his arms and chest. There is just something about a bad boy with tattoos and a man bun all dressed up in something refined that just does something to me.

But what has my toes curling and my heart thumping the most is the way he took care of me. The way he put my needs above his own and made me come in a way he never has before.

He did what I wanted even though I couldn't speak the words—*he made love to me.*

I need *more.* I want the delicious stretch as he enters me. I want his thick muscles flexing over me as he drives inside me. I want to see the soft expression on his face turn carnal as he loses control.

Zeke is still kneeling in front of me, so I lean forward and brush my hands inside his jacket, pushing it off his shoulders. He lets it fall to the floor.

Then I grab his bowtie, tugging it up until he's standing in front of me.

For the last fifteen minutes, Zeke has kept eye contact with me. He's looked into my soul, knowing I needed the deepest connection with him to keep from breaking. To keep from reliving how close I was to being violated.

But my goal now is to make his eyes roll back from pleasure, just not yet.

I undo his bowtie slowly, every movement feeling as much like a tease as our lips brushing together.

The bowtie falls to the floor. I begin undoing every shirt button slowly.

"You're killing me," he says so softly. So kindly. The gentle giant. The man capable of so much pain showing kindness.

My eyes flutter. This isn't what lust feels like. This is what love feels like. But I don't say it. I can't. Because if I tell him I love him, and he doesn't say it back, I will die. Everything I've done for months now will have been for nothing. These last seven years would be for nothing, because fate put in this position—to save Zeke.

Saving Zeke matters more than just saving him for myself. Zeke is meant for greatness. Only he can save more. Save the masses. While I can only save him.

Slowly, Zeke removes his shirt while I unbutton and unzip his pants.

He doesn't wait for me this time. His pants and boxer briefs fall to the floor, and we are both naked.

I suck in a breath. Zeke is standing between my legs, our eyes still together. He doesn't drive into me immediately. He holds my head and locks our lips while maintaining eye contact.

He lets my hands explore his muscular body, getting reacquainted with him. He lifts me from the counter and turns us to the door. At first, I don't know why, and then I hear him—Hugo.

He's ensuring Hugo can't get to me by fucking me against the door. He's letting Hugo hear what Zeke gets that he doesn't.

It turns me on to see how much Zeke needs Hugo to know that I'm Zeke's, no one else's.

"This okay?" he asks, his cock resting at my entrance as he holds me, my back against the door.

I can barely hear Hugo anymore, but I want him to hear everything. I want him to hear what it sounds like when I'm fucked by a real man. By a man I want. A man I love.

This is what Hugo could have had if he had loved me back. If he hadn't betrayed me. If he never tried to hurt me.

"Fuck me, Zeke."

His cock is inside me in one slow stroke.

I suck in a breath.

"No, this isn't fucking. This is more," he says. His forehead rests against mine, our eyes as close as possible without going cross.

He moves inside me. "So much more."

Zeke takes his time thrusting inside me. My slick walls are welcoming him in hungrily. My body is already coming alive for a second time around him.

I kiss him, pushing my tongue and pulling for everything he can give me as my fingers claw at his back.

And he gives me everything. Every thrust. Grunt. Moan. Every scream he has.

He hits each spot he should and somehow finds new spots inside me to turn on and drive me wild.

"Siren! Jesus, I'm close, Siren!"

I tangle my hand in his hair. "Zeke! Yes, Zeke!"

We come, slamming hard against the wall, until it's undeniable what we are doing—fucking each other's brains out.

Zeke continues to thrust, making sure he pulls every drop of my orgasm from me, but he never loses eye contact with me. I'm his world right now.

"Zeke, I lo—oh, fuck!" I say, my feelings almost slipping out.

Zeke just kisses me. I don't know if he realizes what I was about to say, or he just wanted to kiss me.

I hear the angry pounding on the other side of the door.

"I think we might have woken him up. Oops," Zeke says, but he isn't sorry at all.

He stares at the tub. "We should soak, but I don't want you anywhere near Hugo for a moment longer than you need to be," he says.

"We can take a bath in your room. I'm not staying here. Not a moment longer."

He nods. "I don't think we should stay in this hotel tonight. Not after..."

I frown. I'm not sure what he means. Yes, we fucked, and Hugo knows about it, but I doubt he will tell anyone. Unless he thinks one of the night guards heard us, which is definitely possible.

"Okay. Then we will drive or catch a train out of here and fly out on the first flight tomorrow."

He nods.

We both reluctantly get dressed. Neither of us wants to leave this room. Out there, we have to face the world. In here, we only have to face each other.

Once we are both dressed, Zeke asks, "Ready?"

I nod.

Zeke takes my hand and keeps me behind his body, shielding me from whatever we will face on the other side of the door. He switches the lock, grabs the handle and turns, pushing the door open.

Hugo is sitting on the edge of the bed, waiting for us.

As soon as we emerge, he springs up and tries to grab me, but Zeke only moves in front of me more, pushing me further back, shielding me.

"Aria is my wife! She's not your plaything. She's my wife!" Hugo yells.

"No! She's not your damn wife! Maybe on paper, but only because you set some trap in the prenup she signed. But in every other sense, she's mine!" Zeke yells.

She's mine.

I shiver, his words washing through me until they warm my soul. *I'm his. He's mine.*

But for how much longer? The doubt immediately creeps in.

Zeke lets go of my hand, and the looming danger raises the hair on my arms.

I reach for my gun but realize I'm an idiot; I didn't sleep with a gun. I was worried Hugo would grab it while I was sleeping and use it on me. Probably smart since he was able to pin me down in my sleep. *If he had had a gun, what would he have done to me?*

I'm defenseless expect for my fists and wit, standing in my pajamas. Zeke, though, isn't defenseless. He has his gun out and aimed at Hugo within seconds.

I knew I felt danger, but it thought it was an outside source coming in. I didn't realize the danger was coming from Zeke.

"Zeke, what are you doing?" I ask, trying to keep my voice calm.

Zeke ignores me. He looks at Hugo, who has his hands up and fear in his eyes as he takes a step back. Hugo is no match for Zeke. Hugo is just a dumb man who got lost in a world he didn't belong in. Sure, he can fight, but not like Zeke. Hugo isn't ignorant enough to think the security in this hotel would be able to protect him.

"You hurt Siren. You slashed her stomach. You tried to take from her without her permission. Do you remember what I said I would do if you hurt Siren?"

"You said you would kill me," Hugo answers his voice dry.

Zeke nods. "I'm a man of my word."

"No!" I scream, dashing in front of Hugo to protect him.

Zeke blinks rapidly, not expecting me to save this disgusting man again. And shocked from the fact that he almost shot me, instead of Hugo.

"Siren, move," Zeke says.

"No, you can't kill Hugo," I answer. *There is so much you don't know, Zeke. Just trust me. This is what saving me looks like—not getting revenge.*

Zeke's eyes don't leave mine. He will do what I ask even though it pisses him off to not kill Hugo.

Zeke drops his gun wordlessly and walks to the door.

I glare at Hugo.

"Thank you," Hugo says, realizing Zeke really meant to kill him.

"I didn't save you for you."

"I know."

I follow Zeke out the door and back to his room for a brief second to throw his things in a bag and give me time to change out of pajamas and into Nora's clothes. I didn't bother to pack up my own.

Zeke doesn't talk to me the entire time. Nora notices but doesn't ask what's going on between us. She also doesn't ask why we are packing up in the middle of the night.

We got what we came here for—the phone. Hopefully, it's enough to hack into their bank accounts to steal the money.

I look at Zeke, who will no longer meet my eyes. It's going to take a long time for him to be warm to me again, if he ever does. In Zeke's eyes, I chose Hugo over him. I didn't.

I was choosing myself. Protecting myself. And if there was a way I could have chosen Zeke, I would have. But he wasn't even an option. He will never be an option.

We ride a train and then a plane. This time I sit with Nora. There won't be any sneaking off to go fuck in the bathroom on this flight—not this time.

When Zeke finally starts snoring in his chair across the aisle, I bury my head in Nora's chest and let the tears fall. I got what I wanted. I got Zeke to claim me as his. I got one lovemaking session. Then it was all taken away a second later because of Hugo.

"Shh, it will be okay. You're the strongest woman I know. And Zeke knows that. He'll come around," Nora says.

I am strong.

But Zeke won't come around. That hurt doesn't go away.

The good news is I've finally got the missing piece back from Hugo. Any love I once felt for him is now gone. The bad news is all of my heart belongs to Zeke Kane—a man who vowed to stop protecting it. A man who gave me one moment of vulnerability, only to take away any thought of love a second later.

I was hurt by Hugo. I paid for seven years for the pain Hugo caused me. But Zeke has the power to hurt me for forever. The love I have for Zeke is different than the love I had for Hugo. The love I had for Hugo only went surface deep, but the love I have for Zeke is down to the depths of my soul.

Hugo was a slimy man looking for his next lay. Zeke, whether he admits it or not, is the most loyal man and can only do forever relationships. He's too loyal not to be with a woman who will one day become his wife.

And Zeke thinks I'm too disloyal to ever earn that title.

CHAPTER 27

ZEKE

The plane ride back takes a thousand hours. At least that's how the nine-hour plane ride feels.

The distance between where Siren sat on the plane and I sat was less than ten feet. But it might as well have been an ocean between us. Neither of us looked at each other. Or acknowledged each other. We acted like strangers.

A complete one-eighty from how we behaved on the first flight.

But if I thought the plane ride was long, it was the easy part. Once we said goodbye to Nora, the truck ride back to my house was ten times longer.

Again we didn't speak. Or look at each other. We sat in silence. But that didn't mean we both weren't thinking about the other.

I'm missing something. I know I am. But what?

In the bathroom in Paris, Siren would have told me anything. She would have told me the entire truth. She would have vowed to be on my side—declared her love forever.

When we were making love, it felt like that's what we were doing.

But the second we stepped out into the bedroom, everything changed. I no longer felt like Siren and I were on the same team. We were all on different teams. All fighting for ourselves.

Then Siren chose to save Hugo.

Is that her thing? She just likes saving people? Even scum like Hugo?

Or does she still love him? She said she didn't, not anymore, but I can't figure out why she won't let me kill him, especially after what he did to her that night.

A part of me says I should have done it. I don't take orders from Siren. And Hugo deserved to die more than most men I've killed.

But I looked in her damn eyes, the same soft, warm eyes that fell apart at the pain he did to her. The same eyes that held my entire world when I made love to her. And I couldn't betray those eyes.

So Hugo lives, for now.

I need to know why she saved him, for my own sanity. But I have to protect myself. She can't keep hurting me. And whether for self-preservation or because she's devious, she keeps lying to me by hiding the truth. She may not lie with her words, but she lies by hiding the truth, which is just as vile.

I sling my bag over my shoulder when we get to my house. Siren waits for me to unlock the front door before entering, which is unlike her. But she doesn't wait for me to invite her in once I open the door.

I head to the fridge and pull out stuff to make a sandwich. I'm starving. Before I realize what I'm doing, I make one for Siren.

She sits down at my dining room table with her laptop and two coffees. *When did she make those?*

I put one of the sandwiches in front of her. Then I sit down kitty-corner to her with my own sandwich and drink the coffee she placed in front of me.

Neither of us thanks the other for getting the food and coffee. Our eyes both betray us, saying our thanks anyway.

I pull out Mr. Martinez's stolen phone.

We stare at our electronic devices for a second as we drink some of the coffee and eat part of the sandwiches. Then we get to work, still in silence. Siren on her laptop. Me on the phone. Both of us doing business without words.

I pull up Mr. Martinez's bank account on the phone. It has over a billion dollars in it. She picked our target well.

She looks at it and types some more into the computer, probably pulling up Julian's bank information so we can make the transfer.

Her job is easy since Julian gave her the information needed to make a transfer.

Suddenly her mouth drops open.

"I, um..." she speaks for the first time.

"What?" I ask, my first word to her since leaving Hugo in the Parisian hotel room.

"Julian gave me an empty bank account to make the transfer into. But I was nosy and had some time on the plane, so I've been working on hacking into his main bank accounts and..."

She turns the computer screen so I can see what she's looking at.

"Holy shit," I say, my jaw dropping to the floor and my tired eyes widening at the sight of the number on the screen.

It's a huge number. Like Bill Gates big. No, bigger. Like Jeff Bezos big—no, double that.

What is Julian Reed up to? Or better yet, who is Julian Reed? He's not the small-time drug dealer turned human trafficker I thought he was. This man is loaded. He has more money than my old boss Enzo Black ever dreamed of having.

Julian is more dangerous than I realized. *Has he been playing me all along?* He sure as hell doesn't need the billion dollars we are transferring to him.

I look at Siren, studying her reaction. She's a good actress, but the shock on her face looks real enough. And she's doing more than just staring; she's running her hand through her hair, she's grabbing at her chest like she's having a panic attack. I don't know how you fake that.

"Siren? Are you okay?" I ask, standing as she does, prepared for her to faint or be sick.

She nods. "Um...can you finish the transfer?"

"Yes, but—"

"Good. Make the transfer, and then tell Julian we finished the task." She starts walking toward the door.

"Where are you going?"

"I'm sorry. I have to go," she grabs the door with sorrow and fear in her eyes. She's gone, without a word or explanation. I'm left to deal with finishing the job, the shock of this new information about Julian, and the unanswered questions that always arise with Siren. For every answer I get, I end up with more questions.

I stare back at the computer. I need to finish. Transfer the money into the empty account and act like I don't know Julian has money. I need to make sure Lucy is safe ASAP.

Then I need to do more digging into Julian Reed. Because if he's after Enzo Black and our family, I'm not sure we are going to be able to stop him.

CHAPTER 28
SIREN

Everything I thought I knew was a lie.

Everything.

EVERYTHING.

I thought Julian Reed was an evil man.

I thought he was a drug dealer.

Sometimes a human trafficker.

I thought he made above-average money, more than any normal person needed to survive.

I thought he had power, but that it was limited.

All of those facts are wrong. None of them are the whole truth.

Julian Reed is worse than evil. I always thought of him as the devil, but now I know he's the richest devil in all of history.

He may be a drug dealer, but you don't make that kind of money selling drugs from a tiny island.

He may sell people, but not billions of dollars worth of people.

And Julian's power isn't limited; it's far-reaching. He may be the most powerful man on the planet. If another person has more money than him, I've never heard of it.

How?

Why?

How did I not know Julian Reed has this much money and power? Because he doesn't act like it. He acts like he's just growing his business. Like he isn't the most powerful man in the world.

Maybe it's because he isn't? Maybe he's just holding onto the money for his boss?

But Julian Reed doesn't act like he has a boss. I don't think he could handle having a boss. But I also didn't think the man was capable of having this much money.

It doesn't matter what I assumed. It doesn't matter that Julian manipulated me as much as I manipulate other men.

I need to put all of that aside. I have more important things to do now that I know this information.

I need to find out everything I can before Julian realizes I know about his wealth, which could only mean a few hours with the resources he probably has.

Most importantly, I need to find a way to protect as many people as I can. And I know exactly who I'm starting with.

CHAPTER 29
ZEKE

"The billion dollars is in your account," I say to Julian. We are standing on his back deck while Julian smokes a cigar and looks out at the view of the ocean. This isn't his usual spot, but it is a particularly nice day. I guess I understand why we are outside enjoying the sun.

But I can't enjoy anything. Not until I protect the people I love.

"Excellent work. You did that quickly. Three days? Impressive."

"You aren't even going to check your account balance?"

"Aria sent me the bank report earlier today. I already checked."

Siren.

I haven't seen her in twenty-four hours. *Has she been here this whole time? Or did Julian send her on a mission?*

"What did you do to Lucy? Where is she?" I ask, trying to keep the anger out of my voice. I need answers, not revenge.

After I transferred the money, I immediately got in contact with my guys closest to Seattle. They went in search of Lucy. But she was already gone—someone got there first.

I should have moved her sooner; the second Siren gave me her address. I didn't want to disrupt her life unless I had to, but it was the wrong decision.

Julian puffs on his damn cigar. I want to shove it down his throat and suffocate him with it.

"Seattle, as far as I know. I brought my team back when Aria agreed to the date. I kept my word and haven't gone after Lucy. Once I make a promise, I always keep it." He exhales a perfect circle of smoke.

I pull my gun out and aim it at him. I'm done being nice. I need answers.

"Where is Lucy?" I ask again.

He shakes his head. "Shoot me, and you'll never find out. If you want me to find Lucy for you, we can make a deal of our own."

Julian doesn't seem the least bit scared at the sight of my gun. I've threatened him too many times without actually killing him.

Dammit.

I lower my gun. "I'm done making deals with you. I've made my last deal. Two down. Three to go."

"Ready for the next round?" Julian asks with a grin. He knows I'm not ready until I figure out where Lucy is.

I ignore him and walk out. I'll get every contact I can find that has nothing to do with Enzo Black looking for Lucy. But I suspect they won't find her. Whoever took her hid her well.

I walk out of the house toward my truck when I spot Siren heading toward Julian's house.

It all clicks.

"Did you move Lucy? Did you take her?" I ask, my voice threatening. No one touches Lucy without paying the consequences. Not even Siren.

"Yes," she answers without hesitation.

I grab Siren's arms and push her against the side of my truck.

"What the hell? Why?"

She winces but doesn't immediately answer.

"Where is she?" I ask, almost losing it.

"I can't tell you the—"

But I don't let her finish. The second she says she can't tell me, Siren becomes dead to me.

Siren told me her truth; now it's my turn.

"I'll kill you if you hurt her. I'll kill you if she gets hurt because of you."

I release her.

"The only reason you aren't dead right now is so I can torture you to find out where she is."

The words are my truth. I promised Lucy a long time ago I'd kill for her. I never thought that I'd have to kill someone I care about, though.

As I speak the words, as I hear them, as I see the defiance in Siren's eyes, I know my words aren't true. I can't kill Siren. But I can't break my vow to Lucy either.

I don't have a choice. Someday soon, I won't be able to protect them both. I'm going to have to choose. And for a split second, I'm not sure which woman will survive.

CHAPTER 30
SIREN

I moved Lucy. Not for whatever devious reasons Zeke is accusing me of.

I moved Lucy to keep her safe. I didn't have a choice. I don't trust Julian, not anymore, not with anything. Not even with his promises.

Lucy needed to be moved. She needed to be moved securely and quickly and with as few people as possible. She needed to be moved to the furthest corner of the earth. She needed to be moved by the best people.

Zeke could have moved her. But he didn't. I know he was preparing to. To avoid contacting his old world and Enzo Black, he was going to have her moved by people that have no connection to his family. I'm sure they are good men, but not the best.

This job required the best, and even that might not be enough to hide her from Julian forever.

I can't tell Zeke where she is. Not here. Not when Julian is listening to our conversations. Not even in his house where I'm sure there are more security systems monitoring us than either one of us wants to admit. Sure, we both found some bugs, but there's more we haven't found.

"

Zeke said he would kill me. If it came down to Lucy or me, he would kill me. I understand. That's what love does. It makes you crazy.

If it comes down to Lucy or me, I hope he does choose Lucy. That's what love has done to me. I want Zeke to get his happily ever after with the love of his life, even if that isn't with me.

And I'd rather be dead than live in a world without Zeke.

I can't keep living in a world where three men try to control me—Julian, Hugo, and Zeke.

I may not be able to do anything about Julian right now.

And I don't want to do anything about Zeke right now.

But I can do something about Hugo.

Maybe doing something big out in the open, letting Zeke in on one part of the truth so he understands the sacrifice I'm making for him, will be enough to get him to trust me with Lucy, at least for a moment.

"Lucy's safe. You don't have to believe me. Go search for her if you must, but she's safe. You're not the only person willing to protect people we love," I say, coming the closest yet to telling Zeke that I love him.

Zeke shakes his head. "I'm tired of the lies, Siren."

"It's not a lie."

"I can't trust you. You know the stupid game we play—truth or sin? There is no truth in that game. It's always sin, even when you choose truth. You've never told me the truth. You're never going to tell me the truth. And at this point, even if you tell me the truth, I won't believe you."

I start walking, hoping Zeke will follow me. He does. He's not finished with this conversation.

We walk half a mile into the jungle on the edge of Julian's property. It's not remote enough to tell Zeke the truth about Lucy. Julian could still hear. And as Zeke said, I could tell him the truth, and he wouldn't believe me anyway.

But we're far enough away for me to do this.

I pull out my knife.

Zeke laughs. "What? You brought me to the jungle so you can kill me?"

I turn the knife around, holding onto the blade, while holding the handle out to Zeke. He takes it.

Then I turn my back to him and lift my hair up so he can see the three names on my neck.

The first name is Hugo's. The first name was written with love. I wanted a tattoo of Hugo's name; I was so in love with him. The last two—Julian's and Zeke's—were written out of loyalty and pain. Someday all the names will be gone. But today, I get to remove one with Zeke's help.

Zeke reaches out and touches the names slowly with his fingers, unable to resist.

Shivers course through me, but I remain still. I will not let him know how his touch affects me.

"Cross out Hugo's name with the knife," I command.

Zeke doesn't move.

"Zeke, cross out Hugo's name."

He pauses for a second, and then he carefully thumbs the names on the back of my neck before pressing the cold of the metal against my base.

I suck in a breath at the same time he slices through the name. I've never wanted to feel pain as much as I do right now. I needed to feel his name ripped from my body.

I feel strong.

Powerful.

I know exactly what I'm doing—taking my life back, one man at a time. I will own my own life, my own name, and my own heart again. Zeke's name will be the hardest to cross out, but someday, I'll cross it out. When I deliver Zeke safely to Lucy, back to his own world.

Zeke blows on the wound gently, and then he ties my hair up with a scrunchie from his arm, keeping my hair from getting into the fresh wound.

I bite my lip to keep from smiling. *How can he be so kind to me? So protective? So caring?*

My heart is doing flips at the small gesture.

I turn and face him.

"Why did I just scar your neck? Why did I cross through Hugo's name?"

"Because I'm finally ready to divorce him."

He gasps.

"Once I file, once the agreement of the prenup is complete, then you can at least know one truth."

CHAPTER 31
ZEKE

Siren starts to walk away but stops. She looks at me, and I don't see fear like I expect. *I see hope.*

"You're my anchor, Zeke. Don't forget that."

I blink rapidly, not understanding.

"What does that mean?"

She smiles softly, as if the secret her words are hiding is precious and nice instead of what they really are—just one more lie.

"It means you're my strong, unmoving force. You keep me grounded. You ensure I live, even when I should die. You are the one stable thing in my life. You can make sure that I come back—not by saving me, but by never letting me truly go in the first place. You anchor me here."

Her words tell me everything and nothing.

But they keep her here for a second longer—another second for me to come to my senses and realize what she's doing.

At first, I thought she stayed married because she loved him. Maybe she did once, but that love has been lost. I don't know what the prenup she signed says, but it must be bad if it keeps her married to Hugo. Whatever she must do in order to get the divorce they both want will hurt her. And hurting her will hurt me.

"Don't…" I reach out, as if my hand will stop her. It won't. Nothing will now that's she made up her mind.

I'm torn. I want her to divorce him. I want her to be rid of him. I want to have a sliver of hope that we could have a future if we ever forgave each other for all the lying.

But I don't want her to leave. I don't want her to get hurt.

"What does the prenup say?" I ask, scared of what she's going to say.

She sighs. "It says that soon I'm going to be stronger than I've ever been. It says that soon I'll feel a little freer than I felt before."

And then she's gone. Running away from me.

I could chase her.

I could demand she tell me.

I could keep her here until she tells me the truth.

But I won't. If you love someone, you set them free. *Do I love her?*

Maybe.

Definitely.

Is it healthy?

Hell no.

Will our love last?

Doubtful. I doubt both of us will still be breathing a year from now.

Does it stop me from chasing after her?

Absolutely not.

I run once I realize what I want. Her unhurt. Her alive. I don't want her in pain. I don't want her dead. I need to find her. I can't let her go.

But Siren knows the jungle better than I do. By the time I make it back to my truck, she's already gone.

It won't stop me from chasing after her. It won't stop me from saving her if I have to.

I vowed I would stop saving her, but I can't.

If there is a chance I was wrong about her this whole time, if there's a chance we can heal the wounds we've caused in each other's hearts, then I'll never forgive myself for not saving her.

CHAPTER 32
SIREN

I meet Hugo at the house we technically own together, but I've never spent more than a night in it since we got married. The house is small, modest. He doesn't stay on this island often. Just when he wants something from me.

Like now.

The anger flares in his eyes as he stands in front of the front door.

"You have some balls showing up here," he says.

I raise an eyebrow. "This is my house."

"You stole from my parents," Hugo growls. It's not as deep or sexy as when Zeke growls. Hugo bares his teeth during his growl, making it frightening.

"Yea, what are you going to do about it?" He can't do anything to me.

"I was going to add it to your debt and make you pay every penny back with interest," he yells.

"You can't prove I stole the money. Even Julian will back me up. I don't owe you anything."

He huffs. "Then I'll kill that boyfriend of yours."

I laugh. "Not if he kills you first."

Fear—I see the fear in his eyes. It gives me satisfaction, and I smirk a little, trying to be brave for the next step. In a few seconds, Hugo's going to be the one with the smirk, not me.

"What are you doing here, Aria?"

"I'm giving you what you want."

"Which is what?"

"A divorce."

The words alone scare the crap out of me. I'm giving up so much. Possibly everything. I'm chancing everything by divorcing Hugo. It's necessary.

It's the only way to gain everything.

"I don't believe you," Hugo says.

"Let me inside."

Hugo stares at me, trying to understand why I'm doing this. The reason he wrote this in the prenup was because, at the time, he wanted me to stay married to him forever. He thought with this prenup, I'd never divorce him. I'd be his forever. Trapped in a binding contract. He could flaunt it over me for the rest of my life.

Hugo doesn't really want a divorce. He wants control over me. It's all he's wanted since I was eighteen.

He's about to get one last drop of power over me, then nothing, forever.

He marches inside, and I follow him through the house he clearly hasn't kept up. The house is dingy. Clothes and trash clutter most of the rooms. Hugo is headed for one room, in particular, a room he made into an office.

He heads to a filing cabinet and unlocks it, pulling open the top drawer roughly, almost pulling the entire cabinet down. His eyes lock with mine, glaring over the cabinet. Then he's searching through the papers until he finds what he's looking for.

He flings the papers on the desk.

"Read it again. And then tell me you still want a divorce," he says.

I feel my hands tremble. But I fist them and then open them, forcing my body to settle. I'm making the right decision—the only decision. I'm stronger than what Hugo has planned.

I can do this. I can win.

But what if I don't?

I told Zeke not to save me.

Julian might, just to keep his best asset close.

But what if neither of them comes? What if I can't save myself?

Then I'll die happy, no longer married to this asshole.

I flip through the papers quickly, reading the crucial part again, trying to decipher any hidden meaning of the words I haven't realized before. But I find no hidden meaning.

The prenup is on top, along with divorce papers Hugo had drawn up in case I ever wanted a divorce.

"Got a pen?" I ask.

Hugo laughs, likes he thinks I'm bluffing. He thinks I won't really sign the papers.

He continues to chuckle as he opens the desk drawer, facing me head-on. He pulls out a pen and holds it out to me.

He's not going to make any of this easy—not one second.

My heart thumps wildly. My hands clam up. Goosebumps form on my arms. There is no hiding my fear from Hugo. Not this time.

Slowly, I take the pen from him. It doesn't matter that he knows I'm scared. What matters is that I sign the papers. That is my moment of strength.

I flip to the last page, and I sign my name.

Hugo's jaw hits the floor as I toss the papers in his face.

"Do your worst," I say.

CHAPTER 33
ZEKE

It's been one week since Siren left.

Vanished, more like it. I can't find her anywhere. Not a Julian's. Nowhere near the compound. Nowhere on the island. I've even called my contacts to start looking for her, but they can't find her either.

Siren isn't the only person who vanished. Lucy is still missing.

I've done everything short of contacting Enzo Black to find her.

My only comfort is that I don't think Julian knows where they are either.

At least, I don't think so. But I'm out of options. Julian may not care where Lucy is, but he cares about Siren.

I march into his office as his butler tries to stop me.

"Julian," I say as I kick open his door.

"I'm so sorry, sir. He just stormed in," the butler says.

"It's okay, Hanson. Zeke is always welcome here."

The butler leaves in a scurry.

"What do you want?" Julian asks, reading his newspaper.

"Tell me what the prenup said," I say.

His eyes draw up over the newspaper. And he grins. "I told you to ask Aria. It's not my truth to tell."

"I would, except she's disappeared. Know anything about that?"

He scoffs. "She'll turn up again. She made a vow to me. Trust me, she'll never break it."

I glare at him, ripping the newspaper from his hands. "You really think Siren cares about a vow she made to you to save a man she hates?"

"Yes, because you don't understand who Aria is. You don't understand what she's done."

He doesn't realize what's happened. He doesn't realize what Siren's done.

"What did the prenup say?" I ask, my voice gravely and full of anger.

"Why?"

"Because she signed the divorce papers."

"Shit," Julian jumps up faster than I've ever seen him. He's on his phone in a second, barking orders to his men to go search for Siren.

For the first time, Julian and I just got on the same side, if only for a brief second.

CHAPTER 34
SIREN

"He's here," Hugo says, glancing out our hotel window. After I signed the divorce papers, we went to Portugal. Apparently, Hugo wasn't too surprised I signed the papers because he had a whole plan already in place. He put everything in motion with one phone call.

I sit on the edge of the hotel bed. It's a cheap room, and the bed dips wherever I sit on it.

"It's time to go," Hugo says.

"Why?" I ask, hoping for one last chance to convince Hugo not to do this.

He stares at me—really stares—like he's taking a mental picture to remember this moment forever. And that terrifies me. If he's taking a picture, then this is goodbye for real. He doesn't think I'm going to survive this. He doesn't think I'll be coming back next week to chew him out.

"You shouldn't have stolen the money from my parents," he says.

"Maybe not. They aren't bad people per se, they just raised a horrible son."

Hugo frowns.

"But that's not why you are doing this, Hugo. That's not why you added the provision to the prenup that allowed you to do this. Why did you?"

There is a knock at our hotel room door. My time is up.

"Because you were mine. Mine to love. Mine to keep. Mine to hold. And I knew if I had to ever let you go, this was the only way I could bear it."

Those were not the words I was expecting to hear. I wasn't expecting Hugo to admit that he loved me. I assumed he would be doing this for revenge and for his sick twisted pleasure.

"You don't get to claim you are selling me for love," I say.

"No, but love is the reason all the same."

Hugo opens the door, and a man walks in. This isn't the man I'm being sold to. This is his henchman.

"This the girl?" The man asks.

Hugo nods.

"Wow, an obedient one. You don't even need ropes or handcuffs."

Hugo shakes his head sadly. "She's the least obedient person I know. She will fight harder than any woman your master has ever bought. And she will burn the castle down with her. She's not going to submit. She's going to destroy you. Only if your master is smart about controlling her will you have a chance against her. But even then, she will eventually win. She always wins."

Our eyes lock as he speaks so highly of me.

"Then why is she submitting now?" the man asks.

"Because this is the only way to get what she wants. And she doesn't fear being sold. She doesn't fear you. She fears nothing, because she is stronger than you could ever imagine," Hugo says.

"Her name?" the man asks, continuing to talk about me like I'm not here.

I wait for Hugo to say Aria, or maybe bitch, or cunt, if he's in a particularly foul mood. Instead, he says, "Siren."

It feels like a truce. He's admitting who I really am and who I deserve to be with. That I need to be free of him. That I belong with Zeke.

"Is she ready?" the man asks.

"Almost," Hugo walks over to me and holds out his hand, demanding me to turn over my gun.

I do. Then Hugo gives me a quick pat-down. He knows I always carry more than one weapon, but when he finds the knife buried in my boot, Hugo just winks at me and lets me keep it.

I have a weapon, for now at least.

Why is Hugo being nice to me?

Surprising my further, Hugo wraps his arms around me, hugging me. "I could have loved you forever, but that wouldn't have been fair to you. You deserve someone worthy of you."

I blink, rapidly as he pulls away and walks over to the divorce papers. He signs them, knowing I'll keep my word and willingly go with the man. At least until I get to his car, then all bets are off.

"Why?" I ask one last time.

Hugo smiles at me.

"He will only come if you are in danger. You two need all the help you can get in the love department," Hugo says. Then he slings his bag over his shoulder, and walks out the door.

I'm left stunned by Hugo's admission. Maybe the prenup was originally to ensure I never divorced him, but now he's keeping to the contract to push Zeke and me together.

Unbelievable.

It's not true. Hugo is an evil, manipulative asshole.

An asshole I once loved.

But an asshole all the same. A man I won't think of again after today.

Hugo is wrong about Zeke coming for me. I told him not to, and he'll listen. This won't bring Zeke and me closer together. Even if it did, this isn't how I want us to end up together. I want us to choose each other, not be scared of losing each other.

After Hugo leaves, my purchaser's henchman opens the door, and three other men run inside with guns.

Apparently, Hugo had already warned them I wasn't going to go with them easy. I'm a fighter.

They give me no choice but to surrender, binding my hands and ankles. Then I'm dragged to the back of a truck where the three men surround me.

Now doesn't seem like the best time to escape. But I will escape. And I will kill every one of these men.

A truck ride, a plane ride, and another car ride later, I'm dragged into a house and thrown in the basement.

I can save myself. I can escape.

But when I see a dozen eyes staring back at me, I realize it's not just myself that needs saving. I wasn't counting on having to save someone else too.

CHAPTER 35
HUGO

Selling Aria hurt more than I thought it would. I knew I would have to do it someday, even when I added that provision to the prenup. Aria was never really mine. I thought being able to control her would feel like she was mine, even when she stopped loving me.

But it doesn't.

I have no control.

I knew when we said our wedding vows that Aria was too good for me. I knew this is how our marriage would end. But I wasn't prepared for what signing the divorce papers would feel like.

It destroyed me singing my name next to Aria's, telling the world that I no longer care about this woman, and admitting Aria is no longer mine.

In reality, she hasn't been mine for years.

Aria will escape. I won't be here when she does. Being sold is temporary. Aria can never be contained by a man. Never be owned.

Zeke Kane might be the only man who can tame her. And even he will have to fight constantly to keep her his. Eventually, she will get free of even him.

Aria Torres is invincible. She's independent and kind and selfless. And she deserved better.

But so did I.

Aria was the only woman who could give me what I needed. But what I asked for was too great. I needed forgiveness, in spite of who I was. I needed to be forgiven again and again.

Yes, I fucked up. I cheated on her. I broke Aria's heart.

But Aria is forgiveness. She is kindness. So I thought she would forgive me.

We were kids when we got married. I didn't understand what marriage was. I was a drug addict. I was constantly fucked up and made a lot of bad decisions.

The only good decision I made was marrying Aria.

I loved her desperately, but I cost her everything. Ten years of her life she gave to save me. And I paid her back by cheating on her. That isn't something even the highest angel can forgive.

I don't regret falling in love with Aria, because she saved my life more than she knows...

MY HEART IS RACING, JONESING FOR ANOTHER HIT. I NEED IT. I'M desperate. I need a hit right now. My legs are shaking, I'm sweaty, and I can't get enough oxygen in my lungs.

I need the drugs. It's been too long since my last hit.

I bought drugs meant to be sold, but instead, me and my friends used them. Not this time. This time, I'm selling them and only using a little bit. I just need one hit, then I'll be able to function again.

I'm supposed to meet the buyer here, on the edge of this sea town. I'm so damn tired of the sea salt smell and the humid, sticky air. Beach towns are overrated.

I turn down a road and into the alleyway where I met him last time, but I don't see him.

Am I early?

Late?

I don't know. I don't have a watch. Or a phone.

I have no way to figure out if he's coming or already left.

But I'm not going anywhere. For one thing, the alleyway is spinning.

I need to sit down.

So I do.

"Ow," a high pitched voice says.

I stumble over and look down at what I stepped on—an angel.

Did I die?

I must have.

The girl smiles up at me when she sees my reaction. *Yep, I'm definitely dead. No girl looks as sweet as her.*

She's leaning against the wall, playing with something in her hand. Even though she's sitting on the dirty ground in the alleyway next to a trash can, she looks clean and smells like flowers.

"You should sit down; you don't look so well," she says.

I slump to the floor next to her.

"Are you sick?" she asks with big eyes.

I nod. I'm always sick. Except when I'm high, which seems to be less and less these days.

"Here," she says, removing her denim jacket and draping it over my shoulders.

I stare at her with bug eyes.

"You are shaking. You must be cold. The jacket will help."

I nod. It does help. Although not as much as a hit of heroin would.

"What are you doing here?" I ask her, still assuming I'm dead.

Her beautiful bright smile drops. "Hiding."

"From what?"

"Not what, who," she answers. Her eyes drift down the alleyway, looking lost in a cloud of gloom.

Okay, so she's a dark angel. She hides behind her pretty eyelashes and big smile, but I can see the darkness now. She's had a rough past, same as me.

I study her closer and realize she's young. Seventeen, maybe eighteen.

She's either running from her parents or a boyfriend.

"Have a boyfriend?" I ask.

She shakes her head, and I have my answer—she's running from her parents.

"What's your name?"

"Aria Torres."

"I'm Hugo Martinez."

She nods, giving me a polite smile. She tucks her hair behind her ear, and that's when I see it, the blueness around her eye.

If I was in a better place, I'd get up and run after her dad. I'd kill him for touching such a sweet angel. But since I can barely keep myself sitting upright, I don't think I can manage chasing down a grown man.

Aria reaches over and grabs a bottle I didn't notice before. She takes a sip of the beer and then hands it to me. "Want some?"

I take the bottle, the alcohol barely addressing my jitters, but I appreciate the taste and gesture.

"What are you doing in an alleyway like this, Aria? You could be enjoying the beach."

"The same reason you are."

I frown. This girl should be doing nothing I'm doing. I lean my head back against the brick wall behind us.

"So, what do you like doing for fun, Aria?"

Please don't say drink or drugs. You're better than that. Give me hope.

She frowns. "I don't know. I don't do anything for fun."

"Well, if you could, what would you do?"

She thinks for a moment, scrunching her nose. "Sing."

It seems like an admission she's never made to anyone else before. But she made it to me. I feel my jittery heart do strange things—like flip for this girl.

"What do you like to sing?"

"I don't know. I've never tried singing before."

"You want to sing, but you've never tried it before? How do you know you are any good?"

She smiles. "I don't. Don't you have dreams you've never tried before? Skiing, surfing, painting?"

I don't tell her that I've done all of those things. I grew up privileged. That doesn't mean that the darkness didn't find me, too, just like this girl who has nothing. This girl, who has been beaten, abused, and yet she still smiles. She still has hope.

"Well, I think it's about time."

"Time for what?"

"Time that you sing."

She frowns. "But I don't know how."

I laugh. "Yes, you do. Singing isn't something that has to be taught. At least not at first. Sure, to get good at singing on key and harmonizing and stuff, you might need lessons, but you don't have to be good to start singing. You just sing."

"Okay, if you don't need lessons, then you sing," she says with a raised eyebrow.

I walked right into that one.

I think for a moment, trying to come up with something to sing. Then I open my mouth and sing 'Moves Like Jagger.'

Siren smiles. "Did you write that?"

I frown. "No, it's Maroon 5. Haven't you heard it on the radio?"

She blushes. "My parents don't have a radio."

Oh.

Shit.

"I'm sorry, I shouldn't have pushed you."

But then she opens her mouth and starts singing. A song I've never heard before. One I'm sure she's written herself.

You hurt me.

    Destroyed me.

    Made me turn to darkness to survive you.

    The pull is too great.

    I can't resist your temptation.

    It's the only way to survive you.

    Even though it destroys me.

    And yet, I still love you.

. . .

My mouth falls open as she sings. I was wrong about everything. This girl can sing. She doesn't need lessons or practice. This girl could be on the radio right now if she wanted to be. If the right person listened to her, the pain in her life would vanish.

But that's what makes her voice so special—the pain behind it. The life experience.

"It was horrible, wasn't it?" she asks, her voice timid.

I shake my head. "That was the most hauntingly beautiful thing I've ever heard."

She swallows hard, and her mouth goes dry as she stares at me like I'm someone to awe.

Then—an electricity I've never felt with a woman before. I need to touch her. She seems to need it too.

We've found something here, connected in a way neither of us was expecting. We are two lost souls in need of saving. Maybe we can save each other.

I touch her cheek.

She touches my chest.

And then we kiss.

Our lips brush. Our tongues tease. And the beautiful thing that is Aria encompasses me. *I'm hers—forever.*

I don't know how I'm going to hold onto something so beautiful. So precious. So forgiving. But I'm going to try.

Finally, I see it—the needle next to her leg. And I see the darkness in her eyes as I kiss her. She's facing the same monster as I am.

The pull of drugs.

She's not shaking like I am, and she doesn't have needle marks all up and down her arms like I do. She can still be saved from the deepest layer of darkness.

I can save her. I can protect her. And maybe her goodness, her kindness, her ability to forgive will be enough...because I already know I'm going to have to ask for her forgiveness.

My love wasn't enough to protect her.

Her forgiveness wasn't enough to save our marriage.

Love isn't enough to protect against darkness.

What I did was unforgivable.

When I was planning our life together, I forgot one thing—Aria fell in love with me too. And love makes people do unpredictable things. Aria is the strongest person I know, but I broke her heart. I didn't realize how fragile it was since everything else about her is strong.

I know what's coming, and I deserve it. I need it to happen. Despite everything, I still love Aria. But she's no longer Aria. Aria is gone. She left the second I shattered her heart.

She's Siren now. She finally found a man worthy of her. I just hope my plan works. I hope the pain brings them together, like it did us. And I hope, unlike us, they cherish their love instead of letting it destroy them.

But I better not be here to watch it happen, because Aria isn't the only one with a fragile heart. I can't watch her get her happily ever after, while I'm the reason ours ended.

CHAPTER 36
ZEKE

Julian drives me to Hugo's house. I must be crazy to trust Julian, even for a second, to get her back. I don't have a choice—Julian knows Hugo and Siren's history better than I do.

"There," Julian says when we pull up in front of a small beach house on the far end of the island.

I pull my gun out. *Hugo's a dead man if he sold Siren. A dead man.*

Julian pulls a gun out as well. I've never seen him get his hands dirty, never seen him wield a gun, but for Siren, he will. He loves her, which is the only reason I brought him along. He'd die, before he'd let her die.

He may have been a good actor. He may have acted like he would kill her if I didn't behave, but no way can Julian kill Siren. Just like there is no way I can kill her. There is just something about her that lures men in. Only she can decide if we get to live or die.

We march up to Hugo's front door. I pound loudly on the door, my gun in hand, and Julian standing on my right.

Slowly, Hugo opens the door. We don't give him time to talk. We both ambush him back into his house until he's sitting in a chair in the center of his living room with both our guns aimed at his forehead.

The house is a mess. There's trash and empty alcohol bottles everywhere. That isn't what has me worried, though. The track marks on his arms worry me. The redness in his eyes. The brokenness. The needles on the coffee table.

Hugo is high. Who knows if we will be able to get answers from him.

"Where is Siren?" I ask.

"Who?" Hugo asks.

"Aria, your wife. Where is she?" Julian asks.

"Oh, her," Hugo's head drops, and I swear he's seconds away from passing out, puking, or keeling over dead. I'm just not sure which.

He's no longer the man I knew before. He's not the man who would fight for Siren, the man who would make threats. This man is empty, broken.

Julian kicks him in the leg. "Wake up! Where is Aria?"

Hugo's head drops again, and he shakes his head.

I study him, trying to figure out how to play this. How to get the information we need? We need to know where Siren is. If he doesn't tell us, it could take us days to find her instead of hours. I don't want her with another man for any longer than she has to be.

"Where is she?" I ask, calmer.

Hugo looks at me in the eyes, and for a second, I see clarity. He looks over at Julian, and his eyes get cloudy again.

"Julian, make him some coffee or something. He's so high he won't be able to think straight."

Julian doesn't like taking orders, but he wants Siren back just like I do. He reluctantly marches into the kitchen to make coffee.

I squat down in front of Hugo. "Who did you sell her to?"

"Northern Spain. The number is in my pocket," Hugo answers me.

I exhale a deep breath as I reach into his front pocket and find a note. I have her location and a phone number. *I can find her. I can save her.*

Hugo grabs my shirt, holding me close. "Don't break her heart. It's fragile. Protect it at all costs."

I frown, not understanding.

"Promise me!" His voice gets louder.

I don't know why I'm making promises to Hugo, but I am. "I promise."

Hugo grabs my gun and aims it at his heart.

I realize what's happened—Hugo's hurting. His heart is broken. *He really did love her.*

Three men.

Hugo.

Julian.

And me.

We've all fallen for her. Siren's love is the kind that consumes you. It's all any of us can think about—loving her. She's strong, independent, and secretive—a true siren with the power to kill us all. She just has to decide if she wants any of us alive.

Divorcing Hugo was the final straw. He lost. And now he can't survive without her. It hurts too much. She destroyed him.

I don't understand their love story, but I don't doubt now that they loved each other. I don't doubt that he loved her more than she loved him. Even though she traded ten years of her life to save him, he still loved her more. And in the end, it was his demise.

"Do it," Hugo says.

I look at him closer. He's already dying. He's gaunt, just bones. If I don't kill him, the drugs will. For a moment, I feel sorry for him. Ultimately, he simply wasn't strong enough to keep her love.

Am I?

No. I'm not sure any man is.

But that's a discussion for later. For now, I get to kill a man who hurt Siren. I get to get her vengeance. Hugo may love her, but he still sold her. He cheated on her. He nearly raped her. He locked her into a marriage when she was never his to begin with.

The only way to keep Siren's love is to let her be herself, let her be free. Let her be Siren and hope your love is enough. You can't cage her in like Hugo did.

You can't trap her into vows like Julian does.

You can't force her to tell you the truth when she's not ready like I do.

I don't know how Siren needs to be loved, but all three of us are doing a horrible job. All three of us are going to end up dying with a broken heart, just like Hugo.

I consider letting him die slowly and painfully, but it's not my style. And I don't think it's what Siren would want. She loved him once. She wants him to die honorably, before he loses himself completely.

He closes his eyes, welcoming death. I let him die with a bullet in his heart, putting him out of his misery.

Julian enters when he hears the gunshot.

"What the hell? You killed him before you found out where Aria is?"

"No, I found out where she is."

"Where?"

"This is where our partnership ends." I shoot him in the shoulder, not enough to kill him, although I want to desperately. I'm afraid he's working for a more powerful man—the one whose money that really is. I don't want to piss that man off by killing his number two, not at least until I know who he is.

Then I leave. I know where to find Siren. I just hope I'm not too late. And I hope I'm doing the right thing by saving her. If I know Siren, she'll most likely shoot me for saving her.

CHAPTER 37
SIREN

I can do this. I can escape. I can save all these women.

Three men drag me in chains to a grand room, and suddenly I'm not so sure.

No, don't doubt yourself. You've been in worse situations before. You destroy men. Manipulate your new owner just like you do every other man.

"You can go," the man sitting in a large chair says to my guards.

"But, sir—"

"Unchain her, then leave," his voice is loud and booming. It's meant to scare me. It doesn't, but it drives some fear into his men.

They fumble with the chains around my wrists and ankles.

And then finally, they leave. It's just me and him—the man who bought me.

I grin. *This will be too easy.*

No, if I was just trying to free myself, it would be easy. This is harder, saving six other women.

"Who are you?" I ask, wanting to know the name of the man I plan on destroying.

"Bishop," he answers. His answer surprises me. He doesn't tell me to call him mister or master. For all I know, Bishop is his first name and not his last.

"Well, Bishop, it's nice to meet you," I say, walking over to the window to see my escape options. I'm on the third floor—jumping out the window isn't a good route.

"Is it? I would have thought it was the opposite of nice," Bishop says.

"Maybe, but I'm not like most women. I like to know who the monsters are. I don't run from them. I destroy them."

His eyes soak me in. "That you do. But I'm not like most men either."

I smirk. "All men are the same." *Except Zeke, Zeke is different. He's not a monster.*

Bishop stands and walks over to the window I've been studying. His eyes are blue, his hair blonde, and his skin fair. He doesn't look evil. The best men hide who they really are.

"You're wrong. I'm different," he says.

"How are you different?"

"I've felt pain you've never imagined. It turned me into a different man. A man who wants to see others experience similar pain."

"Don't worry about me; I have a high pain tolerance. You're not going to be able to hurt me."

He reaches out and touches my chest. "You're wrong. I know exactly how to hurt you. And I'm going to enjoy every second of it."

"And I know exactly how to hurt you."

"Oh, I hope so. I hope you are the one who can finally hurt me because I've grown tired of the easy ones. It would be good to feel something new."

I frown. *This man is unusual.*

He snaps his fingers. A woman enters in chains being held by a man. She looks awful. She's had enough. But there's something familiar about her.

"Now, you will do exactly what I say, or Peter will torture her," Bishop says.

I close my eyes, trying to reveal nothing, but this man already has me figured out. He knows I will do anything to save someone else from being harmed.

Although, he's wrong if he thinks that will hurt me. There is only one person who could hurt me, and he's thousands of miles away.

"What do you want me to do?" I ask.

Bishop smiles. "Oh, princess. All the darkest things you can imagine."

♡

THERE IS SOMETHING WRONG WITH HIM—BISHOP. SOMETHING fucked up in his head. Something deranged about him.

He doesn't get off raping women. He doesn't get off on control. In fact, half the time, he wants me to hurt him in the same way he's hurting me. That's what he gets off on—the pain.

Someone hurt him bad.

If I don't get out of here soon, I'm not going to be able to walk out on my own two feet.

I realize now, even I have a breaking point. Bishop has done his best in the last three days to find it. And he has.

I'm broken.

Not physically, but psychologically. I haven't slept in three days. I haven't eaten. I've barely had any water.

I'm delusional. All I see is Zeke.

Zeke...Zeke...Zeke...

He's in my head.

He's in my heart.

He's everywhere.

I can't remember if I should be running toward Zeke or away from him.

But Zeke keeps calling me. He tells me to follow him.

There is a reason I'm not supposed to go with him, but I can't remember anymore. I can't think.

I just move.

I sprint.

At least, I think I'm running.

I'm barefoot. Naked under a baggy T-shirt. My hair is a mess. My eyes are exhausted, but I keep them open. If I close them, I feel electric shocks.

Bishop enjoyed shooting electricity through my body. Seeing him do it to another woman made me beg him to give me more and her none. I can't watch others in pain.

Others! I can't run, I have to save them.

You can't save them if you are dead.

Run, get help. That's the only way to save them. You aren't strong enough on your own.

Yes, I am!

No, you're not.

The voices in my head keep fighting as I stumble through the forest. At least I think it's a forest. All I see are ghosts floating through the shadows, telling me to run.

So I run.

And run.

And run.

But I will never escape the pain. Not my own pain, that man's pain. I've never felt anything like it. I want to turn around and kill him just to end his suffering, but I can't. I have to run.

I have to escape.

I am strong enough.

I don't need a man. I don't need Zeke.

Suddenly I feel the hands grab me as I collapse. The hands aren't Zeke's hands. They are the man's—Bishop's.

"Did you enjoy your run? I enjoyed the chase." He pulls me up. "Let's get you home and fed. Then we can do that again. I quite enjoy chasing you."

I collapse in his arms. I'm not strong enough. I can't save myself. I definitely can't save the women. *I failed.*

Zeke.

Zeke isn't coming. He vowed he wouldn't, and he always keeps his word.

CHAPTER 38
ZEKE

It cost me everything to get Siren back.

Every penny I had.

The man Hugo sold her to is more sadistic than any man I've ever met. He would only sell her to me if I gave everything I had. He didn't care if I only had a thousand dollars in my account, he would have taken it. He just wanted me to be poor, to be worth nothing when she returned to me.

I could have fought my way in. I could have fought him, killed him. But it would have taken time, time I didn't have to get her back.

I'll kill him. Eventually, I will. But the most important thing right now is getting Siren back in my arms and away from him.

Hugo didn't tell me his name, and I still haven't learned it. Right now, his name doesn't matter. Hugo gave me the number to call. He told me she was in northern Spain.

I'm there now, waiting for Siren to be returned to me in a coffee shop.

A freaking coffee shop!

That's where he said his men would meet me.

I'm afraid he's going to double-cross me. This dark stranger hides in the shadows and enjoys playing games with me.

He won't break his word because he's watching. And he'll enjoy the show. He thinks Siren won't want me now that I'm nothing. Now that I have no money.

He's wrong.

Siren will want me. The millions in my bank account meant nothing to her. She didn't even know how much money I had. In fact, I'm pretty sure she'll love me more for giving it all away to save her.

Or she'll shoot me for not letting her save herself.

I never know which way it will go when it comes to Siren.

A car pulls up, and a woman is pushed out before it takes off.

I run to her before she collapses in the street.

"You're alive," I breathe into her hair as my tears fall.

She doesn't look too beaten up. She looks whole, but that doesn't mean I know what she's been through. It doesn't mean she didn't suffer.

I lift her up and realize how light she is. How her eyes fall closed. How her breath is weak.

"Fucker. I'm going to kill you," I vow into the darkness. *Whoever you are, you're dead for whatever you did to her.*

Siren doesn't respond to me holding her; she's too weak.

"You're safe now, I've got you," I say as I carry her to my rental truck. I will drive her to the airport where Nora is waiting for us. She hired a private jet that can make the overseas trip, as I have nothing left. No money to save Siren with. No money to bribe anyone to fly us or take care of her.

I have nothing but love to offer Siren.

I drive to the airport with Siren in my lap and my hand on the pulse on her neck, making sure she's alive. I don't know what's wrong with her, but the waiting doctors on the plane will find out.

"Hold on, Siren. Hold on," I say.

I drive faster than I ever have before to get her to the plane. I spot Nora standing on the tarmac as I arrive. Her eyes search for Siren, still limp in my lap.

Nora grabs the door as I lift Siren out.

"Is she okay?" Nora asks.

"I don't know. She hasn't spoken. She hasn't acknowledged me at all."

Nora's eyes tell me everything. She's worried.

I carry Siren up the stairs and onto the plane where the medical team is waiting.

"How is she?" the doctor asks as I lay her on a makeshift table.

"She's unresponsive, but I felt a pulse."

"Let's get to work! Oxygen, pulse, fluids..." the doctor barks orders at his team while Nora and I stand and watch. There is nothing for us to do. We've done everything we can. Now it's up to the medical team.

"What's wrong with her?" I ask, when the flurry of excitement seems to settle down. Siren still hasn't opened her eyes.

The doctor rubs his neck. "She's definitely dehydrated, which is why she's so weak and skinny, but we couldn't find anything else physically wrong with her."

"Was she..." *Goddammit, I can't even ask.* I swallow my anger, needing to know the answer. "Was she raped?"

The doctor puts his hand on my shoulder as if to prepare me for the bad news. "I can't answer that for you. We did a rape kit, but we found no real evidence. Physically, she's fine. She could have been raped. She could have been mentally tortured. So much could have happened that I can't answer, only she can."

"How long until she wakes up?"

"Minutes, hours, days. She's exhausted and dehydrated, so her body shut down to preserve energy. I can't tell you when the body will feel rested enough to reverse course."

I nod. "Thank you, doctor."

"Sit with her. Sometimes having the person we love most close does more healing than medicine ever can."

The person we love most—I love her.

I knew it the second I realized she was sold. There was nothing I wouldn't do. *Nothing.*

I'd even hurt others I cared about or supposedly loved. Siren sucked me in and made me fall for her. I can't explain it. I'm hers. *I'm fucking hers.*

Everything else disappeared.

Lucy.

Kai.

Enzo.

My whole life—no one mattered as much as Siren. Nothing has been as complicated as loving Siren either, but I want complicated. I want messy. I want complex.

I used to think the only way to settle down was a simple life. A life where I met a simple girl who made my life easy. A woman who didn't push me to be better.

But with Siren, she makes me want to learn how to fight harder. How to be better. How to love her deeper.

I want to experience the full range of emotion. The full spectrum of life—with her. I love trying to figure her out. I love that I'm the only man capable of loving her and being loved in return without dying from heartbreak like Hugo did.

I love that this complex, strong, incredible woman chose me. Wants me.

I sit next to Siren.

Nora pokes her head in. "I'm going to try and get some sleep. If you need a break, wake me up, and I can sit with her."

"I won't need a break," I say, staring at a sleeping Siren.

Nora smiles. "I know. Wake me up if there is any change."

"I will."

Nora leaves me in the room at the back of the plane with Siren sleeping in the bed.

I run my hand through my long hair.

"I'm wearing my hair down for you. I know you like it better this way. Open your eyes and see for yourself," I say.

But of course, she doesn't open her eyes.

I sigh.

"This plane is huge, and we have a bed all to ourselves. We could really do some damage to our mile-high status on this plane," I joke.

Nothing.

"Yea, okay, that was dumb."

Just be with her.

Maybe words aren't the way.

I grab her hand, planning on holding it until she wakes up. There's a shock, probably static electricity. I pull my hand back for a second, and her eyes open.

"My anchor," she sighs.

"Yes, I'm your anchor," I say, still not knowing why she calls me that.

I reach out to pull her into a hug at the same time she sits up, but there's that damn static electricity again, shocking us both. It seems to hurt Siren worse than it does me.

"I'm sorry," I say, holding my hands wide and letting her come to me. I don't feel anything when she touches me, but it's clear she feels something painful.

"Never mind, I can hug you in a minute. Do you need anything? Water? Food?"

She shakes her head, smiling. "Just you."

I nod. "You have me."

"My anchor," she says again with a bigger smile on her face. "You've been my anchor this whole time. Thank you for saving me again."

"It seems like you did a pretty good job saving yourself. I just got you the last little bit. Only minor injuries."

She nods, her smile falling a little. *Please tell me he didn't rape you.*

"He didn't rape me."

I exhale. "Thank you," I whisper.

She nods, her eyes watering. "I fell for you, Zeke. I tried not to. Every man who falls for me ends up dead."

Our eyes meet. She knows Hugo is dead. I don't know how, but she does.

I nod, though, confirming her thoughts.

"I don't want you to suffer the same fate."

"I won't."

She swallows. "You want to know when you became my anchor?"

I nod.

"When I saved you. You were weak, out of it on my boat, looking a lot like I look right now."

"No, no one is as beautiful as you." I want to touch her, but I don't want to shock her, so I'll wait until the end of her story.

She smiles. "There was a storm, choppy waves. I knew I had to get you to land as fast as possible. It was the only way you'd survive. So I pushed us faster. Harder into the waves.

"One of the waves was too big. It pushed me overboard. I tried to swim against the current, but I was too weak. You were drifting away. But, somehow, my ankle got twisted up in a rope. A rope tied to the boat. All I had to do was hold on and you pulled me back."

I stroke her face, and watch it turn to pain at my touch.

"I was far too weak to pull you back," I say.

"It didn't matter. We were tied together. When all hope was gone, you pulled me back. Maybe not intentionally, but you gave me strength. I had to save you, and you had to save me. When I got back on the boat, I felt myself falling, my heart beating for you. Call it instant love. Call it fate. I don't know. But it scared me. I needed to get away from you."

I nod.

"God, I need to kiss you."

"Then kiss me."

I do. I devour her. I need this kiss to be fucking everything.

She screams in pain as soon as my lips touch hers.

The doctors fly into the room, and I'm pushed back. Every time they touch her, she screams like she's being shocked.

What did he do to her?

Why can't she handle being touched?

And how can I love her without touching her?

CHAPTER 39
SIREN

It takes the doctors a minute to realize what happened to me. It takes Zeke and me even less time.

I remember. Bishop shocked me. He played games with my head until I hated being touched. Then he sold me to my love, knowing I couldn't handle him touching me.

He thought it would break us. It might have, if something else didn't break us first.

A truth that turned out to be a lie. A truth I found out accidentally. A truth Zeke never thought I'd learn.

The doctors fuss over me most of the plane ride. Zeke speaks to me some, but we don't try touching again. We hardly talk until I'm back at Zeke's house.

Then everything comes out.

"You lied to me," I say.

Zeke stares at me. "What?"

"You said you didn't sell those women. You said you saved them."

"I did."

"You lied."

"What are you talking about? You should rest, and we can talk more in the morning. I have doctors coming who can help reverse what happened to you."

I scream. "This can't be reversed just like that! Is that all that matters to you? Touching me?"

"No, that's not what I meant. I'm just trying to help you."

I grab his hair and yank hard, needing to hurt Zeke without shocking myself.

But I'm already in pain. So much pain. Zeke isn't the man I thought he was. I have high standards for the men I love. I thought Zeke would pass my tests.

I was wrong.

"I've been falling in love with you since the moment I saved you," I say.

"And I've been falling—"

I can't hear him say it.

"I gave up everything to save you. I risked everything," I continue as my tears come.

Zeke stills at the sight of my tears and not being able to do a damn thing to help me. Not because he can't touch me, but because he's just like all the other men in my life.

This is how I get rid of him. This is how Zeke leaves my life.

I have to get through this first. Just a little longer.

"Lucy is safe. I'll make sure you know exactly where she is before I leave."

"Leave? You are in no state to go anywhere, Siren. You're not going anywhere."

But I am. There is no use fighting him on this. I need to leave. I'm not going far. Just to Julian's. To figure out how to cross out his name from my body.

"You're not going anywhere with me, Siren. I know you're free now that Hugo is dead. You no longer owe anything to Julian. Your debt is over."

If only it were that easy.

"I used to love you, you know. Until I learned that you are just like all the rest of the dangerous men in my life."

"What are you talking about, Siren?"

"The women you supposedly saved. The women you said you didn't sell. They had a different story to tell. Two of the women were sold to Bishop. They were sold by you, Zeke. You didn't save them. You sold them."

Zeke doesn't respond. He just blinks at me. "Bishop, who?"

"I don't know, but you aren't even going to deny it?"

"No, you are the only woman I care to save. I love you, Siren. I want you. And I'm the man for you."

I shake my head as he walks closer.

"I'm going to fight for you. I'm going to kill Bishop for what he did to you. I'll rescue any woman I want. I'll spill every secret, lie, and horrible thing I did in front of your feet so that you can make me pay in blood for my sins. You're the person for me, Siren. You, not Lucy. Not Kai. Not any other woman. You're mine."

God, his words are everything. But I've heard them before. From Hugo. From Julian.

I thought they would sound different coming from Zeke, but they don't. They all sound the same. Because all the men in my life are the same—murderous monsters who only care about themselves.

"You're free now, Siren. Free from Julian. Together we can take him down. Together we can find our happily ever after."

Oh god, his words are going to kill me.

But he still doesn't understand my truth. I hope to god the words he's saying aren't the truth. Because I realized one thing with my time with Bishop. I can't be with Zeke, no matter if I love him or not. Whatever his reason for lying to me about selling the women, I might be able to forgive him—maybe.

I won't allow myself. I'm better off alone.

"I'm not free."

"Yes, you are." Zeke grabs my hand, and it burns. I jerk my hand free.

He steps back sadly.

"I'm not free, Zeke. Saving Hugo wasn't the only vow I made. My ten years might be over, but I've saved others. I owe more debts."

Zeke frowns. "None of those men matter."

I shake my head. "Every life matters. Good, evil. Strong, weak. I want to save everyone. Just like I wish someone would have saved me before I became this dark version of myself."

"What are you saying, Siren?"

"I'm saying that I'll never be free of Julian, but I can be free of you. You are the one man I will never save. I used to love you. I would have done anything for you. But you proved to me that all men are evil. That all men hurt women. That you are just as vile."

I did it. I told my first lie out loud to another person. Because everything out of my mouth is lies. And everything I'm feeling is lies too. I don't feel pain when Zeke touches me. I feel nothing but love.

Bishop didn't take my love away from me. He showed me Zeke's fate if I let him fall in love with me—death. Every man who loves a siren dies, whether the siren wants them to or not.

I love Zeke. I'll always love Zeke. Zeke protected those women with everything he had. He didn't sell them. Someone else did. Someone he loved betrayed him.

He'll figure that out soon enough. But for now, this will give us distance. He can think I hate him. That I can't touch him. That I don't love him. It's the only way to protect him.

The fight I see in Zeke's eyes scares me. I'm afraid this time, it's too late. That he can see through my lies. That this time, he's fallen in love with me. And that love will destroy him.

Run, Zeke. Run back to your friends. Only they can protect you from me.

And then I do the one thing that I know will push Zeke away from me. Hopefully, for good.

I pull out a piece of paper with Lucy's new address.

"Lucy needs you."

The lies spill effortlessly from my lips now. *Apparently, lying for love is easy.*

Zeke stares at the address before ripping it up. And then he pushes past me.

"I'll be back," he says, grabbing the keys to his truck before he leaves.

No, you won't.
So this is what real heartbreak feels like...

THANK YOU SO MUCH FOR READING SINFUL! ZEKE AND SIREN'S story continues in BROKEN: A Truth or Lies World Collection.

There is one thing I'm certain of...I have to end this—us.

One-click BROKEN now >

"Gripping and Full of Painful Emotions!"

JOIN ELLA'S NEWSLETTER & NEVER MISS A SALE OR NEW RELEASE → ellamiles.com/freebooks

Consumed by Truths #6

DIRTY SERIES:

Dirty Beginning

Dirty Obsession

Dirty Addiction

Dirty Revenge

Dirty: The Complete Series

ALIGNED SERIES:

Aligned: Volume 1 (Free Series Starter)

Aligned: Volume 2

Aligned: Volume 3

Aligned: Volume 4

Aligned: The Complete Series Boxset

UNFORGIVABLE SERIES:

Heart of a Thief

Heart of a Liar

Heart of a Prick

Unforgivable: The Complete Series Boxset

MAYBE, DEFINITELY SERIES:

Maybe Yes

Maybe Never

Maybe Always

Definitely Yes

Definitely No

Definitely Forever

STANDALONES:

Pretend I'm Yours

Finding Perfect

Savage Love

Too Much

Not Sorry

ABOUT THE AUTHOR

Ella Miles writes steamy romance, including everything from dark suspense romance that will leave you on the edge of your seat to contemporary romance that will leave you laughing out loud or crying. Most importantly, she wants you to feel everything her characters feel as you read.

Ella is currently living her own happily ever after near the Rocky Mountains with her high school sweetheart husband. Her heart is also taken by her goofy five year old black lab who is scared of everything, including her own shadow.

Ella is a USA Today Bestselling Author & Top 50 Bestselling Author.

Stalk Ella at:
www.ellamiles.com
ella@ellamiles.com